BURIED

Also by Kendra Elliot
Hidden
Chilled

BURIED
A BONE SECRETS NOVEL

KENDRA ELLIOT

Montlake
Romance

Published by Montlake Romance
P.O. Box 400818
Las Vegas, NV 89140

ISBN-13: 9781611098983
ISBN-10: 161109898X

For Dan, my rock.

PROLOGUE

Eighteen Years Ago.

He crouched behind the woodpile, carefully watching the little girl through an opening in the stack. She looked about ten years old but exuded the confidence of an older child. She carried a striped kitten into the little playhouse near the woodpile, chatting to the animal about tea and cookies. She was dressed for play in cutoff shorts and a lunch-stained T-shirt.

The plastic playhouse had to be stuffy. The weather was hot and dry, but that was good. It meant he'd been comfortable while sleeping the last few nights in the woods, but during the day the heat could be deadly. He'd spotted the big white farmhouse this morning. His first sighting of civilization in...years. He'd slowly crawled to his current hiding spot, moving between shaded spots, watching every movement about the property. An hour ago he'd seen a couple of older teenage boys leave in a beat-up farm truck and a woman let two gray cats out the back door. She looked kind.

He ached to experience some kindness.

He nestled in closer to the wood, resting his head, blinking hard as his vision blurred. He was days past feeling hunger; food barely interested him. He just wanted water. There was a hose near the back door, but it was a good hundred feet away. Maybe he should just approach the woman and ask for help. But he wasn't going anywhere until he felt safe. He'd wait until dark. By then—

"Tabby! Come back!"

He grasped at the woodpile with both hands as the kitten shot by his feet.

Uh-oh.

The little girl burst around the corner of the woodpile and slammed to a stop as she spotted him, her mouth falling open and her eyes widening. She took two cautious steps in his direction, studying him intently.

He couldn't move.

He knew he looked bad. His filthy clothes blended with the brown of the wood and dirt. Under the layer of grime on his skin, he suspected he was lily-white from lack of sunshine.

Curiosity filled her bright blue eyes, and she moved closer, looking him over. Her gaze slowly traveled from his blistered bare feet to the old, bloody shirt he'd wrapped around his head. She stopped five feet away. A healthy distance if she needed to make a fast exit, but she'd obviously judged him to not be a danger. She was right. He was about as threatening as a baby seal.

"Do you speak English?" she asked loudly.

He bit his cheek. *That was her first question?*

"Do you live in the woods? How old are you?" Her gaze narrowed.

He slowly stood, bracing himself against the wood, feeling his head swell with the movement. Her eyes grew wide. He was thin, stork-thin. She could see his bruises and abrasions, and he knew many more were hiding. "Yes, I speak English. No, I don't live in the woods. And I'm thirteen," he croaked.

She stood straighter, concerned. "Are you alright?"

He touched a gentle finger to his makeshift turban and winced. "Do you have any water?"

She nodded and raced into the playhouse. She reappeared, carefully carrying a blue floral cup and saucer. His hand shook as he lifted the cup to cracked lips. The warm water was heavenly, but he winced as his muscles went through the foreign motion of swallowing. The simple act of her help made him want to cry.

"How did you get those pink circles on your face?"

The cup rattled as he set it back on the saucer. *The scars. Cigarettes. The bunker. Stories he could never share without endangering lives.* "May I have some more, please?" This time she brought out a little pot and refilled his cup. He drank and then slid back down into his crouch before his legs gave out on him. Nausea gripped him. *Did he drink too fast?* "Is your mom home?"

She nodded. "Do you want me to get her?"

"Please. Don't tell anyone else I'm here, okay? Just get your mom." He leaned his head back against the wood and closed his eyes. Bright colors shifted on the back of his eyelids as the world began to gently spin. Speaking had sapped his energy, but he'd escaped the forest and this family would help him. Now he just had to keep his wits about him and his mouth shut.

"What's your name?" she whispered.

He opened his eyes a crack. Her expression was one of simple curiosity. "Chris. Chris Jacobs." His dry lips twisted. "Could you get your mom? Please?"

She turned and ran, tan legs pumping hard.

CHAPTER ONE

Present Day

"No press." Suspicious cop eyes squinted at Michael.

The Oregon farm smelled strongly of manure, but there wasn't a cow in sight. His research had told him the old dairy farm had been out of operation for over twenty years. Wood and wire fencing traced the edges of the fields in crooked, drunken lines. A hundred yards away stood a barn that Michael wouldn't step foot into for a million dollars. He didn't mind taking risks, but this building looked ready to collapse if a bird landed on the sagging roofline. "I'm not here as press. I'm meeting up with Dr. Campbell," Michael lied.

"The medical examiner left an hour ago." The cop tilted up the brim of his hat, doubt in his gaze, knowing Michael was namedropping to get into the recovery site. How many reporters had he chased off today? The discovery of multiple hidden remains tended to draw out the vultures. One brow rose and challenged him to create a more original ruse.

Luckily, Michael had one. "Not that Dr. Campbell. His daughter. Dr. Lacey Campbell."

The cop ran a hand across his sweating forehead and checked his clipboard. His instant lascivious grin made Michael's jaw clench.

"Oh, *her*. Yeah, she's still here."

Jackass.

"Can you let her know—"

"What's your business with her? She's in the middle of an excavation and a murder investigation. I don't think she'll appreciate me bugging her 'cause some stalker is looking for her."

"Oh, Jesus Christ." Michael took half a step forward and lowered his voice. "Pick up your radio and get someone back there to tell Dr. Campbell that Brody's finally here. She'll want to talk to me." He glanced at the fleet of police cars and obvious unmarked American sedans. "Callahan here yet?"

The cop's eyes narrowed at the detective's name, and his hand moved to his radio. "Not yet." He deliberately turned his back and spoke into his radio.

About time. Michael rubbed at the skin of his baking neck and wished for an icy bottle of water. Or beer. Would Lacey drag herself away to talk to him? When she was deep in a case, she had a tendency to forget about the outside world. Her cell was turned off; he'd tried to call a dozen times.

The cop half turned his head and watched Michael from the corner of his eye as he spoke quietly into his radio. Michael ignored him, studying the recovery scene in the ninety-degree heat. It was hot, dry, and dusty. Every time he inhaled, his lungs were coated with fine dirt.

Cops in navy-blue uniforms dotted the brown fields. *God, they had to be dying in this summer heat.* Small white tents hid private procedures from prying eyes and the news helicopters' cameras. Too many tents. More tents meant more bodies. A tall figure in a Tyvek protective suit strode from tent to tent.

Aw, shit.

Victoria Peres. Identifiable at any range. The rangy forensic anthropologist probably wouldn't let him on the site even if Lacey held his hand. Michael blew out a hot breath and felt sweat trickle down the center of his back. He slipped his sunglasses back on and turned away. Might as well start making some more calls instead of wasting his time trying to get into Fort Knox. He needed to know what they'd found buried beneath the dirt; he wasn't here for a story. This was personal.

"Hey!"

At the cop's bark, Michael looked over his shoulder. He'd finished with his radio and had crossed his arms over his chest, biceps bulging below the short sleeves of his summer uniform. His name badge read "Ruxton."

"You're the damned newspaper reporter who raised a stink about our overtime pay," Ruxton sneered. "Had every suit on the city council pissed off about the overtime we get paid."

Not again. Michael briefly closed his eyes.

Ruxton wasn't nearly done. "If the city would loosen its ass to gives us some cash to hire more police, then we wouldn't have to work overtime."

"I didn't—"

"You reporters just write headlines when someone decides to sue us because they dinged their head while running away during an arrest. Or because they broke a rib fighting against being cuffed. You don't know—"

With two rapid steps, Michael closed the distance between them, eyes hot. "I'm also the reporter who helped hunt down that sick son-of-a-bitch cop killer last winter."

The cop's mouth slammed shut.

"Some of my closest friends are cops, and I've got nothing but respect for the job you do, but don't judge me by what you read in the paper, and I'll do the same for you."

Unflinching, the men stared at each other.

"Michael?"

Michael turned at the female voice, his day instantly brighter and the cop completely forgotten. Lacey looked fantastic but tired. The petite forensic odontologist had just stepped out of a micro-thin, crispy jumpsuit and was holding it between one finger and thumb. Her nose wrinkled.

"In this heat, no deodorant can win against these damned plastic bags they make us wear."

Her warm brown eyes looked Michael up and down. Lacey frowned and glanced at the glowering cop. Instant understanding crossed her face. She gave the cop her brightest smile, and Ruxton's spine visibly relaxed. He lazily dragged his gaze from her hiking boots up those shapely tanned legs to her shorts and snug tank top. Wavy blonde hair was pulled back into a ponytail and stuck out the back of her Seahawks' cap.

Michael's strongest ally. A woman who wasn't tall enough to come up to his shoulders. Gorgeous, blonde, hot, kind, sexy, and smart. The whole package. Every man's dream girl.

The cop didn't have a chance. She'd wrap him around her finger just like that new gold band on her left hand. The band with the big-ass diamond.

Not Michael's diamond.

Damn you, Jack Harper.

Lacey flashed perfect teeth at Ruxton. "Mind if I bring him in? Dr. Peres has been waiting for him."

Michael coughed. *Victoria Peres? Not fucking likely.*

Ruxton blinked and looked at Michael like he'd appeared out of a genie lamp. Michael smirked. Lacey had that effect on men. "He needs to sign the log. Here." Ruxton thrust the clipboard at Michael, a wry tilt to his mouth. He'd spotted the ring.

Lacey winked at Ruxton and pushed Michael toward the listing barn. Her steps slowed considerably after twenty feet. Michael pulled her to a stop and lifted her chin with a finger, taking a closer look at what the cop hadn't noticed. Dark shadows hung below her eyes, and her lids were red and swollen.

"Is it bad?" He crushed his lips into a hard line. It took something truly horrid to upset this woman.

She briefly closed her eyes, all flirty pretense evaporating. "They're all children, Michael. One after the other." She sucked in a ragged breath. "At first, only one skeleton had been reported, but the cadaver dog keeps finding more."

His stomach swirled, a deep dread emerging. *No, not now.* "How long ago?"

Lacey shook her head. "I don't know when they died. Long enough. They've been underground long enough to leave nothing but brown bones." Her chocolate eyes filled, and she wiped a dusty wrist under her nose. "So far we've found seven. They're so small…" Her voice faded.

His hands were on her shoulders, squeezing. "Any boys?" he asked hoarsely. He could feel his marrow quake. Several children...something in his gut told him this was the place. *This was the place.*

"Well, yes. Two, for certain. It's hard to tell on some of the youngest. For now we're sort of going by what's left of the hair and their shoes..." She grabbed at his arms as her eyes widened. "Oh God, Michael. I'm sorry. I didn't even think...you don't think..."

"I always think about it, Lace. Every time I hear about child remains, I think about it."

She stepped forward and pressed her cheek against his chest, her arms wrapping tightly around his waist. Michael bent his head and wished her cap wasn't in the way. Right now he'd like to sink his nose into her hair, get lost in her female scent, and simply forget. She had the power to do that for him, but he no longer had the right to take it.

Daniel. His brain screamed with his brother's name, images of the boy ricocheting through his skull. Images that had slowly faded over twenty years. He squeezed his eyes shut tight, willing the images to sharpen, come alive.

"The ME's office already has Daniel's dental records, right?" Lacey sniffed as she stepped back to look him in the eye.

He could only nod.

"I'll check them first thing, Michael." She slipped her phone out of her pocket and turned it on. "I'll have Sara scan them and send them to me right now. That way I can at least try to rule them out against what we've found." She froze mid-dial. "I don't know how many bodies there will be...my gut tells me there are more children out there."

"There'll be eight," he whispered.

CHAPTER TWO

Michael couldn't relax. Sitting still while others were working their butts off was making him antsy. He wanted to jump in and help. But he had no role in the excavation.

"Why don't you go home?" Lacey asked Michael for the tenth time. "I'll call you if something comes up. There's no point for you to be sitting here waiting and waiting. It's not going to speed things up." Hands on her hips, she glared at Michael as he petted the German shepherd in the shade of one of the little tents.

He shook his head, avoided her eyes, and buried his hand in Queenie's soft fur. The dog's tongue lolled in joy. Rule one in an argument with Lacey: *Keep your mouth shut.* Drove her crazy.

He'd watched her fiancé slowly learn the trick over the last few months. At first the poor sap had actually tried to win arguments with the woman. Impossible.

She huffed at him and turned her attention back to the tiny mandible a tech had placed in her hands moments before. "Too young," she muttered, and Michael's spine relaxed. Barely.

But the happy cadaver dog under his fingers had hit on another spot thirty minutes ago, and that Amazon of a woman, Dr. Peres, was supervising the beginning of the unearthing. *Fucking amazing dog.* Michael had witnessed a lot of things in his life, but watching the dog scent death below the dirt had blown his mind.

The handler, a graying, earthy woman who talked a mile a minute, had been working a grid pattern when the dog abruptly sat and refused to move. A hit. Sherrine had rubbed the dog's head and given her a hug, gently backing her away from the place of the hit. Sherrine had nodded at a uniform, and he drove a pole a foot into the dirt at the spot three times, leaving small openings over the area.

Michael wondered how many times Sherrine and the cop had gone through the morbid routine. She'd led Queenie by the holes again, where the dog took one sniff, promptly sat, and wouldn't budge.

No question.

"The holes let out more of the scent," Lacey had whispered at his side. The cop had promptly whipped out stakes and tape and cordoned off another sad square. Crime scene techs covered the dusty farm like ants. Oregon State Police had thrown everything they had at the site. Skeletons of multiple children motivated everyone.

Now Michael restlessly patted Queenie and waited for the results of the current find. Sherrine returned with three bottled waters. "Thirsty?"

Michael took one of the bottles with a nod. Lacey took the other and ground her heel into his shoe. "Wha—thanks for the water, Sherrine," he muttered.

The woman chortled and winked at Lacey. Sherrine pulled a collapsible dish out of her backpack and poured half her bottle into the dish for the dog.

"You don't work for the state police, do you?" Michael asked.

Sherrine shook her head. "Private contractor. Queenie and I have helped out dozens of times. State police, counties all over the state, and at least ten other states." The talkative woman paused to count silently on her fingers. "Thirteen other states, actually. We had a fascinating case last month in Washington. I'd never officially tried Queenie over water. We'd trained for it, but never had needed to use the skill. She found a missing boater trapped between rocks below twenty feet of water." The woman frowned. "Too late, of course. He'd been missing for three days. We've done searches in Idaho, Nevada—"

"The twin towers in New York?" Michael couldn't stop the question.

A flat, blue gaze briefly flicked to his and looked away. "Yes."

She didn't expound, and the silence filled the tent.

"Sorry," Michael muttered. *Idiot.*

"Dr. Campbell?"

Lacey jumped up at Dr. Peres's question. The tall woman had come up behind them with no one noticing. "I want you to look at something." Victoria Peres glared at Michael but didn't say a word. Lacey had gone to bat for him earlier with the woman. Once Dr. Peres had heard about his brother, she'd allowed his presence, but first he'd received a strict lecture on staying out of the crime scenes. Michael had solemnly nodded and replied. "Of course, Vicky."

He swore the woman had growled.

Lacey had rapidly intervened, distracted the doctor, and then given her own lecture in furious tones in Michael's ear.

Both women were so easy to infuriate. And he'd needed something to keep his mind off what was being found under the dirt.

This time he kept his mouth shut. He could still taste his foot in his mouth from his question to Sherrine.

Without meeting Michael's eyes, Dr. Peres flatly stated to the group, "It's an adult. Female." She stalked out of the tent.

Lacey followed after a single, silent transmission to Michael with her eyes. *Don't move.*

No problem. Michael blew out a breath. An adult. Not another boy.

Beside him, Sherrine stretched. "I think we'll head out." She clapped her hands at Queenie, who bounded to her side. "We're done here."

Done? "Wait a minute. You can't be done." Michael stood, ignoring the sweat that rolled down his neck. "There's more."

The woman glanced up from examining her pack. "No. I'm positive we've found everything. Queenie and I have been back and forth over this farm all day. Unless the police decide they want to start gridding the forest on the south side, we're done. It looks like everything was buried in this immediate area."

"But there's more. There's got to be one more."

The woman blinked at him. "And you know this how...?"

"Because...because..." He leaned closer. "There were nine children taken. One walked out. The rest were never seen again."

"What in the hell are you talking about?" Sherrine's hands froze on the zipper to her pack.

"How long have you lived here?" Michael's heart was ready to bust out of his chest.

The woman shrugged. "Eight years."

He swallowed hard. "About twenty years ago, nine kids and their bus driver vanished. The bus, too. One boy showed up two years later, half dead, unable to remember what'd happened to him. The others are still missing. You just found seven children and an adult. This *has* to be the place. *It has to.*"

"You think the woman Dr. Peres just mentioned is the driver?"

Michael nodded urgently. "There's got to be one more child buried here somewhere."

Sherrine looked ready to blow her stack. "How come no one mentioned this to me? Everyone knows what we're looking for but me?"

"No, not everyone," a new voice spoke. "And let's keep it that way."

Michael spun at the male voice and turned to find himself nose to nose with Mason Callahan, OSP Major Crimes detective. Michael automatically glanced over Callahan's shoulder, looking for his ever-present partner, Detective Ray Lusco. Ray flashed him a white grin, his eyes twinkling at Michael's surprise.

"Detectives. Wondered when you'd show up," Michael managed to say evenly.

"We've been in and out since the first discovery yesterday, Brody. Didn't realize we were supposed to report to you. What the fuck are you doing on the scene?" Callahan's dark green eyes glittered dangerously under his cowboy hat.

Lusco fought a cough.

Aw, hell.

"How can you wear that hat in this heat?" Michael asked. At least the hat was a pale straw instead of the detective's usual black felt. Shitkickers and faded jeans made up the rest of the detective's uniform. Lusco looked his usual GQ self in khakis and short-sleeved knit shirt. Michael wondered if Lusco deliberately matched his belt to his shoes. No doubt.

No one had ever truly intimidated Michael, but the aging cowboy detective was near the top of the ladder. Vicky Peres stood a rung higher. Not that he'd ever let her or the detectives know that fact.

"When are you gonna stop dressing like a skateboarder? What are you, thirty-five or fourteen?" Callahan fired back.

Michael had a hunch the detective knew exactly how old he was. And his date of birth.

Michael first crossed paths with the state detectives last winter when Lacey had been stalked by a killer. Michael had been standing in the right place at the right time when the detectives had needed an immediate hand. Had he ever gotten a thank-you? A note? Nothing.

"These are the missing Condon Academy kids. You know it," Michael stated quietly.

"We don't know shit. We've got a couple of bodies that are kids. That doesn't automatically make this related to your brother."

Callahan knew exactly why he was there.

Callahan also believed it was the missing bus, and he hadn't been one bit surprised to find Michael on his scene. He probably had wondered what had taken Michael so long. Damned detective probably knew every relative of every missing kid on that bus. Oregon's saddest mystery was never far from every cop's thoughts.

Nine children from the elite, private Condon Academy. Returning from a field trip to the state capitol building. The bus never made it back to the school. No kids. No driver. No bus.

Until thirteen-year-old Chris Jacobs walked out of the forest two years later on the other side of the Cascade Mountain Range. Emaciated. Near death. No memory.

"You think this is the place," Michael stated.

Lusco's phone beeped, and he stepped away to answer.

Michael held Callahan's gaze and saw something briefly soften in the cop's face. "We don't know," Callahan repeated carefully. "What my gut says and what the facts are might be two different things."

"Callahan." Lusco was staring at the screen of his phone. He looked up, amazement crossing his face. "They just found a decrepit bus in the woods a quarter mile south of here."

Michael looked at Callahan. "What's your gut say now?"

CHAPTER THREE

"I don't understand. If that is the place...where is...Daniel?" Michael's mother whispered.

Michael hadn't wanted to tell her. She didn't look good. She hadn't looked good for months, and Michael still hadn't come to grips with the fact that Cecilia Brody might die. The Senator sat beside her on the huge bed, gripping her hand. He was never "Dad" or "Father." He was "Sir" or "The Senator." Michael had always pictured the title with capital letters, and he'd often written it that way as a child.

The frail woman in the bed couldn't be his mother. Michael closed his eyes. His mother was head of surgery at the prestigious teaching hospital on the hill overlooking Portland. She *had been* the head, he reminded himself. She'd stepped down since her diagnosis. For the past three months, The Senator had been in Oregon more than Michael could ever remember. He'd often wondered what it'd take to keep his father out of Washington DC for an extended period of time. Cecilia had refused to give up her important position at the hospital when her husband was elected, so Maxwell Brody had continuously flown back and forth across the country for twenty-five years.

A tough woman, Cecilia had devoted her energy to her hospital, relying on nannies and private schools to raise her two boys. Working long hours and flying to DC when her husband needed her to make a social appearance. Now she spent ninety percent of her time in her bedroom; a room where Michael had always felt like he'd stepped into an overpriced hotel and shouldn't stand on the expensive area rugs. He glanced down and shifted his feet onto the hardwood.

"They're still looking, right?" The Senator barked. "They haven't finished yet?"

Michael nodded. "Once they found the bus yesterday, they expanded the search area. They're still looking for one more set of remains...Daniel."

Cecilia leaned back against the pale peach pillows and closed her eyes. The Senator glared daggers at Michael, and Michael steadily held his gaze. The Senator had a habit of blaming the messenger, but Michael had learned to ignore it. If anything, the glare showed The Senator's devotion to his wife. That was good. Devotion was good.

Too bad there wasn't enough for anyone else.

Finding the missing bus outside the farm had been a coup. Michael had seen some cops giving high fives and others relating the old story to the younger cops. Callahan and Lusco had practically run to the site. Far back in the woods to the south, an ancient outbuilding had hidden a secret for twenty years. The school bus was one of the short ones, not the giant long buses most kids ride. Michael had hated riding the bus on field trips because outsiders assumed the kids on board were handicapped. It was the only bus the small academy had owned; it didn't offer bus service. All the children had been driven to and picked up from school. Some in limousines. Michael and Daniel were usually dropped off by the housekeeper or gardener.

The frail outbuilding had collapsed onto the bus. A mass of moss, bushes, and overgrown trees hid the building from a casual passerby. Not that anyone ever passed it by. The misshapen building was completely isolated. The narrow access road probably hadn't been used since the bus had been abandoned. Hidden.

No children were in the bus.

The Senator rubbed at his wife's hand, and her eyes opened, meeting her husband's gaze. She gave him a faint smile, reassurance. The intimate moment stretched, and Michael felt like they'd completely forgotten he existed. It wasn't a foreign sensation.

Michael had been told a million times his parents were a handsome couple. They still were. His father was tall, silver, and imposing with a direct green gaze that mirrored Michael's. Cecilia was elegant and slender, always perfectly dressed, frequently surprising strangers with the iron will that hid beneath the soft surface. Successful. Wealthy. Perfect.

The only flaw in their perfect lives had been the disappearance of their second son, Daniel. He'd been eleven years old to Michael's thirteen when he'd vanished with a group of schoolmates. Michael's memories of that time were a blur. Police, news cameras, reporters, more police. The kidnapping of the son of

Oregon's junior senator had made national headlines for weeks. Then faded away as no sightings of the children or their bus driver emerged. No confirmed sightings. Unconfirmed sightings had placed the bus in Mexico, Canada, and Brazil.

Chris Jacobs had appeared two years later, and the story flared up again. The boy had been no help. He'd spent months in the hospital, part of the time in a coma, and more months in therapy for head injuries. His parents had kept the cameras and reporters away, defending their privacy.

Michael had hated the child. Why had *that* boy survived? Why not Daniel?

His mother had walked the house in a fog for months; his father had raged and held meetings with his brother Phillip, detectives, and other statesmen for hours in his study. Michael had hidden at the door, listening, hoping for good news but hearing only angry voices. Uncle Phil had become the family spokesman; The Senator was unable to speak publicly about Daniel and keep his composure. Phillip Brody had been a newly elected state representative. The tragedy placed him in the spotlight, and he drafted new crime bills, using Daniel's case to push them into law. The election gods had shined favorably on Uncle Phil and slowly moved him up the political ladder into the governor's mansion, where he currently sat, holding court for the last four years.

Right now the publicity cyclone hadn't started circling yet, but Michael knew it would. He could feel the pressure of the discovery ready to burst onto the front page and national news. This time Michael had the power to spin things to protect his mother. Nothing would be printed in the *Oregonian* without his okay. Better yet, no one would write about it but him. His editor knew Michael could present things in a balanced fashion and would back him up. The long years of a solid working relationship and award-winning investigative reporting were about to pay off. He was going to call in every fucking favor owed him.

He pulled his ever-present digital recorder out of his pocket and switched it on.

"What in the hell are you doing with that?" The Senator nearly roared. "This isn't the time for an interview."

Cecilia looked like a wounded kitten.

"Time for the spin," Michael said flatly. "You know how this works. You want to deal with the press or with me?"

"Call Evelyn," The Senator snapped. "Now."

Michael had already contacted his father's publicist. "Evelyn agreed it was best I talked to you first. She's going to have her hands full with the television reporters. I'm going to handle most of the print."

Michael's mother squeezed her husband's hand as The Senator opened his mouth to speak and then clamped it shut.

"I'm sure Michael knows what he's doing," she stated calmly.

He shot his mother a look of gratitude.

"If you want to talk to someone, go find that boy. Jacobs." His father's voice cracked ever so faintly on the name. "Maybe he's remembered something after twenty years. Maybe the discovery of so many graves will shake some memories loose." A ribbon of spite wove through the words. The Senator had never forgiven the boy for living while his son was still missing. And he'd believed the boy hadn't told all he knew, believed the police had been too lenient in their interviews, and the boy's parents too overprotective.

"I will." Chris Jacobs was next on his list. After Michael's parents. He pulled a delicate-looking chair from his mother's desk and sat carefully, his heart heavy. He looked at his parents, and his mouth dried up. God, this was going to suck. He took a deep breath.

"I know you've told the story a thousand times, but you haven't ever talked to me about it. I need to hear everything that happened twenty years ago. And every other thought or suspicion you've had since then about who could have done this."

"Mind if I sit in for this?"

This time Detective Callahan's voice didn't surprise Michael one bit.

★ ★ ★

Mason had been standing outside the door for a few seconds. Long enough to know the doctor was tired, the senator was angry, and the reporter used a firm hand when it came to managing his parents.

"Ma'am." Mason nodded at Dr. Brody and then her husband. "Senator. I'm Mason Callahan, Oregon State Police Major Crimes, and I'd also like to talk with you." He started to return his cowboy hat to his head but thought better of it and set it on the desk behind Brody. The reporter hadn't flinched as Mason spoke.

Mason hadn't met the doctor and senator. He knew who they were. Senator Brody had been a familiar face in Oregon politics for over three decades. In the Portland area, Dr. Brody was well known for her philanthropy and important position at the medical school. Mason knew she'd been severely ill, but her appearance still shocked him. She looked like a thin shell of the vibrant, strong woman he'd seen in the paper and on TV. Cancer? Mason couldn't remember what had happened to her. Maybe something with her liver?

"Where's your shadow?" The reporter stood and surprised Mason by holding out his hand. Mason shook it, grateful for Brody's deliberate acceptance of his presence in front of the distrustful parents.

"At the Carling home." Elizabeth Carling had been eight when she vanished with the bus. Mason heard Dr. Brody catch her breath.

"Has she been identified?" Michael asked.

"Your girlfriend made a preliminary ID. I guess the child had braces on her top teeth and distinctive decalcifications on her molars that'd been noted by her dentist long ago." Braces at eight? Mason still didn't quite understand that. The odontologist, Dr. Lacey Campbell, had shrugged and commented that some orthodontists do movement in two stages. The first when the child is young and the second after they've lost their baby teeth.

"Daniel?" Senator Brody finally spoke. His knuckles were white, holding his wife's hand.

Mason shook his head.

"She's not my girlfriend," muttered Michael.

Mason felt a twinge of guilt for trying to push the reporter's buttons. Wrong time, wrong place. "Sorry." Michael nodded diffidently, but Mason saw regret flash in the man's eyes. Sucks to have your woman swept away right under your nose. Been there, done that.

"If you don't mind, I'd like to hear your answers to your son's questions."

The senator's face stated he did mind, but he kept his mouth closed. Mason lifted a brow to Dr. Brody, asking her to go first. The woman wiped at her eyes and began to quietly speak.

An hour later, Mason hadn't heard anything that he hadn't already read in the old police reports and found in newspaper articles. Michael Brody's pointed questions and frustration revealed he felt the same. Mason had let Brody do most of the interview. The reporter was sharp, asking questions as identical ones crossed Mason's mind. And the parents seemed to open up better to their son. Mason made notes and wished Ray was there to take notes instead. Mason could concentrate better if he wasn't writing and listening at the same time. He eyed Michael's digital recorder. He'd ask him to download the interview and e-mail it to Ray. Computers and Mason didn't mix. Ray usually handled any computer work beyond the basics.

"It was never known if just one child was the target or if all of them were," Mason jumped in as Michael paused. "Ransom or blackmail was expected at first, considering the socioeconomic class of the children. Usually, crime motives boil down to money, drugs, or sex." Dr. Brody blanched. Considering the age of the children, the thought of sex as the motive made Mason queasy, too. "If you imagine Daniel was the prime target. Over the years, has someone come to mind, even very briefly, that could do this?"

Dr. Brody looked away and twisted the sheets in a fist. Several times over the last hour, tears had streaked her face, and Mason knew they were about to start again. He shifted his gaze to the senator. The tall man sat on the bed by his wife; his usually stiff shoulders had slowly deflated through the interview. He met Mason's gaze. "No, no one."

Dr. Brody said nothing.

"My wife is tired. Are we done?" The senator directed his question at his son. Mason's ears perked up at the accusing tone, and he saw Michael's back stiffen. The reporter nodded and stood. He picked up Mason's hat and handed it to him.

Mason got the message.

He shook the senator's hand and said his good-byes. He silently followed Michael through the maze of hallways and out of the big house into the blazing heat. Mason wiped at the instant sweat on his forehead and put on his hat. *Jesus Christ.* Seven in the evening and the temp was still hovering around a hundred degrees.

Mason stopped beside Michael on the wide wraparound porch and stared at Portland's skyline.

Stunning view.

What had it been like growing up in such wealth? Michael Brody came from some of the bluest blood in the state but didn't show it. The guy always needed a haircut and dressed like he spent his days at a beachside bar. Except for the watch. Mason knew shit about watches. All he cared about was if it worked, but Ray had once commented that Brody's watch probably cost a third of Mason's yearly salary. *Gross salary.*

Mason struggled to wrap his brain around that. His gaze went to the black Range Rover in the driveway. *Oh yeah.* And the vehicle. Another sign that Michael Brody wasn't the beach bum he presented himself as. Not to mention the dual master's degrees in international studies and economics, the investigative articles Brody wrote about his year in a motorcycle gang, running with the damned bulls in Spain, and jumping out of anything that could fly.

"They aren't telling us everything," the imposter beach bum stated.

Mason nodded. Brody's green eyes were narrowed in deep thought. The brain behind those eyes was one of the sharpest

Mason had ever met. Too bad the guy had a problem with following the rules. Or listening to authority. Oregon State Police
could have used someone like Brody. Or the CIA. But Brody
liked to do things his own way.

"I agree," Mason said.

The men stood in silence until Mason glanced at his cheap
watch. "I need to go." He moved down the steps, leaving Brody
behind.

"Callahan."

Mason turned.

"I'm going to find out what happened to Daniel." Brody
held his gaze.

Mason nodded, unsurprised. He believed Brody would do
just that. Maybe even before he did.

CHAPTER FOUR

Jamie hung her keys on the hook by her phone and, with a smile, dropped her purse on the counter. Summer rocked. It was nearly nine in the evening and it was still light out and toasty warm. As much as she liked seeing the kiddos crowding the halls at her elementary school, she especially liked the quiet and the half-days of work during the summer. The warm afternoons and evenings were hers. No meetings with parents, no lectures on not hitting other students, no complaining teachers. She placed her hands on the small of her back and stretched, inhaling the scent of fresh-cut grass from the fields across the street. Her favorite smell of summer. Right after barbequed steak.

Her mouth watered. Opening the fridge, she took out a Diet Coke and frowned at the sparse offerings on her shelves. Yogurt, cheese, and milk. Dairy group accounted for. Not much else. She snagged a lemon yogurt and kicked her flip-flops onto the mat by the door to the garage. Living alone was great, but sometimes she wished she had a reason to cook a big meal. Meat and pasta and crusty bread. Lots of it. Once a month she met with girlfriends for dinner and wine to catch up on each other's lives. The rest of the month she lived on protein bars, dry cereal, and fruit.

And yogurt, lots of yogurt.

She eyed the yellow, creamy substance. She needed a change. Work, eat, exercise, clean house, mow lawn. A solid and comforting schedule but rather boring. She glanced at the calendar. Next week she was off. She'd planned to paint two of her bedrooms, but maybe she should get out of town. Do something different, unplanned. Like…go to the beach and just read. Heather had been pestering her to visit her in Bend. Jamie could drive over the Cascades and sunbathe with Heather in the dry, baking heat of Central Oregon.

She rinsed out the empty yogurt container and placed it in the recycling. Her spoon went directly into the dishwasher. Who was she kidding? The numbers on the calendar taunted her. She would be painting next week. It needed to be done.

The doorbell jangled. Jamie strolled to the door and looked through the peephole. Male. Big. *Don't know him.* Her stomach stopped digesting her yogurt.

"May I help you?" She spoke through the door.

His left eyebrow rose, and he gave a half smile. Instantly charming. And hunky. Jamie felt a different sensation in her stomach.

"Michael Brody. I'm with the *Oregonian*." A laminated ID suddenly blocked her view.

Jamie wasn't impressed. Anyone could make an official-looking ID, and this guy looked anything but official in his cargo shorts and snug T-shirt. But the name on the ID was familiar...

"What do you want?" She wasn't about to open the door.

"I'm looking for your brother Chris." He lowered the ID and looked directly at the peephole.

Jamie froze. Not again. Every few years, reporters and cold case cops came out of the woodwork to harass her brother. Temper swirled in her chest.

"He doesn't live here."

The man's eyebrow rose further. "I know. Where can I find him?"

Jamie choked out a laugh. Did he think she was stupid?

His mouth twitched at her laugh. "Are you Jamie Jacobs?"

Did he just bat his eyelashes? She swallowed another laugh. "No."

"Do I need to call the police because you're in her house?"

Jamie snorted.

The reporter's face turned serious. "They found the bus," he stated quietly.

Jamie pulled back from the door, heart in her throat. *Oh shit.* "What about the kids?" she whispered.

He heard her. "I'll tell you if you open the door. Do you know who I am now?"

His name echoed through her brain and hit its target. Brody. One of the other kids. She pressed her eye against the hole again. Michael Brody's face had lost all expression, and she instantly saw the resemblance to Oregon's Senator Brody.

This was the brother to the senator's missing son.

Jamie forced her lungs to pump air. She'd never really met Michael Brody. He'd been much older than her at the academy. She mainly knew his name as a byline in the newspaper. Her parents had pulled her out of school and then isolated her and Chris from all media coverage after her brother had returned.

With shaking fingers, she worked the two deadbolts and opened the door.

★ ★ ★

Michael exhaled as he heard the bolts start to slide. He'd wondered if she would talk to him. He'd dug up what he could on the woman. Her parents were dead, and all leads to her brother seemed to end at brick walls. She was Chris's only living relative. Jamie Jacobs had been nine when her brother vanished. Eleven when he returned. Now she was a principal at one of Portland's poorest elementary schools. Fair and sensible was the description he'd heard. Her students loved her and the teachers raved about her. Her yard was perfect. The hedges perfectly trimmed and the trees properly pruned. The grass was cut short and the flowers in a neat border. He eyed the border. Purple flower, yellow flower, purple, yellow. All the way around. Why hadn't she mixed it up a little? It looked...too perfect.

The door opened, and he turned back to face the woman.

Too perfect.

Eyes the color of pale green jade stared at him, fear and anxiety hovering behind them. Long black hair was caught back in a ponytail, with wavy sections escaping to frame her face. What a face. She reminded him of the old-time movie sirens. The ones who seized the screen with their noble aura the second they stepped on camera. The ones who played the roles of queens or empresses. Regal women. Like Sophia Loren...but with bright eyes. She was tall. Nearly as tall as he. He barely had to look down to meet her gaze, and he'd barely need to dip his head if he wanted...*fuck.* He blinked and watched wary shields abruptly cover the anxiety in her eyes. Her black tank showed off toned arms that either spent a lot of time in the gym or working in her yard. She was buff, an interesting mix of athlete and contessa.

Every well-rehearsed question in his brain evaporated.

Why hadn't his elementary school principal looked like this?

Her chin lifted the slightest bit, and he recognized a familiar stubbornness. Lacey looked just like that when she was about to chew him out.

"What about the kids?" she snapped. "What did they find? Where was it? Did you—"

"Hang on." He lifted his hands, unable to process the questions pouring from freaking gorgeous lips. "Can I come in?"

She clamped her mouth shut and blatantly assessed him from head to toe, like she was sizing him up for a round or two in a boxing ring. Her right hand slipped to her pocket, wrapping around something, and he watched the muscles flex in her forearm. What'd she have in there?

He took a half step back.

"Let me see that ID again. And your driver's license." Her voice was calmer but still held the punch of someone expecting to be obeyed. She must be a great principal.

He handed her the newspaper ID and dug in his pocket for his wallet. She snorted at the jam-packed piece of leather. He dug through the mess for thirty seconds.

Where the fuck was his license?

She reached out and deftly plucked the license from the stack of receipts and dog-eared business cards. Balancing both IDs in her left hand, she studied them carefully and then studied his face again. She handed them back, and he noticed her right hand slowly move from her pocket.

"Mind if I ask what you've got in your pocket?" He jerked his head at her hand as he fumbled to put his wallet in some semblance of order. She smiled and his heart skipped two beats. *Christ!* The woman was a knockout.

"Pepper spray," she said coolly.

His hands froze. "Would you have used that on me?"

"Yes." Another calm, regal smile. "If I'd needed to."

"Am I safe now?" He eyed her wide lips. Now she was a movie queen packing a weapon. His stomach tightened. In a good way. In a fucking awesome way.

"Maybe." Her fantastic eyes narrowed at him. "What exactly do you want from me?"

Twenty-four hours in my bed. No. Forty-eight hours.

Where the hell did that come from? He shook the thought out of his head.

"Just to talk."

"Uh-huh. I've heard that before." More suspicion darkened those green gems.

"No, seriously. I just want to—"

"I'm teasing." Her lips quirked, and she stepped back to allow him into her home.

Michael blew out a breath. He was seriously off-kilter. "Don't make me dance, princess," he muttered and stepped into the royal lair.

★ ★ ★

Jamie took a deep breath as the reporter moved past into her air-conditioned home. The scent of slightly sun-toasted male touched her nose, and her senses lit up. She gestured toward her kitchen, and he nodded, stepped into the cheery room, and then positioned himself against her counter in front of her microwave, arms crossing his chest, his dark green gaze on her.

She frowned. He was in her spot.

Her kitchen immediately felt smaller. Michael Brody wasn't a big, bulky guy. He was lean but tall with wide shoulders that seemed to take up too much space. Waves of cool composure rolled off him, and frustration tightened her spine. She was being intimidated in her own kitchen. Her chin jerked up.

"Can I get you something to drink?"

He shook his head, and she reached for her Diet Coke can, condensation running down its sides. She took a nervous sip and felt an icy drop land on her chest and start to roll beneath her tank. His gaze locked on the drop, tracing its path.

Jamie brushed at her chest, and Michael's gaze returned to hers. She glared and he blinked innocently.

"What's happened?" she asked.

His chest expanded and his face closed off as he spoke. She listened in horror at the events of the morning, her drink forgotten.

"One child's body is missing?" she whispered. *All those bones. Buried all these years.* Her eyes smarted.

Michael nodded grimly. "They didn't find my brother... well, there isn't a preliminary age match to my brother, and there should be one more...child's remains."

Jamie closed her eyes. What was he going through? No closure for his family.

"It's been so long—"

"Where is Chris?" Michael stopped her apology.

Jamie bit her lip. The last thing Chris would want was the media hounding him again. "I don't think he'll want to talk to the media."

Michael unfolded his arms and leaned toward her. "I'm not here as the media. I'm here as a brother who's got a lot of questions."

Jamie shook her head. "Chris doesn't remember much from back then. He had a pretty bad brain injury, and the doctors believe he blocked everything. He's never had any memory return."

"So he says."

Jamie slammed her can on the counter. "Get out."

Michael rubbed a hand across his forehead. "Fuck. Sorry. I didn't mean that. I just need to hear it from him."

Seeing red, Jamie pointed at the door. "That way."

He locked gazes with her, and Jamie's stomach did a slow warm turn. Michael Brody exuded a hell of a lot of testosterone that was hammering away at her hormones. She squared her shoulders. "I'm sorry about your brother. I'm certain it's just a matter of time before they find his body."

Michael's face blanked, and her heart contracted. She hadn't meant to speak like a bitch. The words had sounded better in her head.

He pushed away from the counter and brushed past her, avoiding her eyes and leaving that sunshine scent in his wake again. "Nice meeting you, Ms. Jacobs. I'm sure we'll cross paths again soon."

Jamie caught her breath and turned to follow, but he was already out her door and halfway down the walk. She stopped in the doorway, one hand on the frame, and watched Michael climb into a black Range Rover at the curb. His tires came just short of squealing as he pulled away.

Jamie exhaled and leaned against the frame.

Well. That went real smooth.

★ ★ ★

Michael pulled to a stop at the end of Jamie's street, out of sight of her home, and hit a button on his cell to call his invaluable source at the phone company.

"Grace? Brody here. That address I gave you earlier? Any calls go out in the last few seconds?"

He scowled at his cell as he scribbled a number on the back of a napkin. "Where the fuck is that number from?" His writing slowed at her answer. "Really? Who'd want to live out there?"

No wonder he couldn't find Chris Jacobs. He was hiding out in one of the remotest parts of the state.

"Thanks. You're a doll. Dig up everything you can on this number for me, okay? I need to know just where I'm going. And I owe you a big one, Grace. Drinks are on me next time."

Michael felt adrenaline dump into his veins. Time for a trip.

★ ★ ★

Chris erased his phone message and sat in the evening light, his brain spinning. He'd always known the call would come. Now that it had, it was almost anticlimactic. He'd lived this moment a thousand times, dreamed it even more. The call had come and gone, and the world still went on, not stopping like it should.

A large weight lifted from his chest. No more waiting. Time to put the wheels in motion.

He breathed the sweet air deeply and listened to the silence. Only the normal, nearly inaudible sounds of nature reached his ears. The breeze rustled the tall grass around his cabin. No vehicle sounds, no human noise. As it should be.

For ten years he'd speculated every time his cell rang. Would this be the call? Would he be ready when it came? Maybe it'd never come. He'd had his plans in place for several years now. Checked and double-checked every few weeks. He'd thought them through and through, hoping to find a way to avoid them altogether. But there was no way out. He'd known if the call ever came he would have no choice but to act.

An image of the Ghostman flitted across his memories, and he mentally crushed it down. The Ghostman stood for failure; Chris wasn't going to fail. The Ghostman had haunted his dreams for a long time. *Not dreams, nightmares. Nightmares of torture and pain.*

He turned to his laptop and typed the usual words into the search engines. Nothing. How had the phone call come before the computer warning? He shifted in his seat, brow wrinkling in mild surprise. Anyone with a little skill could find whatever he needed. Anyone with a lot of skill could manipulate that information to do as he pleased. Like him. Computers hummed under his fingers, their languages as second nature to him as English. Or Spanish. He had alerts on many phrases and names, but none had been tripped in the last twenty-four hours. Tomorrow would be different. The story would be everywhere. The cursor blinked. Taunting him to run another search. Chris closed the lid.

A quiet cough came from the other end of the bungalow. Chris silently padded down the hall and stopped, pushing open the bedroom door. Brian didn't move. Chris could see the outline of his son under the thin covers and hear the soft sounds of the boy's breathing.

Chris's heart clenched, and he ran a hand over his jaw, feeling the faint raised seam of bone beneath the skin where it'd never healed correctly. His son would never suffer. He would never experience the horrors that men can inflict on children. He would only know love and peace. It was a familiar mantra. One he'd repeated every day for the short eight years of his son's life.

Was that about to change?

CHAPTER FIVE

"I don't want to do that again." Detective Ray Lusco shook his head as he stared into his coffee at the diner. "I don't know if I can face another set of distraught parents like that. Shit. I feel like the bad guy."

Mason nodded in agreement with his partner. The only thing worse than discussing the death of a child with parents was being the one to deliver the news. And that was what he and Ray had spent the day doing. The parents had been informed of the find yesterday, but conclusive evidence hadn't emerged until today. Most of them had long ago accepted that their child wasn't returning, but the parents of nine-year-old David Doubler had always believed their son would walk in the door one day.

They'd talked with several sets of parents in the office of the medical examiner. Weeping and acceptance had been the staples for the day. Until the Doublers. The *Doubters* described the couple better. The parents had brought in tiny dental X-rays of their son's teeth. Twenty-year-old X-rays that the mother had kept in an envelope in case their son's body was found one day. David Doubler Sr. had argued with Dr. Campbell's identification.

Mason shook his head. David Sr. had met his match with the feisty odontologist. Lacey Campbell had calmly placed the films on a viewbox next to the films she'd taken on the skull and proceeded to give the father a calm lesson in reading dental X-rays. Even Mason had seen the match. David Sr. had refused. "Baby teeth all look alike," he'd argued. "Every kid had silver fillings back then."

Dr. Campbell had quietly pointed out the distinctive white shapes the silver created on the boy's first permanent molars. David Sr. had shaken his head. It wasn't good enough for him. The chief medical examiner had stepped into the room at that moment. Dr. James Campbell could tell his daughter was about to pull out her hair in frustration.

"Maybe this would help," the gray-haired ME had said and held out a plastic baggie to the parents. "You recognize this? It was found with the remains of this child, about where his neck would have been."

Mrs. Doubler had stared at the silver strands in the baggie and promptly burst into tears. Mason had swallowed hard. He'd known the shape of the pendant on the chain. His son had worn one for years after being diagnosed with juvenile diabetes.

Ray took a sip of his coffee. "Thank God, that was the last one."

Mason said nothing. Ray was wrong. There had to be another body. One boy was missing, and Mason had already met his parents.

Dr. Brody was a tough woman. She knew her son wasn't coming back, but Mason wasn't certain about the senator. The senator had a look of denial that matched Mr. Doubler's.

"Doesn't feel right. Why would one body be in a completely different place? Why weren't all the bodies found on that farm?" Ray asked.

Mason stirred his coffee. His thoughts exactly. His gut was telling him something wasn't right.

They sat in silence for two minutes, letting the conversations of the other restaurant patrons flow around them.

"Went home and hugged my kids last night." Ray had two preteens. A boy and a girl who creamed Mason at their video games every time he visited. Ray was looking him straight in the eye. Most cops would have mumbled the words into their coffee. Not Ray. The big guy was never afraid to show his emotions when it came to his kids or sexy wife.

Ray was looking at him expectantly.

"Yeah, I called Jake." Mason fought the urge to look out the window instead of meeting Ray's gaze. Jake had been his usual smart-assed self, making Mason struggle to get a complete sentence out of the teen's mouth. Jake's stepdad had originally answered the phone. Mason would rather talk to his urologist than the cheerful superdad. The man had done everything right in his life that Mason had done wrong. Now he had Mason's wife and kid. *Ex-wife.*

All Mason had was frozen pizza and an empty bed.

Ray's cell rang, and Mason exhaled in relief. He'd seen the look in Ray's eye. The one that said his wife, Jill, had been talking about more blind dates for Mason. Jill tried to set him up several times a year, and Mason talked his way out of them. Not easy considering Jill had once been a trial lawyer.

"It's where?" Ray's voice raised an octave. "They think this is it? How far?"

Mason's spine tingled as he watched Ray scribble in his ever-present notebook. Something big. Mason could feel it

"Oh fuck. Oh fuck!"

Mason froze. Ray rarely swore.

His eyes angry, Ray moved the phone from his mouth and whispered to Mason. "They think they found the place where the kids were kept. Before..."

Mason nodded. *Before he killed them.*

★ ★ ★

Jamie studied the calendar on her office computer, tapping her sandaled toe to the soft classical music from her speakers. Two more days. Then she was out of here for a week. Last night she'd painted a dozen paint samples on the bedroom walls, unable to sit still, trying to put all thoughts of the sad crime scene out of her head. She flipped open the color chart from the paint store. How many shades of beige were there? Cappuccino, wheat, sand, Hawaiian sand...

Her gaze lingered on the dark greens. Forest green really would be great with her wood floors and throw rugs. She flipped the brochure closed and buried it in her inbox. Too many choices. Why did she suck when it came to these types of decisions? She had the same problem at Baskin-Robbins. She had to read every flavor and study the look of every ice cream twice before making a choice. And she always ended up with chocolate chip mint.

A throat cleared, and her gaze flew to the tall figure at her door. Her heart stopped.

"Jesus Christ." She glared at Michael Brody leaning insolently against her doorframe. "How long have you been standing there?"

Emerald eyes sparked at her. "Long enough to tell you can't decide on paint." A slow smile widened his mouth, and Jamie drew a deep breath. He was tan and tall, and his legs and arms were solid, lean muscle mass. She blinked as she caught herself staring and jerked her gaze up to his face. And found herself staring again. His light-brown hair had sun-bleached highlights that her friends paid hundreds for. Not fair that a man should have eyes of that rich color and freaking long black lashes to set them off. Jamie thought of all the tubes of black mascara she'd bought over the years.

"What are you doing here?"

"I'm still looking for your brother." He strolled closer and stopped, studying her perfectly organized desktop.

Jamie stood. Michael was using his height, looming over her desk. He probably had lots of physical tricks to get answers out of his victims, er...interviewees.

"I don't need to tell you where my brother is. He doesn't like press and just wants to be left alone."

Michael pressed his lips together and leaned forward with his palms on her desk. "How much does he remember?"

"None," she snapped and took a step back to lean against her office windowsill.

"Have you talked to the police?"

"They called last night."

"Callahan?"

Jamie straightened. He knew the detective? Or was he messing with her head? "Yes."

"Have you heard from him today?" His eyes were green ice as they studied her intently.

She shook her head and felt her stomach painfully knot. "What's happened?

"How much therapy did your brother have after he came back?"

Jamie sucked in a breath. "Get out."

"He was tortured, wasn't he? He probably had nightmares for years."

She simply stared. "Why are you doing this?"

Michael's eyes softened, and she couldn't look away. "I'm not trying to be mean. I'm trying to understand how your brother thinks. They've found a place they believe the children were held. There's evidence of...Maybe seeing it could help your brother with some memory recall."

What was in that place? What'd the police find? *Oh, Chris...*

"No. He shouldn't see it. I won't put him through that." Chris's screams rang in her head. How many times had she awakened to hear his screams in the middle of the night? His body had finally healed, but his mind...his mind was never the same. Her happy, joking older brother had never returned.

"Where is he?" Michael spoke evenly, drawing the words out.

"I'll tell you the same as I told the police," Jamie snapped back. "I have a phone number. I leave a message on a voice mail. Sometimes he calls me back or texts me, but the number is always blocked, so I know it's probably not the number I leave the message at."

"Did he come home when your parents died in the car accident?"

Jamie swallowed hard. "No. I don't think so."

Michael tensed in a way that reminded of her of a hunting bird spotting its prey. He jumped on her words. "Don't think so? Was he here or not? How long ago was the accident? Two years?"

"Two and a half." Tears smarted at the corners of her eyes.

"Was he here?"

"I didn't see him."

"But?" His eyes wouldn't release hers.

"But I could tell someone had been in my parents' home. Some photos were missing. And there was a sketch left on the counter."

"A sketch? Like a drawing?"

Jamie nodded.

"You didn't tell the police that someone had been in the home?"

"No one forced their way in. Someone had a key. The sketch told me it'd been Chris."

"Why? What'd he draw?"

Jamie shrugged. The sketch was matted, framed, and on her bedroom wall. It wasn't a big secret. "A mountain range. He did lots of drawing after he came back. Especially mountains or beaches. Part of his therapy..." Her voice trailed away.

"You didn't see him at the funeral? He didn't make contact with you?"

"I haven't seen him since he left," she whispered. A small crack widened in her heart.

"When did he leave town originally?"

"It's been close to ten years."

Surprise crossed his face. "You haven't seen your brother in ten years?"

Jamie shook her head.

"What an ass."

She jerked. "Don't call him that. You don't know what he's been through."

"You've been through a lot, too. Your parents died and your brother won't even see you? Sounds selfish. Really selfish to me."

"He...it was okay. I didn't mind. I understood. He'd been through so much. I handled everything for their funeral."

Michael was silent for two seconds, his gaze penetrating. "I bet you handled everything."

Jamie lifted her chin. "I managed."

He was silent for another ten seconds. Jamie could nearly hear the wheels and gears working in his brain.

"Why haven't you seen him? Why does he hide from you?"

Jamie licked at her lips. "He likes to be alone. He doesn't want people talking to him or staring at him. It's always been that way. Ever since he came back. His face...his face wasn't right. His jaw was broken..." Her voiced cracked. "And he had burn scars and cuts that never went away. Even with all his plastic surgery. He didn't like people staring."

"But he's an adult now."

"I don't know if that matters. As soon as he finished high school, he left."

"Your parents let him leave?"

"They didn't try to stop him. They pretty much let him do whatever made him happy. He'd been through hell. He couldn't tell us what, but at night—" Jamie closed her lips.

"Nightmares. Screams?"

She nodded.

"Do you think he's still struggling with that?"

"I think he would come home if he wasn't." Jamie finally looked away from those green eyes. *Why was she telling him this?*

"Maybe it'd be good for him to face some of this. Put it in his past."

"He did so much therapy. Physical and mental, emotional. But he wasn't stupid."

Michael blinked. "Of course not. I didn't say that."

"He was smart. Chris was the sharpest kid in school. Just because he got bad grades didn't mean he was stupid. He could have gotten a scholarship to college—he was so smart. Or a scholarship for his art. His paintings are amazing! He always helped me with my homework because everything was a breeze for him. He was just bored."

Michael stared at her. Her rant had obviously surprised him. He'd been working to pry answers from her, and now she was running off at the mouth. Jamie blinked hard. She wanted Michael to know how intelligent Chris was. She didn't want him to think Chris was some psycho hermit in a hut, in the forest, planning to blow up buildings. Her brother wasn't like that. He was good and sharp and couldn't help it if he felt things very deeply. He needed to be away from crowds. He needed peace. Cities were too fast for him. He'd needed to live where he could move at his own pace, working where his talent was appreciated but not in an office with cubicles. Chris lived and breathed through computers. He freelanced. His clients never met him face-to-face. He only interacted with others through cyberspace.

Or so he'd told her.

Jamie didn't know exactly what her brother did. They stuck to generalities when they talked. No specifics. She'd learned a long time ago not to ask questions.

"After I left yesterday, you made a phone call to Eastern Oregon. Is that where he is?" Michael asked.

Jamie stared and heat flushed her face, her spine straightening. *How in the hell did he do that?* "Isn't that illegal?" she choked out, her words tripping. "How can you get away with that?" What else could this man find out about her? Or Chris?

Michael shrugged crossing his arms. "It's my job."

"I seriously doubt breaking the law is part of *your job*. That's outrageous…snooping into other people's private business. And my brother and I are not part of *your job*."

He looked at the ceiling and blew out a deep breath. "No, you're not. But I've been dealing with a missing brother for twenty years, and this is the first solid lead. I'm going to dig and rip at it until I've exhausted every bit of it." He brought his gaze to hers, dark green eyes hard and cold as granite. "Excuse me for snooping, but right now I don't give a rat's ass."

A missing brother. Understanding and guilt flooded through her. She'd always felt that part of Chris was still missing.

"I don't know where he is," Jamie said quietly. "If he's in Eastern Oregon, this is the first I've heard about it." She refused to be embarrassed that she knew so little about her brother. It was how Chris wanted it. He'd claimed it was for her own good.

Which made no sense at all.

Michael glanced at his watch, and Jamie watched his tan arm muscles ripple as he twisted his wrist.

Christ.

She turned her back on him and looked out the window. Now she wouldn't stare. She focused on the empty swings of the playground but lost concentration as she noticed in the window's reflection that Michael was stepping closer. She whirled around, arms crossed, and he stopped.

His mouth turned up at one side. He'd known she was watching him even with her back turned. "I'm heading to the recovery site right now. Do you want to come?"

Jamie shuddered. "God, no. I don't want to see where…"

All those children.

"I've got someone working on the source of that phone number. Hopefully, I'll have a lead pretty soon. I'd like to narrow the field before I head over to Eastern Oregon."

"You're going to the other side of the state? A seven-hour drive?" The questions burst from her lips. Was he nuts? He'd never find her brother.

His forehead wrinkled. "Of course. How else I'm I going to talk to him? I wouldn't mind some company for that trip. He'd probably be more open to a visit from me if you're with me. Unless you can convince him to talk to me on the phone."

Jamie shook her head. Chris deserved his privacy. "I also told the police I couldn't convince him to talk to them." She gave a harsh laugh. "I guess Chris knew what he was doing when he wouldn't tell me where he was. I was completely useless to the police, and I didn't even have to lie. He always said the lack of knowledge was for my own good."

"What? What do you mean?" Michael had that "I see prey" gaze again. Jamie stared. Had his eyes actually grown darker?

"He always said it was for my own good that I didn't know where to find him. I didn't understand that explanation until just this second."

Again, Jamie watched the gears churn behind those stunning eyes.

He broke the moment by glancing at his watch again. "I need to make some calls. I've got a line on a sheriff from the remote area where I think your brother is at. I'm outta here. Last chance to come." He gave her a sly glance, letting heat infuse his gaze.

He was teasing her, trying to make her uncomfortable. *Men.*

She shook her head again. No question. That was the last place she wanted to be. Buckled into a seat next to Michael Brody in a car for seven hours.

"Fine." He gave a wink. "Till later, then." He turned and vanished out her door.

Jamie sat down hard in her chair, making it groan in protest. She sucked in a deep breath and was rewarded with the reporter's toasted sunshine scent that made her brain spin and her stomach growl. The man was getting under her skin. She'd told him more about her brother than she'd told anyone else in the last ten years. It was those eyes, she mused. He obviously used some sort of Jedi mind-control skill with them to make her talk.

Must be nice to pack up and take off for where-the-hell-ever when his job called for it. She stewed for a few seconds, resenting her job and lack of wanderlust. She wasn't the type to simply up and take a trip. Proper travel took planning and scheduling. Who takes off at the drop of a hat?

Michael Brody—steaming hot reporter and manipulative Jedi mind-bender—did.

CHAPTER SIX

Thank God for fir trees.

The temperature wasn't nearly as staggering under the giant trees. Michael scanned the area. Same official responders as the other horrible day at the old farm. Only the stage was different. No dry, dusty fields smelling like old cows. Today it was tall trees and the smell of moist dirt. Three miles from the old dairy farm and buried deep in the Cascades, the police had made two discoveries. They first found what appeared to be an old bomb shelter under the Oregon dirt.

It wasn't a bomb shelter; it was hell.

Michael gave a shiver in the ninety-degree heat, and goose bumps covered his arms.

From what he'd gathered from the terse statements by OSP Detective Mason Callahan, the bunker was a small space that housed one ancient, disgusting single mattress, rusting food cans, cuffs, chains, buckets, and rope. A high school–aged cadet had tripped over the metal entrance during a search line. Michael thought the opening looked like a hatch to a submarine. Round, small, metal, and it opened up like a tuna fish can.

The police had followed a barely discernible trail from the bus. Almost as faint as a deer path. When the cadaver dog hit on a spot, they initiated a search line and found the bunker. The hit from the cadaver dog revealed their second discovery under the dirt: a deep pit.

So far, the pit had revealed two adult male and two adult female skeletons in a single hole. No children yet. Forensic specialists continued the dig under the eagle eye of Victoria Peres, looking for more remains. Two areas of intense work. One group at the bunker and one group at the growing body pit.

Where was Daniel?

Michael had stood in the same spot behind the yellow tape for an hour, gaze locked on the crew with Vicky. Four times she'd glanced his way and shaken her head. He pressed his lips together. How many more bodies were below the dirt?

"It's got to be related."

Michael turned to see Detective Lusco standing at his side, his gaze also on the group of diggers. The detective moved silently for such a big guy. Or else Michael was severely distracted. Michael figured it was a combination of both.

"Is there any question?" Michael asked.

Lusco shrugged. "Not making any assumptions. Until we find a direct link to that other site, this is a separate investigation. So far there's just the proximity to tie the two together."

Michael nodded. Lusco plainly believed it was part of the first investigation, but he wasn't about to state it out loud until there was some concrete proof. Anyone with half a brain knew it was related. "Where the hell did these adult remains come from?"

Lusco shook his head. "Beats the shit out of me. Fucking crazy. We were expecting to find kids."

Michael's stomach tightened, and he said nothing.

"We'll find out what went on here," Lusco stated. "When we find the son-of-a-bitch that did this—"

"He might be dead," Michael broke in. "It's been twenty years. Or he might be locked up for something else."

Lusco snorted. "If we find out he's already locked up, our job will be easy. Just spread the word that he's a child killer and that'll be the end of him. They aren't partial to child abusers and killers inside. Cheap trial. Save the taxpayers a little money."

Or give me two minutes with him.

A small hand slipped into Michael's. He didn't jump. He instantly knew her touch. He pulled Lacey to him and gave her a tight hug. She fiercely hugged him back, nearly cutting off his air.

"I'm sorry, Michael," she whispered to his shirt.

He gave her a final squeeze and reluctantly let go.

"Hey, Dr. Campbell. Thought we'd see you today." Lusco smiled sadly. Lacey gave the big cop a quick hug. Michael waited for the unreasonable jealousy that always came when he watched a man touch Lacey. It didn't come.

What the fuck?

Michael zoned out as she asked Lusco about his kids. Was he finally accepting that Lacey belonged to someone else? His gaze slid from her blonde ponytail to toned, tanned legs. Huh. Maybe his heart was finally catching up with what he knew in his head.

He watched Lacey step into her Tyvek suit while talking of her wedding flower decisions with the detective. Ray Lusco was the only cop Michael knew who could discuss dressy heels, baby colic, and flower arrangements with women. It'd surprised the hell out of Michael at one point, but now he was used to it.

Voices rose at the hatch, yanking everyone's attention. Lacey and Ray went quiet and watched Detective Callahan emerge from the small opening. The salt-and-pepper-haired detective scanned the scattered groups until his gaze landed on Lusco. He pulled the booties off his cowboy boots, dropped them in an evidence bag, and headed in their direction, his face expressionless. *Not good news.*

Michael felt Lacey's hand slip into his again as they waited for the detective to come closer.

"What is it?" Michael spoke first. His gut churned woozily around the Big Mac he'd had for lunch.

Callahan's gaze went to his partner and exchanged silent words.

"Mason?" Lacey gripped Michael's hand tighter. "Do you need me down there?"

The detective shook his head. "No remains in there."

Michael's stomach instantly calmed. *Daniel wasn't in that bunker.* He exhaled and heard Lacey do the same.

His gaze darted to the pit, and his stomach clenched again. If not in the bunker, then Daniel was probably in that pit. Thrown away like garbage. Faintly he heard Lacey give a small gasp and realized he was hurting her hand. He let go. She didn't.

"What is it, Mason?" Lusco spoke low and stepped in to close their small circle.

Callahan's steady brown gaze went to Michael's. *Here it comes.*

"We've found a bunch of kid backpacks."

Michael couldn't breathe.

"Daniel's name is on one," Callahan said quietly.

"Navy blue, Ninja Turtles," Michael automatically said, the pack's image clearly in his mind. Along with Daniel's jacket with the Portland Trail Blazers' logo, blue jeans, and red Nikes. *What was your brother wearing when you last saw him?* How many times had he answered that question?

Callahan nodded, disappointment briefly touching his eyes.

Michael understood. He'd hoped the detective had been wrong, too.

"Anything to offer an explanation for those adult remains?" Lusco broke the silence.

Callahan's face told nothing. "Possibly."

Michael wanted to grab the detective and shake him, yell at him to spill every word about what he'd seen in that underground prison. Instead, he held tight to Lacey's tiny hand. The diamond on her engagement ring dug into his palm.

"Do the other backpacks appear to belong to the other children we...found?" Lacey's soft voice cracked.

Callahan nodded. "Each one is labeled with the child's name. Clearly marked on the outside in black marker."

"Wait a minute." Michael shook his head. "No. They weren't marked. It's unsafe to have a kid's name plastered across his backpack where anyone could learn his name. The school wouldn't allow that. Sane parents wouldn't allow that." Lacey nodded her head in agreement.

A look of distaste crossed Callahan's face. "Someone wrote on the packs. The print seemed the same on each one. I assumed it'd been done at their school."

Michael felt Lacey's hand give an abrupt quiver.

"He did it. He wrote on them. Why would he do that?" she whispered. "Did he want us to find them? Know we'd found the right place? Or was it for a reason back then? A way to tell them apart."

Michael briefly closed his eyes. "I don't know, Lace."

"Those children. All those children." Tears sounded in the back of her throat.

Lusco spoke slowly. "Looks like we've got our definitive connection. This is a single investigation."

Michael met Lusco's gaze and then Callahan's. "We...you could use a witness. Did you ask Jamie Jacobs where her brother is?"

Lusco looked surprised, but Callahan didn't blink. "Leave the Jacobs woman alone. We'll find Chris Jacobs and question him again. You don't need to go hunting for him."

Michael should have known Callahan was keeping an eye on him. "No problem. I'll stay away from her brother."

Jamie Jacobs was another matter.

★ ★ ★

The man stared at the Yahoo! news stories.

Adults? They were finding the bodies of adults? What the hell?

He stood and crossed over to the bottle of single malt he kept handy to impress guests. He poured a generous drink and swore at his shaking hand. He threw back the scotch and relished the smooth burn on his throat. Inhaling deep and meeting his gaze in the mirror, he waited for the calm to flow through him.

He'd interfered with several people's lives so long ago, but he'd never felt bad. Not at all. If he hadn't acted, what would have happened?

Sometimes a few need to suffer for the greater good. He'd done the right thing.

Twenty years.

Secrets had been hidden for twenty years. And now they were exploding out of the ground like land mines. One small trip wire had set off a chain reaction.

The chain would never connect to him. He flicked a speck off his jacket shoulder and straightened his tie, lifting his chin. Never. He'd prepared too well. He'd taken every precaution, and the chain would end right where he wanted it to. He'd picked the perfect scapegoat.

Empowered, he stepped over to his desk and hit a button on the phone.

"Sir?" The voice was tinny through the speaker.

"In my office, please. We've got a situation."

"Right away, sir."

★ ★ ★

The old man gazed at Chris with shrewd eyes that nearly glowed in the dark of the evening. "This the real thing or another practice run?"

Chris shook his head. "Don't know," he lied. "Doesn't matter. Same rules apply."

Dark eyes held his for a second and then looked to the boy wrestling with the rangy yellow dog in the feeble light from a single light bulb. "The room's ready."

Chris nodded. "I appreciate it." He sucked in a deep breath, gaze automatically checking the shadows of the shop. Juan's bakery was ancient. The equipment had been old when Juan's father opened up shop. He kept the place spotless. No dust dared spend any time on his floor or shelves. This time of night the single room was still, but the smell of fresh bread lingered heavily in the air. His mouth watered.

A cackle answered him. "You've paid me well. Wouldn't be able to keep the shop open without your rent." He snorted. "Rent for a room that you never use."

"We've been there a time or two." Chris handed over some bills. The money didn't matter to him. It was like payment on an insurance policy. He was purchasing peace of mind.

He could watch the cameras positioned around his home from his computer. And wait. See who would come looking for him. See whom the stories shook out of the brush, moved to action. No one knew he rented the room. Juan lived alone and had been sworn to secrecy. Chris had noticed the window above the shop four years ago and had convinced the old man to let him borrow the space. It was a win-win situation. Juan kept his shop, and Chris felt safe.

The question was, how hard would he be looked for? If he put the old man in danger, he'd never forgive himself. The dog splayed his front legs and bent low to the ground, giving a playful growl. His son gave a high-pitched giggle and growled back. Chris silently watched.

He'd die before danger touched his son.

He'd figured he had two or three days after Jamie's call before he had to make his move. The news had finally hit the Internet, his Google alerts filling his inbox. *Oregon school bus. Missing children. Kidnapping.*

The names of his schoolmates.

Each one had burned in his brain for twenty years. Their names and their faces. It'd been a shock to see their old school pictures online. And his own picture from that year. Short hair, innocent smile, so trusting. He'd avoided school picture day when he returned, citing his scars, telling his parents that he didn't want anyone to see pictures of him.

Over the last twenty-four hours, he'd been glued to the Internet, reading every word he could find on the grisly discoveries. He'd shed tears over the descriptions of the tiny skulls, picturing them as the friends he'd once played with. Kendall with her long black hair and lisp. Jeremy with the lopsided grin and mass of freckles.

Why was he the one still alive?

Memories had spilled over as he studied the pictures. And he was there. In the hellhole again. Reliving it all. The man's lifeless pale eyes, the skin so white Chris could almost see through it. The Ghostman had released the youngest girls first. The other kids had cried and begged to be next. He'd seen Kendall leaving with her hand clasped in the Ghostman's, a wide smile on her face as they climbed the ladder out of the stinking hole. Had it been a gift that they never knew each other's fate?

His stomach heaved, and he felt sweat start at his temples. Breathe. In. Out. In. *Damn it.* This was a certain sign there'd be nightmares tonight. Fine. He simply wouldn't sleep. Laughter pealed as Brian was knocked over by the dog and it vigorously licked him in the face.

Old Juan cricked his neck to look at the two tussling on the ground. "That's a good boy you've got there." Brown eyes cannily read Chris's face. "Parents do anything for their kids, yes?"

Chris nodded and tried to swallow the lump in his throat. "Anything."

★ ★ ★

"Yes! We've got a match." Ray Lusco thumped a fist on his desk in the OSP building.

"On one of the bodies in the mass grave?" Mason asked. Sitting directly across from Ray at his own antique metal desk, he opened the digital file with the photos of the grave, and thumbnails filled his screen. A few lessons from his son, Jake, had improved Mason's skill with the computer. He had about ten sticky notes for different procedures dotting his monitor. Patiently outlined by Jake.

Mass grave weren't quite the right words to describe the pit. Each body had been buried at different times. One on top of the other. Why would someone reopen the same site each time? Curiosity? Had he wanted to see what the previous body now looked like? Or maybe the earth was easier to dig since it'd been disturbed several times before.

The dig had been a forensic nightmare. Bodies mixed together. Remains disturbed every time the killer had added another body. Had he purposefully mixed them together?

Five adults had been found. Not old, according to Dr. Peres, the forensic anthropologist on the scene. Late teens or early twenties. The woman had been in full work mode. Mason swore the challenge of the pit had put the anthropologist in heaven. She'd called for a dozen assistants and painstakingly photographed and removed every bone. Mason had seen her eyes light up each time a skull was uncovered. For the most part, she worked silently, keeping her theories to herself, barking curt orders to her workers, and simply telling the police the sex of the victims as each was uncovered.

"Steven James Monroe. Age twenty-four. Arrests for prostitution and possession. Last known address is nearly twenty-five years old. Reported missing a year before our bus vanished. Parents filed the report."

"Twenty-four years old," muttered Mason as he studied the old photo of Monroe. The kid looked innocent, young, fresh. How'd he end up in their hole? "Somebody was active before our kids were taken. How much you want to bet the others will be prostitutes, too? Maybe a Jeffrey Dahmer type had been in the area. But I guess this guy liked men *and* women."

"If they do turn out to be prostitutes, it adds weight to a sexual motive." Ray's voice tightened, and Mason knew he was getting angry. "Coordinates with the shit we found in that underground tank."

"Just because the first one had a shady past doesn't mean the rest of them will. They could be missing college kids for all we know. Think he kept adults in the tank first?"

Ray nodded, and Mason heard his teeth grind.

"Why the switch to kids?"

Ray shrugged. "You're asking the wrong person."

"Wonder if our unsub is still alive?" They could be chasing a goddamned ghost.

Mason grabbed up the receiver as his desk phone rang.

"Callahan."

"Detective Callahan? This is Cecilia Brody."

Mason's grip tightened on the phone. "Dr. Brody, what can I do for you?"

"I've been giving some thought to your questions from the other day."

Right, Mason thought. *You mean you've finally decided to share something you held back.* He'd felt both parents weren't saying every-thing that day in the sick woman's room. At first he'd thought it was because of the presence of their son, but Mason had rapidly discarded that theory. The parents had talked dispassionately to their son like a stranger.

"What have you thought of, Dr. Brody?"

The line was silent for a long second, and Mason worried the woman had changed her mind.

"You'd asked if there was anyone we could think of who would want to hurt us through Daniel."

Mason stayed silent.

"I've been thinking, and I remember about a month before Daniel was taken, I'd had an issue with a patient."

"An issue?"

"A death. He died on my table."

Mason straightened in his chair, making it squeal in protest. "He died? Like during surgery?"

"Yes. And the family laid the blame on me." Her voice was steady, emotionless. "He was high risk. It was do something or he would definitely die. It was worth a chance, and his wife knew it. I presented my case to her, and she gave me permission to try to save him."

"What happened?"

"I couldn't save him. Once his chest was open, I saw it was even worse than we'd expected." Dr. Brody abruptly went quiet.

Mason waited, wondering if she was about to lose composure. He sincerely doubted it. The slight woman had a spine of steel.

"Mr. Jeong wasn't old. He was young, considering the type of medical issues he faced. He'd been in the country visiting family when he collapsed in one of the local shopping malls. He was transported to my hospital—"

My hospital?

"—and the family was immediately told the outlook was grim. I was amazed by the number of family members present. It seemed to grow by the hour. The man's father arrived and took command of the large group. He only spoke Korean and didn't live in the US either."

Dr. Brody cleared her throat.

"Language was a bit of a problem. The patient's wife was pretty fluent but couldn't calm her father-in-law. After the death, the man repeatedly sent me threatening letters and tried to bring lawsuits against the hospital and myself. He was rich. Loaded with money. He threw it around, trying to get me fired, trying to get the media's attention. It didn't work."

"What happened with the lawsuits?" Mason wondered how much money someone had to have to warrant a comment about wealth from the affluent Dr. Brody.

Mason printed on a yellow legal pad. *Lawyers? Court records?*

"Nothing came of it. There was some minor harassment. I was blatantly followed by Asian men for several days after the lawsuits were thrown out."

"Did you contact police?"

"No. They never came close. Just followed at a distance and made certain I knew they were there."

"You think this man was angry enough to hurt your son?"

A long silence filled the line. "I don't know," she said slowly. "You asked me to consider everything. I was haunted by this man's anger for a long time. I've never seen anyone's gaze show so much hate...I can still see his eyes. He truly believed I killed his son."

Mason heard the words she didn't say. *He may have killed mine in revenge.*

"Thank you, Dr. Brody. We'll look into this. Can you forward me the records you have? We'll contact the hospital and their legal department, too."

"It could be nothing," she said quickly.

"It needs to be ruled out."

"Yes, well...whatever it takes. I want to know what happened to Daniel. I need to know before..."

Mason blinked. He'd nearly forgotten the steely woman was ill. "Doctor...what is your medical condition?"

"I need a kidney," she stated simply. "Without it, I'll be dead within the year. My husband and Michael can't donate. They each only have one kidney apiece. A hereditary issue. We need a special match for me to lower the rejection risk."

Mason mentally squirmed, her utter frankness throwing him for a loop. "Ah...okay...that's not good...I hope they find—"

"Thank you, Detective. Good day, Detective."

The phone clicked in his ear.

Shit. Mason slowly lowered the receiver and rubbed a hand across the back of his neck. Ray watched him intently from across their desks.

"Dr. Brody?"

Mason nodded. "She had a patient who died a few months before her boy disappeared. The patient's father sounds like a nutcase. A rich, foreign nutcase. Possible revenge motive."

Ray nodded. "That's more than any of the other parents have thought of. Kendall Johnson's mother had an argument with her daughter's music teacher the day before she vanished. That was the only incident she could think of. The music teacher was seventy-two at the time." Ray's voice twisted wryly. "Passed away eight years ago."

"The Brodys never mentioned this patient to investigators twenty years ago." Mason scratched at his chin. "I wonder why not. Why now? I didn't think to ask her a minute ago."

"She's had twenty years to think about it," offered Ray.

"The senator must have known. I could tell there was some-thing more he wanted to say that day in her room. He must have wanted his wife to bring it up." Mason tapped his pen on his desk. How did this fit with what they'd found out in the woods?

An angry Korean father and a local male prostitute.

Two and two weren't adding up to four.

"Lotta missing pieces," stated Ray. His logic was following the same path as Mason's.

"Yep. And it's our job to find the rest."

CHAPTER SEVEN

Jamie shut off the news. She didn't want to see any more body bags or people digging in the dirt. She didn't want to hear more vague police statements or reporter speculation. She was sick of TV. She'd caught a quick glimpse of Michael Brody standing behind the yellow tape, his hand clasped in a gorgeous blonde's.

It was a brief shot. Less than a second as the camera had panned over a group of police and detectives. Why was it stuck on replay in her brain?

She'd recognized Michael's stiff stance immediately. He'd looked like he was clamping down on every emotion he had. Just like he had at her school this morning. When she'd made a fool of herself by telling him those personal things about Chris.

And when he'd invited her to travel with him...He hadn't been holding back all emotions at that point. She'd seen the dark sparks in his eyes. She could have said yes. After all, it was her brother he wanted to see. Not spend time with her. Jamie shook her head and marched into her kitchen and attacked the dishes she'd left in the sink. She never left dishes in the sink. Where was her mind lately?

Earlier she'd locked her keys in her car. She'd stood there, staring dumbly at the empty pocket in her purse where the keys belonged. Then she'd peeked through the window and did a double take. There they were. In plain sight on the console. Blowing out a disgusted breath, she'd searched under her car for the little magnetic box she'd hidden years ago when she'd first bought the car. She believed in preparing ahead, but she'd truly never thought she'd need that box.

Her doorbell rang. She moved to the door and pressed her face against the wood to look through the hole.

Speak of the devil. Her porch light illuminated his face in the dark of the late evening.

He winked, and her heart did a double flip.

Sheesh.

Fuming at her reaction, she threw the bolts and opened the door. "What do you want?"

"I need you to come with me to find your brother."

"No. I already told you I wouldn't go. Leave him alone." She shook her head with each word. "He doesn't need to be a part of this. He doesn't do well with media attention. I told you he struggles with nightmares. This is just going to make it worse."

"Is it your brother you're protecting, or his son?"

Jamie's knees twitched, and she held tight to the doorknob. "Son? His son? Chris doesn't have children." *What?*

Sympathy and anger flashed in those green eyes. "He does. You didn't know?"

Jamie couldn't speak. She shook her head. *Chris? Son?*

"Looks like he was protecting more than just you," Michael said quietly. His gaze abruptly narrowed. "Hey. You need to sit down." He grabbed both her arms and turned her toward the living room, guiding her to sit on the couch, and sat beside her. His weight on the cushions nearly caused her to tip into him. She fought to stay upright.

She couldn't breathe. Confusion spun in her mind. She had a nephew? Had her parents known? "How old?"

"How old is what?"

"The boy. How old is my nephew?" she croaked.

"About seven or eight years old."

Jamie squeezed her eyes shut and brushed angrily at the tears. "He never told me."

"Yeah. I see that." Sympathy filled his voice. "I'm sorry."

"He's married? He never told me?" *Why? Why hadn't Chris told her?*

"Doesn't look like he was ever married. The mother died when the boy was one."

More tears streamed. Tears for a motherless baby and his lonely father. "She died? Who was she?"

"I have a name, not much else. Elena Padilla. She was twenty-two when she died."

Jamie looked down and saw she was holding both of Michael's hands in a death grip, her knuckles white. She released and her fingers felt like they'd been frozen in place. They fought to straighten. She shoved them between her knees and turned to look at him.

Concern wrinkled his forehead. He watched her like he expected her to crack in half.

"I'm sorry," she mumbled, her tongue feeling numb. "It's just that...Chris is all..."

"He's the only family you have left. And now it turns out he was hiding more."

"What's his name? What's the boy's name?" she pleaded. Her mind wouldn't stop spinning. *She had a nephew? And Chris never said a word?*

"I don't know," Michael answered.

"Are you certain?" she asked again, searching his gaze. "Are you absolutely certain he has a son?"

"No doubts," he said softly.

She looked away, unable to face the pity in his eyes. "Do you know where he is?" She was done wondering how Michael dug up information or the accuracy of that information. Her instinct told her he didn't let words cross his lips unless his facts were triple-checked.

"I have a good idea. A good starting place anyway."

Jamie's heart clenched tight, overwhelmed with a need to see the faces of Chris and his son. "How do you know? How did you find out?"

Michael shrugged. "The phone call you made indicated a general area in Eastern Oregon. It's pretty sparsely populated. I made some calls and got a hold of the sheriff in the area. He knows a Chris Jacobs who lives off the grid as far as possible. He says it's the type of area where people go to avoid the rest of the world. Sound like your brother?"

"Yes, unfortunately."

"The reason he remembers your brother is because of how Chris's wife—well, not his wife legally—died in a car accident. I can't find a record of a marriage, but I did find newspaper clippings about the accident. And it talks about the child. The information matches what the sheriff told me. It was pretty bad and sounds like a scene that would stick in your head for a long time."

"Don't tell me. Please," Jamie burst out, meeting his gaze. She didn't want the gruesome death of a young woman playing through her mind.

He nodded at her request. She could see a shadow in his eyes that hadn't been there before. From the description of the accident? How many horrific things had he witnessed or covered for the newspaper over the years?

"Now will you go find him with me? Your brother is more likely to talk to you than some stranger. Chris may not believe I'm not looking for a story. This is personal. I'm going because I need to know what happened to my brother."

An urge to see her own brother hit Jamie like a blow to the chest. It'd been so long…

But to-do lists flooded Jamie's brain. "Umm…I need to stop the paper and mail and talk to my neighbor about feeding my cat, and I'm supposed to meet with a parent late tomorrow…"

Even to her own ears, her excuses were weak.

"Christ, princess. Yes or no? I'm leaving tomorrow morning. It's a long drive. Some company would be nice."

She froze, unable to agree. "I need a few days." She couldn't make that type of immediate decision without thinking it through. For a trip, she had to have a plan before she began. After Chris had vanished, her parents no longer let her out of their sight. A simple afternoon to hang out at a friend's home involved a visit by her parents first. And a sleepover at a girl-friend's? Forget it. She'd been in college before she slept without her parents under the same roof.

It was a habit that was hard to break.

Michael glanced at his watch. "Fine. I get it." He stood and locked gazes with her, dark green eyes flashing.

Jamie blinked. His heated gaze didn't match the tone of his words. It said, *I want you to come with me now.* And he didn't want her simply for the convenience of speaking with her brother. He wanted her for...something else.

Heat flooded her belly. What would it be like to be alone with this man and his energy? Silent sparks erupted every time he was near her. He was dangerous.

Jamie avoided danger on principle. She rose to her feet and stepped away. "I can't. I can't leave on a moment's notice."

"Why not? You don't have family to arrange for. Just a cat. You're on summer break. It's time to move on impulse for once."

His words stung. She was well aware of the lack of spontaneity in her life, but she didn't need other people to point it out. It was understandable. It was her parents' reaction to the kidnapping of her brother. It'd created in her a sense of precaution and the need to think through every move she made. Sure, she'd sacrificed some impulsiveness. But there were worse habits to have.

Michael had highlighted her biggest shortcoming, and he barely knew her. She lifted her chin. "Call me if you find him. And his son. I want to know about my nephew."

Silence choked her living room.

A sad smile crossed his face. "I will." He turned and strode to her door. He opened it, looked over his shoulder at her, and vanished.

The sound of the closing door echoed in her empty house. Jamie exhaled and plopped back down on the couch. Would Michael find Chris? Chris had made it clear over the years he wanted to be left alone. He hadn't responded to the voice message she'd left yesterday. Maybe she should leave him another one? Warn him a reporter was looking for him?

She shook her head. Plenty of people had searched for Chris over the years. He knew how to stay hidden. As tenacious as Michael appeared to be, Chris knew how to avoid reporters. But, boy, her brother had some explaining to do about her nephew. When the publicity died down, she'd pressure him to let her meet the child.

But why did she feel that she'd just missed an interesting opportunity with Michael Brody?

★ ★ ★

The man was angry, pacing in his office.

"What the hell were you thinking? What was that place? A torture chamber or sex dungeon? I told you to get rid of them. Not keep them as personal slaves for your twisted lusts. Jesus fucking Christ."

Gerald sat silently. He'd heard different versions of this lecture before. The man just needed to vent. What did he care?

"I can't believe you left that bunker full of crap. Who knows what they'll find in there? These days, fucking forensics can trace you from a grain of rice you dropped. You left a treasure trove of kid junk for the police to sift through. Your fingerprints could be everywhere. And I *know* your fingerprints are in the system." The man halted his pacing to stare him in the eye.

"I never went in there without latex gloves," he said. That wasn't quite true. The gloves came off for certain things.

"Did you leave any gloves? They can get fingerprints off the insides of those damned things."

"Of course not."

His boss held his stare, and Gerald understood why people respected him. He could convey every emotion in a way that made the listener feel it deep in their gut. Right now he was telling Gerald that he didn't believe him.

He was pretty sure there were no gloves left inside. His last visit to the bunker had been over a decade ago, and he'd cleaned out any incriminating garbage. He'd left all the kids' stuff. It didn't point any fingers at him. It just showed that children had been there.

He'd eliminated most of the kids pretty fast. Girls first. Then the younger boys. The two oldest boys had appealed to him the most, so he'd kept them the longest.

For the millionth time, he wondered about Chris Jacobs. Did he really have no memory of those years? Or was he just covering his ass? Gerald had made it clear to the boys what he could do to their families if they disobeyed. And he'd sent that reminder basket to the kid in the hospital. A strong message not to talk.

Either way, the kid had stayed silent for twenty years.

His boss was having the same train of thought. "That Jacobs kid might have some memories stirred up by all this publicity."

"He doesn't even live in the state anymore. At least, I can't find him. I look every now and then. He's put as much space as possible between him and his past."

The boss gave a withering stare. "The fucking story has gone national. Maybe worldwide. Dead kids do that to the media."

Gerald shrugged. "He doesn't know who I am or where to find me."

"They could put out a description. You're a little *distinctive* looking." The man looked him up and down.

Gerald cringed inside. He'd done everything he could to look as normal as possible, but he constantly wondered if people were staring at him. He'd been a small child when he first realized he didn't look like the other kids. And kids were cruel. He'd read that some animals ostracize based on appearance. Society acted like those animals. He'd always been the outcast.

"The important witness died. Daniel," Gerald argued. "He's the one who could've done some damage. He could have messed things up real bad, if he'd survived."

"You're fucking lucky Daniel's dead." His boss looked ready to pop a nut. "If I had known you were keeping those kids alive instead of getting rid of them, I would have strangled you with my bare hands back then.

"You've got some loose ends to tie up. Find Chris Jacobs *now* and get rid of him. You've put this off too long. I don't know why I've put up with it. You should have taken care of it the minute he appeared. You'd told me they were all dead. Fucking lied to me that you were hanging on to some."

His boss was starting to repeat himself. His face was red, and his silver hair stuck out in places. Usually he was impeccably groomed, but the situation was wearing on him.

Gerald ran a hand through his own hair. "I've looked for him. Every few years, I look. I've done every computer search possible. Either he doesn't exist on paper or he's changed his name. My money is on him changing his name."

"He could still come forward. Maybe consent to be hypnotized to see if they can pick some shit out of his brain."

"And what's he gonna say? I remember a guy with white hair and some tattoos? I lived in an underground can for two years with another boy? How can that lead back to us?"

"Daniel lived for a long time. Daniel could've told him what he knew." His boss wiped at the sweat on his temple.

"No one knew we were connected back then. A kid wouldn't have figured that out."

"Daniel was smart. Everyone said he was a fucking mini-genius."

"Even a genius can't add one and one together to come up with five," Gerald argued.

"What the hell does that mean?"

"He didn't have enough facts to figure it out."

"You ask the sister where Chris Jacobs is?" his boss asked.

"Everyone has asked the sister. Police, media. She doesn't say shit."

"She's got to have an idea of where her brother is. Start there. Finish the damned job. I don't know how I've trusted you with anything. Now get out."

Gerald hated him. "Yes, sir."

There was a very good reason his boss trusted him. And Gerald hoped one day he'd have the opportunity to ram that reason into his perfect face.

★ ★ ★

"I'm sorry I cut it short today, Lisa. You gonna keep going?" Balancing on one foot, Jamie pulled her other foot behind her until it touched her shorts, stretching the muscle in the front of the thigh. "I don't know why it's cramping so bad."

Lisa jogged in place. "I'll do another circuit. Want to try tomorrow?"

"Yes, I think it'll be fine. I'll see you tomorrow morning."

Lisa spun around and dashed off. "Alternate some heat and ice!" she yelled over her shoulder.

Jamie nodded and gingerly headed up the walkway to her front door. *Damn.* Her thigh was really sore. They'd only covered three miles. Half of what she and Lisa usually did several times a week. She'd dig out the heating pad and do some gentle stretching. Drink lots, too. She didn't think she was dehydrated, but the days had been getting ridiculously hot. It could happen.

Suddenly very thirsty, she pushed her front door open and made a beeline to the kitchen. And froze. *Jesus Christ.* Every drawer in her kitchen had been emptied onto the floor. Every cupboard was open. She slowly backed out of the room, eyes wide at the disaster.

Get out. Now.

"Don't move. Don't turn around," a male voice uttered behind her.

She didn't.

Something small and hard pressed against the back of her skull.

Her heart started to pound its way out of her chest, her mouth instantly dry, and her vision tunneled.

"I want you to slowly lie down on the floor. On your stomach and put your hands behind you."

He's going to rape me.

Jamie didn't move. If she got down on the floor, she wouldn't have a chance.

"Get down, now!" he growled.

She shook her head, unable to speak, unable to move her legs.

"Fucking bitch." He rammed his hand into the small of her back and ground the gun into her neck. "Move it!"

Jamie fell to her knees and winced. He grabbed one of her arms and wrenched it behind her back, the gun still digging into her neck.

"Where's your brother?"

Chris? "What?" Her voice squeaked.

The gun dug deeper. "Where's that fucking brother of yours? The one with the pretty round scars down his face." He moved the gun around to her cheek and shoved it into her flesh. "You want some matching scars? I've got a pack of cigarettes handy."

Tears rolled down her cheeks. The gun hurt, but not as bad as the image of Chris's skin burning.

"Where is he? I know that reporter is looking for him. Everybody wants a piece of Chris Jacobs right now. The famous survivor." He spit the last sentence. "Does he really not remember where he was and what happened to him? I bet he remembers my cigarettes."

Jamie frantically shook her head. "Nothing...he doesn't..."

Oh my God. He's the one. He's the one who hurt Chris. He killed all those children.

"I don't believe that. And all this publicity is bound to stir up some old memories. I bet he won't be sleeping very good once he hears about all those little discoveries at the farm. Now. Be a good sister and tell me where he is."

"I don't know! I really don't know! I call a number and leave a message...he gets back to me eventually. I called yesterday, but I haven't heard back. But Michael..." Jamie clamped her mouth shut.

He burned my brother. All those children...

She felt her skin tear as the gun dug into her cheekbone.

Chris's nightmares...the screaming...he's the one...

"Michael? The reporter? He found something? He knows where to find that skinny bastard?"

Jamie shook her head, trying to pull away from the tip of the gun. "He doesn't know."

"Why don't I believe you?" He yanked on the arm behind her back, and her vision blurred.

"I don't know...I don't know what you want!"

"I want your brother!" He gave a hard shove, and Jamie's face slammed into the wood floor.

Every self-defense article she'd ever read scrambled in her brain. One rule stuck out: Fight back and scream!

She rolled over and lashed out with her legs and feet, kicking him in the shins and knees.

She screamed. Every ounce of energy went into her screams and her legs.

Years of running powered her legs, and he stumbled backward in surprise. The gun slipped from his hand, and she scrambled for it. He dove forward, grabbed it, and backhanded her across the face with the gun. The metal tore her lips.

She screamed more. He was on her level now, and she kept kicking and kicking. Arms, legs, gut, ass. She connected everywhere. He scrambled backward, crablike, slamming the gun against the floor each time his hand moved.

Keep kicking! Keep kicking! Jamie pushed forward, scooting on her butt, using the most powerful part of her body to hammer him with her feet. He grabbed a cupboard door and heaved himself off the floor. He whirled around the corner, out of the kitchen, and ran.

Jamie clambered to her hands and knees and shot up after him. Catching her balance on the doorframe, she saw a glimpse of his shirt as he dashed out her front door.

She grasped the kitchen doorframe with both hands as she stared down her hallway and out into the bright sunshine. Jamie slowly slid down the frame and sat on the floor.

He's gone. He's the one...the children...Chris...

She couldn't breathe, and her heart wouldn't stop thrashing inside her chest. Her arms shook. She crossed them on her chest, squeezing tight. They didn't stop.

She needed to call 911. *Now.*

The phone on her counter seemed a mile away.

Oh my God, he almost killed me...

She blinked, seeing the cupboards start to shimmy and warp. Her stomach heaved.

Oh crap.

She grabbed a bowl from the mess on the floor and vomited.

★ ★ ★

Michael threw another pair of shorts in his bag.

"Fuck." What was wrong with him? He'd planned to be on the road an hour ago, and he wasn't even packed. His internal alarm clock had failed for the first time in his life, and he had a good idea of why.

He'd been awake half the night thinking about Jamie Jacobs. And spent the other half dreaming about her. It wasn't until after he'd stepped out of the shower that he realized he was running late.

He'd been disappointed last night when she'd refused to go to with him. He'd wanted her to help deal with Chris when he found him. He wanted her there to smooth his way. And he ached to get to know her better. He scowled into his bathroom drawer, digging for a new razor. Jamie was different. She didn't feel like a temporary female distraction. His entire focus was on this woman and how to spend more time with her.

He hadn't known something was missing from his life until it punched him in the gut.

Jesus Christ. He sounded like a religious convert.

He shoved his feet into leather flip-flops and headed for the front door, his carry-on slung over his shoulder. He checked his pockets. Keys, wallet, phone. Good to go.

His front door slammed behind him, and the heat of the morning slapped his face. It was in the high eighties already, and it was only seven o'clock. How hot would Eastern Oregon be? The east side of the state's weather was more extreme than the west. Either hotter or colder. He jogged to the black SUV parked in front of his garage, feeling his phone vibrate in his pocket. He ignored it, planning to return the call once he was on his way.

He was on a search for answers about Daniel. All his life he'd wanted to know what'd happened to his brother, and he was getting close. He could feel it.

Once out of his neighborhood, he shoved the phone in the holder on his dash and glanced at the screen. No name, just a number. His heart pounded. Jamie's number. He'd never dialed it, but her cell, home, and work numbers were all filed in his memory from his research.

"Return call," he requested.

Did she change her mind about the trip?

Nearly missing a stop sign, he hit his brakes and commanded his heart to slow.

"Michael?" Her panicked voice filled his vehicle, and his chest tightened.

"Jamie. What's wrong?"

Sputtering breaths filled the line.

"Damn it, Jamie, what happened?" He grabbed his phone, turned off the speaker, and pressed it to his ear. "Are you okay?"

"I'm fine...well...yes, I'm fine—"

"You don't sound fine,"

"Um...someone broke into my house—"

"Get out. Get out of the house right now." His grip could have crushed the phone.

"No...it's okay. The police are here and I'm fine."

Michael blew out a breath. *Thank God.* "Let me talk to one of them." It was going to take an hour to get the story out of Jamie. He put the phone back on speaker and pulled a U-turn. *Fuck the airport.* He headed toward Jamie's.

"This is Officer Byers."

"Byers. Is she really okay? What the hell happened over there?"

"She's gonna be okay. She's a little banged up. The EMTs bandaged her face. She's lucky, considering he was armed."

"He had a gun?" Michael hit his brakes.

"The guy dug into her cheek with it. She fought him off."

"What?" Michael ground his molars together.

"She fought him off. Who knows what else he would have done."

"Ah fuck. You find him?"

"Not yet. She got a good look at him. We'll get him."

"Let me talk to her again, please." Michael exhaled a breath that lasted a full five seconds. *She could have died.*

"Michael?" Her voice was steadier.

"Hey, princess. I'm on my way. I'll be there in ten minutes."

"I'm not sure why I called you. You don't have—"

"I'm coming. Don't argue." *Nothing would stop him.*

"Okay," she whispered.

"And we're gonna have a little talk about fighting with men who have guns."

She gave a choking laugh that ended in sobs.

"Sit tight, I'm coming."

"Don't hang up, okay?" she rasped.

"Wouldn't dream of it."

★ ★ ★

Two police cruisers were parked in front of Jamie's house when Michael pulled up. Jamie and three uniforms stood outside on her walkway, talking in a tight circle. She had on snug black running shorts that left nothing to the imagination and made him catch his breath. *Holy crap.* Did she actually wear those in public? Anger blew away his shock as he realized the backs of her upper thighs were bandaged.

All four turned as he slammed his door and jogged across the street. Jamie's arms were tightly folded across her chest like a protective shield, her face pale under her tan.

Her face. Michael wanted to strangle her intruder. She had a large white bandage on the right side of her face, and her lips were swollen and starting to scab.

He strode straight to her and pulled her against his chest in a bear hug, not caring if she thought he was being too forward. After what she'd been through, she had to need a human touch. She stiffened for a second and then blew out a deep breath and relaxed as he rubbed his hands across her back. Her Lycra tank was smooth to his touch, but not nearly as smooth as the silkiness of her skin. She kept her arms across her chest but carefully leaned her forehead against his cheek. She shuddered.

"I'm okay."

He rubbed her back for a few seconds longer and then stepped back, keeping a firm grip on her shoulders and looking her in the eye. "What happened?"

One of the uniforms coughed, and Michael glared his way. "Is the house clear?"

"Yes, we cleared it. Ms. Jacobs hasn't gone back in to see if anything is missing yet." The cop raised an eyebrow at Jamie, and Michael wanted to kick him for pressuring her. His name tag read "Byers."

"I'm ready now," she said. She reached up and took one of Michael's hands off her shoulders, gripping it. "Will you go with me?"

Like anyone could stop him.

She started toward her front door, and Michael glanced at the cops just in time to see their gazes drop to her ass. "Christ," he muttered, and their gazes immediately bounced up. Protectiveness washed over him, and he bit back a growl.

Jamie stepped through the doorway and slowly walked down the hall. Michael felt a tremor in her hand as she turned into the kitchen. "Should I be walking in here?" she asked. "Am I going to ruin evidence?"

"Just don't move anything till they get some pictures," Michael said. "It's not a murder scene."

It looked like a tornado had ripped through the room. His gaze focused on three big zigzagging brown smears on the floor. "Is that his blood or yours?"

Jamie blinked at the smears. "Mine. I think that one is from my face." She pointed. "And the others must have happened when I was kicking him from the floor. I cut the backs of my legs on broken glass. I didn't even feel it." She touched the bandage on her right thigh, a bewildered look on her face. "The EMTs spotted the blood."

"Is anything missing?" Byers patiently asked.

Jamie surveyed the room. "I don't think so. Nothing of value in here. Unless he likes Mauviel."

Simultaneously, Michael snorted and Byers asked, "Likes what?"

"Cookware." Michael pointed at the shiny copper pans strewn on the floor. "Spendy."

Byers raised a brow at him.

"My mother likes it," Michael explained.

A five-minute walk-though of the house turned up nothing missing. But someone had been thorough. Every drawer was pulled out and overturned. Closets emptied. Byers's partner silently snapped digital shots. Jamie discovered her jewelry intact and her electronics untouched. The tenseness left Jamie's shoulders, but she paced the kitchen, unable to relax. Nervous energy bleeding out her pores.

"They dug through everything," Michael said. "How long were you gone?"

"About twenty minutes. I usually run for an hour, but my leg was bugging me."

"You run every day?"

"Most days."

"Same time of day?"

"Always at seven."

Michael exchanged a look with the cops. "Someone knew your schedule. He thought he knew exactly how long he had. You must have surprised him before he could take off with anything."

Jamie shook her head. "He wasn't looking for valuables. He was looking for Chris."

Electric shocks shot through Michael's nerves. "*What?*"

The uniform taking notes said, "He kept asking where her brother was."

Michael clutched at Jamie's arm, whirling her to face him. "He wanted Chris? He said that?"

She nodded. "He said Chris would remember his cigarette burns. He's the one, Michael, he's the one who hurt Chris. He must be the one who killed all those children...and your brother."

Daniel. Michael eased his grip on her arm and rubbed at it in apology. His mind felt ready to explode. *The man who killed Daniel is still here. I will find him.*

"Sorry, princess." He turned to Byers. "You've got to contact Detective Callahan in OSP's Major Crimes."

The cop's eyes narrowed. "Major Crimes? Why? We've called out one of our robbery and assault detectives."

Michael shook his head. "You've got to contact Callahan. This is related to a murder case he's caught."

Byers glanced at Jamie for confirmation. She nodded, still silent. "What the hell?" Byers asked. "Everyone out. Out of the house now." He stepped closer to Michael. "You better know what you're talking about. Why the fuck didn't the two of you say something to start with?" His glare included Jamie.

Michael's hackles rose. "Because I didn't know till she mentioned her brother, and she was in too much shock from fighting for her goddamned life." He challenged Byers's stare.

"I'm sorry—" Jamie started.

"Not your fault. Not your fault at all." He rubbed his hands over her shoulders. "Did you get a look at him?"

She nodded and then started to shiver.

"Christ. Let's get out in the sun. You got a coat you can grab?"

"Don't take anything out of the house yet," Byers interjected. "I've got a Mylar blanket in the car she can use."

Jamie's teeth started to chatter.

"Jesus," said Michael. "Outside. Now."

★ ★ ★

She couldn't get warm. She was wrapped in two Mylar blankets and in full sun, lying flat on her back in the middle of her front yard. Michael had wedged a backpack from his truck under her feet and knelt by her head, rubbing at her hands.

"Just a little shock, princess. You'll feel better in a few minutes."

"Why do you keep calling me princess? And make them go away." Her teeth still chattered as she glared at the circle of uniforms staring down at her. Wasn't she conspicuous enough? What were her neighbors thinking?

"Back off," Michael directed. The cops obeyed. "Princess popped in my head the first time I saw you. Actually, I thought you looked like a queen. Something about the way you carry yourself. You've got a regal bearing. Not snooty or stuck-up. Just...calm, kind, and self-confident."

Regal? "I'd call it my principal posture. Makes the kids listen to me." Her damned body wouldn't stop shivering. "I can't get warm."

Michael leaned closer, green eyes concerned.

Jamie blew out a long breath, closed her eyes, and concentrated on making her muscles relax. The shivering dropped to short spurts, down from continuous attacks.

"That's better," he said softly. "Do you think you can talk now?"

She opened her eyes. The concern in his gaze touched her deep in her chest. She nodded. "Sit me up."

He shook his head. "Not yet." He gestured for Byers to come back.

"How much description of the guy did she give you already?"

Byers consulted his flip notebook. "Caucasian male, probably six foot one or six foot two, medium build, late forties or early fifties, sandy-blond hair, blue eyes, navy light running pants, long-sleeved white T-shirt, tattoos on backs of both wrists."

Jamie nodded in agreement. "I think the tattoos went up his sleeves. Like they covered his arms. I could see faint patterns through the material of his shirt."

"Probably why he was wearing long sleeves in the middle of July," Michael commented. "Wonder if the long pants were for the same reason?"

"More tats?" Byers asked.

Michael shrugged. "Possibly."

Jamie'd had enough of being on her back and having people speak down to her. "Sit me up."

Michael gently pulled her into a sitting position and steadied her with a hand on her back. And left it there. Its heat soaking into her skin felt heavenly.

"I don't recall getting a glimpse of his legs or even ankles." Jamie mentally reviewed her struggles with the assailant. "But he looked weird."

"Define weird." Michael's lips curved up on the right.

She paused. "His eyes weren't right. The color seemed fake."

"Lenses?" Byers asked.

She nodded slowly. "Maybe. It was the same with the hair. The color seemed forced. Like a home dye job."

"Christ. Vain," Michael said wryly. "Can't handle a little gray hair?"

"Maybe his hair was actually really dark, almost black. And he lightened it to throw her off. Same with the eyes. Maybe they're brown or hazel," Byers theorized. "You feel positive about the colors being changed? I mean, I had no idea my wife's been coloring her hair for the last five years until her sister mentioned it. How can you tell?"

Uncertainty crept into Jamie's brain. Maybe she was wrong. "Women look at hair. Most men don't. It's just a gut instinct with this guy." She fumbled about for a way to explain. "You asked for his hair color. I pictured it and stated what I remembered, but something bugged me about my answer. I think it didn't feel accurate because I'd imperceptibly picked up that it was colored. And that didn't register till a minute ago."

Both men stared at her. Byers's pencil hung motionless above his notebook.

"Women can tell these things," she asserted.

Byers recited as he wrote in his notebook: "Female instinct says hair colored and colored contacts."

★ ★ ★

Gerald crammed his latex gloves in his pants pocket. That hadn't gone well.

Rephrase that. It'd been a fucking disaster.

Sitting in his car in the McDonald's parking lot, he sucked on a Coke and took inventory of his injuries. His legs were going to be bruised for a week, and he had a finger sprain that'd swollen to twice its size. Damn thing had better not be broken.

Christ, she'd fought hard.

He'd never had a woman fight so hard. Surprisingly, in the past it'd been the women who put up the biggest fights. For some reason the men hadn't. Maybe he'd simply picked men who didn't mind being victims. The women had all minded. For prostitutes, they'd pissed off easily when they realized things weren't going as planned.

Jacobs had surprised the crap out of him when she returned early from her run. From his observations, this woman never varied her routine. He should have left. Attacking her hadn't been the smartest move, but he'd been frustrated with his empty search of the house. And his "interrogation" hadn't accomplished anything either.

Except that the Jacobs woman had seen his face.

It didn't matter.

He bit at the inside of his cheek. *It didn't matter.* He kept his hair colored and his real eye color covered up. Maybe it was time for a change? Darken the hair a bit? Eyes too? He had every contact lens color available. He usually stuck to nondescript blues and greens. The people he worked with never noticed that his eye color slightly varied some days. Lots of people's eyes normally do that.

No fucking way was he telling his boss that she'd seen him.

And he still didn't know where Chris Jacobs was. He'd found nothing in the house. No addresses, no mail, no pictures. Nothing that indicated she had a brother.

If she hadn't said she didn't know where Chris was living, he'd almost think the guy was dead. People don't vanish. There's always a record, somewhere.

Now what?

Angry pale jade eyes filled his brain. She'd been scared, but determination had also shone from those eyes. Jamie Jacobs was quite a specimen. She was tall and lean and fit. No spare fat on that woman's body. He could still feel her muscles under his fingertips. And her long, glossy dark hair. She reminded him of her brother a little bit. Chris Jacobs had been tall and lanky. Well, he'd *grown* tall and lanky during his two years. To start with, he'd been kind of a pudgy kid. At the end, both boys had been incredibly thin. Gerald had found it was easier to control them if they didn't have much energy. He kept their calorie intake at a minimum.

How they both had managed to escape was a mystery.

Their escape was a personal affront to him. A score he'd wanted to settle for a long time. No one else had ever humiliated him like that. Not since he was a teen.

He'd been visiting the boys about once a week before they vanished. His day job was a nine-to-five requirement, and sometimes he was simply too tired to make the long drive to visit the boys. Truth be told, just thinking about his captives in their prison was enough mental fantasy fuel to get him to the weekend. He'd kept people before. Adults. Both men and women. People he'd found on the streets of Portland or Salem who seemed like they wouldn't be readily missed.

Disposable people.

Male or female didn't matter to him too much. Both were useful. Both served the needs he had. He'd been surprised to find that almost-teen boys worked as well. The younger children he'd snatched were a waste of time. He'd disposed of them quickly. But the older boys...that had been different.

He closed his eyes. When he was younger, boys had been the enemy. They hit him, kicked him, spit on him, and called him names. Girls had simply looked the other way. When he was thirteen he'd fought back. Bruce had been one of the worst bullies. He and his buddies had been taunting Gerald on the bus. It was his usual daily ride from hell. When they'd got off the bus, Bruce's mouth hadn't stopped. As they walked past the apartment garbage dumpsters, Gerald snapped. He remembered seeing red, feeling his anger bleed into rage. He'd dropped his backpack, grabbed the gate to the dumpsters, and swung it into Bruce's face. Wailing, Bruce dropped to his knees, his hands covering the blood that dripped from his nose.

And Gerald felt the rush. The rush of pleasure and adrenaline and high that came from the dominance. He'd stood over the groveling boy, his heart pounding, and was instantly addicted.

It'd changed his life.

It'd awakened a bloodlust he'd never dreamed existed. The sight of the boy in pain from his action was energizing. And it proved that he had the ability to take control.

It was better to be the executor than the victim.

In the bunker, one of the kidnapped boys had fought back immediately. He couldn't recall which one. But it'd been eye-opening. The rest of the children had cowered and annoyed him. But the older two boys had shown fight.

He'd kept the boys.

He would have never believed boys could do that for him as an adult if it hadn't been for a phone call twenty years ago from the prosecutor.

He hadn't seen the county prosecutor in two years. The prosecutor had dropped several of the charges pending against him when the police couldn't produce key evidence. He'd sweated during the hearing, knowing full well the police had collected plenty of evidence that proved he'd been present at Sandra Edge's murder. They didn't have proof that his hands had touched her, but they definitely had proof that he'd been in the room with her and his buddy, Lee.

But then the blood and trace evidence from the sheets and carpets went missing. Not just a little bit of evidence, a lot of it. All the important parts were completely gone.

The prosecutor scared him. He'd been a sharp, intense, and intelligent man. Gerald had firmly believed he was going to prison for a very long time. Instead, he served a few months on a much lesser charge.

He'd gotten away with accessory to murder.

Lee ended up getting the murder rap. Which he'd deserved. He'd been the one who'd actually finished strangling Sandra, and he was stupid enough to admit it.

For two years, Gerald had stressed, waiting to hear that the evidence had turned up in a dark corner of a storage room somewhere. Instead, when the phone call came, the message and the person who made the call were unexpected.

Yes, the evidence was still in existence. No, it hadn't been lost. Yes, the evidence would stay away from the courts if Gerald would do him a favor.

"What kind of favor?" he'd asked.

"I need a kid taken care of."

A kid?

The former prosecutor had gone on to say he was fully aware of Gerald's role in Sandra's murder.

"Why me?"

"Because I know what you're capable of. And if you don't, you'll be in prison for the rest of your life."

"And after I take care of this for you?"

There'd been a long pause on the phone. "I might have a permanent job for you."

Gerald had been interested in the job. He'd done it well for over two decades now and wasn't about to let his employer down again. He knew when he'd kept the boys that his employer wasn't going to be happy, so he didn't tell him. His boss had been royally pissed that so many children had been affected when only one needed attention.

Gerald had shrugged. "I handled it the way I saw best. You needed fast action and you got it. No witnesses to anything. Plus, it confuses the motive. With so many kids gone, who was the primary target? Or was there a mass target? It'll keep the police scratching their heads for years."

After that his boss had no complaints about his job. He'd been impressed for two years when no evidence of the missing children had been found. No sign of the bus or the driver anywhere. His boss had never asked for details about how he'd accomplished the feat.

Then Chris Jacobs had walked out of the woods. Half dead, no memory, and miles from the underground bunker.

His boss had nearly blown a gasket. But when he learned of the boy's brain damage, he relaxed a bit. At that point, he grilled Gerald on the fates of the other children and then relaxed a bit more.

Gerald had been crazy to hang on to the two boys for as long as he did, but they'd fueled his soul in a way that adults never did.

Now Jamie Jacobs was proving to be a challenge.

He watched the line of vehicles snaking through the drive-through, reliving the events of that morning. Jamie was the type of woman who made men turn around and watch as she walked by. He hadn't been with a woman in over a month now, and he could still feel the silkiness of her skin from this morning. He shifted in his seat.

He needed to get laid.

He had a list of phone numbers of women who weren't too expensive. *Damn it.* Every woman on that list belonged in Walmart, and he was craving Saks Fifth Avenue.

Gerald's phone vibrated in his car console. He popped it open and scowled at the screen. *Already? He's asking for an update already? Shit.* He hit the green button.

"Yeah."

"What the fuck happened this morning? What did you do? There are cops crawling all over the Jacobs house."

Gerald's chest tightened. *An adult bully.* Gerald overlooked it because he knew it meant his boss was sweating a bit. And he liked the pleasure from putting his boss in that situation.

He had control. Not his boss.

"I was looking for a lead on her brother. You knew that. I didn't expect her to come home so fast. She might have got a bit banged up on my way out."

He wasn't about to mention that the woman had neatly handed his ass to him.

"What'd you find?"

"I've got a stack of paperwork and mail to look through. A couple of address books, too." He lied.

"I got something that'll work a bit faster for you."

"Like what?"

"Michael Brody, a reporter, is showing an unnatural interest in Jamie Jacobs."

"I figured he was watching the story pretty close because of his brother, but you mean a personal interest in the woman?" Gerald's gut twisted in an odd way. Something about Brody and Jamie together didn't sit right with him.

"Exactly. *A personal interest.* And I know this guy. When he's got his nose deep in a story, nothing gets in his way. He's gonna dig until he unearths Chris Jacobs."

"You want me to wait and follow him?"

"See? You're smart. That's why I hired you. Other than the one big fuck-up way back, you usually pull things through."

Gerald swallowed the bitter words he wanted to hurl at the man. "You know me best, boss."

"Damn right. And don't ever forget I own your ass."

Ditto.

★ ★ ★

"You want to explain to me what you're doing in the damned bull's-eye of this case?"

"Not my fault," Michael said into his phone. Detective Mason Callahan could bitch all he wanted, but Michael knew the man held a grudging respect for him. And vice versa.

"I could swear I told you to stay away from the Jacobs woman."

Michael ignored him. "They told you he beat her up pretty good?"

"Yeah, she okay?"

"She will be." Michael leaned against the fender of his truck, twisting to catch sight of Jamie. She still sat on her lawn, the Mylar blanket next to her on the grass, trying to recall the tats she'd seen. A cop handed her a bottled water and squatted beside her as she sketched, studying her drawing.

"I was told the attacker wanted to know the whereabouts of Chris Jacobs. And that he told her he'd made the scars on her brother's face."

"That's right," said Michael. "And threatened to do the same to her."

"Doesn't mean he's the one who actually made the marks on her brother. It was even in newspaper articles back then that the boy had been burned with cigarettes," Callahan stated.

Michael didn't have an answer for that.

"What reason could he have to want her brother if it's not because Chris might get some of his memory back and identify him?" Michael argued.

"Maybe he owes him money," Callahan quipped.

"Fuck you."

Callahan laughed. "I'll interview Jamie. Hear what she has to say."

Michael wasn't done. "She thinks he was in his late forties, maybe early fifties. That'd put him at the right age to pull that shit twenty years ago."

"I'm not saying he didn't. Christ, Brody. I'll follow up. Right now I've got a stack of children's autopsy reports on my desk. I take a break from reading them every fifteen minutes to go punch the wall, I get so pissed. After I get through those reports, I have a smaller stack from the pit with the adult remains. I'll make you a deal. I'll swap jobs with you. You read, and I'll drive around town in the sun, getting a tan and sticking my nose into other people's business."

"I get it, Callahan."

The detective's voice lowered. "I'll get to her, Brody. I want the bastard as bad as you do."

"Impossible," Michael muttered.

"Too bad he's so average looking. Nothing really stands out visually."

"What?" Michael stood straighter. "Didn't they mention the tattoos?"

"Tattoos?" Callahan asked sharply.

"Tats on the backs of his wrists. Jamie got the impression they went a lot farther up his arms."

Callahan's swearing made Michael pull the phone away from his ear.

"What?" Michael said when Callahan stopped to catch a breath. "What the fuck is up with the tats?"

"We've got pictures."

"Pictures? Pictures from what?"

Callahan had turned away from his phone and was urgently talking to someone in the background.

"Callahan. What pictures?" Michael spoke through clenched teeth.

"Lusco's pulling them up. Fucking pervert."

"Lusco?" Michael could hear the other detective's voice in the background now.

"No, Jamie's attacker."

Michael was ready to strangle the detective. "What the fuck are you talking about?"

Callahan cleared his throat. "We found pictures in the bunker. Old Polaroids. Sick Polaroids. They weren't even hidden. They were just left on one of the shelves for anyone to find."

Michael's stomach turned to pure acid. *Daniel?*

"The creep took some nasty pics of those kids. His hands, or someone's hands, show in some of them. There're tats on the wrists."

"His wrists?"

"Yeah, they don't look like they go up his arms. Forearms are clear. It's just a few Asian characters on the backs of the wrists. Pretty big, though. About an inch and a half in diameter."

"You can't see his face?" Michael asked. His head suddenly felt weightless. He leaned on his elbows on his hood, head down.

"Not of him. Just the kids. Nothing else shows of the adult."

Michael didn't want to know any more. No details. His brain was supplying too many details of its own.

"What'd Jamie say the tattoos looked like?" Callahan asked.

"She didn't say. She's working on some sketches with the cops. I don't know if she saw specifics. She said there were a lot of them."

"He could have added to them."

"Hang on, Callahan." Michael strode over to the lawn where Jamie sat. "Hey, princess, you come up with any images yet?"

Jamie gave him a weak smile. "Don't call me princess, please." She looked down at her paper. "I don't know what I'm doing. I can't picture them."

"I told her to start with just colors," the cop next to her said. "Then add stark lines or shapes."

"Let me see." Michael held his hand out for the paper.

It appeared she'd traced her own hands and wrists for the outlines. She'd made muted multicolored swirls that started at mid-forearm and spread nearly to the knuckles. The colors intensified on the backs of the hands. Blues, reds, greens.

Directly on the wrists, over the colors, she'd drawn thick black crisscrossing slashes, like pound signs.

Acid from Michael's stomach burned up his esophagus.

"It's him," he said into the phone. "We'll be downtown in thirty minutes."

CHAPTER EIGHT

At the police station, the young woman in front of Mason looked like she'd been brutalized, but she held her chin up, her stance solid, her back straight. Jamie Jacobs was tough, and he admired that. Looked like Brody was admiring her, too. Mason hadn't ever seen him hover over a woman like this before. He'd been plenty protective of that little dentist, Lacey Campbell, but that was in a big-brother type of way.

Mason caught his partner's gaze, and Ray Lusco nodded with a wry smile, agreeing. Looked like the reporter had been hit in the head with a love stick.

The bandages on her face pissed him off, and Mason knew she had more under her light pants. She was agitated, trying to reach someone on her cell who wasn't picking up.

"Are you sure it's the right number?" Brody asked her.

"Yes! It's in my contacts and in the call history. I know it's right, but it's been disconnected."

"Has he ever left you without a way to reach him before?"

"Never. There's always been a phone number. Sometimes he doesn't get right back to me, but he's never done anything like this before."

Mason interrupted. "You're talking about your brother?"

Unusual light green eyes looked to him.

Holy crap. No wonder Brody's smitten.

"Yes, and no, I don't know where he is. But he's always left me a number to call in the past. Maybe someone got to him... like that guy got to me today."

Brody carefully took her hands, getting her to look at him. "Jamie, you've told me how smart your brother is. I think he's well aware that someone from his past could one day seek him out. I think that's part of the reason he left and why he doesn't let you know how to find him. I have no doubt he's gone deeper into hiding."

Mason raised a mental eyebrow at Brody's soft and reassuring tone. *Yep. He's in deep.*

Jamie stared at Brody for a few seconds and then nodded. "We need to warn him, though. He should at least know what happened to me today."

Mason cleared his throat. "Let's talk about that." He waved a hand at two chairs. "Have a seat."

Ray tactfully and thoroughly led Jamie through the events of the day. Surprisingly, Brody kept his mouth shut but watched everyone in the room like a hawk.

Mason only interrupted once, directing a question to Brody. "You traced his call?"

"Yep."

"How?"

Brody said nothing and just looked back at Mason.

"Okay. Fine. I suppose you're still planning a trip to find him?"

Again, Brody just looked at Mason and then asked a question of his own. "Tell me about the tattoos in the pictures."

Mason noted he didn't ask what else was in the pictures. He only wanted to hear about the tattoos.

Mason moved Jamie's sketch of hands and wrists to the center of the table. "There's a lot more color and detail here than in the pictures. Possibly, he's added ink." Mason pulled out four hazy close-ups of wrists that they'd created off the Polaroids. The pictures weren't the greatest, but anyone could see that the tattoos in the pictures were in the exact same position and same size as the black marks on Jamie's drawings.

Jamie stared at the close-ups. "Those are them. They've been enhanced with design and colors. It must be the same person."

Mason shook his head, but Ray spoke up first. "No, we have to keep open the possibility that two people could have the same black tattoos. Maybe they're associated with each other. Maybe some sort of private, sick club."

Brody snorted.

Mason agreed with Brody's sentiment, but he knew better than to jump to conclusions. "We know it's unlikely to be two different people, but we won't rule it out. Yet. I've passed the Polaroids and drawing to a detective in the gang unit. No one knows more about tattoos than this guy. And if nothing jumps out at him from the images, then he knows who to ask and where to look."

"I doubt it's gang related," Brody argued. "We're talking about a white guy with tattoos from twenty years ago. To me that makes the tattoos sound more military related or foreign."

Mason nodded. "Agreed. Obviously this guy isn't a gang-banger, but the people who work with them are our tattoo experts. They'll know where to turn next. It's our best lead so far."

"Why would someone leave something so incriminating as pictures in that place?" Jamie asked. "You said you haven't found fingerprints anywhere, but you found photos? That doesn't sound like the same person. This"—Jamie paused, eyebrows narrowing—"crook...murderer...isn't being consistent if they're not leaving fingerprints but are leaving pictures."

"Agreed," Lusco said. "We might be dealing with more than one person."

"Someone else had to take the pictures," Brody added.

"One of the other kids could have been behind the camera." As Mason spoke, he saw Brody imperceptibly flinch. "Not willingly, of course," he added.

Jamie's face flushed. "I've seen a lot of child abuse in my position. I do what I do because I want to help kids better their lives. Nothing makes me sicker than a defenseless kid." She met Mason's gaze straight on. "My brother was horribly abused, and I've sat back, thinking I was letting him heal and doing the right thing by not pushing for answers. It was how my parents handled him, and I continued it. Now I think it's time for him to actively help. The man who attacked me could still be hurting kids. I don't care if my brother claims he remembers nothing, I'm gonna drag him to every therapist and hypnotist in the country until he gives you something to help find who killed those children, before this person hurts more."

She turned to Brody. "I'm ready to go with you to find Chris."

★ ★ ★

It was evening by the time Jamie and Michael drove into the outskirts of the dry, beige town of Demming, Oregon. The trip east had taken six hours, and Michael drove the entire stretch. Jamie had offered to take a shift, but he'd turned her down.

"I get antsy if I'm sitting in the passenger seat. Driving helps me focus."

Their conversation had been minimal. If Michael wasn't on the phone with an editor or co-worker, his music was blasting through the SUV. His taste was eclectic, ranging from traditional rap to the most heart-stirring classical she'd ever heard. She'd relaxed and simply let him drive, taking the time to study his profile and the world outside.

The scenery changed as they moved east. Dryer, browner, flatter. Once they'd left the Portland metropolitan area and passed through the Cascade Mountain Range, it was as if they'd entered a different state. More pickup trucks, longer stretches between towns, and less greenery. The fir trees were few and far between, while the cowboy hats grew in number. Gun racks started to appear in the back windows of the pickup trucks. Bumper stickers told politicians to keep their change to themselves and keep their laws off their guns.

They were now on the red side of the blue-voting state. By the square mile, the east side of the state was nearly twice as big as the west, but much lower in population and income. Oregon

was a state divided in half by the Cascade Mountains, economics, and politics.

Jamie suddenly craved a handcrafted iced cappuccino and
knew she wasn't going to find one. The self-service machines at
7-Eleven didn't count.

"The sheriff is expecting us, right?" she asked.

"Yes, but I didn't tell him exactly when we'd get in. We'll
stop at his office in Demming, see if he's available to talk a bit.
He wants to give me better directions out to your brother's. I
guess it's hard to find. Also cautioned me to not sneak up on
anyone. People in these remote areas have a tendency to shoot
first, ask questions later."

"Chris wouldn't do that."

Michael raised a brow at her. "He's hiding from something.
That's the only reason for a man to live like he does and not
introduce his son to his sister."

Jamie looked out her window. The words stung deep. "He
doesn't like to be around people. After he recovered…he avoided
everyone. He has burn scars on his face."

"I've known plenty of people with disfigurations who oper-
ate just fine."

Jamie was silent for a few moments. "What were you doing
that day?"

Michael didn't ask what day she meant.

She saw him swallow hard and then run a hand across his
forehead. He kept his gaze forward on the road.

"I'd stayed home sick from school. I knew there was a field
trip to the state capitol building scheduled that day, and to me
nothing was more boring." He snorted. "Daniel was pumped.
He had a freaky fascination with politics."

"Your father was a US senator at the time, right?"

"Yes, the junior senator. He'd just started his second term."

"Your father liked Daniel's interest?"

"He was thrilled. He had Daniel's political future mapped out."

"That's insane. What kind of pressure does that put on a kid?"

Michael laughed. "The Senator and Daniel used to talk about it for hours. Where he could go to law school, where was the best school for undergrad—"

"And you? What were your plans?"

"I had no plans." His voice went flat.

A small stab of sorrow touched Jamie's heart. She'd seen too many kids in her school ignored by their parents. "That didn't mean he had no reason to love you."

Michael twisted up one side of his mouth. "I know my parents loved me. It just didn't feel like they *liked* me. I wasn't the type of kid they'd planned to have. I wasn't interested in school. I just wanted to skateboard and ski. I used to pay high school kids to take me along when they skipped school and went skiing. I got caught over and over, but I didn't care."

"How'd your parents know you went skiing?"

"You know what raccoon eyes are?"

Jamie laughed. "You didn't know to use sunscreen when skiing?"

"Naw, sunscreen was for wimps."

Was he trying to avoid her original question by distracting her? "So were you really sick that day?"

He shook his head. "Not at all."

"When did you find out?"

"Phone calls started coming in. Daniel wasn't home from school, the bus never returned to the school, no one could locate the bus driver. The Senator was in Washington DC and immediately flew home. My mother didn't go back to the hospital for three days. I'd never seen them so panicked."

"Of course they were. Their son was missing. They would have reacted the same way if you'd never come back from skiing."

The wry look on Michael's face said he doubted her words.

She sat straighter in the SUV's seat. "You think they would have simply brushed it off if you vanished? That's ridiculous. No parent reacts like that!"

★ ★ ★

Michael tried to control the expression on his face. The absolute indignation on Jamie's was killing him. His parents had never been the same after Daniel disappeared. Before DD—long ago Michael had divided up his life into *Before DD* and *After DD*—he'd simply thought his parents connected better with Daniel, as if they understood the chemical wiring in Daniel's brain versus the ricocheting impulses that bounced through Michael's.

At many points in a child's life, one wonders what it'd be like to be an only child. Michael had experienced that daydream often, assuming all his parents' focus would be on him...as an adult he'd often thanked God that hadn't happened. He and his parents would have gone nuts if they'd tried to shape Michael into their own image. Looking back, he'd been grateful that Daniel had meshed so well with them and kept the focus off himself. Once Daniel was gone, the focus never shifted. It'd stayed on Daniel. And Michael had spread his wings. And spread. Usually to the point of risking his neck.

Mountain climbing, check. Run with the bulls in Spain, check. Crab boat trapping in the Bering Sea, check. Infiltrate a Los Angeles biker gang for an exposé on crime, check. That one had nearly cost him his life. He still had the knife scars on his gut and an intense dislike of the harsh tequila that they'd all drunk by the gallon. No margaritas for him, thank you.

"I know my parents cared," he said. It felt like an over-spoken line in a play. Lifeless and meaningless. Deep down, he knew they'd cared, but for some twisted reason, they couldn't show it. A therapist had once theorized that they were afraid of the pain of losing another child, so they tried to keep their distance, protecting themselves if something happened to Michael. And perhaps that was why he thrived on risk. Trying to coax a reaction out of his parents.

Michael had stared at the therapist, pulled three hundred dollars out of his wallet, slapped it on the table, walked out, and never returned. Why pay money for what he already knew? What he wanted was someone to fix it. Fix them. Fix him. Give him the family he'd never had, the one that lived in movies and books. It existed; he just had to find it.

Lacey Campbell was the closest thing he had to family. She was the little sister who mothered him when he needed it, sent him to get a haircut, and stocked his fridge when it only held beer and three-day-old pizza. They'd tried romance, but it'd failed. Miserably. Friendship worked best. For a long time, he'd pretended the friendship was fine with him, believing that if he stuck close and waited, it'd evolve into more and it'd be right the second time around. That dream had crashed and burned with the presence of her fiancé. He'd wanted to murder the man at first, but now...he accepted it.

Michael stopped his vehicle in front of a squat brick building in the small town, a large sheriff sign over the door. The town was quiet, one main drag through a row of storefronts, a couple of people moving from store to store. A few empty storefronts echoed the recession that'd stomped on the nation in the last few years. He killed the engine and rolled down his window, surprised that it wasn't as hot as he'd expected for the dry town in the middle of summer. The elevation must keep it a bit cooler. Jamie lowered her window, too.

"Most parents care in one way or another," stated Jamie. "But some just have a fucked-up time showing it. I've seen parents who can never look their child in the eye but threaten to kick my ass if their child flunks an assignment." She rolled her eyes.

Michael snorted. "I know my parents cared," he repeated. Perhaps if he kept saying it out loud he'd really feel it. He shifted in his seat. He wasn't ready to go into the sheriff's office just yet. Jamie hadn't moved either. There was an aura of openness in the vehicle that he didn't want to lose. Jamie looked at the sign on the building, and her eyes softened.

"Luna County. I love the sound of that. The word *Luna* sounds so much prettier than moon. I wonder if the moon seems bigger out here. I went camping in Central Oregon once. The sky seemed so big, the stars brighter, and the moon closer."

Michael stared at her profile. He grabbed every available chance to study her features when she wasn't looking at him. The woman was gorgeous. Gorgeous in the way of fresh and healthy. Not because of makeup and hair product. She dressed minimally, shorts and tanks. Little makeup or fussing with her hair. She let the glow of her skin and toned muscles subtly grab attention. And her eyes...that color...outlined with the black lashes. He could stare forever. He'd memorized the outside, now he wanted to know what was inside. He didn't remember her from their private school. She had been several years behind him and too young to go on the field trip. Then her parents had yanked her out of school and homeschooled her after the children vanished.

"What did your parents do that day?" he asked.

Her gaze fell to her hands, playing with the hem of her shorts. "They were in shock. The school called and told my mother they were trying to find the bus. She simply sat by the phone for the rest of the day and stared into space. I remember watching cartoons, thrilled that she didn't care how long I watched that day. Usually there was a strict time limit. That day she didn't care. She called my father, but he couldn't leave work. When he got home, he joined her...waiting at the table. I was the only one to eat dinner. They sat there and watched me eat. It felt weird, but I knew my brother would be home soon. I figured the bus was just lost." Jamie turned her face away, looking out her side window as her voice went quieter. "It was like they knew he wasn't coming. Looking back, I swear they had no hope at all."

"And the day Chris returned?" Michael felt a brief rush of jealousy at the survivor and his family. It faded rapidly as Jamie turned her green gaze to him.

"They didn't believe it. It wasn't until they actually saw him in the hospital that they let themselves believe. They'd lost all hope. Absolutely all hope. Those two years were so dark. I look at pictures from Christmas during those two years. I can see the despair in their eyes even as they smiled for the camera. My mother stayed in the hospital with Chris until he came home. She wouldn't leave."

"Wasn't he there for three months or so?"

Jamie nodded. "It seemed like forever. He was in a coma for a few weeks. I think the doctors induced it to allow his brain injuries to heal. He had five surgeries on his face and more on his right leg. I kept waiting for everything to return to normal, but his medical issues dragged on and on. It never was the same around our house. I thought joy would return. Instead, I still heard my mother cry at night and watched my father's liquor supply dwindle and refresh.

"Christmas pictures from then on weren't much different. My parents still had shadows in their eyes, and Chris would never look at the camera. The left side of his face was so bad, he always turned it away, hating his looks. My parents finally stopped taking pictures of him." Jamie frowned. "That seems so wrong now. But it wasn't because they were ashamed of him; it was what he wanted. He was so withdrawn. He acted like he didn't want the world to know he existed. When reporters would come around every few years, he wouldn't come out of his room for days. I think it was nearly a relief to my parents when he moved out."

"That's horrible."

"I agree," she nodded thoughtfully. "But the stress was hard on them. Of course, it was worse when he'd vanished, but living with the shell of the child who returned was difficult. Therapy went nowhere. He was only content being alone, working on his computer. It's hard to be a parent when your child is untouch-able. When you want to help but nothing works."

Silence filled the vehicle. Not an uncomfortable silence. A commonality. A connection. Michael reached over and squeezed her hand. Jamie glanced down at the gesture, a small smile curving her lips, and then she met his gaze.

"I'm sorry," he said.

"You have nothing to be sorry for."

"Yes, I do. I hated your family for years. I hated your brother, I hated your parents, and I hated you for getting your brother back when I had nothing."

Jamie's face blanched.

"But I didn't get it," he added quickly. "I was a kid. It was my outlet. It was easy to hate faceless people. I just wanted my brother back. Still do. I think any shrink would say it was a pretty normal reaction."

Color slowly seeped back to her cheeks. "I understand. I probably would have been the same way."

He held tight to her hand and felt the pressure returned. Warmth spread through his chest, and she smiled. A real smile, not a fake I-don't-believe-a-word-you're-saying smile.

"God, you are gorgeous," he blurted.

Her eyes crinkled in mirth, and she chuckled. His heart double-thumped. If he'd thought she was beautiful before...

She pulled her hand from his and touched his cheek. "You're not so bad yourself, Brody." Her gaze moved from his eyes to his mouth, and the heat in his chest flared.

"Christ." He couldn't breathe.

She chuckled again and ran a finger across his upper lip. "Ready to go find that sheriff?"

Michael blinked. He'd completely forgotten their purpose. How did women shift gears so fast? "Uh...sure." He didn't sound sure at all.

Jamie unbuckled her seatbelt and opened her door, swinging sleek legs out. Michael bit the inside of his cheek. She slammed her door and glanced at him through the open window. He hadn't moved.

"You coming?"

He felt glued to his seat. And it wasn't from the heat. Something about their conversation and the touch of her hand on his face had utterly undone him. His heart had moved into a foreign position, and he was clueless how to handle it. He swallowed hard, feeling like he was about to step out of a plane. With no parachute. He reached for his door handle.

"Always."

CHAPTER NINE

Michael looked like he didn't want to get out of the SUV, like he didn't want to break the connection they'd created. Jamie hadn't wanted it to stop, but she needed a breather. This reckless, impulsive man was pulling her close and opening her up in a way she'd never experienced. She'd never discussed Chris with anyone outside of her parents and Chris's psychiatrist. But she hadn't been talking about Chris; she'd been talking about herself.

Michael's emerald eyes had made her mouth keep moving and her breathing grow deeper. His face was all planes and angles, no softness. She'd felt the need to touch with her hand to add some softness to those hard surfaces. And the heat that'd erupted from his eyes at her touch had nearly unraveled her. She wasn't the only one feeling something. In those brief seconds, she'd known every thought in his mind. And they weren't about her brother.

She stepped up to the sidewalk in front of the sheriff's office and watched Michael emerge from the SUV. He moved with confidence, like every muscle had a supreme purpose, exuding a tightly coiled energy. He was the kind of man who drew a woman's eye, who made a woman wonder what it'd be like to be in ownership of that kind of male. But he was also the type of man who made a woman step back. He didn't expel the commitment pheromone most women sought. His pheromones screamed temporary…but what a temporary ride it would be.

Jamie didn't need temporary. Jamie didn't need excitement. Long ago, she'd decided she needed a man who offered security, stability, and solidity. She didn't see that in Michael.

But a tiny voice in her head kept telling her to consider the ride he was offering. And she was weakening. Once they'd figured out what was going on with Chris, she was going to take a hard look at the man Michael Brody was.

He stopped beside her on the sidewalk and tilted his head toward the door. She nodded and started to reach for the doorknob, only to see his hand grab it first and hold it open. She paused and then passed through, acutely aware of the warm hand he'd placed on the small of her back. The dim coolness of the office helped her relax.

"Can I help you?" A small, fluttery bird of a woman smiled brightly at them from behind a large desk. She was in civilian clothes, a floral shirt and faded blue jeans that Jamie immediately labeled as "mom jeans." She wore way too much black mascara, but her smile was warm and open. Her name tag read "Sara."

"We're looking for Sheriff Spencer," Michael answered.

Sara's gaze took a quick measure of Michael, and Jamie could tell she liked what she saw. Too bad she was older than him by at least twenty-five years.

"He went down the street. He's grabbing some dinner at the diner. Might be stopping at the grocery, too. We're out of coffee." Sara focused more intently and tilted her head in a rapid way that reminded Jamie of a bird again. "You the reporter from Portland?"

"Yep. You think he'd mind if we wandered down to find him? We need to check in at the hotel, too."

Jamie stiffened. She hadn't thought about the sleeping situation. Until now. Too many images peppered her brain. Some very hot.

Separate rooms. No exceptions.

Sara abruptly pinned her focus on Jamie, blinking rapidly, and Jamie knew she'd picked up every nuance of her body language.

"Not at all. He'd probably like to have someone to gab with over dinner. You eat yet?"

Jamie couldn't remember eating at all.

"No," answered Michael. "Food good?"

"The best," Sara proclaimed proudly. "Try the enchiladas. And keep hitting the bell at the hotel desk if no one is right there. Chuck's a little hard of hearing."

Michael thanked her and steered Jamie out the door with his hand on her back again. She blinked at the sun that was starting to set.

"I'm freaking starved," Michael muttered. "Let's eat and find the sheriff, then find your brother."

Jamie silently agreed, feeling her stomach rumble at the thought of enchiladas drowning in melted cheese. A sign a block away indicated it was the town diner. She locked her gaze on it and walked faster.

Michael moved his hand from her back to firmly hold her hand. She gave him a smile, but his gaze was focused ahead on three men lounging in front of the tiny grocery store. One man wore an apron with the grocery store logo, and the other two men each held a soda can—Coke and Diet Coke. Jamie's mouth was instantly dry.

"Simon, your break is up." A heavyset woman with black hair piled on top of her head stepped out of the grocery door. Spotting Jamie and Michael, she grinned and offered a greeting. Her name tag read "Janet."

"You two look parched," Janet said. "The air's real dry here. Not too hot today, but it'll still drain your fluids. Better pick up some waters."

Obviously, this was a town where everyone knew everyone else. She and Michael probably stuck out like pigs in an opera.

"We're headed to eat but probably should put some in the car," said Michael. Janet followed them in the store. Behind her came Simon in his apron and the two men with sodas. They watched Michael select two bottled waters like they hadn't seen outsiders in months.

"Sheriff Spencer been by?" Michael asked. He plopped the bottles on the counter, ignoring the scrutiny. Jamie lifted her chin. *What was their problem?*

Janet lifted a brow at Simon, who spoke as he scanned their bottles. "About twenty minutes ago. Bought coffee."

"What you needing the sheriff for?" Janet asked. "Everything okay? You just got to town, right? Surely you haven't run into a problem already."

Jamie swallowed her laughter. Small towns.

"We're just looking for someone," Michael replied.

"Well, you're standing in the right place." Janet gestured at herself and the other men. "Between the four of us, we know everyone around here. Who're you looking for?"

Questioningly, Michael met Jamie's gaze. She shrugged. Why not?

"Chris Jacobs."

The four stared at Michael and Jamie and then exchanged glances.

"What? What's the deal?" Michael folded his arms over his chest. He studied each townie intently, almost hawk-like. Jamie swore she saw his nostrils flare like he was scenting prey.

Janet wrinkled her nose. "What do you want with him? I've never seen him even speak to another person. Well, he talks some to old Juan. But that's it. That boy of his doesn't seem to ever speak either. Doesn't even go to school. Delores went out to his house, told him the boy needed to be in school. He said he was homeschooling the boy and meeting the state standards and told her to keep her nose to herself." Janet let out a huff. "Boy should be in school. Needs socializing, otherwise he's gonna be a hermit just like his father. There's more to schooling than books."

Jamie's heart cracked. Her nephew. Janet was talking about her nephew. How on earth was Chris raising him?

"What happened to the boy's mother?" Michael asked.

The question surprised Jamie. Michael had already read what'd happened, but as a reporter, she figured he always wanted to hear what others had to say.

The four townsfolk exchanged looks again.

"Car accident," Diet Coke man stated.

Michael and Jamie waited in silence for someone to continue. Jamie saw Janet start to open her mouth and then close it.

"Sad business that," Simon expanded. All four nodded.

Janet fidgeted with her apron, frowning. "She was driving. Alone. Went off the road into a tree. Not a mile from their house. Sheriff said she probably died instantly. Old car didn't have an airbag."

Michael's hawk brows shot together. "What ran her off the road? An animal? She drunk?" The man wasn't nearly satisfied with Janet's story.

Janet shrugged. "Who knows? She wasn't drunk. No alcohol at all in her."

Jamie grabbed her water. "Let's go. I'm starved." She didn't want to hear gossip. These people obviously weren't fond of her brother. Any words out of their mouths would be biased. She had a hunch they were about to blame her brother for the car accident.

"Nice to meet you," Michael said over his shoulder as they headed out the door.

"You too. Sheriff's probably down at the diner. He usually eats dinner about this time," Janet called after them.

Jamie power-walked down the sidewalk, and Michael grabbed at her hand. "Slow down," he said, pulling back on her. "What's wrong?"

Jamie shook her head. "Those people. They don't know Chris, but they judge him anyway. That's how it's been his entire life. People just look at the outside."

"Well, sounds like he's not letting anyone see inside."

"And that poor little boy. I don't even know my nephew's name! No mother. And it sounds like Chris is raising him to be as introverted as he is."

"Well, at least his dad is spending time with him."

Jamie stopped and turned to look at Michael. He had a shut-tered look on his face. "That's true. It's important to have that connection. But the boy needs more in his life. I'm going to talk to Chris about moving back home. Janet has a point. The boy needs to be around other children."

"Think he'll be open to that?" Michael's tone wasn't optimistic.

"I hope so." Jamie felt a heavy weight on her heart as they started walking toward the diner. It'd been so hard for Chris to adjust when he came home from the hospital. School became the enemy. No, the children and many of the adults in school had become the enemy. People in general were the enemy because they stared at him and talked about him like he wasn't right in front of them, hearing every word.

She'd been confused as a child, unable to figure out her big brother's thoughts. Her big brother was home...but he wasn't. For two years, she'd prayed for God to send her brother home. He finally did, but Chris was seriously damaged inside and out, and Jamie didn't understand.

She could see the outside damage. The marks on his face, the scars on his arms, the bony protrusions at all his joints, the lopsidedness to his jaw where it'd been broken and never healed right. She remembered the first time she'd seen him in the hospital. He'd been so still, his eyes closed and his face swathed in bandages. She'd gently held his fingers, the only part of him that looked like it didn't hurt, and they'd softly squeezed back. Jamie had studied his hospital bed, so many tubes and machines.

Her mother hadn't left his bedside since he'd been found. Her father had driven back and forth between the hospital and his job, seeing Jamie at dinnertime where he'd promise Chris would be coming home soon.

Looking at him in that hospital bed, Jamie knew it was going to be a long time before her brother truly came home.

Over those next few weeks, she lost count of the number of times she said, "Chris is doing good, and he'll be home soon." This was in reply to neighbors, teachers, and even strangers who somehow knew about her brother. That was probably from the TV. Chris's story was frequently on the TV, even though the reporters never talked to him or her parents.

Her parents whispered to each other all the time. Outside his hospital room, in the car, in their bedroom. Sometimes it sounded like they were arguing in whispers. Jamie heard them mention brain damage and burns and therapy. Her mother cried a lot, not nearly as much as when Chris first went missing, but more than a mother should when her lost boy has finally come home. Jamie played silently with her Barbies, read books, watched TV, and waited for someone to tell her when her family would be back to normal.

Chris missed another year of school. Three years total. His parents had pushed for him to return when he could walk without needing to rest every ten feet, but Chris said he wasn't ready. He was nearly fourteen and should have been starting high school with his friends. Instead, he'd avoided his friends, telling them he was too tired and telling his parents he didn't like the way his friends stared at his scars. Eventually, they stopped coming around. When he could look at a book without getting headaches, he'd started studying. And studying. His parents had bought their first computer, and Chris took it over. After a lot of discussion, his mother had designed a path for him to get his GED. That decision seemed to alleviate some of his stress.

He'd helped Jamie with her homework, tugged on her black braids, and called her "Licorice," like he had before he'd vanished. His own light-brown hair grew back uneven and patchy from where he'd had the surgery on his skull. He kept it buzzed short, making him look like he was from Auschwitz, not Oregon. He never gained enough weight to resemble the healthy, heavy athletic boy he'd been before. Until the day he moved out, he'd looked anorexic and pale.

Looking back, Jamie understood why her parents didn't force Chris to go to school, but was it the wisest decision? Would he be the hermit that he is today if he'd been forced to socialize? Or would he simply have more internal scars?

She knew absolutely nothing about her brother.

Everyone had tiptoed around him. Were they simply enablers of his condition? Jamie had spent years learning about educating children and their behaviors, but suddenly it all went out the window when it came down to the emotions stirred up by her brother. Had they done right by Chris? First her parents and then her. Had she done the right thing by letting him dictate the limits of their relationship? Should she have pushed for him to give her more?

"Ouch!" Michael said, jerking them to a stop and dropping her hand.

"What?"

"You're about to break my hand. You've got a grip like a nun who likes to whip with a ruler." He cradled it like it was broken.

Jamie glanced at his hand. Sure enough, she'd caused the blood to blanch out of his palm.

"I was enjoying holding your hand, but you seemed to not be focusing on the romance of the moment."

"Romance?"

"Yes. You and me in this quaint little town. Walking to dinner, holding hands."

She tried not to roll her eyes. "I was thinking about Chris's recovery and the situation with his son. Sorry, I wasn't seeing the romance of the moment."

Green eyes gazed deep into hers. "I liked holding your hand. I can hold your hand and still look for your brother, right?"

Jamie caught her breath and felt her heart do the tiniest flutter. *That shade of green…*

Who the heck was Michael Brody? *Jedi knight and hand-holder?*

"I like you, Jamie Jacobs. I like you a lot. And I have no problem letting you know."

She blinked. He was so direct. It was…refreshing.

Michael was figuring out how to push her happy buttons in a fast way. Charmer or not, she was buying what he was selling. Something told her he was much deeper than the casual image he presented. She'd learned to look to the heart of people; it was part of her job. She could spot a bullshitter at ten yards. Michael was sending out true, clear signals of honesty.

"When you called me after your attack, I was ready to rip someone's head off. The thought of you being hurt didn't sit well with me. *At all.*" Sparks lit inside his eyes.

Oh my. Her heart did the flutter again. Bigger this time.

He leaned closer, running a warm hand up and down her arm. "Hungry?" His tone said nothing about food.

"Starved," she said. "For dinner," she clarified.

A slow smile stretched across Michael's face, and he took a firm hold of her hand, leading her toward the diner.

★ ★ ★

Michael looked around the diner. The sheriff was easy to spot by the beige uniform and cowboy hat on the table. Half the tables had patrons, and at the counter, nearly every stool was full. The diner had a tired aura, like it was working on autopilot. Taking in the dated decor, Michael figured that nothing had changed since the midseventies.

Several people glanced over as he and Jamie stepped inside, their looks lingering a little longer than was polite, but eventually turned back to their food. Sheriff Spencer made eye contact, held it for two seconds, and then waved them over. Michael let Jamie walk ahead of him. Watching the customers, he realized Jamie in her snug shorts drew every man's gaze, not just his own. He met the gaze of one younger man who'd discreetly watched Jamie walk by.

Yep, she's with me.

Let them stare. He was the one who'd be walking out with the woman.

Michael inwardly frowned. Well…Jamie was with him. But not in the way he wanted. Not yet. Once he set his mind to something, he succeeded. And his mind was set on Jamie. She just needed a little convincing. He was good at that.

Sheriff Spencer was shaking Jamie's hand, introducing himself. He reached out to Michael, and they shook. "I knew the minute you walked in the door you were the folks from Portland. We don't get a lot of visitors through here."

"So we've found out," Jamie commented.

The sheriff gestured for them to sit at his table and waved the waitress over. "You hungry? The enchiladas here are incredible. The owner's married to my receptionist and really knows his food."

That explained Sara's restaurant recommendation.

The sheriff didn't look at all like he'd sounded on the phone. His voice was low and raspy like an older, bigger man, but he couldn't be a day over forty or a pound over one-sixty. Thin and wiry, he looked like a runner who'd been jogging in the sun. A lot.

Michael and Jamie both ordered cheese enchiladas and dug into the bowl of tortilla chips the waitress plopped down on the table. Michael took a bite and felt it melt in his mouth. Damn, they were good. Hot, fresh, crisp.

"Watch the salsa," warned the sheriff. "It's got some kick."

Jamie dipped a tentative corner into the salsa, took a bite, and sighed in appreciation.

They made polite small talk as Michael tried not to make a pig of himself with the chips. Their drive, the weather, the food. The salsa rocked. The sheriff was right; it had kick, but an awesome kick.

The sheriff rubbed his hands together. "I know you're not here for the food. Let's talk about this guy you're looking for. Chris Jacobs. Now, the reason I asked you to check in with me before heading out there wasn't just for the directions. You'll need to watch your odometer, keeping track of the tenths of miles to know where to turn; there's no signage out that way. You could drive around for hours and not find it. What I really wanted to do was warn you to be careful. That boy's a crack shot with a rifle, and the rifle usually greets any visitors before he does."

Michael noticed Jamie stop with a chip halfway to her mouth and slowly lay it back on her plate. "He shoots at people?" Her voice cracked.

"No. I'd say he's just well prepared. I haven't been out there for a while, but around the time of Elena's death, I made several trips. I always saw the rifle before I saw the owner. That's okay. There's a lotta people around here like that. You just need to make your presence known. He doesn't have a landline. If he has a cell phone, I don't know what it is, and I doubt he gets much coverage if he does."

"Back to the rifle," interjected Michael. "He hurt anybody?"

"Nope."

"But you know he's a crack shot?"

"Yep, my deputies have watched him out at the firing range. Said they've never seen anything like his accuracy. Rifle and handgun. Seems to have quite the arsenal. They've seen him with half a dozen different weapons."

Michael glanced at Jamie. She shook her head. "That's news to me. I didn't know he could shoot."

Shrewd eyes studied Jamie. "How do you know him? He doesn't speak to anyone except old Juan, his closest neighbor. Even he lives half a mile away. Jacobs has lived out there as long as I've been sheriff, and that's been over ten years."

"He's my brother," Jamie said simply. "He moved out when he was eighteen."

The sheriff nodded slowly, his eyes sympathetic. "He keep in contact?"

Jamie shook her head. "Not really."

Sheriff Spencer looked away for a few seconds, pressing his lips together as he thought. Michael watched the man wrestle with a decision. There was something he didn't want to share, and it didn't speak highly of Chris Jacobs.

"Spill it," Michael ordered. He took Jamie's hand under the table and gently squeezed. Her hands were cold.

"Well, I'm not one to gossip—"

"Then don't. If you don't know it to be true, then I don't want to hear about it," stated Jamie. Her grip tightened on Michael's hand.

The sheriff rubbed a hand across his mouth. "The woman. Elena. They never married. That's no big deal, and having a kid while not wed wasn't a big deal to most around here. They looked happy whenever I saw them. Can't say I've ever seen him smile since she died—"

"What's his name? The boy?" Jamie interrupted again.

The sheriff's eyes widened. "You don't know his name? Jesus H. Christ. That's a hell of a brother you've got there. The boy is Brian."

Michael watched Jamie's lips move as she silently spoke the name. Her eyes grew wet.

"I can't believe he wouldn't tell you," Sheriff Spencer snorted. "Why in the world would he refuse to tell you Brian's name?"

"I didn't know about him. Brian. I didn't even know he existed." Jamie's voice drifted off.

"That's even worse." The sheriff shook his head, wonder in his eyes.

"What were you about to say about Jacobs?" Michael brought the sheriff's focus back to the matter at hand.

A blank look crossed his face for a split second. "Crap. Lost my train of thought. I was about to say people think Chris was in the car with Elena when it crashed. Maybe somehow caused the crash. He had a big bruise on his face that day, but claims he'd accidentally whacked himself with something...I don't remember what. It was enough to make people talk, wonder why he'd not admit to being at the scene of the accident. Made him look guilty in some way."

"He said he wasn't there?" Michael asked.

"He said he was home."

"Why would he want to cause an accident? You said they seemed happy."

The sheriff shrugged. "Elena was a Mexican gal. Probably illegal. I figure that's why they never married. She just appeared around town one day, no family, looking for work. I'm not certain how she hooked up with your brother. Anyway, some stuff didn't make sense at the accident. The passenger door was open. Elena's blood was on the outside of her door, but her door and window were shut. Someone had been there after the accident. Jacobs seemed the most likely. The accident happened close enough to their home. He could have easily walked home."

"Who found her?" whispered Jamie.

"Dean Schmidt. Driving by. Swears he didn't touch the driver's door. He'd noticed it was bloody when he got there. He checked Elena from the passenger side and said that door was open. He had to drive a few miles to get a cell signal to call it in."

"He could have messed up the scene," stated Michael.

"He could have," the sheriff agreed. "Dean is eighty-eight years old and sharp as a whip. I guess he watches CSI all the time, said he knew not to touch anything. He checked for a pulse and that was it. A lot of the blood had already dried, and she was nearly cold by the time he found her."

"So anyone passing by could have tampered with the scene."

"I'd usually agree with that statement, but that road only goes to the Schmidt place or your brother's place. The chances of anyone else driving by are slim to none."

"Chris was never arrested for anything, right?" Jamie asked.

"Nope. I was the one to deliver the news. I saw the look on his face. That was the look of a man who'd just lost the love of his life." The sheriff blinked hard. "I asked some questions and was satisfied he knew nothing of the accident. I'm not sure who first spread the story of him causing the accident—I'd like to kick their ass. Damn town loves gossip."

"And telling us? That's not spreading gossip?" Michael raised a brow.

"I've never repeated the story to another person, and I've told plenty of people to shut up about it. I'm just giving you some background on what your brother's experienced here because you're related. I'd say he's rather bitter. Now you know why."

A waitress set two huge platters of food on the table. Michael inhaled. Christ. It was heaven. He didn't even look at Jamie as he dug in. "Holy shit. That's good."

Jamie nodded, her mouth full.

Sheriff Spencer grinned and pulled a piece of paper out of his shirt pocket. "Here's your directions. Like I said, watch the odometer, otherwise you'll never know which road to turn on." He stood, picked up his hat, and glanced at his watch. "Kinda late to drive out there tonight. You're gonna want better light. I'd wait till morning. It's up to you. Hotel's just down the street."

Michael stood to shake his hand. "Thanks for your help."

The sheriff touched the brim of his hat at Jamie. "Good luck."

Michael sat back down with a sigh and picked up his fork. Tomorrow morning was fine with him. He wanted to eat and then sleep. Nothing else.

"All this cheese," Jamie said, focusing on her plate. "I'm gonna have a ton of calories to work off."

Michael suddenly lost his need for sleep.

★ ★ ★

Mason Callahan did not like autopsies. He sat in his car outside the medical examiner's office, air conditioner blasting, and wished for a cigarette. His partner, Ray, was home with a nasty flu bug, so Mason was on his own today. It was easier when Ray came along. It gave him someone to man up to. By himself, it was too easy to wimp out, stalling by sitting in his car, no peer pressure to get his ass inside and listen to what the ME had to say.

He tried to attend the autopsies related to his cases, but usually it was a single victim. Today, it was the adults found in the pit by the bunker. Was this even called an autopsy? What do you call it when there are just bones left? It's more like a puzzle to put back together instead of a body to take apart. That should be the opposite of an autopsy.

Christ.

Can you say stalling?

It was just bones. But he still didn't like stepping foot in the building. It had *that smell.*

He forced himself out of his car, felt the heat slam him in the face, and put on his hat. People always asked how he could wear a hat in this heat. He liked his hat. The brim shaded his eyes and his neck, and the light straw color reflected back the sun. Without his hat the top of his head got hot.

He'd taken two steps when his phone rang. An unfamiliar number showed on the screen. Any other day he'd let it go to voice mail, but maybe this was something important. Something that needed him to get his butt there right away. Away from the ME's building.

"Callahan," he answered.

"Detective. This is Maxwell Brody."

Mason instinctively stood straighter. "Yes, Senator. What can I do for you?"

"After our talk the other day, I've been thinking hard, trying to remember if there was anything else odd going on when Daniel disappeared."

Here it comes again. Mason closed his eyes. There was always something the family held back, feeling it was none of the police's business or had an aspect too embarrassing to reveal. What in the hell had the senator waited twenty years to talk about?

"I had to go back to my calendar. In my type of position, there's always a permanent calendar, a permanent record of what I'd done that day."

Mason heard another male voice speaking in the background.

"Hang on, Detective." The senator's voice was muffled as he answered the other male. He came back on the line. "I'm sorry. My brother, Phillip, is here. He's been helping me review my calendar and diaries from that time."

Mason stood straighter, fighting the need to remove his hat. The governor was there, too? This was what you'd call a power phone call.

"A few months before Daniel vanished, I started having problems with...well, I guess you'd call it a stalker."

Mason's ears perked up.

"I always associate the word *stalker* with a woman being followed, but I don't know how else to describe what I had to deal with. It started simple. The usual crap in the mail. Bullshit letters. The kind of stuff we roll our eyes at but always date-stamp and file away. Just in case."

"What type of letter would you call a bullshit letter?" Mason asked.

"Oh, stuff like he hated my policies, I don't remember which in particular. Someone always hated everything. The eye of God is upon me. I'm not doing God's will, or I'm leading the people away from the path of righteousness."

"A religious fanatic," Mason stated.

"Believe me, I've heard them all. You can't survive in this position without a very thick skin. I don't engage the odd ones. You get a feel for it after a while. You instinctively know who isn't playing with a full deck, and you don't engage."

"This was a half-decker?" Mason heard the senator snort and then turn to repeat the question to his brother. Low laughter rumbled in the background.

He'd made the governor laugh. A proud moment.

"Definitely a half-decker. Anyway, the letters came more frequently, and then the phone calls to the office started. His message was always the same. 'God will punish you.' Like I said, I don't remember which issue he believed God had it in for me. I ignored it until the calls started going to the house."

"Do you know how he got your phone number?"

"No, I never figured that out. But then he started showing up outside the building at work, then at the house. He must have followed me home one night."

"Shit. No kidding? You called the police, right?"

"Of course. He left by the time they showed up. He never came up to the front door, but I saw him pacing outside the gate. You've been to the house; you know the iron gate at the walk-way entry to the yard."

Mason remembered the gate. He'd had to hit a buzzer to get a maid's attention and then show his badge and ID to the camera before she'd unlock the gate.

"He didn't ring the buzzer?"

"No. We didn't have the buzzer and cameras at that time. He could have easily pushed the gate open and walked up to the house, but he didn't. We added them soon after Daniel vanished."

"So why do you associate this guy with your son's disappearance?"

The senator was quiet for a moment. "I guess it's the timing more than anything. And his phrasing that God will punish me. I don't know what punishment is stronger than the death of a child."

Governor Brody spoke low in the background.

"I'm getting to it, Phil," the senator said. "Detective, this guy was arrested for trespassing at the capitol building, so there is a record of who he is. But after his arrest, I never saw him again. I haven't contacted Salem police to try to track down the arrest record. I thought I'd run it by you first."

Mason scribbled in his little flip book. "I'll look into it. You said this happened within a few months of...of the disappearance date? How close to the date do you think the arrest was?"

"I'm guessing within four weeks."

Mason wrapped up his power phone call. The senator didn't have much other information. He scanned his notes from the call, an odd buzzing in his stomach. It wasn't the buzz he got when he knew he had a hot lead. This was different. This was a dire, impending buzz.

Or maybe his stomach felt that way because he was still outside the medical examiner's building. And now he was late.

He hustled across the parking lot and through the double doors. The girl at the front desk waved him in. "They were just asking if I'd seen you. They're in op six!" she hollered after him as he strode down the hall.

"Sorry!"

Mason took off his hat and wiped at the sweat on his temples. The building was icy cool compared to the stiff heat outside. He wrinkled his nose as *the smell* entered his nostrils. There was no getting away from it. Tonight, he'd have to wash his pants and shirt and take a shower before going to bed. It didn't matter if he was in the building for thirty minutes or three hours. The scent still clung. Dr. Campbell claimed the building had the best air filtration system available. And he didn't doubt her. Clearly, nothing had been invented to eliminate the odor of decaying flesh.

He added a medical examiner's perfect air filter system to his mental list of *how to make a million bucks.*

Mason paused outside of op six, took a deep breath through his mouth, and pushed the door open with his shoulder. Dr. Victoria Peres and Lacey Campbell were shoulder-to-shoulder, bent over a skull on one of the silver tables, as Dr. Peres pointed at the nasal opening. Dr. Campbell was nodding emphatically, her brows narrowed in concentration.

Scanning the room, Mason took in four other tables with full skeletons. Each arranged as if the person had simply lain down and his flesh had melted away.

How had they separated the skeletons?

The pit had been one giant hole. The bodies tossed in like trash, their bones and flesh commingling over the years.

"Mason. Over here." Dr. Campbell gestured, her eyes lighting up at the sight of him.

Actually, he figured her eyes were already bright from her fascination with the case. It took a special breed of person to get excited over old bones. Dr. Campbell was one. Dr. Peres was another. They were so deep in bone heaven, they probably hadn't noticed he was very late.

Dr. Peres nodded at him. "Detective." She glanced at the clock on the wall.

Scratch that. The forensic anthropologist missed nothing.

He moved closer, his boots sounding too loud on the hard floor. "Morning, doctors." He stopped next to Dr. Campbell and forced himself to take a good look at the remains. The bones were a muddy brown, not the ivory color he'd expected. He glanced at the other tables. The other skeletons were the same. "Why are they dirty?"

Dr. Peres bristled and Dr. Campbell smiled, putting a calming hand on the other woman's arm. "They aren't dirty. They absorbed the color of the dirt they were buried in for twenty years. It's pretty common. And they've been cleaned. There was some tissue still attached in a few places."

Mason grimaced. "Tissue? There was still flesh left?"

"A bit. A simple soaking in a few different solutions takes care of it."

Mason knew she'd purposefully left out details. In the past, he'd stepped into the room when bones had been simmering to remove the flesh. It'd smelled like a restaurant. He swallowed hard.

"How'd you get them separated? How do you know you have the right bones grouped together?" he asked.

"Very carefully." Dr. Peres spoke. "I'm glad I was there for the unearthing. That's where the first mistakes are always made. Luckily, he'd buried them one at a time. There was a small layer of dirt between each skeleton, enough to help us keep each separate."

"Layers of dirt? How long apart between each burial?"

Dr. Peres bit her lip, and Mason knew she was frustrated that she didn't have a perfect answer for him.

"I can't tell. We can have each dirt sample analyzed, but I'm comfortable saying all five were buried within a ten-year period."

Mason nodded. Once they had identified the bodies, he had a hunch each one would have been reported missing around the same set of years. He needed to get them identified first.

"What else can you tell me?" He pulled out his notebook and pen.

Dr. Peres's face shifted into lecture mode. "This is number three. He's a Caucasian male, approximately eighteen to twenty-five. Six feet tall with a well-healed fracture of his tibia." Dr. Peres pointed at a bone in the lower leg. Mason bent closer and saw the thickened, slightly lumpy area along the sleek bone. "It can take three to five years for a break to look this good. It's an old one...compared to this one." Dr. Peres moved to a different table and indicated the smaller lower arm bone.

The bone had a jagged break that ran across the bone. "This happened pretty close to death. And this particular break on the ulna usually indicates a defensive wound." She lifted her arms and crossed them in front of her face as if protecting her head. "Imagine defending yourself against a swing from a baseball bat. Where is the impact going to be?"

Mason nodded. Her visual worked very well for him. "But how do you know it didn't happen while transporting the bones? Old bones have got to be brittle. I wouldn't think it'd take much to accidentally break one."

Dr. Peres smiled and picked up the thin arm bone. "Every break tells me a story. See here?" She ran a gloved finger along the break. "See the darkness? It's a stain from the bleeding because of the break. The broken ends would be a lighter color than the outer bone if it happened during the recovery or transport because there would be nothing to seep in and stain the break. And see how notched the broken surface is? When fresh bone breaks, the ends are jagged and angled. When a bone breaks long after death, the break is almost flat, because the bone is brittle... like a dry stick snapping. Ever try to break a green tree branch?

It's a jumbled mess. A fresh stick will never break cleanly. Same with bone."

Mason blinked, remembering his attempts to break some small tree branches to roast marshmallows with while camping. It'd been a disaster. He'd used an ax to finish the job. "So someone took a bat or mallet to him, and he tried to protect himself?"

Nodding, Dr. Peres gently laid the bone back in its place. "He was hit with something hard. And his skull shows three blows that are perimortem...close to time of death. I can't tell you what the weapon was other than it was large and blunt. The imprints on the skull are too large to be a hammer." She lifted the skull, showing Mason three impact sites with radiating fractures.

"Were those enough to kill him?"

"Easily."

Had the man been beaten to death?

"But I don't think that's what killed him." She rotated the skull and showed him a small circle at the back of the skull. "This is probably your cause of death."

"Christ," muttered Mason. "Entry or exit wound?"

"Entry," stated Dr. Peres. "See how there's no beveling of the bone around the wound? Entry bullet holes are flat around the holes. The bevel is inside. I didn't find an exit wound or the bullet. It either exited through the eye or never exited at all." She frowned. "Though I would have found the bullet if it had stayed inside."

Mason made a few notes. "Do the others have gunshot wounds?"

"Three of the skulls do," answered Dr. Campbell.

"Do you have ages for the rest of them?"

"They're all in the same age range," said Dr. Peres. "Three are white, two African American."

Mason looked up from the notes he was scribbling. "Oh? An equal-opportunity killer?"

Dr. Campbell's eyes narrowed. "Does the race matter?"

"Usually killers will stick to one race. Not always but more often than not."

"I prefer the word ancestry over race," added Dr. Peres.

Mason held up his hands. "I just want to find who did this. Sorry I'm not the most PC person in the world. Frankly, I can't keep up with what's okay to say and what's not. But yes, a pattern in the type of victims does help direct us to the killer." He met both women's gazes. "Now. Tell me how you can tell someone is black…African American…whatever. He's been killed, and I want to find the murderer."

The women exchanged a glance, and Dr. Campbell picked up the closest skull. "Common to African Americans is the wide nasal opening and the rectangular eye orbits."

"Rectangular? Seriously?" Mason asked.

Dr. Peres picked up a different skull. "See? This one is Caucasian."

Sure enough, the other skull had eye openings that looked more angular.

"There are many things to take into account when determining race," said Dr. Campbell. "But the nose is one of the most useful."

In Mason's opinion, the noses were fucking gone. All that was left were holes. He felt his phone vibrate in his pocket.

"Damn it." He dug the phone out. It was the same unknown phone number from before. The senator.

"Callahan," he answered, avoiding eye contact with Dr. Peres. No doubt he was getting the evil eye for answering his phone in the middle of her lecture.

"Detective, I thought I'd save you some time. I made some calls and tracked down the arrest record of the man I told you about earlier."

Already? Mason couldn't get results that fast.

"I'm having a copy e-mailed to you. The man's name was Jules Thomas."

"Thank you, Senator. I'll look it over."

"Glad to be of help." The senator signed off.

Mason slipped his phone back in his pocket, shaking his head. The man knew how to get things done. Fast.

"Senator?" asked Dr. Campbell. "Senator Brody?"

"Yes, your ex-boyfriend's father. He dug up some information for me." He didn't volunteer more information. Dr. Campbell personally knew the senator and his son. If she had questions, she could ask them.

"I've enjoyed the anthropology lesson, but I need to head back to the office." Mason touched the brim of his hat. "I look forward to your reports, Dr. Peres. As soon as we can figure out who these skeletons are and match them to missing persons' records, we'll figure out who did this to them. And who did it to that bus full of kids, too. Goodbye, Dr. Campbell."

He kept his walk to a steady pace as he exited the operatory. Pushing open the door to the outside heat, he inhaled deeply three times.

Fresh, clean air.

★ ★ ★

Michael did a double tap on the desk bell for the second time. Jamie glanced around the small room. The little town's only hotel turned out to be a bed-and-breakfast two buildings down from the restaurant. The house was charming, but it had that old lived-in smell to it. The one where you figure the carpets have been vacuumed twice a day but not cleaned in several years.

Michael looked ready to jump the counter and check them in himself. Jamie put a hand on his arm. "The woman at the sheriff's office said to keep hitting the bell because the guy's a little hard of hearing."

Michael's answer was to whack the bell again. Finally, a muffled voice came from upstairs.

"What'd he say?" Michael asked.

Jamie shrugged. "Beats me. But at least he heard us."

Someone came slowly thumping down the stairwell. The cadence of the steps was odd, unrhythmic. A gray-haired man smiled at them as he rounded the corner. One of his legs was slightly shorter than the other and didn't bend. Jamie responded to his contagious grin as he limped behind the counter.

"Well, you must be the two Sara called me about. She said you'd be checking in. You from Portland?"

The power of small towns.

"Yes. That's us," she replied. "Are you Chuck?"

His brown eyes beamed. And Jamie fell in love. If she could remember her grandfather, this is who she'd want him to be like. Smiley and kind. "I am. And I've got your room all ready for you."

"That's great," said Michael, bending to grab his bag. "We're bushed."

Jamie froze. "Wait—"

Green eyes and brown eyes looked quizzically at her. The green ones twinkling innocently.

"We need two rooms," she pleaded.

Chuck's face fell. "Oh…well. Then we've got a problem. I'm full up."

"Full? The whole place is full? I thought this town rarely got any visitors," grinned Michael.

"Now, that's true. But I've only got five rooms. And four are full. It's kind of a busy week for me. The Hensens have relatives in town but no room to put them, so they take up two of my rooms. Jordeen Gold's mother-in-law is here, but she won't sleep at Jordeen's because Jordeen is her son's second wife, and she's still rather partial to the first." Chuck ticked off the rooms on his fingers. "And Bill Norman has been staying for the last two nights since his wife kicked him out. I figure he'll be here another two nights. That's usually about her limit." He looked up with a grin. "That leaves one for you."

"Perfect," said Michael. He leaned a little closer to Chuck. "Jamie just didn't want the town getting the wrong idea…seeing as we're not married and all. But you seem like an understanding kind of guy."

Jamie wanted to elbow him. "We don't want to put you out. Is there somewhere else where one of us can stay?"

"You ain't putting me out." Chuck patted her arm. "That's my job. And I'm the only place to stay for thirty miles. Unless you feel like camping."

Jamie's stress level was floating somewhere close to the ceiling. A night alone in a room with Michael Brody. Hormones had been bouncing between them since they met, and now they were going to be trapped in a small space with a bed?

Wait a minute. What the hell was she worrying about? She took a few deep breaths. She was a grown woman, not a teenager. This man had been flipping all her switches into the on position for the last two days, and now she had a chance to be alone with him. This was an *opportunity*, not a situation to run from. She needed to look at this differently.

Peeking from the corner of her eye, she saw Michael was pleased with the arrangement. Why didn't this sort of situation stress men?

She needed to start thinking like a man.

If she wanted something from a man, she needed to show him. Or ask him.

What's he gonna do? Say no?

She doubted it.

"Well," said Chuck slowly. "I do have the attic room. I don't rent it out during the summer because the air-conditioning doesn't—"

"That'll work. We'll take it, too." Jamie exhaled as her argument with her inner vixen suddenly became meaningless. She had her own room. Disappointment surged, surprising her. An opportunity had slipped through her fingers. But more so, she was missing out on taking a chance. She rarely risked anything. But she'd nearly talked herself into risking...risking what? A moment of embarrassment when he refused? Losing out on one of the hottest nights she'd ever experience? How often did men like Michael Brody come along?

This was the first time in her life.

Would there be a second chance?

God, she was confused.

Beside her, Michael's shoulders shook in a silent chuckle, as if he knew what was going through her mind. She glared at him. "Michael will take the attic."

★ ★ ★

Chuck was cool. Michael liked the old man a lot. He'd given Michael a wink as they'd headed up the stairs to the rooms.

"I need a few minutes to check out the attic room," said Chuck. "I'm gonna let you guys wait in the first room. I'll go open the windows up in there, but it's gonna be hot. You better give it some time to cool off." He handed Michael the key. A real key. Not a key card. "I was just putting a bottle of wine in here when you guys showed up. It's still cold. Enjoy." Chuck closed the door behind him, and Michael heard his uneven steps trudge up another set of stairs.

"Perfect," said Jamie. "I need some wine." She picked up the bottle, glanced at the label, and deftly used the opener to slide out the cork. She poured a large glass and raised a brow at Michael in question. He nodded and she poured a second glass, handing it to him.

The room was clean, and the king bed looked comfortable. The decor was dated and faded, but Michael could not care less.

Jamie's wine vanished. She refilled her glass and disappeared into the bathroom. Michael could hear her banging little makeup jars and brushes and shampoo bottles and whatever else women traveled with. She would probably come out in a sweatshirt and sweatpants, even though it was ninety degrees outside. And then send him to his hundred-degree room.

Michael sighed, set down his wine, and flopped on the king bed, tucking his arms under his head. Tomorrow they would talk to Chris and hopefully find out some leads on what happened to Daniel. There was nothing more he could do about it tonight. Thinking endlessly about it wasn't helping; time to put it aside and pay attention to what was in front of him.

Jamie.

What did he want from this woman?

Sex.

Was that all?

He frowned. No. Not even close.

His body was craving sex. That was obvious. He simply had to be in her presence and he felt his hormones hit overdrive. But he wanted more than that. Michael studied the ceiling. He wanted that part that came after, too. The part where you wake up the next morning and roll over to pull the woman closer to you, knowing neither of you had to leave. The part that sits on the back deck and drinks coffee together, sharing the Sunday newspaper, and discussing where to vacation next.

He could still hear that overpowering voice that'd spoke in his head the first day he'd seen her. The one that'd told him to hang on to this woman. End statement.

Now...how did he let her know? Without her walking out on him or laughing in his face?

Aw, fuck. He was in deep.

And she had the shovel.

He couldn't blow it tonight. He patted his pocket, checking for his cell phone, feeling an urge to call Lacey and get her advice.

How would it look to Jamie if she came out and he was on the phone with another woman? Not cool.

Think, Michael. WWLD? What would Lacey do?

Lacey would talk. She'd say exactly what was on her mind to Jamie.

He could do that. Just filter out the sex stuff.

He wanted to know what Jamie was thinking. They'd had several moments where he felt like she'd let her guard down and spoken to him like she'd known him forever. And several moments where the hormones were off the charts.

Lacey would tell him to simply ask Jamie how she felt.

No problem. He sat up, feeling clearer in the head, ready to talk.

The bathroom doorknob turned.

Michael took a deep breath.

Why hadn't Chuck left a bottle of vodka?

★ ★ ★

It's now or never.

She'd had a second chance dumped in her lap when Chuck said he needed to check the attic room. Only a stupid girl would ignore it. Jamie held her breath as she reached for the bathroom doorknob. She'd spent the last five minutes arguing with herself—and finishing that second glass of wine—as she changed into the black bra and matching thong that she'd coincidentally packed.

Some coincidence. She'd known exactly why she'd thrown that black duo in her bag. Because she might end up in a hotel room with Mr. Hottie. And here she was.

The only thing holding her back was herself. She was certain he wouldn't turn her down. She'd caught him staring at various parts of her body multiple times, and he'd been putting out that protective vibe since her house was trashed. She could almost smell the pheromones.

Today had been one of the most stressful days of her life. There was someone back in Portland, looking for Chris, desperate enough to attack her in her home. But putting nearly an entire state between them and the attacker felt good, and being close to Michael made her feel safe. Tomorrow he'd help her find her brother, but tonight...

He'd held her hand.

That's what'd touched her the most and made her melt inside. When he'd taken her hand at dinner with the sheriff as they talked about her nephew, she'd wanted to curl up on his lap and bury her head in his neck.

But tonight she wasn't seeking comfort. She wanted a taste of the wild ride that the man promised. It leaked out of every pore of his body. Pure testosterone pumped up with smooth male confidence.

What was the worst that could happen? He fucked her and never called? Yes, that would suck, but she'd live. And probably have a memorable night.

Damn it, she wanted that memorable night.

She wanted it bad. Bad enough to make her step outside her comfort zone. She wanted to be a different woman tonight. Not Principal Jacobs. Not perfectly neat and organized Jamie who didn't take a step without a plan.

She looked in the mirror and ran her hands over flat abs. Boobs looked good. A thong made almost every ass look good. She could feel the wine warming her limbs, giving her the courage she needed. She wanted Michael Brody and was about to let him know it. She lifted her chin and opened the door.

★ ★ ★

He stared.

A goddess had emerged from the bathroom and stood in front of him in black lace. Her chin lifted, and she held his gaze, inviting and fearless.

He had no voice. He reached out to touch one thigh and pulled back. He needed to simply look some more, mentally soak in the sight. Jamie was all smooth skin and long limbs, with legs that didn't end. She brushed her hair over one shoulder and his heart nearly stopped.

"Sweet mother of pearl. You are smoking hot."

Her laugh warmed his heart.

"What are you doing?" he choked out. She looked ready to go several rounds in bed with him. And he'd just talked himself into having a conversation with her.

His brain shifted mental gears. "Wait. Don't answer that. Don't say anything. I don't want you talking yourself out of this."

Jamie's lips turned up. "You're learning me well. Because if I overthink this, I'll be back in that bathroom in a heartbeat, and I'll put all my clothes back on." A touch of nervousness appeared in her gaze.

And if he made a wrong move, she'd run.

"God, woman. I want you so much at this moment, I think I'm about to explode."

The nervous light in her eyes evaporated.

"While you were in the bathroom, I convinced myself to spend our evening talking about our feelings."

Her eyebrows arched.

"I know. Stupid, huh?" This time he did touch her thigh. *Silky.* Just like he'd known it'd feel.

"You have feelings to tell me about?"

"Oh yeah." He placed both palms on her thighs, staring at the skin under his fingers. *I want to feel you everywhere.*

"Michael. Really. What did you want to talk to me about?"

He blinked. And looked up into questioning light green eyes.

Talk to her.

He didn't want to talk right now. Every thought except one had blown clear out of his brain. He scrambled to get his thoughts together and removed his hands from her legs, because the feel of her skin was short-circuiting his mind even more. She sat on the bed beside him, holding his gaze, and reached for his hand. Hers were slightly damp. This close, he could smell the wine from her mouth.

He licked his lips.

He'd read somewhere that women were turned on by what they heard? And men by what they see?

Too true.

"Don't get me wrong," he started. "I want this. I want what you're…offering. I've wanted that from the first time I saw you at the door at your house. You're the full package, you know? Brains, beauty, and some balls."

She scowled slightly.

"That's a compliment." He wiped at his forehead. *Compliment?* "I mean, you went through some tough shit and came out great."

Her expression didn't change.

"Ah, fuck me. *Damn it.* You'd think I don't know how to talk." He grabbed both her hands, turned toward her, and looked at her in earnest. "Listen. You *do it* for me, princess. In an amazing way. You get me hot with one look, but that's not all of it. I don't want just *that*. I want to wake up in the middle of the night and stretch out a leg and feel yours against it. I want to open my bathroom cabinet and see your makeup next to my stuff. When I pour my coffee in the morning, I want to pour two cups."

She simply blinked at him.

"I want to know your opinion on the next election and that stupid kid beauty pageant TV show and if you like Indian food." He sucked in a breath. "I don't know if you like to travel or see movies or go camping, but I want to find out! What I'm saying is that I *like* you, Jamie. A lot. I don't want to just have an awesome night of sex—and it will be awesome—I want to keep moving forward. Does that make sense?"

A wicked gleam touched her eyes and she smiled. "Perfect sense. You're saying I'm not a one-night stand." She touched the collar on his shirt and then the skin just below it, her gaze following her fingers.

Fire lit at his neck and shot downward.

He lunged forward and kissed her.

She met him kiss for kiss, and the next few minutes flew by in a flurry of hands and mouths. Tugging at clothing, undoing hooks, grasping at bedding as they flung back the covers to get bare skin on cool sheets. He moved her back against the mattress and stretched out beside her, touching every inch of that silky skin of hers with his own. She clung to him, gripping as she rubbed her thighs against his, her chest pressed tight to his.

He wasn't done talking with her, but there would be time to talk later. She ran her nails through his hair, and his body lit up like fireworks. He continued his deep assault on her mouth as they rolled on the bed, taking turns for control. His hands traced her smooth skin, touching and memorizing every dip and curve. It was fast and hungry, no calm, soothing sex here. He felt like a starving man.

And Jamie was delicious.

He pulled back and stopped, holding her at arm's length, pinned against the mattress, so he could look his fill. Her eyes were dark and her pupils dilated, her lips open and wet, her chest heaving as she paused. Her gaze held his, saying she was giving him a moment to look but not much more. Something possessive gripped him.

"It's not just sex," he repeated. He needed to know she truly understood before this went further.

"I know." The pulse at her neck throbbed.

Her leg shifted between his, stroking his rigidity with her thigh. Michael tried not to moan. Instead, he bent his head to her breast and took her nipple gently between his teeth, teasing the silky tip with his tongue. She hissed and clutched at him. The scent of her skin shot heat down his spine and put every hormone in overdrive.

There wasn't time. He parted her with a hand, stroking her, and found her slick wetness, which nearly made him release on her stomach. She pressed a condom into his hand. He ripped it open and sheathed himself as her knees came up and her head tipped back. He pressed against her and slid deep.

Their bodies arced together, their pace frantic and feverish. It was mindless, hormone-driven sex. Exactly what he'd needed and apparently she'd needed too. She scratched his back, and the small pain magnified his anticipation. White lights danced behind his eyelids as he heard her gasp, felt her clamp and pulse around him. His tension built.

Michael came, his brain and spine exploding with sensations.

Later, he wrapped his arms around her, relishing the feel of her skin pressed against him. She'd drifted off, but he didn't want to sleep. He didn't want to relinquish the moment. He wanted to stretch it out as long as possible, savoring the intimacy they'd shared. He still wanted more, more of everything she had to offer him. Physical, emotional, and mental. He was keeping Jamie around for the long haul.

But he couldn't wait to pour two cups of coffee in the morning.

CHAPTER TEN

Gerald had packed a small duffel bag for a few nights, filled up his gas tank, and parked his vehicle a mile from Jamie's house at a local gas station. He read the latest Lee Child novel as he waited for his boss's man to update him. There was no way he was going near Jamie's home after the break-in that morning. Thankfully, his boss always knew someone, somewhere. And to get one of the cops, who was currently keeping an eye on the Jacobs home for twenty-four hours, to give an update of any movements at the home took a simple phone call.

Something was going to happen, he could feel it. Sure enough. Just as Child's Jack Reacher character was about to raise bloody hell on four beefy idiots with his bare hands, Gerald's phone rang. According to the source, Michael Brody's black gas guzzler had pulled up to Jamie's house with her in the passenger seat. It'd parked at her home for ten minutes until the two of them emerged with Jamie carrying a small suitcase. And the SUV was headed his way.

Gerald reluctantly closed the novel, carefully marking his place. Were they headed to the airport? He was prepared if it came to that. Brody's SUV blew past the gas station, and he pulled out after it. The SUV passed the airport exit and continued east on the highway, following the Columbia River through the gorge where the river cut through the Cascade Mountain Range. Gerald kept his gaze glued to the Range Rover, ignoring the wide blue river on his left. The river was the northern boundary of Oregon, separating it from Washington. On his right were towering steep cliffs with the occasional waterfall.

To Oregonians, the Columbia River Gorge was one of nature's miracles. Gerald ignored it.

Hours later the cliffs eventually became flatland. The sights grew drier and browner. They crossed over into what Gerald mentally classified as redneck country. The eastern side of the Cascade Mountain Range was home to ranchers and cowboys. How far east were Brody and Jamie going? Boise? Montana? He believed it wouldn't be too much farther. If they were going as far as Boise or more, it really made more sense to fly.

About fifty miles before the Idaho border, the SUV exited the main highway. A series of dusty two-lane roads and ninety more minutes of driving placed them in a tiny country town. Gerald stopped at the single-pump gas station to fill up and kept an eye on Jamie and Michael's vehicle down the street. It'd pulled up to the sheriff's building and they'd gone inside.

Fuck, it was hot. Gerald stretched the kinks out of his back as the attendant filled his vehicle. Hopefully this was nearly the end of the journey. Why'd they stop at the sheriff's office? Did they not know exactly where they were going?

He had a hunch Chris Jacobs was hiding out in this shitty little town.

He noticed the attendant eyeing the tattoos peeking out on his wrists. Gerald tugged at his sleeves, hating to pull them down to hide the color. The guy probably thought he was nuts for wearing a long-sleeved shirt and jeans in this heat. The shirt was athletic fabric, the clingy, stretchy kind that wicked moisture away from the body and showed every sculpted muscle of his arms and chest. It really wasn't too bad in the heat.

He pretended to make a phone call and held the phone to his ear for a few seconds.

"Shit. What the hell?" he said, loud enough for the attendant to hear.

"Problem?" the kid asked. He looked like a typical country boy. Tanned skin, dingy cargo shorts, and a T-shirt that had been white at some point. He just needed a grass stem hanging out the side of his mouth or a tobacco can ring in his back pocket.

A brief flash of the teen boys from his childhood hit his brain. This kid would have been one of the popular kids. Normal looking, confident. The kind who made fun of Gerald, the freak. Gerald stood straighter, expanding his chest. It was one of the reasons he stayed in top physical shape. It was a confidence builder. And his tattoos gave him confidence. Sometimes he wanted to shed his clothes and show his colors to the world, but that wasn't their purpose. They were for him. They allowed him to look at his body with pride, boosting his morale. In private moments, his victims had seen his skin of many colors. It'd intimidated them, helped them recognize his power.

Gerald held up his phone. "Keeps going to voice mail. I've called five times."

The kid nodded. "That sucks."

"Well, hell. I drove all the way from Boise today to buy a truck from a guy, and now I can't even reach him. He'd told me to give him a call when I got to town, so he could give me directions. I told him I had a GPS, and he just laughed. Said his address doesn't work on those things. That common out here?"

White crooked teeth grinned at him. "Totally. A GPS can get you to Demming, but none of the mapping companies are going to waste time with the local addresses when there's one house every twenty miles."

Gerald looked over the tiny town. "I guess I'll sit and wait somewhere and hope the guy gets back to me. I hope he doesn't think that I changed my mind."

"Who're you buying a truck from?"

Yes! Gerald gave the kid a surprised look. "You think you might know him? This area that small?"

The kid shrugged and glanced at the ticker on the gas pump. "I know most folks."

"The name's Chris Jacobs. Sound familiar?"

One eyebrow rose a bit. "Yeah, I know him. Didn't realize he was selling his truck. That thing's a piece of shit. Why'd you drive so far to buy that?"

Gerald tried to look concerned while inside he was shooting off fireworks. "You think it's a waste of money? I'm just looking for a beater vehicle for my nephew to drive to school."

"Oh. Yeah, it'd be fine for that."

"You know where I can find him?"

The pump turned off, and the kid clicked the handle a few times, topping off the tank. He slammed the handle back in the holder and punched a few buttons on the pump. "Sure. But you better keep trying to call him. Chris doesn't like surprise visitors. He nearly shot my buddy, Justin, when he cut through his property going after a coyote. I'll write the directions down for you. If he's not home, you could stop by the bakery and ask. Old Juan, the baker, is about the only guy Chris ever talks to. He might know if Chris is out of town for some reason."

Gerald hid his excitement as the attendant scribbled on the back of his gas receipt with a grimy pencil. Only in a small town does everyone really know everyone else. And willingly give you directions to where they live.

Now he could get down to business. He pictured how to end Chris Jacobs's life as impatience rushed through him. He imagined Chris fighting for air with Gerald's hands around his throat, knowledge of his killer's identity visible in his eyes. Or Chris seeing the spray of his own blood on a wall from Gerald's knife to the neck. The two men had a history together; it was time for the climax.

★ ★ ★

Chris studied his monitor in the dim light. Four camera views showed different angles of his home. Three outside and one in. He'd thought about investing in some motion detectors to trip the cameras, but there were too many small critters wandering around. The black-and-white images were still. No one had gone near his home.

Brian made a small sound in his sleep. It was a good noise. A contented noise. It was an adventure for the boy to spend the night above Juan's bakery. It was one of Brian's favorite places to buy a treat, so sleeping above the little shop was even better. The boy definitely had a sweet tooth. Juan created some incredible baked goods. Chris loved the smell and the taste of the baked breads, but he could do without the sweet, dessert-type foods.

He hadn't eaten sweets in decades.

Sweat beaded down his back, and feeling slightly nauseous, Chris ran a shaky hand over his mouth. No cakes. No frosting. Not for him. He closed his eyes, breathing deep.

He remembered being back in the hospital. He didn't know how long he'd been there. According to his parents, he'd spent months getting well enough to be released. To him, the time was a big haze. Doctors, nurses, police, detectives. He'd spoken to none of them and looked away at their questions. He couldn't even face his parents. He knew he looked bad. The burns ran up and down his face, and his hair had been pulled out in places. Later, he'd learned that both his cheekbones and his nose had been broken, probably more than once.

Although most of the hospital days were a complete fog, there were some clear memories. Jamie. He remembered the first time he saw her. Her blue eyes wide in wonder as she stared at his bandages.

And he remembered the Twinkies. They'd been in a small gift basket. His hospital room had been packed with bouquets and balloons and gift baskets. Gifts from people he'd never met. People who'd read about his plight in the paper. People who'd prayed for two years for all the kids to come home safely. He was an answer to that prayer.

One gift basket had caught his eye during one of his foggy moments. Individually wrapped cellophane Twinkies filled a red toy bucket, clear wrap fastened with a red bow at the top. It'd sat across his room nearly hidden by balloons, but it stood out like a spotlight to him. He'd stared at it, unable to get himself out of bed. He'd drift off to sleep, but the bucket was still there each time he woke. Sometimes moved to another tabletop to make room for more gifts. When he finally woke with a nurse in his room, he'd pointed at the bucket. Shock had crossed her face. He'd never made eye contact with any of his caretakers before, but he was making contact now. He pointed again. And met her eyes.

"You want to see your gifts?" she'd asked, excitement in her voice. She reached for a stuffed animal. Chris shook his head and pointed again. She hesitated and placed the animal back, trying to follow his line of sight. "You want the red bucket?"

He nodded.

"I'll let you look at it, but I don't think you should eat any right now. I can ask a doctor later if you can have one." She lifted the bucket and peered inside.

Chris emphatically shook his head. No way would he eat a Twinkie. The nurse faltered at his head movement, assuming she'd grabbed the wrong gift again. He gestured for her to bring it closer. She set it on the bed next to him, and he reached for the envelope. Correction. He tried to reach for the small envelope. His hands wouldn't obey his brain.

The nurse gently lifted the note and slid out the card. "Looks like it's already been opened and read." She scanned the note, a small crease appearing between her brows. "It's not signed. But some of the arrangements from the public haven't been signed." She smiled at him, "They can't help but send you things. You've been missing for quite a while, and they're happy you're home."

Chris did an awkward "hurry up" gesture with his hand, his stomach starting to churn.

She looked back at the note and read out loud: "Get well soon, Chris. Your family is extremely lucky to have you back. I hope these Twinkies keep your mouth full until you go home."

Chris vomited all over his bed.

In Juan's attic, Chris's vision blurred. Bile came up the back of his throat, and he lunged for the garbage can. He heaved. And heaved.

I hope these Twinkies keep your mouth full.

He heaved again, the nurse's voice ringing in his memory. He sank to his knees, leaning over the can, waiting for his stomach to hold still. Sweat dripped from his forehead into the can. Chris fell back against the wall, sliding to sit on the floor, the can clutched between his hands.

Fuck.

He hadn't had a reaction like that in at least six months. The discovery of the children's remains had brought everything fresh to the surface. He spit into the can, wincing at the acid taste. Not ready to get up, he leaned his head against the wall and closed his eyes. He needed a few more minutes. He breathed deep through his mouth in an attempt to not smell his own vomit. That technique semi-worked.

Twinkies. Fucking Twinkies.

His empty stomach churned.

The Ghostman had a Twinkie fetish. Healthy food was rarely available in the Ghostman's pit, but Twinkies always were. At first the kids were thrilled at the constant supply of the junk snack. But watching the Ghostman eat one…cleaning out the center with his tongue…that was enough to make a kid put the little cake back up. Then later…when the Ghostman wanted the boys to hold the Twinkies in their mouths…

Chris's stomach found more fluids to hurl into the can.

I hope these Twinkies keep your mouth full.

Fucking nut job. Perverted child abuser. Salty wet tracks ran down Chris's face.

At that moment in the hospital, Chris had known he could never say a word about his two years with the Ghostman. The Ghostman had found him. And proved that even in a hospital with a cop standing outside the door to keep the media vultures away, the Ghostman could touch him. The note was a reminder directed at his family.

Your family is extremely lucky to have you back.

If Chris told his family anything, the Ghostman would make his threats against their lives come true. His only way to protect his family was to be silent. He made a vow to himself. No matter the cost, Chris would never speak of those days.

Brian sighed in his sleep. Chris had made another vow. His son would never know the touch of a pervert like the one who had owned him. His son would never have his life turned upside down and inside out. Chris had kept that promise. Brian never lacked for company or stimulation. Chris was his best friend, teacher, playmate, and confidant. Brian didn't remember his mother. Occasionally he asked, but the answer that his mommy was an angel satisfied him. For now. The harder questions would come later.

He blew out a deep breath. His stomach was quieting. He slowly pulled himself off the floor and carried the garbage can to the bathroom. He flushed the contents, rinsed the can three times, and flushed it again. He silently walked through the little room, glancing at his laptop. All quiet at his home. Perhaps he was being too cautious. Too overprotective.

He will never touch Brian.

No. Chris wasn't overprotective. Until he knew that the Ghostman was dead, he had a son to safeguard.

He reached through the window and placed the can out on the roof. The smell still lingered. He considered closing the window, but the room was too warm. The odor should dissipate. He gazed out over the quiet street and thought about Brian playing with Juan's dog. Every boy should have a dog. Maybe when things calmed down, he could find a dog. One who needed a good home. Perhaps a rescue dog. It would be a good situation for both of them.

A small sliver of the moon hung low in the dark night. Chris stared. He liked the quiet of this town. He liked the open sky and the open land. He didn't want to move again. This was the only home Brian had known. He wanted to keep that sense of stability for the boy. But if he felt threatened or unsafe, he and Brian would be on the road before the sun came up. He had a dozen plans in place if he ever needed to leave. It gave him peace of mind to know the two of them could vanish without leaving a trace. He prayed he never needed to implement those plans. He felt good here. He felt like he could breathe. Like he could heal.

Chris stretched, feeling his right shoulder pop. It'd never been the same since the Ghostman's hands. He massaged the joint as he went to close his laptop. Enough monitoring for tonight. He was about to fall asleep standing up. He put his hand on the lid and froze.

A man was standing outside his home, his back flat to the front wall, peering in a window. The small sliver of moonlight found the gun in the man's hand. Chris stared at the man's hair. He recognized the man's stance, the angle of his face.

It was time to leave Demming.

★ ★ ★

It was four in the morning, and no one was at Chris's home.

Gerald had easily found the small house. A double-wide trailer surrounded by a swatch of tall firs standing alone on a small rocky plateau. He'd left his vehicle a half mile away in another group of trees and brush. He hadn't seen another car since he left the town.

Talk about rolling up the sidewalks. The small town had shut off every light in the "city" area by eight p.m. Even the gas station had closed by seven. Last evening, he'd kept a distant view of Michael and Jamie as they'd eaten dinner at the diner. After that, they'd gone to a bed-and-breakfast and not come out. Apparently, they were waiting until the following day to meet up with her brother.

By the pale light of the moon, Gerald went through the drawers, pulling out everything. He figured if Chris wasn't home by now, he wouldn't be coming home at all tonight. Clothes piled at his feet as he ran his hand under and around each drawer. He was beginning to wonder if he had the right house. He wasn't finding any sign that Chris Jacobs lived here.

He steamed. He'd had a plan, an expectation. And it was all going to hell. Every ounce of him wanted to put an end to the man who'd eluded him for years. And it looked like he'd slipped away again. His hands and psyche were aching for blood.

He stalked to the small kitchen and did the same number on the drawers in there. No scraps of mail, no bills, nothing with Jacobs's name. There weren't any photographs either. The only things hanging on the walls were the artwork of a child. Looking at the toys and clothes, it was a young boy. Younger than ten. Gerald bent over and started on the cupboards. Pots, pans, bowls. Nothing that indicated who lived in the house.

He opened the fridge. He'd seen those fake bottles before that people hid important papers or money in. He checked the small amount of condiments and found them all to be legit. He grabbed the carton of milk and peered at the date. It didn't expire for another seven days, so someone had been here recently.

Would Jacobs have a child? He hadn't found any women's clothing or women's touches around the house. The bathroom only held male toiletries. Where was the child's mother? Divorced? Again, Gerald wondered if he had the right house.

He pulled the cushions off the couch, unzipped them, and ripped the covers off. Nothing.

Damn it!

There was no landline, no computer, but there was a desk that looked like it was missing a laptop. A printer sat close by, and there were several bookshelves full of computer programming books. He marched back to the main bedroom and stared, letting his eyes travel the room. What had he missed?

He scanned the blank walls. Whoever lived here, lived like they'd never settled in.

He froze as the thought hit him. Or lived like they were ready to leave at a moment's notice, without leaving a trail.

No papers, no pictures.

Satisfaction flowed through him; he was definitely standing in the right house.

This was the house of a shadowman. Who now had a son to hide.

★ ★ ★

Within fifteen minutes of seeing the Ghostman on his laptop, his heart racing, Chris had Brian packed in the truck. The sleepy boy leaned against the side rest of his booster, unable to keep his eyes open. He hadn't asked a single question about being awakened in the middle of the night. Chris was always ready to travel light. Every item he owned had a mentally attached tag of "take" or "leave" on it. Everything he'd ever bought, he'd considered whether it'd be something he needed to abandon if he had to leave town fast or if the item was light and necessary to pack.

He didn't say good-bye to Juan. The old man was a light sleeper and had surely heard them leave. Years ago, he'd briefly told Juan that someday, someone might come looking for him, but he kept details to a minimum. The old man easily read between the lines, and he knew Chris would run without stopping if he thought Brian was in danger.

Through numerous mental dry runs and the occasional real one, Chris had packing and vanishing down to a science. And now it was paying off. He and Brian had made long car trips south into Mexico, and he knew exactly where he wanted to go. There was a tiny, sleepy town on the western coast of Mexico. Life was slow, and the people seemed kind and not nosy. Not like here. The town gossips tried to stick their noses in his life every now and then, pretending concern for how he was raising his son. He'd considered making the move a few years ago, but he couldn't bring himself to leave the US. He'd lost almost everything. His parents, Brian's mother. Living in the US was one of his last connections with his previous life.

Elena had shown him the small Mexican town. Her grandparents had lived there, and she'd visited often as a child.

Elena. His hands tightened on the steering wheel.

Her death had left a gaping wound in his heart. She'd been such an innocent. He'd fallen in love with her simple ways and immediate acceptance of his scars. She saw past them to who he was inside. Only she could calm his nightmares, and she brought him peace. He still felt that peace at times with his son. Brian was a little living piece of Elena.

He had a strong suspicion of what'd happened the night she died. Elena had been out of communication with her family for several years. Her brothers ran drugs, and violence surrounded their lives. She'd wanted nothing to do with it and had left. A few weeks before her accident, she'd finally been contacted by her oldest brother, who'd demanded that she return home. She'd refused. When the brother realized she was living with a man and had a child out of wedlock, he'd flipped. A strong Catholic, her brother increased the pressure.

That night, she'd gone to meet with her brother, the first time she'd seen him in three years. Chris didn't believe her brother had harmed her in any way, but he'd known Elena was extremely upset by the visit. She'd called as she left her brother. Hysterical with tears, saying her brother had ordered her back to Mexico and called her a whore. Chris had made her hang up the phone because he wanted her to focus on driving.

Driving too fast? Possibly. Chris suspected her brother had been the one to see the accident first; perhaps he was driving behind her, following her after she ran out of their meeting. The next thing he knew, the sheriff was at his front door and Elena was gone. There'd been some tampering at the accident scene, which Chris suspected had been from the brother checking on Elena after the accident. She'd died instantly, according to the coroner. No immediate action could have saved her.

The brother had vanished. Chris hoped he lived with the vision of Elena's death in his mind every day.

He'd never heard from her family. Their rejection didn't bother him, but the idea that they'd rejected Brian as part of their family did. Not that he wanted his son to associate with criminals—or the man who possibly drove Elena to wreck her car—but every child needs to know they have extended family that cares.

Chris had Jamie. That was it.

Jamie was persistent about keeping in touch. But he ached for that larger circle of blood to call his own. His parents were gone. Wiped out in a single moment by a drunk driver. How ironic that the people he'd loved the most were all killed in car accidents. He forced himself to keep Jamie at arm's length for her own good. And tonight was proving that he'd been right all along. Where he was, trouble would eventually follow. He had to keep moving.

He glanced at Brian in his rearview mirror. The boy's mouth was open slightly, his black hair mussed from bed. Keeping Brian's existence a secret from Jamie cut him deeply every day. But if she knew about his son, she'd force the two of them out into the open, where it was dangerous.

Chris looked at his son, and his heart ached. In a good way.

Brian was his number-one priority in life. He would do everything in his power to keep his boy safe. Safe from predators like the one who'd scarred him. The boy shifted in his booster, and Chris eyed the seatbelt to make certain it still crossed Brian's chest in the right spot. How careful parents were these days. When Chris grew up, children had avoided seat belts, lying down in the backseat or in the back of station wagons. He'd had a friend who liked to lie down against the window above the backseat as his parents drove.

Today, a parent would get pulled over for a stunt like that.

His parents had shielded him from the outside world after he'd returned from the forest. Which was good. He hadn't wanted to interact. He'd spent years simply wanting to stay in his room. School had been a nightmare. His mother had finally resorted to homeschooling. Actually, Chris did most of the learning on his own. He'd outline each month what he planned to learn, and his mother had approved. She was available if he needed help, but frankly, schoolwork was a breeze.

His brain was a sponge. He read history for pleasure, did math because he was curious, and studied computers because they fascinated him. His idols were Steve Jobs and Bill Gates. Their lifestyles were too public for his taste, but he understood how their brains worked.

When Jamie was studying fractions as a sixth grader and struggling to master them, he'd written a simple computer program for her to watch and interact with. Seeing her face light up as she finally understood had been like a hit of crack. He wrote more programs. And more. Back then, there were simple message boards that programming geeks posted on, asking other geeks for help. That became his social life. The other geeks couldn't see the external and internal scars.

The Internet exploded, and he was perfectly positioned to take advantage. His simple websites for local businesses caught the attention of other businesses. By the time he was eighteen, he was making more money than his father. Life was spinning along quite comfortably. Plastic surgeries had improved his scarring... or so he thought, until he'd stepped out in public and caught the children's stares and the quick glances of adults who rapidly looked the other way.

Only once had he asked to see some of the other children who'd vanished with him. He'd been lucid for a few days between surgeries, during the second month, and asked his mom if he could talk to David Doubler, who'd been released a few months after they'd been kidnapped. He still remembered the shock and pity on his mother's face.

"David is still gone, Chris. No one but you has come home."

He'd nearly blurted out that he'd seen the other children released one by one. But he bit his tongue in time. If he admitted he'd seen them released, he'd have to admit he remembered where they'd been held and describe who had held them.

He kept his mouth shut.

But the minute he had the ability to search the Internet when he was older, he looked for all of them. And found nothing. Except families who still waited and grieved for their children.

How many nights had the belief that his friends had been released helped him stay sane in that bunker? He'd hated the children who were released, yet he was overjoyed for them at the same time.

He would never study his son's face on a missing-child poster.

Now he knew where all the children were. They'd been buried in the dirt for two decades while their families waited for their return. At least the families finally had their answers. At least now the families could give up hope that their children were still alive and move on. Living with the unanswered questions was the worst. He'd wanted to tell the families he believed the children were dead, but he had no proof. He didn't know what the Ghostman had done with them. And he had to continue his charade of memory loss.

His heart clenched at the thought of Daniel's family. Their son hadn't returned home. His body wasn't found with the other children.

What was that lack of knowledge doing to his parents?

Their wounds had been freshly reopened. No doubt, Daniel's parents had learned to cope without their son for so long. But while all the other parents had answers, they still suffered from the unknown.

Should he tell them what had really happened to Daniel? How they'd escaped from the Ghostman together? For nearly two decades, he'd wanted to tell the senator and his wife what had happened to their son. But he'd had to keep his mouth shut. If he'd told, there would be blood spilled. Innocent blood and guilty blood. He didn't give a damn about the guilty blood, but he would do his best to protect the innocent. That meant being silent.

It'd been an enormous burden to bear.

The quiet highway stretched out before him. He'd passed very few cars at this hour. The sun was just starting to peek over the horizon on his left side. The more miles he put on the road, the safer his son would be. He loosened his grip on the steering wheel. His fingers were cramping, he'd been holding on so tight. He forced a long exhale and tried to relax.

Just keep moving.

But his mind kept returning to the same question over and over.

How had the Ghostman found him in Demming?

The car jerked in response as a new realization shocked his system.

Jamie. He hadn't given Jamie his new phone number.

He'd been in the process of setting up a new number for her to reach him when the news of the found children had started filling the Internet. He changed the number every few months, and he'd immediately changed it after Jamie had called to tell him the children's bodies had been found.

Christ! Had she tried to call? What sort of panic would she be in if she couldn't reach him? He steered the vehicle to the side of the highway and parked. He hit the button to call her house.

Shit! Voice mail. He couldn't leave a message.

He tried her cell phone. Voice mail again.

He didn't dare leave a message that anyone could hear. At least he'd had his number set up to show as a restricted number. Hopefully, that would let her know he'd at least tried to reach out to her. She knew he'd never leave a message.

What if she can't get to her phone? What if the Ghostman already got to her? Is that how he found me?

Chris leaned his head against the wheel, heart pounding. Slow sweat started to drip down his temples. Could that have happened? Could the Ghostman have traced him through Jamie? He'd been so careful. But it made sense for someone to start with her if they wanted to find him. He'd always made certain Jamie knew nothing, and he'd hoped that was enough to keep her safe from anyone who decided to look for him. But what if someone wasn't satisfied with her answers? What if they hadn't believed her and decided to force answers?

He couldn't move. How could he leave the US not knowing if she was okay?

He had to go back to Portland.

Bile churned in his gut, and a headache bloomed behind his temples.

He had to see for himself that she hadn't been touched. A quick trip. He'd keep trying her phone numbers on the way. Then he'd head to Mexico.

He pulled a U-turn on the empty highway.

★ ★ ★

No one was coming back to Chris Jacobs's little house. Gerald was certain of that. Somehow, Jacobs had instinctively fled. Possibly Jamie had said something to scare her brother off, but she was still in town. And Jacobs wasn't with her. As far as he could tell, the sister was planning to head out to the Jacobs house sometime today.

Last evening, he'd asked a few questions in the market, and he'd found out Jamie had asked the sheriff for directions to Chris's home but not driven out there. Instead, she'd shacked up in a bed-and-breakfast with Brody.

Gerald snorted. *Wonder what they'd spent the night doing?*

According to the checker at the market, the only person Chris Jacobs spoke to was the town baker. Some old Mexican with an ancient bakery off the main drag in town. The kind of place where living quarters are behind the shop. He'd said Jacobs was a regular at the bakery. It matched the story he'd gotten from the kid pumping his gas.

Did Chris still have a sweet tooth? Gerald doubted it.

Gerald decided the bakery wasn't going to be opening up shop today. He'd made a hand lettered sign to place in the window stating Juan wasn't feeling well. That would be sufficient to keep small-town people away. He needed to have a private talk with the baker. Might take a few hours.

He silently let himself into the bakery, sneering at the pathetic lock. He'd dismantled it in fifteen seconds. The bakery was dark, the windows facing the street quite small. That was good. He inhaled deeply though his nose. God, it smelled heavenly. Small glass cases stood empty, ready to be stocked with that day's goods. The bakery was old but spotless.

Gerald moved behind the cases and into the back room. Old stainless steel equipment littered the room, the walls lined with shelves and stocked with canisters. But he only had eyes for the door to the right. He held his breath as he listened outside the door for a full five seconds. Pure silence. He placed his hand on the knob and slowly turned, pushing the door in to another dark room and tightening his grip on his gun.

He heard the movement before he felt the metal pole crash into his face. Lights exploded behind his eyes, and Gerald's head felt separated from his neck with the blow. He dropped to his knees in pain, losing the gun. He heard it hit the floor and slide away. He flung himself in that direction, and the bar hit him in the back of the head. Blindly, he cast about the floor for the gun. Hands scrambling. Nothing.

Shit! Where the fuck was it?

His attacker yelled at him in Spanish and struck him in the back of the head again. Gerald powered forward, aiming low with his shoulder in the direction of the voice, and rammed something solid. Swearing in Spanish, the attacker fell backward and landed hard on the concrete floor. He heard the air rush out of the man's lungs, and he lunged forward again, hands grabbing and punching. Adrenaline lit up his brain with fireworks. He got one hand on the metal bar and yanked, flinging it behind him.

His attacker was old. The voice was scratchy, and the movements were of a weak man. Easily overpowering the attacker on the floor, Gerald rolled the old man onto his stomach and knelt on his back, yanking his head up by his hair.

"You the baker, you useless piece of shit?" he hissed in the man's ear.

The man struggled underneath him, and he pulled harder on the hair, overextending the man's neck.

"You want me to break your neck? Is that what you want me to do? Because I can. I can do it so fast you'll never even know."

Gerald punctuated his threats with more yanks, and the old man gasped for air. "My fucking head hurts! You old bastard!"

He squinted in the dim light and spotted an electrical cord plugged into the wall. Stretching, he jerked it out, and a phone fell to the floor. He wrestled the old man's arms behind him and spun the cord around his hands. He grabbed the old man's head with both hands and slammed it into the floor. The baker went still.

He slid off the man's back and collapsed on the floor, gasping for air, trying to slow his heart rate.

Jesus Christ! He'd nearly been taken out by a senior citizen.

He'd been sloppy and overconfident. He was lucky he wasn't flat on the ground with a metal bar sticking out of his skull. Gerald spotted the bar across the room and rose on shaky legs to retrieve it. It was rough and heavy in his hands. Rebar.

Primitive.

He rubbed at his skull. But effective.

His foot kicked his gun. He put it back in his shoulder holster and eyed the prostrate body on the floor.

Dead? He'd smacked his head pretty hard.

Gerald squatted and held two fingers to the old man's neck. A weak pulse fluttered.

Good. Not dead. He needed some answers.

He stood up and blew out a breath. He was still seeing stars and desperately needed a drink of water. By the light of his cell phone, Gerald found a tap and a glass and drank deep. He filled the cup again and poured it over the old man's head.

Nothing.

He checked the pulse and barely yanked his fingers away from the snapping teeth of the old man.

"God damn it!" He gave the baker an angry kick in the ribs and was rewarded with the sound of a painful grunt. He hauled the old man up and thrust him into a chair. Finding some twine, he tied the man to the chair rungs and flipped on the single light bulb over the kitchen sink. Gerald slammed a chair directly in front of him and sat, staring the old man full in the face. The man shrank away in horror, averting his eyes.

"*Diablo blanco,*" he whispered.

"Ah. I see you've heard of me." Gerald grinned. Apparently, Juan was closer to Chris than the townspeople knew. Gerald doubted Chris shared stories from the old days with many people. Gerald kept the memories to himself, visiting them late at night when he was alone. It'd been an addiction, that intoxicating rush of power to his brain back then. Nothing else had ever matched the high of those boys under his thumb.

Now, he was seductively close to having Chris again.

"You can guess why I'm here."

Old Juan was silent, his gaze on the floor. Blood oozed from a cut above his eye and from his nose.

"Where's my buddy Chris?"

Nausea crossed Juan's face. Gerald stood and grabbed him by the chin, forcing the man to look in his direction. "Look at me! Do I look like I'm fucking around? Where is he?"

Terror widened the old man's eyes, but he looked straight at Gerald.

Silence.

Gerald smiled. "Fine. We'll do it your way."

CHAPTER ELEVEN

Mason had showered twice last night but swore he could still smell the ME's office stench clinging to his skin. He shifted restlessly in his office chair, checking his e-mail, hoping Dr. Peres had sent some reports. No dice. It was too early in the day to expect something. Heck. He'd just been there yesterday. He lifted his wrist to his nose and sniffed.

"Why in the hell do you keep doing that?"

He looked up to find Ray glowering at him from across their desks. Their two desks were pushed together, divided only by their computer monitors and various other desk crap. On his desk, the crap was messy piles of files. On Ray's desk, the crap was neatly stacked horizontal dividers with the files perfectly tucked inside. Mason kept forgetting to requisition some to clean up his desk.

"I keep smelling the medical examiner's office. I swear it's fused to me."

Ray sniffed the air. "I can't smell it."

"I can. I fucking showered twice last night. What is the deal with that place?"

"I hate going there." Ray shook his head.

"Don't we all. I don't know how they work there."

"My wife would kill me if I came home smelling like rotting death every day. She doesn't like the way I smell when I go to the practice range. And I think that's a good smell."

"Do you think they have showers available? And maybe a laundry for their regular clothes? I mean, I know they wear scrubs and have them laundered. But what about their own stuff?" Mason asked. "It's got to pick up the odor."

"Christ, I'd build a room in my garage for taking care of it. I wouldn't want that laundry getting washed with my kids' stuff." Ray tapped on his keyboard. "Hey, speaking of…just got an e-mail from the ME."

Mason refreshed his e-mail and opened the new message. He scanned it quickly. "Dental records have identified two of the others from the pit. Both with arrest records. Old arrest records."

Ray made a celebratory horn-like noise with his mouth. "We're getting closer."

Mason kept reading. One skeleton belonged to a twenty-nine-year-old woman who had two arrests for prostitution in Portland back in the eighties. The other was a twenty-five-year-old male. One arrest for prostitution. Same city, same decade.

"Our unsub is a perv," stated Ray.

"Already knew that."

"Looks like he swings both ways."

"Or we're looking for more than one guy," Mason countered.

"Shit. Why do you always complicate things?"

"I call it being thorough. Makes sense, though, handling all those kids? I would think that would take more than one person."

Ray sighed. "Give me five minutes alone with one of them."

"Amen, brother."

"Anything on those tattoos yet?" Ray scratched at his chin. "I like that lead a lot."

Mason shook his head. "My tattoo guy over at the gang unit was real interested. He couldn't tell me anything at the first look. Said he was going to have the symbols interpreted and then dig through the archives and run them by other big-city gang units."

"Think one of the symbols stands for child-killer or pervert?" Ray muttered.

Mason snorted. "I'll put my money on bed wetter."

"I'll settle for one being his name."

"That'll work, too. Doubt he'd let that be photographed."

"Crap." Ray's tone lost its teasing note, and Mason looked up sharply. Ray was focused on his monitor. "That Jules Thomas lead the senator gave you? The nutcase who threatened him?"

"Yes?"

"He's been dead for ten years."

Mason mulled that over. "Any mention of tattoos? Obviously, he wasn't the guy who attacked Jamie Jacobs the other day, but he could still be our guy in the Polaroids. Like I just said, we could be looking at more than one guy."

Ray shook his head. "I'll get someone to contact next-of-kin and ask about tattoos. All I have here is a date of death."

Mason mentally shifted Jules Thomas to the *Unlikely but Not Eliminated* column in his brain. "I still don't have any news back on Cecilia Brody's Korean patient. Jeong."

"Aw, fuck! What if those are Korean symbols on the wrists? Why the hell didn't we think of that before? That would lend a hell of a lot of weight to her lead!" Ray started digging through one of his files.

Mason blinked. *What the hell?* He'd been asleep at the wheel. How had he missed something so obvious?

Ray pulled out the Polaroids, handing half to Mason. "Any other evidence we've missed that can indicate our guy is Asian? Outside of the marks on the wrists? I see so much of that sort of thing tattooed everywhere these days that I didn't even consider that the wearer could be Asian."

Mason stared at the photos while mentally running through other evidence from the underground bunker. *Had they missed something huge?*

The photos had discolored with age. The colors were faded, the whites yellowed. He studied them carefully, trying to ignore the pain of the children in the pictures. Mercifully, the children were dead. No longer suffering at the hands of the monster.

He remembered Jamie's words.

My brother's nightmares…

No doubt Chris Jacobs was still suffering. Suffering emotionally and mentally from this killer's hands. Mason and Ray had tried to locate Chris Jacobs. They'd hit dead ends. The man knew how to stay off the grid. Frankly, Mason was content to wait until Jamie contacted her brother. She'd convince him to come in for some questions. If not, Brody definitely would. Brody would tie Jacobs up and lash him to the roof of his Range Rover to get some answers on his brother's death.

Was Daniel Brody dead? Why hadn't his body been with the others?

In his gut, Mason believed the boy was dead. The odds were not in the child's favor.

Mason studied one photo and ground his teeth. Their killer's wrist and forearm with the tattoo was laid across the scrawny naked back of a young boy. The boy's face was not in the picture, so it could have been any of the boys. The boy's back was a mess of bruises, the colors deep purples, yellows, and browns. Small round red and pink marks indicated possible burns with a cigarette.

He tightened his grip on picture. Something was hovering just out of his subconscious, something important. *Bruises, burns, colors...*

He blinked and focused on the tattooed arm. Stark black and white. Even though the photo colors were discolored, the colors on the arm were distinct.

"Say, Ray..." He paused, searching for the words to describe what he was seeing. "Do any of your pictures show the unsub's arm against the skin of the kids?"

Ray grimaced. "Yeah. Several."

"Let me see them."

Ray passed over a small stack. Mason scanned them, feeling a small victory start in his chest. "Look at the color of his arm compared to the kids' skin. I don't mean to sound racist, but that skin doesn't look very Asian to me. Hell, it doesn't look Caucasian to me, either. It's fucking whiter than snow. It's like see-through white."

Ray held out his hands for Mason's pictures.

"Hell, I'll use the term Dr. Peres used to correct me yesterday. I don't think this asshole's *ancestry* falls anywhere near Asian."

Ray nodded, flipping through the pictures. "Even with the distortion of the colors because of the age of the pictures, he is consistently one *very, very white motherfucker.*"

Mason grinned. Ray rarely swore. When he did, it was an event.

"Jamie Jacobs stated in her report she thought the guy colored his hair and wore colored contacts—"

"—and she said he wore long pants and shirt sleeves on a hot day." Mason cut off Ray's sentence. "I thought he was just covering up tats, but what if he was covering up something more distinctive. Like baby-butt, lily-white skin?"

"You're thinking he's an albino?" Ray asked. "People still have that?"

"I think so. It's not a freaking disease that we immunized for. You're born with it."

"I know that," grunted Ray. "I'm just saying you don't see much of it. Now all I can think of is that Tom Hanks movie with the sicko priest who was an albino."

Mason reached for his phone. "I'm gonna check with Jamie Jacobs. See if she thinks there's a possibility that her attacker was albino."

Mason felt good. *Real good.* His gut said they were headed in the right direction.

CHAPTER TWELVE

"Do you think this is it?" Jamie whispered. She gripped Michael's hand tightly. They'd stopped in front of a dingy, tan mobile home, flanked by some large firs. The bushes and plants in front of the home were neat and organized but lacking in color. Jamie didn't see any indication that a child lived here. She was glad they hadn't tried to find it in the dark last night. The roads weren't marked at all.

Michael honked his horn, making Jamie jump. She glared.

"The sheriff said not to sneak up on him. I'm just letting him know someone's here. It's pretty early in the morning for some people." He squeezed her fingers in reassurance.

"I don't see anyone. Or a vehicle." Michael scanned the area with a hawk-like intensity, still holding her hand. "Let's give him a few minutes. I'm gonna honk again." He laid on the horn as the words came from his mouth. At least it was a partial warning.

Jamie took a deep breath and forced herself to sit still. She wanted to leap from the truck and pound on the door, demanding to see her nephew.

"Relax. Your brother is going to be happy to see you, and your nephew will love you on sight. How could he not? Look at the beauty you're going to bring into his life. He doesn't know how lucky he is."

She turned toward Michael, distracted by his words. He was smiling, his gaze studying her face, making her lips tingle as if he'd touched them. She was discovering that he often said random things, indicating their brains were on different wavelengths. She was worrying about her brother, and Michael was giving compliments. It was slightly disconcerting but also slightly erotic.

"You're not thinking about Chris," she stated.

"Nope. I'm thinking about you. Us. Last night. Awesome."

Yes, last night rocked. "I'm thinking about Chris."

"No, you *were* thinking about Chris," he corrected. "Now you're thinking about last night because I can see your cheeks are pinker. And your eyes are glowing a bit. You don't fool me. You've got sex on the brain again."

She laughed. She couldn't help it. His words were constantly unexpected and so refreshing. She'd never met anyone like him. His brain was quick and nimble, and his thoughts were always miles ahead of hers on different tangents. But it was all good. Sometimes, he slowed down and savored the moment. Like right now. He was still looking intently at her, and his attention made her feel beautiful.

He wasn't the type of guy to deliver a line, hoping to hook a woman. He simply said exactly what he was feeling and thinking. She'd been suspicious of his blunt talk before, but now she knew it for what it was. A man appreciating what was in front of him. She was even getting used to being called "princess." No one else could get away with it. Michael Brody could because he made it sound like pure tenderness.

"Are you excited to see your brother?"

"God, yes. I'm excited, worried, and nervous all together."

Michael looked at the house, his intensity shifting to the little building. "I totally understand. I've got some questions for your brother. And I plan to get some answers. Good answers. I'm not going to accept 'I don't remember.'"

"But he doesn't remember."

"Yes, he does. He knows something. That's why he's living in the middle of nowhere and impossible to find. I suspect he's avoiding the man who broke into your house."

What? "No, you don't under—"

"Your brother behaves like a man hiding," Michael said emphatically. "Not a man trying to avoid people. I've got neighbors I've never seen because they rarely come out of the house. That's how someone acts when they want to avoid people. They don't move to the middle of nowhere and keep their kids out of school. That's a man who is scared...protecting what's his. By keeping you out of the loop, he thought he was protecting you. Instead, you got the crap beat out of you, and it could have been a lot worse. You bet I have some questions for him."

Jamie's mind spun. *Did Chris remember? But why not tell some-one? Why hide?*

"Why hide the truth?" Her voice rose. "If he knows who killed all those kids, why isn't he telling?" She shook her head. "That makes no sense at all."

"I agree one hundred percent." He nodded. "No sense at all. I've thought this through backward and forward and inside out. But the only person who can tell us the truth is Chris or Mr. Tattoo." He squeezed her hand. "Let's go meet your nephew."

In his green gaze, she saw complete support. Michael might be there because he had questions for Chris, but he was also there for her. She squeezed his hand back and slipped out of the vehicle.

Michael pounded on the front door of the home. They waited. And he pounded again.

"Well, we've made enough noise to not be a surprise." He stepped to a window and cupped his hands to peek in.

"Michael—"

"Jamie, get back in the truck. Lock the doors." Michael ducked away from the window, keeping his back against the wall of the home.

She froze. "What—"

"Do it. Someone's trashed the house. Go, now!"

"But—"

"Now!" He turned a razor-sharp gaze her way, and she stumbled backward. Sweat instantly dampened under her arms, and she reached out a steadying hand to grip the rail to the steps.

He's here. The man with the tattoos. He's here.

She backed down the stairs, surprised to see a pistol had appeared in Michael's hands. *Where had that come from?*

"Move it," he hissed at her.

She turned and ran. Locking herself inside the SUV, she ducked behind the dash the best she could while keeping an eye on Michael.

Chris? Oh dear God. Is Brian hurt?

Tears streamed down her cheeks, and she could hear the tattooed man's voice in her head. *Goddamned bitch!* Her thighs quivered from the awkward position, and her torso started to shake.

Michael tried the doorknob to the house. Then opened the door.

No! Do NOT go in, Michael!

With his gun stretched out in front of him like a character on a cop show, he entered the house.

Jamie stopped breathing, her ears straining for any sound outside of the pounding of her heart. Her gaze stayed glued on the open door, occasionally darting to the sides of the house, checking for surprises. It felt like ten minutes, but it was probably thirty seconds before Michael reappeared, his stance relaxed. He scanned the outside of the home and surrounding brush, and then he waved her out of the vehicle.

"No one's here."

Legs shaking, she opened the door but simply sat in the passenger seat. She didn't trust her legs to carry her weight just yet. He came over, the gun tucked in his waistband, and reached out for both of her hands.

"Your hands feel like ice." He rubbed them between his. "I didn't mean to scare you. I just needed you out of harm's way."

"Yes, you scared the hell out of me!" Jamie blew out a breath. "God damn it. That's twice in two days I've been rattled like that." A full-body quiver shook her in the seat. "No one's here? What's inside?"

Michael's jaw tightened. "The place has been torn apart. But there's no sign that anyone was hurt. I think your brother split first."

"Maybe he trashed it to confuse people."

Michael shook his head. "Someone ripped up some kid's drawings and deliberately left them on the floor in the kitchen. It'd take a lot for a parent to act like that, I think. Only someone who was really pissed that they didn't find what they wanted would do it. And there're no toothbrushes in the bathroom. Most people grab their toothbrushes when they leave."

"We need to call the police," Jamie said. Her mind reeled with images of the tattooed man hurting her nephew and brother. "Oh God. I hope they're safe."

"I've got Sheriff Spencer's number. I'll report it directly to him. And I'll let Callahan know that we've hit a dead end here."

"Did you see any pictures of Brian? Were there any pictures of the two of them?" Jamie was suddenly hit by an overwhelming urge to see her nephew's face.

Michael thought for a second. "No, I didn't see pictures. Wasn't looking for them."

She looked at the house. "Do you think I could go in? I won't touch anything. I just need to look..."

"Not a good idea, princess. There could be some evidence in there that'd lead the police to Mr. Tattoo. Let's not mess it up." Michael thumbed through his phone contacts.

"I'll just check the walls and look around. We're so close, it's killing me to be this close and not see them," she pleaded. "Pictures could help us identify Brian if we see him without Chris."

Michael held her gaze and then reached to softly touch her cheek. "I'd want to do the same. Okay, but touch *nothing*. Watch where you place every foot. Don't step on anything or shift anything. No opening drawers or cupboards. And I'll be right behind you." He lifted the phone to his ear, and Jamie could hear a faint ring.

With unsteady legs, she made her way into the tiny house. Michael was right. It was trashed. And eerily reminiscent of the mess in her own home. Bile rose in the back of her throat and she forced it down, focusing on not stepping on the debris on the floor. As if from far away, she heard Michael talking to Sheriff Spencer. She continued her slow trek.

There were no pictures. She stood at the doorway to Brian's room. The room told a story of a boy who loved outer space. Everywhere she looked there were science books on space or fiction that took place in space. There was a hanging model of the solar system and movie posters of space movies. She smiled at the poster of the Muppets from *Pigs in Space*. Chris loved that segment of the old TV show. She had, too.

"There's something I haven't seen in forever. *Pigs in Space*." Michael spoke directly behind her. "My brother and I used to watch that."

"Me too." Jamie turned and tried to smile at him. "There's nothing here. I thought for certain there'd be pictures of Brian. Chris avoids pictures, but I don't know why he wouldn't take pictures of his son."

"Dunno." Michael frowned. "We need to head back to Demming."

Jamie didn't like the grim expression on his face. "What's happened?" She held her breath. *Not Brian, please don't tell me something has happened.*

"Spencer is at a murder in town. His first murder in eight years, and he says the victim's a friend of your brother."

★ ★ ★

Three sheriff's cruisers and one state police vehicle crowded the street in front of the town's bakery. It looked like a simple concrete block building. The only clue to its purpose was the sign that read BAKERY painted over the door. Locals scattered about the sidewalks, talking, pointing, and wiping at tears.

Michael glanced at his watch and felt it slide in the sweat on his arm. It was ten a.m. and over ninety degrees. Welcome to Eastern Oregon.

At least it's not humid.

For as many times as he'd heard that phrase, it should be the state's motto.

The locals avoided him and Jamie. He caught a few glances thrown their way, some curious, some unfriendly. No doubt a lot of the town had heard the two of them were looking for Chris. And now Chris's best buddy had been brutally murdered. "Best buddy" might be a stretch of the description. "The only person Chris talked to" was sounding more accurate.

The sheriff's men were giving them the stink eye, too, as they waited to talk to Spencer. Like he and Jamie were the ones who'd brought murder to their perfect town. Michael inwardly sighed and wrapped a tighter arm around Jamie's shoulders. She'd been looking over her shoulder since Michael had told her there'd been a murder. She'd asked few questions on the ride to town. Michael had few answers.

No sign of Chris and Brian.

No sign of the man who had done it.

Michael knew she was thinking the same thing as he.

Were we followed from Portland? Did we lead someone to Chris?

Sheriff Spencer stepped out of the bakery, took off his cowboy hat, and brushed his forehead with his sleeve. Close behind him was an officer in an Oregon State Police uniform. Michael wondered how many square hundreds of miles the OSP officer was responsible for. He'd heard they were spread pretty thin on this side of the state. Spencer caught Michael's eye and jerked his head. Michael moved in his direction, bringing Jamie with him.

"Brody. Ms. Jacobs. This is Sergeant Tim Hove with OSP." Spencer made introductions. Hove was cadaver thin with red hair and pale skin that must hate the intense sun of the east side of the state.

Hands were shaken all around.

"Who exactly is the victim?" Michael asked.

The two police officers exchanged glances. Spencer spoke. "Juan Rios was sixty-eight and owned the bakery. He lived behind it, same as his father had done for decades. Lived alone. No known family." He took a deep breath, glanced at Jamie, and then returned his gaze to hold Michael's. "Someone broke in. The door lock was busted, weak-assed lock. Juan was tied up in a chair. He's got abrasions from head to toe, at least six broken fingers, and cigarette burns on his cheeks."

Jamie made a small sound in the back of her throat and moved closer beneath Michael's arm. He felt a small shiver speed through her shoulders. Rage reddened Michael's vision.

If I have the chance, I will kill Mr. Tattoo.

"Looks like the cause of death will be strangulation. He's still got the cord around his neck. We'll see what the medical examiner says.

"Juan may have had some overnight guests at some point. There's evidence that someone, possibly two people, slept in his upstairs room recently."

"Chris?" Jamie asked.

Sheriff Spencer shook his head. "I don't know. No one we've talked to said anyone was known to sleep here except for Juan. There are some crayons on the table. So one guest may have been a child, which makes your brother a possibility. Chris never talked to anyone else in town." He scowled. "I don't like that it appears your brother has left town, Ms. Jacobs."

Jamie stood taller. "You don't think Chris killed that man, do you? That's crazy. Why would he break in if you thought he was sleeping in the man's home?" She pushed Michael's arm off her shoulders, and she stepped closer to the sheriff. "Chris's home has been ripped up inside, just like mine was, and it was probably by the same guy who did this. And you said cigarette burns? How do you think Chris got those scars on his neck and face? You've seen them, right?"

The sheriff's face clouded, but he nodded.

"He was tortured as a kid by a sick pervert. And I think that pervert or someone close to him killed that old baker, trying to find Chris."

"But how did the killer know to go to the bakery?" asked Michael. "Someone had to have said something. Has anyone new around town been asking questions about Chris? I mean, anyone besides us?"

"I don't know yet," Spencer replied. "I've got a lot of people to talk to and questions to ask."

"We'll give you whatever support we can," Sergeant Hove offered.

"You need to talk with Detective Callahan in Major Crimes back in Portland," Michael said, turning his attention to the OSP officer. "He's looking for the man who ripped up Jamie's place in conjunction with some older murders. I think Jamie's hunch that this is the same guy is a good one. He is a cold-blooded killer. And has done the cigarette burns before."

Sheriff Spencer's face flooded red. "Wait a minute. Yesterday you never said anything about a murder. All you said was that you were looking for her brother. What the hell have you been holding back?"

Michael shook his head. "I had no idea this guy was on your side of the state. I assumed that he was still in the Portland area where he'd attacked Jamie—"

"Wait a minute." Spencer reached out and gently moved Jamie's chin to the side so he could better see her bruised cheek. "Start from the beginning."

Michael did. He started twenty years back.

Both police officers were rubbing the backs of their necks and shifting their feet by the time he'd finished.

"Holy crap," muttered Spencer. "We need to find Chris Jacobs before your tattoo man does."

"I wouldn't mind finding Mr. Tattoo first. I wouldn't mind that at all." Michael forced back the anger that tightened his throat.

"Do you think you were followed from the city? Obviously, someone found the house before you, but that's only because I told you to wait till this morning so you had some light. Do you remember seeing anyone?" Sheriff Spencer asked.

Michael shook his head and looked to Jamie. She looked ready to puke. He knew she was thinking they'd led a killer directly to her brother and his son.

"I've tried to find Chris through all the usual and unusual online searches. He doesn't exist on paper or in cyberspace. I don't know how anyone else could have found him unless they were following us."

"Anyone else know you were headed over here? You tell anyone your plans?" Hove asked.

Michael shook his head. "Callahan at OSP knew we were following a pretty good lead, but I didn't give him any specifics, and he didn't ask." He smiled wryly. "Callahan knows I'd tell him if I had something concrete. And concrete means I've looked Chris in the eye and shook his hand to be certain he's real. I don't give out or print information unless I've checked and triple-checked it."

"Print?" Hove frowned.

Michael looked the red-haired officer in the eye. "I'm a reporter for the *Oregonian*. I'm not looking for a story. I'm looking for personal answers; I'm looking for my own brother."

He felt Jamie take his hand and give a small squeeze.

Hove's expression relaxed. A bit.

Michael was going to find Chris. And Chris would tell him what'd happened to Daniel.

★ ★ ★

Jamie didn't want to see the murdered old man. The description by the sheriff had been more than enough. She didn't need an actual look. And she knew she was right about who'd done the murder. It had to be the same man who'd attacked her.

It could have been my death that cops were standing around and discussing.

Jamie's chest quaked, and she concentrated on breathing evenly. She'd fought back against the tattooed man. She'd survived.

But would he be back? And did he have Chris and Brian?

She closed her eyes, tuned out the cop talk, and leaned into Michael, inhaling his scent. Male, strong, protective. She took a few deep breaths and felt his energy flow into her, calming her and giving her strength. He was a power source that she simply touched to recharge. Her phone beeped. She moved away from the discussion and saw that Detective Callahan was calling. Her heart double thumped, and her fingers clenched at the phone.

"Hello, Detective."

"Ms. Jacobs. Sorry to be bothering you. I wanted—"

"Detective, has anyone called you about this morning? About the old man who was killed in Demming?"

"What?"

Jamie closed her eyes. "I didn't think so. Michael just told the OSP officer that someone needed to contact you."

"What the hell happened?" He nearly roared in her ear.

"I'll let the police tell you everything, but the short version is we found Chris's house and it'd been torn apart just like mine. Chris and his son were gone." Her heart was threatening to pound its way out of her chest. "Then this morning the police discovered a friend of Chris's in town had been murdered and t-t-tortured. It looks like Chris has been here. But I know he didn't do it. I think the same man—"

"Our tattooed man? You think he was there?"

"Yes," Jamie said, thankful Callahan could read her mind.

"Crap. You think he followed you guys?"

"I don't know. I didn't tell anyone where we were going. Neither did Michael. I asked a neighbor to watch the cat but didn't say anything. We were in such a big hurry."

Jamie could hear Callahan speaking to someone in the background. A second male voice rumbled in answer. He came back on the line. "Who's there from OSP?"

She glanced at the pale officer and checked his name tag. His name had completely escaped her brain. "Hove."

"Okay. I'll get a hold of him. But hang on a minute. I was calling to ask you about the tattoo guy. Anything else that you remembered about him? Anything descriptive?"

Jamie's mind was spinning at insane speeds. "I don't know. No, I can't think of anything new."

Callahan paused. "I was looking back over the officer's notes. The part about where you said you thought he dyed his hair and wore colored contacts?"

"I still feel that way," she started to say. "I don't know how to explain—"

"You felt his coloring was unnatural."

"Yes. Exactly."

"What about his skin color?"

Jamie thought hard. "He was so covered up…"

"But you saw his hands. His wrists where the tattoos were."

She could see the tattoos in her mind. She slid her view down to his fingers. *Pale. Pink fingertips. Very pale hands.* "Very light-skinned. Really white, I'd say."

"Would you say unnaturally pale?" Callahan prodded.

She thought of the tattooed man's face. "I don't remember his face being so pale."

"Could you see his neck?"

Jamie shuddered. An angry face was filling her vision. The hatred and the fury emanating from his eyes…

"His neck was also white, very white I think. Paler than his face. But that's normal for most people, I think," she babbled.

"Ms. Jacobs…would you say he was possibly albino? And was covering it up?"

Her eyes flew open. *Albino?* Her brain skittered to a stop. "Yes, that makes perfect sense. The hair, the eyes, the long sleeves, and pants. I can see that now."

"I didn't want to put the thought in your brain," Callahan stated. "I wanted to see if you would come up with it on your own. It's a theory we have, and I just wanted your input."

"What made you ask, Detective?" *Had someone else seen him?*

"The old Polaroids. We were so focused on the tats, we didn't notice the condition of his skin. It's freakishly white."

"Well, I'd say he's learned to blend in pretty well," Jamie answered. "Albinism didn't cross my mind, but I knew something was off."

"I'll touch base with Hove in a bit. There's no sign of your brother?"

"No. Not yet. If he doesn't already know, someone needs to tell him about the tattooed guy."

"Ms. Jacobs, I suspect he already knows."

★ ★ ★

"Son of a bitch." Mason shook his head. "I think our tattooed freak followed them to Eastern Oregon."

"Sounds that way," answered Ray. "I don't think anyone knew where they were going. Unless Brody told someone his plans."

"Brody doesn't tell anyone crap."

"Agreed. What about Jamie? She tell anyone?"

"She says she didn't. She asked one neighbor to watch the cat but didn't say where she was going."

"Either they were followed or he found Chris Jacobs on his own."

"On the same day?" Mason highly doubted that. "So far we can't even find the guy to interview him. And we've got the best computer system in the world, right?"

Ray choked.

"Either way. Where the fuck is Chris Jacobs now, and where is our tattooed man? They've left one dead body in their wake. I don't want any more. I gotta call this Hove."

"Hove? Tim Hove?" Ray perked up.

"Beats me."

"I know him from my trooper days. Good man. Actually likes living in the boondocks."

Ray knew everybody.

"Jamie didn't disagree with our albino theory. Sounded solid to her. Lends a little more weight to this being the same guy as twenty years ago and not multiples with similar tattoos. Now I want to know what they've found at that scene."

"Think we need to get over there?" Ray didn't sound excited at the idea of the long drive.

Mason knew there was no need to waste the hours on the road. "I'll touch base with Hove and Luna County and see what they've got. Maybe we'll get lucky and their scene will turn up something useful to point us in the right direction."

CHAPTER THIRTEEN

Gerald washed his hands in a surprisingly clean men's room at a gas station thirty miles from Demming. The kill had been relatively clean, but he still felt the need to scrub his hands several times. Once the old man had been tied in the chair, the interrogation had been easy. And he'd gotten shit for answers. The old Mexican knew nothing.

His skin suddenly goosebumped from small electrical pings in his nervous system. The residual effects of the high from the kill. He closed his eyes, exhaled slowly, and relished the small rush. It was almost like a mini-aftershock-orgasm. The abrupt quivers that continue to shoot through the limbs after the sex is over.

196 • KENDRA ELLIOT

At the bakery, the old man had said he didn't know where Chris would go, claimed he had no friends and no family. Gerald had shown him a picture of Chris's sister, and the old man had shaken his head. He'd never seen her or even known about her. Said Chris's wife was dead. Had died in a car accident when the boy was a baby.

The boy was a surprise.

Gerald wondered what the child looked like. Did he look like his father? Chris had started as a hefty kid when he'd first met him, but by the time he'd escaped, he'd been a tall twig. He laughed out loud in the restroom. Was Chris paranoid about the boy's safety? There were a lot of sick people in the world, people who would abuse a little boy with a lot of pain. No wonder Chris lived like a hermit. He probably was nervous for his kid's safety every day.

If only he could get his hands on that kid.

That would teach Chris for putting him in this position.

Where did they go?

The Mexican knew that Chris had visited Portland in the past but didn't know why. He'd also admitted Chris had been to Mexico a few times. Gerald pondered that statement. Was that good or bad? If Chris was headed to Mexico, he probably had no intention of ever returning. Especially once he heard his buddy Juan was dead. He could probably just let him go...

And the boss would say...

Fuck. He had to push on until Chris Jacobs was dead. He'd let the issue slide for two decades, confident in Chris's lack of memory. But now he was starting to wonder. Jacobs lived like a man who had something to hide. The question was: Did he have sufficient motivation to keep it hidden?

Moot point. The waiting time was over.

It was time to clean up the mess that was Chris Jacobs. And he was stoked to do it. This little adventure from the boss had gotten his blood pumping. He'd kept his sordid side buried for a long time, keeping his other business only to himself. This time it was like he'd been given permission. Sometimes it felt like he had two lives. One to show the public and one just for him. This time his boss knew exactly what he was doing; it was almost like having an observer. God, that felt good.

His boss hadn't given him an assignment like this in years. It was great to know he was needed for something besides the other mundane daily tasks he did for the boss. He had skills. Lately, there hadn't been any use for them.

He finished up in the restroom and stepped into the tiny convenience store to pay for his gas. The overweight clerk was alone, his gaze glued to a tiny TV set mounted behind the counter near the ceiling as he sipped on a straw from the biggest soda cup Gerald had ever seen. He glanced at Gerald and then bounced his gaze back to the TV.

"All set?" There was black decay between all of the clerk's front teeth.

Probably sucks on sugary Coke all day long.

Gerald nodded and pulled cash out of his wallet, eyeing a Hostess display with Twinkies and Ding Dongs. The clerk's teeth made him change his mind.

"I can't believe it's been almost ten years since someone was murdered in Luna County," the clerk said as he punched buttons on his register.

"What?" Gerald looked at the TV. A news reporter was standing on a familiar street in Demming. He couldn't make out her words. "What happened?"

"Someone murdered the bakery owner in Demming last night. They're clueless on what happened." The clerk slapped the change in Gerald's hand without counting it back.

Rude. Lazy. Sloppy.

Gerald felt a slow burn of anger start in his chest and swell outward.

"Stupid police out here don't even know what to do with a murder." The clerk picked up his cup, sucked at the straw, and turned his back on Gerald, his focus on the TV.

Gerald envisioned the clerk unconscious on the floor behind the counter with blood seeping from his ear. Gerald's skin prickled in a good way.

"Look at those idiots. Just standing—holy crap! *Check her out.*"

Gerald looked.

Jamie Jacobs stood out from the circle of cops. Next to her, Michael Brody held her hand. The scene was shot from a camera across the street, as the reporter droned on. But Jamie stood out. Long legs, long black hair, perfect ass.

"Fuck. I ain't never seen a piece like that around here. I'd like to tap me some of that." The clerk took a long, noisy suck at the straw.

Gerald stared at the clerk and swallowed the small bit of bile that had risen at the thought of the sloppy man with someone like Jamie. Revulsion curled his upper lip.

"Looks like someone's already gettin' some," the clerk chortled. "Lucky dude."

Gerald glanced at the TV. Apparently, the cameraman found Jamie pleasant to focus on. He'd zoomed in on her and Michael Brody, who'd moved his arm around her shoulders. Even Gerald could pick up the protective waves flowing off Brody and across Jamie.

What'd Brody think of the mess inside the bakery? *Coulda been your girlfriend...*

Did they know where Chris would turn up next? They probably wouldn't be standing around if they did. Gerald twisted his lips. He had to figure out Chris's next move. Following the sister had worked pretty well, but now she looked lost and confused.

Too bad her time with Gerald had been so short. They could have had a lot more fun. Kinda like he'd had with the old Mexican.

Maybe...

Maybe the sister simply didn't know that she held a clue to where Chris was going next. Maybe she just needed motivation like he'd given the old man. Or would Michael Brody be more motivated to hunt down Chris Jacobs if his girlfriend was threatened?

Gerald knew of two men who would probably do anything to protect Jamie Jacobs. There had to be an advantage for him in that fact. An idea started to simmer in the back of his brain, hovering just out of sight.

What if...

He was in the middle of nowhere, and all the police for hundreds of miles were focused on a tiny bakery. They didn't even know what they were looking for. And he knew where Jamie and Brody were staying in Demming.

What would Chris do if the police found a bunch of Twinkies in place of Jamie?

Would that bring him out of hiding?

Gerald dumped his change on the counter and fished a few more bills out of his pocket.

"How many Twinkies will that buy me?"

CHAPTER FOURTEEN

Mason headed out to look at the bunker again. All the evidence had been collected. It'd been enough to fill a small U-Haul trailer. Mason was a bit overwhelmed by the huge amount of crap that'd been taken from a bunker that, at first glance, had seemed sparse and bare. But when it came to children, they overlooked nothing. Anything that could give them a hair or fiber had been pulled. The state lab was going to be backed up. Again.

He'd looked over everything the techs were removing, but he'd been focused on the big items. The kids' backpacks, the cameras, the pictures. The state crime lab would let him know if a grain of dirt yielded any amazing clues.

The scene beneath the big firs was quiet. One lone trooper held the assignment to keep away the curious public. The OSP navy sedan with its distinctive gold swoop was parked in the shade but blocked the pathway to the scene. Its driver sat in the front seat. Mason saw him put down a novel as he pulled closer and then stepped out of his vehicle. Mason parked beside the sedan and pulled out his ID for the trooper. He didn't recognize the cop, but he figured Ray would have known him instantly. The trooper waved off the ID.

"Afternoon, Detective." He waved his wide-brimmed hat to fan his face. "I wasn't expecting anyone today."

Mason shook the trooper's hand. "Robertson," read his name badge. "I wasn't planning to come out. I just need to look around again. How long have they got you on guard duty?"

Robertson snorted. "Tomorrow should be it. Haven't had any Curious Georges to turn away since yesterday. You guys are done here, right?"

Mason nodded. "I think they took away everything but the bunker itself. And there were a couple of guys who wanted to do that."

"They're gonna have to do something with it. Fill it up with concrete or weld it shut. Don't need any other assholes deciding to make use of it."

"There's been talk of the welding idea. That's probably what they'll do. I'll be out of your hair in a few minutes."

The trooper gave an informal salute and went back to his book.

Mason used his own hat as a fan. The forest was giving off a dry, dusty smell that reminded him of a woodstove burning old wood. It was going to be a bad summer for wildfires if they didn't get some rain. In Oregon, usually you could count on rain off and on until July 5th, but this year had been hot and dry since April.

He strolled to the bunker entrance and stared at how the earth had been flattened and trampled around the hatch. So many feet over the last few days. The quiet of the forest was overwhelming. No sounds at all. Was this how it'd been for the children? During the investigation, the site had been crawling with people. Now it felt empty and lonely.

How long had the children been in there?

Mason looked up. The firs blocked his view of the sky. A few pieces of blue shone through here and there, but the dark-green ceiling felt ominous. Like it was smothering something, keeping something hidden from the rest of the world. Which was exactly what it'd done for twenty years. But it was still hiding one thing.

Where was the body of Daniel Brody? The forest hadn't revealed that secret.

Mason stared into the dense woods. Another boy was in there somewhere; Mason imagined the trees hiding his final resting place. *Why hadn't Daniel been buried with the other children?*

The cadaver dog and her handler had been through the immediate surrounding woods several times. Her amazing dog had found nothing. He'd had her walk the farm again, too. Daniel's final resting place was staying buried for now.

When Mason had a suspect in his hands, he was going to get that answer. No matter what it took. Cecilia Brody deserved to know the fate of her son before she died.

His phone buzzed in his pocket. Ray was calling.

"Yep."

"Got a minute?" Ray asked.

"You bet." He hadn't decided if he was going back down in the bunker today. His previous two descents had given him emotional nightmares that he didn't care to repeat. He moved toward the pit and stared into the abyss where five bodies had been hidden for years.

"We've put together another ID on one of the bodies from the pit."

Mason stepped back from the yellow caution tape, slightly disturbed by the coincidence of his location. "I'm fucking staring into the thing right now. That's freaky. What did you get?"

"One of the females was reported missing fifteen years ago."

"Fifteen?" Mason pressed the phone tighter to his ear. "She was seen that recently?"

"Yes, she was reported missing by an aunt who'd seen her the week before."

"So our unsub brought vics here after Chris Jacobs escaped. What's her history?"

"One solicitation arrest. Eight years before she vanished."

"Nice. Let's hope our guy keeps sticking to the same MO. We'll pin him down."

"Even better. She had a previous address in the same neighborhood as the other victim we identified."

"They were neighbors?" Mason wanted to rub his hands together. Would the other victims come from the same fishing pond? Enough dead fish from one area and they could start narrowing in on the common denominator. History had proved serial killers were creatures of habit. They liked routines. When something worked well for them, they had a tendency to repeat, trying to match that success.

"Dawn Henderson. She was thirty when she went missing. Had a decent job as a receptionist at a car dealership, no steady relationship at the time, and no issues with past boyfriends that we could find back then. One day she was at work, and the next day she wasn't. Basically, she vanished."

"Basically, *all* these victims vanished. That's part of this guy's MO. He really knows how to take people without leaving a freaking clue. They vanish off the radar without a blip."

"I haven't gotten in contact with Henderson's aunt yet, but there's an interview with her in the file that the vic had been distraught in the past over the murder of her roommate several years before but had received therapy at some point and had been doing well. For a while, she'd been nearly suicidal."

Mason's Spidey-sense went off. "How many years before she vanished was her roommate murdered? Was that in the same neighborhood?"

Ray shuffled papers in the background. "Nine. Almost ten years. Ugly scene. And the address is close to where Dawn was living when she disappeared. The roommate was attacked in their home. Name was Sandra Edge. She was sexually abused and then strangled. Dawn Henderson wasn't home at the time, but she found the victim after."

"They catch him?" Hope rose in Mason's chest.

"Yep. He's in Salem."

Shit. "The state pen?" Mason asked. "He's been locked up this whole time?"

"I'm looking...yeah, he hasn't been out at all."

"Name?"

"Lee Fielding."

Mason's brain was working at full speed. There was something here...he could feel it. But the guy had been locked up the whole time? "I still want to talk to him. And would you run a search for the registered sex offenders who were living around the residence…aww crap! That's before they had to register with the state, isn't it?"

"The roommate's murder occurred a few years before state law had sex offenders registering. And they only had to register for five years at first, but I'll see what history I can find for that area."

"Our tattooed man is plainly a sex offender. Something tells me he's got to be in the system somewhere. And I still haven't heard back from the gang unit about his tattoos." Mason filed a mental note to follow up. "I'll call and tell the state pen I need to talk to Lee Fielding. Maybe I can get in this afternoon or tomorrow morning." Mason paused. "I've got a good feeling on this one, Ray."

"Damn it! Don't say that! You'll jinx it, Mason!"

Mason smiled into his phone as he strode back to his car.

★ ★ ★

Mason paced the small interview room at the state prison. The room was so stereotypical; he'd nearly rolled his eyes when he walked in. Painted cinderblocks, small window with bars, and a metal table fastened to the floor with two fastened stools. Impossible to budge. Or use to hit someone over the head. Mason hadn't had time to review the Sandra Edge murder case. Ray was digging through the files and would get him the highlights as soon as he could.

Didn't matter. He just needed to see Fielding. Get a feel for him. The right questions would come when he saw the murderer's face.

Two guards appeared with Lee Fielding between them. Fielding had handcuffs attached to his leg irons and shuffled

206 • KENDRA ELLIOT

as he walked. The prisoner looked about sixty years old, but Mason knew he was closer to fifty. He was soft everywhere. Soft face, soft hands, soft belly. It looked like the man hadn't attempted physical exercise since he'd been imprisoned. Mason instinctively sucked in his gut. This guy was too close to his own age, and Mason couldn't help but compare. He knew he looked decent for his age. The damned graying hair and lines on Mason's face announced his age, but he made sure his body stayed fit. A home gym and runs through the neighborhood kept away the middle-aged spread. He exercised more out of stress relief than anything else.

Fielding glanced curiously at Mason as he shuffled by and then plopped himself down on one of the stools with a sigh. His hair had grayed to completely white but had left his eyebrows black. The puffiness of his face kept away most of the lines men get on their face in their fifties, but his demeanor added invisible lines, aging him. He radiated *old*. He gave off the emotional waves of an old man who'd been beaten down. The guard attached a link to the big silver loop on the table and Fielding was fastened into place. A flash of anger crossed Fielding's face as he studied the fastener and then vanished, and his face took on the doldrums look again. Mason noted the anger.

Can't fool me, buddy. You just try to look lazy.

There was a pissed-off man inside that soft body.

"Mason Callahan, I'm with OSP."

Fielding raised his gaze to meet Mason's. And shrugged.

Silence.

Mason internally rolled his eyes. You'd think the asshole would appreciate the opportunity to see and talk with someone new. A break in his boring routine.

"Sandra Edge. It's been a while," Mason stated.

Fielding's puffy face didn't flinch.

"Why her?" Mason asked.

Mason saw a touch of surprise behind the lazy eyes. The directness of the question had caught Fielding off guard.

"Why not?" Fielding's voice was surprisingly high pitched for an older man. He sounded like a thirteen-year-old. A thirteen-year-old girl.

It was Mason's turn to be surprised, and he wondered if Fielding was gay. *Dumbass. Like a voice indicates sexual preference.*

"Did you know her before?"

Annoyance crossed Fielding's face. "Why are you asking questions that you already know the answers to?"

"Humor me. I didn't have time to read your case."

Fielding's gaze narrowed. "In a hurry? What's the rush?"

Again, Mason was treated to a glimpse of the person hiding inside the soft figure. Fielding wasn't dumb.

Of course he's dumb. He's sitting in prison for murder.

"Sandra's roommate disappeared nine years after she was killed. Dawn Henderson. Her body just turned up, and we're looking into it."

"Can't help you there. I've been inside."

"Again. Why Sandra?"

Fielding shrugged and looked away. "A lack of planning on your part does not necessitate urgency on my part," he stated as if reading from a rule book.

Mason's anger tightened his throat. *He's fucking with me. He's bored.*

"I saw that on a sign in a public health office once," Fielding said. "Seemed typical of public employee attitudes. Roles are reversed here, aren't they?"

Mason leaned forward, his hands on the metal table.

"Why Sandra? Where'd you meet? And don't give me shit about wasting your time with information that's already in your file. You've got plenty of time to waste. Why don't you just enjoy talking to my pretty face and see it as a break in your boring-assed routine. All the other prisoners should be so lucky."

Fielding's mouth twitched at one corner. "Okay, Detective. I'll play. I met Sandra at a local bar. She was selling it. I was interested. I was stoned. Things got out of hand. The end."

"Local bar? You both lived close by?"

Fielding shrugged. "My buddy lived close by. I was in town and camped out on his couch for a few days."

"Where did you live?"

"Nowhere."

"Transient?"

"Sometimes."

"So you had no money to pay her. No money for a roof over your head and no money for the hooker. But you had money for the dope and beer. Fucking typical."

The anger flashed through Fielding's eyes, and Mason knew he'd perfectly nailed Fielding's life at the time.

"You must be loving prison. Three squares a day, a roof, cable. And it doesn't cost you a dime. In fact, as Joe Taxpayer, I'm paying for your stay at the Ritz." Mason paused. "And you're very welcome. Anything to keep shit like you off the street.

"Your buddy must have been thrilled when you went to prison and got off his couch. I bet you weren't there for just a few days, you were probably sponging off of him for weeks."

"Fuck you. He went in, too."

"Went in? Prison?"

"Yeah, he was there. You really should read the fucking file so you don't sound like an idiot. Gary and I both went away for

Sandra's murder. He got off easy because they lost half the damn evidence."

"And because you were the one who actually killed her. He was probably just there to party," Mason prodded. "You fucked up his life, too. What was his name?"

"Who, Gary? You're coming off as a dumbshit because you haven't reviewed the case." Fielding's face reddened. "You're like a high school newspaper reporter who doesn't know what the fuck he's talking about."

"Gary what?"

"Gary Busey."

"Oh, for fuck's sake. Grow up."

"Gary Hinkes."

Mason wrote the name in his mental notebook. "Was that so hard?"

"Are you really a cop? 'Cause you don't seem to know shit."

Mason smiled, showing all his teeth. "I'm all cop. Now pretend I'm your best friend and tell me everything you know about Hinkes."

Fielding shifted on the metal stool, his black brows coming together. "Fucker fell off the face of the earth. He went to Shutter Creek for his time."

"In Eastern Oregon?" Mason had never been to the medium-security prison.

"Yeah. I'd get a letter now and then. Then mine started coming back to me. I tried to find out if he'd been released or transferred. He was only supposed to be in for nine months, I think."

"That's it? Accessory to murder and he got nine months?"

"Naw, it was for breaking probation and something else. I don't remember. I've searched for him online but can't figure out where he went."

"Online?" These guys get Internet access? "I bet you were looking at dating sites, right?"

Fielding didn't even blink. He kept rambling, his eyes focused on a spot on the table as he thought about Hinkes. "He's probably dead somewhere or locked up somewhere else. He couldn't keep his hands to himself."

"What does that mean?"

Now Fielding looked up. And grinned. "He liked it. He liked getting it from anyone. The rougher, the better. A lotta pain involved, all the better. Men, women, didn't matter."

Mason froze. Every neuron in his brain firing at once. *Bingo.*

"Where is Hinkes?" *This is our guy.*

"I just told you that I don't know. I've looked. Nothing else to do in here. I figure he served his sentence and got out. Who knows what the fuck he's up to, but asses like that don't change. It's in his blood. I've never seen anyone who likes the pain along with the sex so much."

"Fucking pervert."

Fielding just nodded. "Gary fit most pervert descriptions."

"What'd he look like?"

"Gary? Oh, he was a freak. One of those white-skinned guys. You know, the genetic shit? Albinos? But he dyed his hair. Used the cheap crap...it always looked like shit. He wanted colored contacts but couldn't afford them. Had some pretty amazing tattoo work done. Don't know how he paid for that...I can guess, though. His back looked like a piece of oriental artwork. Fucking amazing."

Blood was pounding in Mason's head. He strained to hear past the noise. "Did he have tattoos on his wrists?"

"No, his upper arms were tattooed. Not his wrists. That could have changed. He had a serious addiction to tattooing.

Loved them. I never understood. That shit fucking hurts."
Fielding pulled up his sleeve to show a small phoenix on his
upper arm. "I did one. That was enough."

Mason stared at the small figure. "Why a phoenix?"

Fielding looked away and pulled down the sleeve, rubbing
at the fabric over the tattoo like he could wash it off. "Stands for
new beginnings. Change."

Mason snorted. "Maybe someday, eh?"

★ ★ ★

"How can he just vanish?" Mason asked. He was seriously frustrated. His best lead, the name from Lee Fielding, was hitting
a stone wall. After his prison interview, Mason had called Ray,
pointed him in the direction of searching for Gary Hinkes, and
sped back to the office, hoping Ray would have fantastic news
by the time he'd arrived.

Ray shook his head. "It's crazy. I went to records to pull the
file. Everything is still on paper from back then. The whole file
on Hinkes is missing. The only info I can get is from Fielding's
file. And I swear, there's shit missing from there."

"There's no record of Hinkes's arrest and sentencing?"
Mason didn't like this one bit.

"There is. I can find that he was arrested. I can find that he
was sent to Shutter Creek. But that is it. Everything else is flat
gone."

"What about previous arrests? Fielding said he'd broken probation, so there has to be something previous."

"Nothing."

"What? How can that be?" Mason tapped his desk with a
pencil and then spun it in his fingers, mind churning. Noting the

slightly blunted tip, he thrust the pencil into the electric sharpener and let the noise clear his brain. He added the pencil to the other perfectly sharpened dozen pencils in a mug on his desk.

"What about pictures? There's got to be at least one photo of the guy somewhere. One we can show to Jamie Jacobs."

"Nothing," Ray stated again. The cuffs of his white dress shirt had been sloppily rolled up to his elbows, and the lines between his brows hadn't left his face since Mason had walked into the office.

Mason stared at Ray's cuffs and noted the tie askew. Ray was feeling the pressure, too. The man was usually the picture of beefy male elegance. Unlike Mason, who strove for matching socks inside his cowboy boots.

"We're close here. What's bugging you? Spit it out."

"How can all this information be missing?" Ray asked. He looked over his computer monitor at Mason. "It's just Hinkes's info that I can't find. There's plenty on Fielding. I can tell you exactly what he's been doing since his arrest, what he eats for dinner, and when he takes a shit, but everything on Hinkes is gone."

A small buzzing started at the base of Mason's skull. "What are you saying?"

"Someone made all this info go away. I can find a half dozen pictures of Fielding. Why can't I find any of Hinkes?"

"Did you check newspaper archives? Maybe his face ended up there."

Ray nodded. "Most papers have their archives accessible online. Nothing is coming up. Same with driver's licenses. No photo available."

"That's fucked up." The buzzing was getting louder.

"Agreed."

CHAPTER FIFTEEN

Michael was pumped. He fought to hold in his excitement. Lusco and Callahan had figured out that Jamie's attacker was albino. And that the kidnapped children were probably held by a person with the same coloring. How many albinos could be wandering around Oregon? Or with blood on their hands in Eastern Oregon? He was about to do a Google search to find albino numbers compared to the rest of the population. Either way, the window was narrowing on their suspect.

He shared the info with Hove and Sheriff Spencer.

"White skin? Don't they have red eyes?" asked Spencer. His expression was perplexed.

"Sounds like he wears contacts." Michael bit his lip to keep from laughing. Spencer looked like he was thinking about a zombie wandering around his county.

"The tattoos are probably the more noticeable flag," said Hove. "He can cover up his hair and eye color, but he's gonna be wearing long sleeves in this heat unless he wants everyone to perfectly remember the man with the colored arms."

"No luck on Chris's truck?" Jamie spoke up. She'd been listening intently to the men speak, but Michael noticed her body language stiffen when Hove started talking about the tattoos. No doubt the images were still sharp in her mind.

Spencer shook his head. "I put out a description and the license plate. Frankly, there just isn't a lot of law enforcement patrolling the roads on this side of the state. But the traffic's lighter too. We'll find him."

Two of the state's crime scene investigators continually passed the group, going back and forth between the bakery and their Suburban. Hove had called in the state's team to take evidence at Spencer's request. Spencer's tiny evidence kit was in a fishing tackle box in his trunk, consisting of fingerprint powder, lift cards, evidence collection envelopes, a special light, and ancient gloves. For this murder and its connections to the large number of murders on the west side of the state, no one wanted to miss anything.

"Chris'll turn up," Michael stated. He pulled Jamie against him and rubbed her back. He knew she was thinking of Brian, too. It wasn't just about Chris. Jamie was passionate about protecting children and especially this nephew she'd never met. She knew the boy was out of her reach and incredibly close to danger.

"Can we go back home now?" she asked into Michael's chest. "They don't need us here, do they? And Chris has clearly left. Maybe he's going to Portland. I'm worried about him."

Michael looked to Spencer and Hove. The two cops exchanged a glance.

"Yeah, I don't see any need for you two to stick around," answered Hove. "We'll call if we have more questions."

Spencer's cell phone buzzed, and he left the circle to answer.

"What about the baker's family?" asked Jamie, before she turned around and wiped at her eyes. Even in the supreme heat, the sudden absence of her head left a cold spot on Michael's chest. He hadn't seen tears, but her eyes were definitely red. "Has someone notified his relatives?"

"We haven't found any family yet," Hove replied with a swipe at the sweat on his forehead. "Spencer has someone looking into it, but they're coming up empty so far."

"Say what?" Spencer exclaimed into his cell, pulling the attention of the group. He turned to make eye contact with Hove but kept listening on the phone. "Where'd they find him?"

Spencer clenched his jaw, and his chest expanded. Michael saw his hand tighten around the cell. Every cop in the area perked up as if a strong scent had entered the air. Michael felt the hair rise on his arms. Jamie's hand gripped his arm, and he stepped behind her, placing his hands on her shoulders, feeling her tremble, her breathing escalating.

Chris?

Spencer shoved his phone in a pocket. "A kid's been killed. His mom found him in their garage a few minutes ago. Looks like he was shot."

"A kid?" Jamie gasped. Michael held on tighter to her shoulders.

"A teenager. Ethan Buell."

Michael felt Jamie deflate. *Thank God. But that poor mother.*

"Ethan works at the gas station. He was on duty yesterday when you two got to town." Spencer gave Michael a hard look.

"We didn't fill up here," Michael said. What was Spencer getting at? Was he implying—

"Ethan's a good kid. Friendly and outgoing. Has a tendency to talk a lot."

Something clicked in Michael's brain. "You think he got a good look at our suspect? Maybe asked him too many questions?"

"I've got two dead people in twenty-four hours in a town where no one has been murdered in almost a decade. Do I think there's a connection? You bet your ass I do. Now I'm changing my mind on you two leaving town today. Plan to stick around a bit." Spencer looked at Hove, who was dialing his phone. "Looks like we've got a murder weapon left at the Buell scene. A Ruger revolver. Damn thing's like twelve inches long." He paused and looked at Michael and Jamie.

"Don't look at me, I don't like revolvers," Michael muttered.

"No, my officer on the scene is saying it looks like one that Chris Jacobs has used for practice on the firing range."

"That's bullshit!" Jamie yanked out of Michael's grasp and stepped forward. "You can't say it looks like someone's gun. This is Hicksville out here. Everyone owns a gun or five. Don't even think about Chris for that boy's death without better evidence."

"I didn't say that." Spencer stepped back, startled by Jamie's vehemence.

"You just did!"

Michael kept his mouth shut. Spencer had just stuck his foot in his own mouth, and Jamie was efficiently taking him to town for it.

"If he was working at the gas station, shouldn't there be video from yesterday? Can't you see who he talked with? Maybe even see license plates?"

Spencer cleared his throat. "Like you said, ma'am. This is Hicksville. And I doubt Jim Graham ever put video surveillance up at his gas station. But I will definitely find out."

Jamie stepped back. "Thank you," she said sincerely. "I didn't mean to yell. I'm a bit protective when it comes to my brother, and I'm tired and—"

"It's been a long morning," added Michael.

"God, yes," sighed Jamie.

Sheriff Spencer touched the brim of his hat at Jamie. "Not a problem. I need to get over to the Buell home. Sergeant? Can I get another evidence team? Or should I just wait on these guys?"

Hove headed into the bakery. "I'll see how things are coming here and let you know," he said over his shoulder.

Spencer touched his hat again and left. Jamie leaned against Michael. She was worn out. He was worn out. It was damned hot, dry, and dusty, and all he wanted to do was crawl into a cool bed with Jamie and hold her.

"Hungry, princess?"

Jamie shook her head. "I can't believe that boy was killed. When he first said a kid, I thought—"

"I thought the same thing. I thought for sure it was Brian. Although, before he got off the phone, I thought they'd found Chris. And not found him in a good way."

"He's still alive. I can feel it," said Jamie. "That man hasn't gotten to him yet. Do you think that boy saw the tattooed man at the gas station? And told him how to find Chris?"

"I don't know. Somehow Tattoo found Chris before us. He might have followed us from Portland, but we didn't lead him directly to Chris. I have to think he asked somebody."

"We have to find him first. Where do we start?"

"That's the magic question."

"I'm ready to go back to the hotel. Actually, I'm ready to go home and see if Chris has turned up there, but—"

"Hey, Brody." Hove stepped out of the bakery. He had on purple nitrile gloves and held a few papers in his hands. "Can you two look at these real quick?"

Hove held a child's drawings. Without touching them, Michael and Jamie studied the crayon pictures as Hove shuffled through them. There were pictures of animals, not certain what types of animals, but Michael guessed dogs by the ears and tails. A picture of Chris's home, obvious by the tan paint and tall fir trees. Another picture was a man, woman, and boy all holding hands. The woman had wings.

"Oh," gasped Jamie. "It's his mother. Chris must tell him she's an angel. How lovely." Her voice cracked.

Hove flipped over the family drawing. On the back, in faint pencil, was another drawing. But it was a quick sketch by an adult. A woman's face. A woman with dark hair and dark eyes.

Jamie sucked in her breath. "Elena."

Michael's chest tightened. Chris had sketched the boy's mother for him. The lines were sure and true and smooth. A drawing that had probably been done many times in the past. It conveyed a gentle personality, a calmness in the woman's eyes. Chris had talent or else he'd drawn the same sketch a million times and could do it perfectly. Michael figured it was both.

"Turn them all over," Jamie begged. Michael knew she was hoping for a sketch of Brian or perhaps Chris. The back sides of the papers were blank. Disappointment rippled across Jamie's face.

"I want them," Jamie said. "When you're done with them, I want them."

Hove nodded. "I'll make sure you get them."

★ ★ ★

Chris continued to dial Jamie's phone numbers every hour. Her cell wouldn't even ring. It kept going straight to voice mail, which told him her phone was dead, off, or out of range. Scenarios kept dancing through his head, and none of them were pleasant. Several times, he'd pushed his old truck past the speed limit on his return toward Portland but then brought it back down. The last thing he needed was a ticket. He was a firm believer in staying off of the radar. Everyone's radar.

But how had the Ghostman found him?

Please let his sister be okay.

"Dad, I need to go to the bathroom," Brian spoke up.

Chris glanced at his watch. It was past lunchtime, and they needed to grab a bite to eat. "Okay. Next exit that has food."

"McDonald's?" Brian's eyes lit up. "Please?"

"We'll see." Every parent's fallback; every kid's most hated reply. "Depends what we find." Chris tried to stretch his legs in the truck. He was tired of driving. A place where he could sit back and relax for a bit would be nice. Preferably not McDonald's. He took the next exit, which promised Food, Gas, and Lodging.

"McDonald's!" Every kid's reaction to spotting the golden arches.

"Umm." Chris eyed the brick diner next to the fast-food restaurant. It looked cozy, like someone's grandma was the owner. "How about that place next door? It looks like the type of place that has grilled cheese on the menu." Brian's all-time favorite.

And beer.

"You think so?" Brian twisted up his mouth in deep consideration.

"Let's check their menu." If not, Chris would beg them to make one. Surely they'd throw one together for a kid.

They parked. Brian cast one wistful glance at the golden M and pushed open the door to the diner. Cool air rushed by them from the nearly empty dining room. Chris sighed. *Perfect.* A waitress with a coffeepot in one hand and two cups in the other scooted by them.

"Seat yourself. I'll be right with ya."

Chris steered Brian toward a large booth in the back, near the bar, and plopped down on the overstuffed bench. The other five people in the restaurant barely glanced their way, and the only sound came from the television screen behind the bar. Menus were on the table. Brian immediately found the kids' selections.

"Grilled cheese. And fries," he announced. He pulled crayons and a coloring book out of his backpack and focused on Iron Man, his current obsession.

Thank you, God.

Chris scanned the menu and stopped at a bacon and bleu cheeseburger. He set the menu down, leaned his head back, and briefly closed his eyes. Parenting was a twenty-four-hour job. A job he was thankful for, but he often wished he had help. After Elena's death, focusing on Brian had helped him get through her loss. At times, he'd considered moving back to Portland and enlisting Jamie's help with his son. But that would mean placing his son where he could be easily found.

Wasn't going to happen.

They were safest away from everyone. Away from society, crowds, reporters, sick men.

"What can I get for ya?"

Chris's head came up, his eyes flew open, and he double blinked. The waitress was darn cute. She couldn't have been much over twenty years old. She tilted her head and repeated her question, with a knowing smile that said she was used to second looks from men.

Chris pointed at Brian. "Grilled cheese, fries, and milk. I'll take the bleu burger and a Coors Light."

"Gotcha. Be right back." She bounced away, stopped behind the bar, poured his beer, grabbed Brian's milk, and was back to them in under a minute with a cheery smile. He sipped at the cold beer and appreciated the iciness on the back of his throat. Brian kept his head down, concentrating on his coloring. His son didn't talk continually like some kids. Like Chris had... before. He'd been one of those kids who gave a running commentary on everything he saw to anyone around him. After he came back, he spoke as little as possible. He still watched his surroundings closely but kept his words to himself.

"Bathroom?"

Brian was staring at his father, his hazel eyes confused, and Chris had the impression Brian had asked the question twice. Chris spotted the bathroom sign past the bar and stood up.

"I can go alone," Brian whined, but he stood and started to follow his father.

"I'll just walk you in." Chris pushed open the men's room door and checked the stalls. All empty. "I'll be back at the table. And wash your hands good."

Brian nodded.

Chris slid back into his booth. Sure his son could use a public restroom alone. After he checked the inside and watched the door after. That wasn't overprotective. That was smart parenting. He shuddered as he remembered how he used to run wild around his neighborhood when he was growing up. One dinner he'd been late and his father had been furious. Looking back now, his father hadn't been worried about Chris; he'd been upset that his mom had been worried.

His son being snatched by a pedophile hadn't crossed his father's mind.

Chris didn't look away from the men's room door.

The waitress set a skinny basket of saltines on the table. "In case he's got the munchies," she said with a perky smile. Chris thanked her. And watched the door.

The door swung open, and Chris relaxed. He took a packet of cellophane-wrapped crackers and ripped it open, setting it on Brian's coloring book.

"Awesome!" Brian proceeded to munch down on the crumbliest crackers ever created. Chris never bought them. They required too much clean-up.

A word from the television caught his attention, and his focus swiveled toward the bar.

...murdered...

A female reporter was standing in a city Chris knew all too well, a serious look on her face. Across the bottom of the screen, it said, "Murder in Demming." He couldn't make out her words.

Chris stood up, moving toward the bar, his gaze fixed on the screen. The waitress crossed his path with two plates.

"Your lunch is ready."

He gestured in the direction of the table, attention on the television. Suddenly, he wasn't hungry. Closer, he could make out the reporter's words.

"...deceased is the owner of the bakery, Juan Rios, who was killed during a break-in of the bakery overnight..."

Juan. Chris's knees wobbled. He reached the bar and rested his hands on it, leaning heavily.

"Police haven't revealed the exact cause of death but say it appears to be a result of homicidal violence."

Juan.

What if Chris hadn't been watching his house and hadn't seen the Ghostman and decided to leave? Would she be reporting three deaths?

How had the Ghostman gone from his house to Juan's?

He had no doubt who'd killed Juan. Chris thought hard. There'd been no evidence at his home that could have led anyone to Juan. But people knew he often visited old Juan. People knew he took Brian to play with Juan's dog. The Ghostman must have talked to someone in town who mentioned his habits.

He glanced over his shoulder at Brian, who was busy devouring his grilled cheese. The boy hadn't noticed the television story.

"...so far no suspects..."

Of course not. He's a ghost.

The camera switched views to Juan's bakery, a group of cops and onlookers milling outside. Chris recognized Sheriff Spencer from a distance. The cop was okay. He'd kept out of Chris's business for the most part and had delivered the news of Elena's death with a lot of tact and concern. The camera zoomed closer, and the back of a woman with long black hair caught Chris's attention.

Elena.

He immediately shook that thought from his head. Elena was dead. The instant confusion happened frequently to him. Eastern Oregon had a large percentage of Native American and Hispanic women, many of whom wore their hair long like Elena had. From the back, they often resembled his dead wife, making him catch his breath and his heart stop. The woman turned to the tall man at her side, exposing her profile.

Jamie.

What the hell? His sister, who he'd been worried sick over, was standing on the street in his town? *Christ.* Chris blew out a breath. *Holy crap.* First Juan and now a glimpse of Jamie. He wanted to cry and laugh in relief at the same time.

The camera shot moved in on the group, and Chris soaked up the sight of his sister, healthy and whole. The stress he'd held in about her safety evaporated, giving him a release-activated, instant throbbing headache in his skull. He rubbed at a spot near his temple. Jamie spoke to the man at her side, and Chris felt his heart skip a beat. The man turned his head to the side the tiniest bit.

Chris stared.

The man turned more, and Chris felt all the veins in his skull swell.

Michael Brody. The man placed his arm about Jamie's shoulders. Chris's world shuddered, spun off kilter, and he grabbed at the bar. This wasn't happening.

Why in the hell was Michael Brody with his sister?

CHAPTER SIXTEEN

Jamie flopped on the bed at the bed-and-breakfast. It had to be twenty degrees warmer in their room than the first floor. She'd felt the temperature rise as they'd climbed the old stairs. The bed-and-breakfast was charmingly quaint, but there were times when quaint didn't cut it and you wanted modern hotel results. Like instant cold air, immediate coffee, and fast room service with cheesecake. "I'm beat," she said. "And it's too damned hot in here."

"Trying to avoid sex with me already?" Michael asked as he cranked up the air-conditioning. "I thought that didn't come till later in a relationship. Isn't this where you say you have a headache?"

A deep laugh bubbled out of Jamie. She couldn't help it. He was so damned frank. "To tell you the truth, knowing two people were just killed has my mind on other things right now. I really don't know how I'm supposed to be feeling. Chris and Brian are missing. There are two people dead...possibly by the same man who attacked me yesterday. Should I be terrified, worried, or angry?"

"You need to be told how to feel right now? I think every one of those emotions is right on ticket with what you've been through. You don't need to pick one, you know. Or write in your planner how many minutes to spend on each one."

Choking on her laughter, Jamie wiped tears from her eyes. He was right. And he'd nailed exactly how she handled stress. "You are very good for me. Did you know that?"

"Of course. I took one look at you and thought, 'There's a woman who needs more laughter and adventure in her life.' I made it my personal goal to help you be spontaneous. Not everything in life needs to be planned."

"I like order. I like to know what will happen next. I'm not fond of surprises. Even surprise birthday parties upset me as a kid."

Michael's head jerked in surprise. "Who doesn't like surprise parties?"

"Me!" She was dead serious. "They made me want to hide. Still do. I don't like being the center of attention. Especially if I'm not expecting it."

"But you deserve to be the center of attention. All the time."

Michael did an expert belly flop onto the bed next to her. He reached over and pulled her tight into his arms and simply held her. She inhaled deeply, seeking his scent to calm her. He smelled like sunshine; his usual smell. With a tint of sweaty, salty male included that made her hormones wake up and stretch. He nuzzled against her cheek.

"Just don't be throwing me any surprise parties, okay?"

"Agreed. I'll always check with you before I surprise you."

"Well, little surprises are okay. Like chocolate. You can bring me chocolate anytime."

"Noted." His face pressed against hers as he kissed his way up her jawbone to her ear.

He hasn't heard a word I said.

"I don't care if we're in the middle of Hicksville right now. Anywhere you are is where I want to be," he said, moving his lips to her mouth.

God, Michael knew how to kiss. His lips were strong and soft at the same time. His manner was authoritative and caring. He was impulsive but smart. The man was a walking contradiction in too many ways, and Jamie knew she was falling hard. He was so unlike the staid, steady men she'd dated in the past. Michael knew how to bring excitement and the unexpected into her life. But how long could that last?

Doesn't matter. Enjoy the ride.

"Speaking of chocolate, are you hungry?" he asked with his lips against the back of her neck. He'd found a place just below her hairline that was sending pleasant chills down her spine and cooling her off quicker than the old air-conditioning unit.

"Starving."

He pulled back. "Me too. I can't even think straight, I'm so hungry."

Jamie wanted his mouth back on her neck. "Eat first?"

He nodded reluctantly. "Sucks. But we'll be happier later. I don't want to get started on something and discover the damned town rolled up its sidewalks at sundown, leaving us to get food at the mini-mart."

Jamie's stomach growled. Noisily.

He chuckled. "My stomach's complaining, too. And it's not the only thing." He disentangled their limbs. "Fuck. I don't want to move."

"Those enchiladas last night were heavenly," Jamie stated, blinking innocently.

"You are evil." Michael stood and then leaned over the bed, his hands resting on both sides of her face. "You relax. I'll go get you some food, and then you can take care of me, agreed?"

Jamie looked at the green eyes so close to her face and felt her heart expand two notches. This man was growing very dear to her. "You're not getting anything for you to eat?" she teased.

"I might get something for me since I'll be there anyway."

She stretched off the pillow to kiss him in response. "You're incredible, did you know that?"

"Yep. I'm awesome that way," he said, kissing her deeply.

Jamie's bones melted into the soft bed at the touch of his mouth.

He slowly pulled away, holding eye contact. "I'll be right back." Extreme reluctance to leave shone from his eyes. "Don't go anywhere."

Jamie watched the door close behind him. She sank back into the pillow and stared at the ceiling, and sighed. One of the bleakest moments of her life had brought this man to help her cope. Lord, she was getting in deep. Deep with a type of man she'd never known before. But she didn't care. It felt fabulous.

★ ★ ★

Michael inhaled as he strode back to the tiny bed-and-breakfast and felt his saliva try to drown him. The scents wafting from the food containers in his hands were incredible. Holy crap, his stomach was complaining big time. He'd ordered the exact same thing they'd eaten the day before. Memories of melted cheese and spicy meat...and then the night spent with Jamie.

Jamie Jacobs was turning out to be that once-in-a-lifetime woman. He hadn't thought such a thing existed. He'd been head over heels for Lacey Campbell for years, but looking back now, it seemed like puppy love. He'd trotted around after her in total infatuation. She loved him, he knew that, but Lacey loved him like a brother. And that echoed his feelings for her now.

Then there'd been Sam. Actually, Samantha didn't live too far from Demming, he suddenly noted. Probably another hour or two away. They'd had a good run for a few weeks, but Sam had responsibilities with her business that sucked up all her time. She knew she'd never leave her small-town life. Michael knew he wasn't suited to live in a town with a single-screen movie theater that was only open on Fridays and Saturdays, showing six-month-old releases. Looking back, he realized Sam had been his rebound woman after discovering Lacey was in love with Jack Harper.

Now there was Jamie.

Smart, sexy, and learning to come out of her shell. He was the one poking away at that shell, because he could see the woman underneath waiting to explode. He liked the buttoned-up Jamie, the strict school principal. If he saw her with her hair up in a librarian's bun, reading glasses, and a high-necked blouse, he'd want to tear into it, revealing the Jamie he'd seen before in that smoking thong and bra. Last night had been hormone and lust-driven on both their parts. He suspected that wasn't something she gave in to very often, but damn, he was glad she had. It'd totally opened her up to him, exposing soft parts that he'd suspected were under that principal shell. And sexy, hot, roaring parts that a guy could only dream about.

Jamie Jacobs was a keeper.

Chuck waved at him, and Michael tossed back a greeting as he strode through the lobby and pounded up the creaking wood stairs. He didn't want to stop to chat. He had one thing on his mind. Well, food and then one thing. Mouth watering, he fumbled to get his room key out of his shorts pocket and balance the food in one hand.

The door swung inward as he pushed his key into the keyhole.

Every sensor in his brain shot to high alert as he shoved the door completely open and stepped into the room. The empty room. He tossed the to-go boxes on the bed, scanning the small room. "Jamie?" The door to the bathroom was open. He checked the quiet shower.

"Jamie?"

Sweat started on the small of his back. *She just stepped out for a minute.*

He pushed aside the lace curtains of their window and scanned the hedged backyard. The rear gate in the hedge was open from the yard to the back alley, but the tables and chairs on the patio were empty. No tall women with long hair. All quiet.

Too quiet.

Michael thundered back down the stairs and into the lobby.

"You seen Jamie?" He shot the question at Chuck, who was straightening a shelf of books. Michael's chest heaved like he'd run a sprint. He slowed his breathing. *Christ. Keep your head on straight.*

Chuck stiffly turned his head. "No, she hasn't come down that I've seen. She got a phone call a while back. I put it through to her room, and it didn't ring back, so I assume someone answered up there."

"A call? Who was it? How long ago?" Michael barked.

Chuck looked thoughtful. "Maybe twenty minutes. Maybe a little more. I can only tell you that it was a male voice, and he asked specifically for Jamie Jacobs."

"Young voice? Old?" Michael's heart was doing flip-flops.

Chuck shrugged. "Neither?"

"Where's your phone system? It'll show the number of who called." Michael started for the man's office.

Chuck chortled. "I ain't got one of those fancy phone systems. Just the basics."

Michael froze. "No caller ID?" *Seriously?*

"Nope. None of that call-waiting stuff either. Always thought that was kinda rude."

Michael exhaled. "And she hasn't been downstairs?"

"I've been in and out of the back. I mighta missed her if she went through."

"You were here when I left twenty minutes ago."

Chuck nodded. "I've been doing some paperwork in the office. I try to keep an ear out for people coming through, but I don't hear footsteps so well these days. That's why I've got the bell on the desk."

Michael swallowed hard and scanned the room. The lobby was the old living room and dining room of the former house, with the reception desk tucked in the corner farthest from the front door. A small kitchen and Chuck's office were through the swinging door across the room. Horses could have pranced through the lobby and Chuck would have missed it if he'd been in the office.

"Mind if I look in the kitchen?" Michael pushed through the swinging door before Chuck could reply. A quick look in the adjacent office and the neat kitchen confirmed no Jamie. Sure enough, Chuck's phone looked straight out of the 1970s. Michael strode out the front door and stood on the wide wraparound porch, seeking any sign of her. Nothing. He stepped back inside and nearly ran over Chuck.

"What's wrong, son? You look like you're ready to strangle a cat."

"I can't find her." *Understatement.*

"Well. She can't have gone far. There's nowhere to go," Chuck said reasonably.

Michael shook his head. "No. She was waiting for me. She wouldn't have left." He checked the time. "I need to call Sheriff Spencer. This isn't right." He left Chuck standing in the lobby and pounded up the stairs. "Would you ask your first-floor guests if they've seen her?" he shouted back to Chuck.

Michael's bedroom door was still open. He looked inside again, hoping...still empty. He whirled around, moved into the hallway, and pounded on the other three doors in the hall, not waiting for someone to answer each one. One door opened and a middle-aged woman with thick eyeglasses glanced out. She reminded Michael of an owl.

"Chuck?" she asked.

"Chuck's downstairs." Michael gestured at his open door. "I'm staying next door, and I'm looking for my girlfriend. Have you seen her?"

Annoyance crossed the owl's face, and her nose lifted into the air. "No. Not today. Last night, I heard her though. Last night...I heard *both* of you. I would have called Chuck, but I assumed he was asleep, and I figured it'd be rude to disturb *his* sleep." She shut the door.

"Ah...sorry about that," he said to the closed door. He pounded again on the other two doors. No answer.

"Fuck." He dashed back down the stairs. His heart was doing a serious drumbeat in his chest, and it wasn't from all the stairmastering.

Chuck stood in the center of the lobby. "I asked. No one's seen her."

"How the hell can she just leave and no one notice?" Michael yanked his phone from his pocket and dialed Sheriff Spencer.

"Well...both rooms down here were watching TV. Usually folks don't pay much attention to what other people are doing around here."

Bullshit. The townspeople had watched every step he and Jamie had made since getting to town. Someone had to have seen her.

"Spencer," the sheriff answered his call.

"Sheriff, this is Michael Brody. Jamie is missing." No point in mincing words.

"What?"

"We're at Chuck's place. I left to get dinner, I came back, and she's gone. Chuck said she got a phone call a while back from a man. Fuck! I think he's got her." Michael's brain screamed as he voiced the thought. He'd been holding off, not giving credence to the theory, but now he'd said it out loud, and he couldn't think of anything else.

"Our tattoo man? Are you sure? Maybe she walked to the store. She's got to be somewhere. Did his phone show who called?"

"Guess how old the phone system is." Michael jogged out the front door and down the street to the little grocery, holding the phone to his ear. "I'm going to check the store, but I'm telling you, she wouldn't leave."

"I'm still at the Buell house. Somebody did a number on this kid. A fucking execution. One bullet to the back of the head. I've got a sobbing mama who wants to know why her son was killed, and I can't tell her I think he said the wrong thing to a stranger. I've got a female deputy on hug-the-mother duty, and she's starting to wear down from this woman's hysterics. State is still taking evidence from the garage, but it looks like a clean scene to me."

"Christ." Michael didn't want to think about a teenager collapsed on his garage floor and his frantic mother. He had Jamie on the brain, and there wasn't room for anything else. He threw open the door to the market and searched the few aisles for Jamie's black head.

Nothing.

"Help you?" asked a clerk as she leaned against the counter. She held a nail-polish brush in one hand, ready for action with her other hand in painting position on the counter. Her eyebrows had shot up as Michael abruptly entered the store. He didn't recognize the young woman from the day before.

"Seen a woman with long black hair come in during the last twenty minutes or so?"

The woman shook her head. "No one's been in for over an hour." Her hand still held the brush in midair. "You buying anything?"

"No."

"Okay." She focused on her nails and applied the brush.

Michael left. "She's not in there," he said into his phone. He looked up and down the street, pacing the sidewalk. He jogged across the road to get a better look to the south. The sun had just started to set on the late-summer night, and the dimming light made him strain his eyes to see into the gray shadows.

Where was she?

Spencer was speaking to someone in the background.

"*Spencer.*"

"Yeah." The sheriff's distracted voice rang clear through the line.

"She's not at the store. I don't see her anywhere on the street."

"Did you call her cell?"

Fuck! Why hadn't he done that? Michael jogged back toward Chuck's. "I will."

"Okay," said Spencer. "I'll send someone your way as soon as I have a free pair of hands."

Michael didn't want to pull help away from the teenager's murder. A few country deputies couldn't help him. "Just spread the word, tell Hove to have his guys keep an eye out."

"Done."

Michael hit End and immediately called Jamie's cell. The phone rang five times and dumped into voice mail. He hung up, disappointed that her voice mail was computerized instead of her own voice. He took Chuck's porch steps three at a time, flew through the door, and across the lobby. He raced up to the second floor. His door was still open from earlier. Stepping through the doorway, he nearly knocked over Chuck for the second time that day.

"I could hear a phone in here ringing a minute ago," Chuck said.

Jamie's phone?

Michael hit Send on his phone again. A delicate melody sounded from the nightstand. He yanked open the drawer and stared at a familiar iPhone.

She'd left her phone. Right next to her wallet.

Michael ended his call and dialed Mason Callahan.

CHAPTER SEVENTEEN

The stretch of freeway between Mason's home and Portland was one straight, flat line. A boring line. If he pushed it, Mason could be in his office within fifteen minutes, depending on the traffic once he hit Portland. He was making excellent time, until he hit a traffic jam south of the city on the interstate and came to a complete stop. And sat.

And stewed.

Steaming, he mentally reviewed his interview with Fielding and conversation with Ray. Where was Hinkes? How could his information simply vanish?

Fuck it.

Mason forced himself to face the one question he and Ray hadn't been able to voice out loud. Who'd made Hinkes's information vanish?

Files can be lost, mistakes can be made, but every bit of information on Hinkes was gone. That took some string pulling to accomplish. Somewhere, someone had dirty hands.

Maybe he was put in witness protection.

Mason nearly spit out the coffee he'd just sipped. Clearly, he was losing his mind from watching too much television. But he didn't like the other option, that someone with power had stuck his fingers into the police system and stirred. He hated that option. It took cooperation from his brothers in blue to make it happen. Mason knew some cops broke rules here and there. He'd pushed his own line a time or two. But to do his job well and keep his sanity, it took faith in the system. Faith that the system worked to put away the bad guys. And left them there.

Mason's faith was being rattled.

Who'd erased Gary Hinkes?

Gary Hinkes was the Tattooed Albino Man. Mason knew it in his gut. Now if only his gut would give him answers to his other questions.

What name was he using now? Who'd cleared his history and allowed him to kidnap and kill all those kids? And why the hell would someone grab a group of kids? Talk about making it tough on yourself. Was the guy sick enough that he needed a group of kids? Or was just one kid the main focus and the rest got in the way?

It'd been the question asked for twenty years. All the parents had been thoroughly interviewed about who would want to harm their kid or hurt the parents in the process. The Brodys had seemed to be the biggest target with the father being a public figure. The senator's latest lead had turned out to be a bust with the death of his stalker ten years ago. The man they were hunting for was plainly alive.

Mason had talked with Hove in Eastern Oregon. The sergeant was giving plenty of consideration to Jamie's—and Mason's—theory that the same man had attacked her, wrecked her brother's home, and murdered the old Mexican.

Someone was cleaning up a loose end.

Chris Jacobs was that loose end.

But why now? Why hadn't Jacobs been targeted when he'd first returned? Someone had waited nearly twenty years to take out the kid and now was frantically burning a path to get at him. What had changed? Had Chris revealed that he remembered something? Something to make someone very nervous?

Or was it simply the exposure of the case? All those children's bodies coming to light? Was there a clue there that pointed at someone who the police had missed? Or was the Tattooed Man concerned the press coverage would stir up lost memories for Chris Jacobs?

Mr. Tattoo was taking huge risks to silence Chris Jacobs.

Somebody had big motivation.

Mason couldn't wait to get his hands on Somebody.

The traffic inched forward. His exit was still three miles away. At this rate, he should be back in the office by midnight. He glared at the man in the adjacent Prius yakking on his cell phone. Looking around, he saw two other drivers texting. Talking and texting while driving was illegal in Oregon...unless your job required it. Like delivery guys. Or police.

He crammed his Bluetooth in his ear. He hated the little earpiece. But not as much as the dorks who walked around with the plastic hanging out of their ears 24/7. He called Ray.

"Where are you?"

"Sitting motionless on I-5 watching the other assholes around me text on their phones."

"Wave your badge at them."

"Why?"

"They're gonna kill somebody someday by not focusing on the road."

"I'm gonna kill someone if this damned traffic doesn't start moving. Got anything new for me?"

"Yeah, heard back from my guy in the gang unit. They can't associate the tattoos with anything they've seen before, so he's definitely doing his own thing. If he was trying to start something with the ink, it's not caught on."

Mason snorted. "Nothing like throwing a party and no one coming."

"I got a translation on the two wrist tattoos. And they're Chinese characters, not Korean, like we'd wondered."

Mason's ears perked up.

"One stands for enlightenment—"

"Oh, for fuck's sake."

"—the other is chaos."

"That seems appropriate. The ass has been causing chaos for these families for decades. I don't get the snooty enlightenment symbol. This isn't a highbrow character we're dealing with."

"Ever watch that show on cable about people who hate their really bad tattoos? Some of the stories are hilarious. Usually at one point, the tattoo had seemed like a good idea and the image really spoke to them. Then later, they realize how stupid it looks."

"After they sleep off the alcohol?"

Ray's chuckle filled the line. "You'd be surprised how many of them are sober and let unknown artists mark them up permanently. Now they're paying through the nose to have it fixed. I'm thinking this is steering us away from the lead Cecilia Brody gave us about her Korean patient. I'm gonna keep Mr. Jeong on the back burner while we give this more priority."

"Definitely. He's looking less and less likely to be involved. So maybe Mr. Tattoo was trying to better himself with a classy message on his wrist? A message that showed in the pictures of those kids with his hands around their necks? That worked real well. Totally distracted me from the *sick prick's intentions!*" Mason glanced at the cars nearby. Had anyone heard him yell at Ray? He blew out his steam and ran a hand over his head. "Sorry," he muttered into the phone.

"You're just saying what I'm thinking."

The phone line was quiet for a few seconds as Mason tried to get those Polaroid images out of his brain. His Bluetooth did an odd double beep in his ear, and he glanced down at his phone screen in his console.

"Hey, Ray. I've got Michael Brody trying to call. Have you talked to him recently?"

"No, haven't heard from him."

"I'm gonna take this call and get back to you."

"Okay. I'm going to return a call to the ME's office. They've got something they want to run by us."

Mason switched over the call. Brody was breathing heavily. *Oh shit.*

"What happened?" Mason barked.

"Jamie's gone. I left her in the hotel room for thirty min-utes...not even that long...and I came back and she's gone." His words ran together. "No one has seen anything, she didn't go to the store, her cell phone is still in the room." He drew in a deep breath. "But a male called her room. Sounds like right after I left. He must have said something that would make her leave. Damn it, Callahan, I think he's got her."

"Silence.

"Fuck."

"I talked to Spencer. They're still processing the scene of that kid who was killed in the garage. Spencer thinks he was killed because he talked to Mr. Tattoo. Thinks that might be how he found Chris's house and knew of his friendship with the baker. Jesus Christ! I'm pulling out my hair here, Callahan!"

"Calm down—"

"Don't fucking tell me to calm down!"

"What'd Spencer say to do? Did you talk to Hove?" Mason thought hard. He was hours away from Brody's position. As much as he wanted to jump into the scene boots first, he'd be too fucking late. *Damn it!*

"He's putting the word out and contacting Hove. I shouldn't have left her alone! That sick asshole's got her. He's killed two people in the last twenty-four hours. Maybe more if he already got to her brother."

"If he's gotten to her brother, he wouldn't have needed Jamie. Now concentrate, Brody! Did you see any vehicles by the hotel? Did you see anyone? Hear anything?" Usually the reporter was unflappable. This level of alarm from Brody was rattling Mason.

"Nothing! I've already gone through all that."

"Where are you now?"

"I'm out in front of the bed-and-breakfast. Spencer is supposed to be sending someone over. I've checked the hotel room. It's immaculate. No signs of a struggle at all."

"So he probably did get her to leave."

"Why would she leave her phone?"

"Maybe she thought she'd be right back. Like she was just going down to the lobby to meet someone or get something."

"Shit."

Mason heard the reporter exhale forcefully. "We'll find her," he said lamely.

"I know. I just need something to do. I'm stuck here with my hands tied because no one knows where to start—*what the hell?*" Brody's tone shot up an octave.

"What?" asked Mason. He could hear a car engine through the line. Brody was silent, and Mason heard the vehicle shut off. "That someone from county?"

"What the fuck," Brody stated. "I'll call you back in a minute."

"Wait! Is it Jamie? What happened?"

"No," said Brody. "I think Chris Jacobs just pulled up."

The phone call clicked silent.

Mason grabbed at his phone and stared at the end call screen. "Jesus fucking Christ, Brody!" He tossed the phone on the passenger seat and pounded both palms on his steering wheel. "You can't do shit like that to me!"

★ ★ ★

Michael slid his phone in his pocket and studied the battered Ford pickup that'd pulled to the side of the road. The truck had been passing by, hit the brakes as the driver glanced at Michael, and then jerked the wheel to pull over. Through the back window of the truck's cab, Michael could see an adult male and the top of a black-haired head of a child in the second-row seat.

Chris. And Brian.

Michael stood frozen, staring at the window.

Maybe Jamie was with them.

There wasn't a third head visible, but his heart fervently made the wish. The adult turned to speak to the child, and then the driver's door swung open. A long, lean man slid out. He was wearing fatigue-print cargo shorts and a black T-shirt. Attire similar to Michael's everyday wardrobe. From twenty feet away, Michael stared at the scarred profile, pocked with large, pale scars down one side of his cheek and neck. Chris had clearly been battered at one point in his life. He turned and locked gazes with Michael, his crooked nose and jaw coming into view, and Michael felt a chill punctuate his spine. His ears started to ring.

Michael focused on the hazel eyes and the bearing of the head and shoulders. Cautious. Protective. Feet apart, hands and arms ready to defend his child. A man who had spent his life looking over his shoulder and preparing for the worst. He stood motionless, assessing Michael.

Michael rubbed a hand over his eyes. And looked again. Chris still hadn't moved. Michael took two steps and halted, scanning the man from head to toe. Movement from the truck pulled his attention, and he looked at the small, chubby face studying him through the back window of the cab. Everything in his peripheral vision vanished. He saw Brian as if looking through a tube.

He looks like Daniel. Daniel as a child. Coloring is wrong…but…

"Michael," said the man.

Not Chris Jacobs.

The man's hair was buzzed short, Marine length.

"Make them look like Marines," said The Senator to the barber.

Michael's mental picture of his hefty younger brother morphed into the lean man standing before him. He blinked.

Daniel.

"Michael," he said again. "I know—"

Michael *knew* that voice. It belonged to The Senator but was coming out of this man's mouth. He focused on the young man. *"Holy shit!"*

Daniel. His brother was standing in front of him. Joy and relief washed over him, and his knees shook. He took a stuttering step toward his brother, unable to take his gaze from that face.

Why didn't he let us know he was alive?

Michael froze.

"What the fuck, Daniel? Why the hell—why haven't you— *God damn it!"* Michael's mind spun into a swirling mass of joy and anger. He didn't know what to feel. He strode forward, a red haze tunneling his vision. "Why in the hell did you let us think you were *dead?"* he spit out. He stopped three feet from Daniel, his gaze drinking him in. He didn't know whether to hit him or hug him.

Daniel subtly shifted into a defensive posture. "I can explain."

"No, *you* can't explain! There is no fucking reason to explain away twenty years of us wondering about you!" Michael expanded his lungs, searching for oxygen. His ears were still ringing. *"Thank God, you're okay!"*

"I'm sorry, but—"

Michael made a cutting motion with his hands. "Save it! You have no idea—"

"You have no idea what my life—" Daniel leaned forward, voice rising.

"God damn you! Do you know what you've done to our parents? Couldn't you have called? You forget which family you belonged to?"

"No, I've known—"

"Does Chris Jacobs even exist? Are both of you out here? Hiding from your families?"

"Chris didn't make—"

"Does Jamie know you're not Chris?"

Daniel's shoulders slumped. "She thinks I'm Chris. I am Chris. To her. And everyone else."

Pain shot up Michael's spine. "Shit! I can't find Jamie!" *How could he have forgotten her for even two seconds?* "I think he's grabbed her. He's been trying to get to *you*!"

Daniel straightened, his brows coming together. "What? When? I just saw you two on a news broadcast. Are you talking about the Ghostman? Who grabbed her?"

"The Ghostman? The tattooed freak?"

"Yeah, that's him. We always called him the Ghostman because he was so fucking white."

"Jesus Christ. *We?*"

"Us kids."

Michael pulled out his cell phone. "You have a fucking lot of explaining to do, but right now we need the police."

He punched Spencer's contact and held his phone to his ear, staring at Daniel.

Daniel?

His hand touched wetness on his cheeks. He brushed at it and looked blankly at the evidence of tears on his hand. A lot of tears.

What the hell just happened?

CHAPTER EIGHTEEN

I didn't handle that well at all.

Chris watched Michael talk on his phone. He didn't know what to do. When he'd seen Michael on the sidewalk as he drove through town, he'd simply reacted. He'd known he had to reveal himself to Michael and Jamie. That's why he'd come back to town. Once he'd seen on TV that Jamie was safe, and that she'd linked up with his brother, he knew he had to make contact.

He was sick of hiding. And running.

Did the Ghostman have Jamie?

He closed his eyes. All the stress that had vanished after seeing her alive on TV came roaring back. One of his worst nightmares had just been confirmed by his brother. *His brother.* Chris mouthed the words. For two decades, he hadn't let himself think or say the phrase. He'd insisted in his brain that he no longer had a brother. It was the only way he'd been able to stay sane and function in Jamie's family. He'd had to believe he was no longer a Brody to protect them.

The Ghostman had said he'd kill Michael and his parents if they ever found out that Daniel was still alive. During his captivity, the threats had been daily. Every day in that metal hole in the ground, the Ghostman had regaled Daniel and Chris with stories about what he would do to Daniel's family.

Daniel never understood the focus on his family. Why the obsession with his family? Why not threaten Chris's?

When Daniel managed to escape, he took on Chris's identity. It wasn't hard. After two years with Chris, he knew everything about him. The only activity to do in the bunker was talk and tell stories of their families and lives. And they were both walking skeletons by the time it was over. Their eye color was similar. His hair was lighter, but hair changes color. If Chris's parents had ever doubted that Daniel wasn't their son, they never said a word. Sometimes you overlook inconsistencies if you want something bad enough.

He was Chris Jacobs now. He'd been Chris for almost twice as long as he'd been Daniel.

The Ghostman wasn't out to kill Chris's family. Daniel had planned to just pretend to be Chris until he felt like it was safe. But after he'd received the Twinkies in the hospital…

No one was safe.

It was best if he just kept his mouth shut and kept his eyes down. Everyone was safer that way. And it worked. There were a few moments when he thought he was about to blow it, but nothing ever came of it.

Jamie became his little sister. Her parents became his parents, and he grew to love them. He missed his real parents, but from what he could see in the newspapers, they were getting on with their lives. Cecilia still ran her hospital, and the senator still ran politics. And they had Michael. At least they hadn't lost all their children.

He'd followed Michael for years. Once the Internet blossomed, he read every article under Michael's byline. The Internet had been his savior, allowing him to keep an eye of sorts on the people he cared about. Cecilia and the senator were often in the news.

When Brian was born, Chris had wanted to tell everyone. But he couldn't. Jamie and his parents would have wanted to see the boy. He'd have to return home, exposing himself to anyone and everyone. He never knew if the Ghostman was simply waiting for him to make an appearance. The Ghostman might have decided that it was time to eliminate the final witness. And what if the Ghostman saw he had a son?

He couldn't let his son get onto the Ghostman's radar.

He knew what the Ghostman did to boys. He relived it most nights.

The nightmares were less frequent now. Although they'd escalated since the bodies of the children were found. He doubted he'd had more than four hours of sleep any night since the children had been found. The nightmares were made up of old scenes and new. The new scenes were the worst because he wasn't the boy in the Ghostman's grip; the boy was Brian.

Eight months ago, he'd read about a ten-year-old boy who'd been attacked in a fast-food restroom. It was a single restroom where the main door locks. The father had tried to beat the door down when he heard his son screaming inside. A manager had to unlock the door. The boy went to the hospital, needing surgery for his stab wounds. The attacker had been a sexual predator, released early from prison for previous sexual crimes.

Chris had thrown up. And never let his son enter a public bathroom without a look-see first.

The attacked boy's physical wounds would heal; the emotional wounds would last forever.

How was he going to make Michael understand?

Michael glanced at him as he talked on his cell phone. Over and over. Chris was doing the same. Studying the face, the bone structure, the hair, the mannerisms. The way his brother tipped his head, and his gaze darted about. *Exactly like Brian does.*

He went over to his truck, the driver's door still opened. Brian had scooted over behind the steering wheel and was solemnly watching the two men.

"Who's that?"

"That's Michael."

Brian tipped his head, studying the reporter. "Do you know him?"

Chris took a deep breath. "I do. But I haven't seen him in a long time. Michael is my brother."

Brian's gaze darted to his father's, eyes searching. "I thought you only had a sister."

Why did I ever lie to my son?

Chris took both of Brian's hands and squeezed them, holding that serious gaze. "I should've told you I had a brother, too."

"Is he angry?"

Chris nodded. "He is. There were some things I didn't tell him. Like I didn't tell you. It wasn't the right thing for me to do, and now he's angry at me. He's not mad at you."

"Did he know about me?"

Chris closed his eyes. The plaintive tone in Brian's voice ripped at his heart. He'd been so wrong to keep Brian from his family. "No. You're a surprise. A good surprise. And as soon as he's done being mad at me, he'll be thrilled that he has a nephew."

"He's my uncle." Brian tried out the word, and looked at Michael over Chris's shoulder. "I think he's done being mad."

Chris gripped Brian's upper arms and helped him jump down out of the truck. He took the boy's hand and turned to face Michael. Michael had finished his call and was brushing at his eyes. The anger had vanished from his demeanor; his shoulders slumped.

Chris raised his chin. "This is Brian. Your nephew."

A slow smile crossed Michael's face as he looked at the boy. "Hey, Brian. How's it goin'? Did you know you look just like your dad did when he was your age?"

Brian shook his head. "Nice to meet you, Uncle Michael," he said in his best-manners voice that Chris had taught him.

Michael froze, and his jaw dropped the slightest bit. "Aw, darn it," he whispered as fresh tears spilled from his eyes. He reached out and roughly pulled Chris to him in a bear hug. After a few brotherly slaps on Chris's back, he reached out and ruffled Brian's hair.

Chris wiped at the wetness on his own face.

★ ★ ★

Michael sat on the wooden steps to Chuck's bed-and-breakfast, waiting for Sheriff Spencer, his mind still spinning over the events of the last thirty minutes. He was ready to jump out of his skin with worry for Jamie. Spencer had told him to stay put until he got there, so he was. Didn't mean he had to like it. His brain was running wild with images of Jamie in the hands of a killer. Daniel...Chris sat beside him, and Brian was trying a balancing act on the low rail around the deck. Michael was trying to wrap his head around calling his brother Chris.

"Brian's only heard me called Chris. I've called myself Chris in my head for almost twenty years."

"Mom and Dad might struggle with that a bit," Michael replied. Chris paled a bit at the thought of their parents and asked Michael to hold off on notifying them just yet.

Right now they had a much bigger issue. "We need to find Jamie." Michael rubbed at the back of his neck. "Where would he take her?"

Chris shook his head. "I don't know. I'd hoped the Ghostman was dead, but—"

"What's his real name?"

Chris shrugged with one shoulder, and the familiar movement triggered a dagger of pain in Michael's memory. *How many times in the past had he seen Daniel make that move? Chris, not Daniel.*

"I don't know. He made us call him 'sir.' When he wasn't around, we called him the Ghost or Ghostman."

"There's got to be something you remember—"

"I remember everything," Chris said forcefully as he leaned toward Michael, gazes locked. "I've relived every memory a thousand times, searching for something to zero in on this guy. Something to identify him so I could sneak in his house and murder him in his bed. If he was dead, then I could get my real family back. I've had this goal since I was thirteen. Do you know what it's like to want the same thing year after year? *I wanted him dead and all you guys safe.* I have worried about you, Jamie, your parents, and Brian *every day* of my life." Chris looked away, across the street. "But he's a fucking ghost, impossible to pin down. And he turned me into one, too.

"I feel like I don't exist. I live a made-up life and pretend everything is hunky-dory so my son won't see my stress and worry."

"Brian has to see it. He has to pick up on it. Maybe it's subconscious, but Brian is aware on some level that your life isn't right." Michael watched Chris's gaze sweep the landscape, noting every rock and tree. The man was on high alert. How did he keep it up 24/7?

Michael was struggling with a similar level of mental stress. With Jamie out of sight and his hands currently tied, he had the energy to run a marathon boiling under the surface. He struggled to focus on his brother.

"He asks sometimes about other kids to play with. There're hardly any kids in town, and I homeschool him. Juan's dog..." Chris rubbed at his face. "Juan's dog was probably his best friend. *Shit.* Do you know what happened to the dog?"

Michael shook his head. "I didn't see a dog around."

"Juan lets him wander. Not the smartest thing to do...sometimes he's gone for a day or two. I'll check for him later."

"How come..." Michael looked Chris up and down for the millionth time. "How'd they not see that you weren't Chris?"

"They? My parents?"

"Yeah. I can plainly see Daniel in you now. I don't see Daniel the kid...but I can see that you're Daniel as an adult."

Chris shook his head. "I was a mess when I came back. I looked like I'd survived a concentration camp. My face and skull had been beat to hell. I think they saw what they wanted to see. Our hair and eye color were close. I said I was Chris, and they accepted it.

"Do you remember the story a few years ago about the two teenage girls? I think they were in a car accident. One died and the other was severely injured and in a coma for a week or two. Anyway, they misidentified the one who'd died. When the other girl came out of the coma, it wasn't her parents pacing her hospital room. It was the dead girl's. Parents see what they want to see. I was in a hospital for months, my head covered in bandages, multiple surgeries on my face. My parents were simply thankful I was alive."

"I've got to tell our parents. We can't put it off any longer. They've been living in hell for two decades."

Chris shook his head. "Not yet. We don't have the time to give them the attention this kind of news will take. Another day or two won't matter. We've got to find Jamie and take care of the Ghostman. Then we can tell them together."

Michael looked at his watch for the millionth time. *Jamie was getting farther away every minute, and he was sitting here on his ass.* "Damn it! Spencer is taking forever. He said he was done at the Buells'."

"Buells'?" Chris's focus jerked back to Michael. "What happened at the Buells'?"

Michael brought him up to date.

"They think it's my gun? I have one like that back at the house...or I had one. *Fuck!*"

Chris pushed off the stairs and paced to the end of the walkway and back, lips silently swearing. Brian abruptly stopped his balancing practice long enough to watch his father. Michael glanced at Brian, gave him a wink, and after a pause, the boy resumed concentrating on his foot placement.

Brian knows more than Chris realizes. He watches out for his father probably as much as his father watches out for him. Not healthy.

"No one can live like something's gonna jump out of the bushes every minute," Michael said.

Chris stopped pacing and planted himself in front of Michael. "Then I have to eliminate the threat."

"Eliminate the Ghostman. That's already on my to-do list. And every cop in the state of Oregon. I think you've got some support going on."

Chris took a deep breath. "Why our family? Why did the Ghost want to destroy our family? He never talked about... Jamie's family the way he did ours. It was like he had a mission to mess us up." He glanced at Brian, but the boy had found a bug on the far side of the wraparound porch to poke at.

"What are you saying?" Michael said slowly. *Was the kidnapping aimed to hurt The Senator?*

Frustration crossed Chris's face. "He never threatened the other kids' families. Just mine. And I always felt like his focus was on me...I mean...like the other kids were there accidentally."

"The kidnapping was because of you? To get at The Senator? Or Mom?"

Chris scowled. "But he never said that. I inferred it, I think. The real Chris and I talked about it over and over. Why was the focus on me?"

Michael's stomach coiled. "Fuck. You didn't say what happened to Jamie's brother," he whispered. "It's not good, is it?"

Chris shut his eyes. "No. It's not."

★ ★ ★

"Come on, Chris! Move it!" Daniel begged. "We can't stop now."

Chris looked like he couldn't take another step. Daniel had been almost carrying him for several hours. He'd hooked Chris's arm about his neck and simply dragged. They hadn't seen water since they'd left the hellhole. And that was yesterday morning. Daniel looked up, trying to judge the time, but he couldn't see the sun. The forest was too dense.

They would never find a way out of the woods.

Daniel didn't care. He'd rather die in the woods than spend another minute with the Ghostman. The boys had made an agreement. Death was preferable to the life they'd been living, and they would do it together. It'd been Chris who'd figured out how to keep the bunker lid from fully latching when the Ghostman left. They'd tried for years to get it open. Blocking the latch had taken coordinated timing and distraction during a visit. One boy to distract and the other to slip the small piece of wood into the latch's socket. From the Ghost's perspective, the lid had fully locked as he left.

Before they escaped, Chris had been struggling with a fever for a few weeks. The Ghostman had given him some medicine, and Chris had seemed better, but then he was suddenly sicker than he'd been to start with. The last three days he'd had a cough that'd shook his whole body. Today, he'd spit blood when he coughed. Last night had been so cold... Daniel didn't want to think about sleeping in the dirt again.

He'd covered up Chris with dirt and leaves, trying to get him warm, then slept with his arms around him for body heat. Had he even slept? It felt like he'd woken up every ten minutes to strange sounds in the woods. He'd expected the Ghostman to leap out from behind every tree. Chris's bony body didn't offer much in the way of body heat. He swore both of them had shivered all night, but at least it hadn't rained.

He knew it was summer. He didn't know the month, but he did know the year. This was the second summer since he'd been taken. To him, summer meant the hole was slightly less cold. And the Ghostman would wear shorts.

He breathed deep. The air smelled so rich and clean. The hole had stunk. It'd stunk after the first week. If only the clean air was enough to give Chris the energy to keep moving.

Just before full dark last night, he'd seen a light. A moving light far off in the woods, and he'd known HE was looking for them. At least he didn't have anyone to help him. He'd told them hundreds of times that the hellhole was his special secret that he'd shared with no one. Daniel didn't think he'd reveal his secret now.

Chris's legs stopped moving completely. Before, he'd at least helped balance or propel himself as Daniel dragged him along.

"I can't. I can't go any further. Just let me rest for a little bit. Then I'll walk."

Chris's cracked lips alarmed Daniel. And he was so hot. It was like a fire was burning him from the inside out. His skin seemed lightly scorched everywhere. Almost scaly.

Daniel feared stopping. He didn't believe he'd be able to get Chris going again. But he stopped and eased Chris down next to an ancient fallen tree. Chris sighed and closed his eyes, leaning his head back against the bark.

"I'll just rest for a bit."

Daniel studied his best friend. Chris's bones stuck out everywhere, but so did Daniel's. But Chris's skin looked stretched so tight over the elbow when he bent his arm. The arm that he could bend. The other arm had been broken months ago and never healed right. Chris barely ever used it. The Ghostman had fashioned him a sling that he wore nonstop. He said his arm hurt whenever he took it off.

Daniel sat down next to his friend. Hot tears leaked out of his eyes, and he swiped at them angrily. Crying wasn't going to get them out of the woods.

"Daniel?" It was a whisper.

"Yes?" Daniel wiped at his eyes again.

"I don't think I'm going to get back up."

Daniel's heart froze. "You just need a rest. Take a short nap, and you'll be ready to go again."

"No, Daniel. Really—"

"Shut up, Chris! Just shut up! You're going to be fine!" His voice cracked.

Chris opened his eyes and looked straight at his friend. Daniel could see the defeat in his eyes. "We both know I'm not going any further. I can't feel my feet, Daniel."

Daniel flung his arms around his friend and squeezed him tight to his chest, throwing Chris into a coughing fit. Daniel didn't let go. "No, Chris," he whispered. "I can't do this alone. It's supposed to be you and me. Both of us till the end."

Chris laid his head on Daniel's shoulder. It felt as light as a kitten. "I know. But if something happens to me, promise you'll keep going."

Daniel bit back a sob. Why was Chris talking like this?

"If you were in my shoes, you'd be saying the same thing," Chris said. "You're my best friend. And one of us has to get out of here."

Daniel watched his friend's knobby chest slowly rise and fall. As long as he stuck with Chris, they'd both be okay. Chris just needed a break. Daniel closed his own eyes. He might as well rest, too. He'd just take a short nap.

★ ★ ★

Daniel startled awake. It was lighter than it'd been when he drifted off to sleep. And a little warmer. Probably closer to the middle of the day. At least he hadn't slept the whole day away. He and Chris should get moving again. He shook Chris's shoulder. The boys had lain completely down as they slept. Chris was curled up on his side as close to Daniel as possible to stay warm.

"Chris?" He shook him again.

The boy didn't move. Daniel felt his empty stomach clench tight. He ran his hand across Chris's forehead. It was cool.

"*Oh God!*" *Daniel scooted away from the dead boy, his hands and feet scrambling on the dirt floor of the woods. He collapsed, staring at what had been his best friend. Tears flooded his eyes. He slowly crept back, keeping his gaze locked on Chris's face. "Chris?" he whispered.*

Chris didn't answer.

Daniel touched Chris's face with a shaking hand, pushing the hair off his cheek. His friend's fever was gone. The stress in his face had relaxed. He actually looked restful, peaceful. Envy flashed through Daniel's mind and vanished. He wanted that peace, too, but not like this. Daniel sat beside his friend and leaned back against the old log, and placed his friend's head on his lap, stroking his hair.

CHAPTER NINETEEN

"I left him there by the log. I couldn't do anything else. I covered him with some brush and stuff. Then I got up and started to walk. I'm not sure how many more days went by before I stumbled into civilization. Three? Maybe four? It's all a blur.

"After I left home for good, I went back to try to find his body. It took three different trips and a lot of camping in the forest before I located that log. I started at the farmhouse where they found me and worked my way back, taking the path of easiest resistance each time. When I finally found him, half the bones were gone. Scattered by scavengers.

"I buried what was left. And marked the site and coordinates. He was my other brother."

"Did you look for the bunker?" Michael asked.

"God, no. I didn't ever want to go back there. You know, before I escaped, I thought the other kids had been released. That's what he told us he was doing."

Michael shook his head. "He didn't."

"The recent news reports didn't say how the other kids died."

Michael thought for a second. "You're right. I know there weren't any bullet holes in skulls of the children at the recovery site. I don't know if they could tell how they died."

"We never heard any gunshots. It's driven me crazy for years wondering what exactly happened to them. Once I was told they'd never returned, I knew he'd killed them. I've had nightmares where I see him doing...things to them. Sometimes not knowing is the worst part. Your brain makes up its own details."

Tell me about it. Michael understood too well.

"Hang on. I think I know who could answer that question." Michael dialed his phone.

"Michael? Where are you?" Lacey Campbell's voice spoke in his ear.

"Eastern Oregon still. You following what's been going on out here?"

"Yes. I've spoken with Detective Lusco. Is everything all right?"

Michael rubbed at his eyes. "No. Jamie is missing. We've got every cop in Oregon looking out for our tattooed man, because we think he managed to nab her. Maybe tricked her to leave our hotel room somehow. I'm going crazy not being able to do anything."

"God damn it! When are they going to stop him?"

"Lacey, I wanted to ask you if the ME's office figured out how all the kids were killed."

Lacey was silent for a second. "Why are you asking about that?"

"I need to know. I need to know what he does to them. Were they shot? Stabbed? Can you guys even tell?"

He heard her exhale noisily over the phone. "None of the bones show signs of gunshot or stab wounds. Could there have been those types of wounds and they didn't touch the bones, yes, but it's doubtful. Usually the bones tell. Dr. Peres didn't find a single knife nick from a stabbing on any of the kids or the adults from the pit."

"So how'd he do it?"

"Two of the bodies from the pit had broken hyoid bones."

"The bone at the throat?"

"Yes. Sometimes it breaks during strangulation."

"But none of the kids had that?"

"In children, the bone hasn't fused. It starts as three pieces and then fuses into one as they age. Usually by age thirty, most people have fully fused hyoids. We just can't tell on children."

"How can you tell the difference between a broken bone and one that hasn't fused? They're both in pieces. Those bodies in the pit were all in their twenties, right? Maybe they weren't strangled, maybe their hyoids hadn't fused yet," Michael theorized.

"Fractures cause jagged ends on the bones. Unfused bones have smooth ends. The broken adult hyoids were very jagged."

"Got it. But strangulation wasn't ruled out on the children."

"No," said Lacey. "We couldn't rule it out. But my gut says that's what was done."

"Mine too. Chris says he didn't hear any gunshots."

"Chris?" Lacey said sharply. "You found him?"

"Oh God, Lace. I haven't told you. Fuck. He found me." Michael rattled off the events of the last thirty minutes.

"It's Daniel? Are you sure?" Lacey said softly.

"Never been so sure of anything in my life." Michael stared at his brother as he examined Brian's bug. The boy was gesturing excitedly as he pointed out the finer parts of the bug to his father.

"Oh, Michael. How wonderful."

"Wonderful doesn't begin to describe it. Now I just need Jamie back. I don't know where to start looking. Christ, Lace. It's the absolute worst and happiest day of my life! I want to hit something and cheer at the same time."

"They'll find her. She'll be okay."

"Don't simply say meaningless words. I need answers."

Lacey was silent, and Michael felt like shit.

"I'm sorry, Lace. I'm absolutely at my wit's end. I don't know what to do, and I've never felt this way before. I always know what direction to head next."

"She's something special," Lacey stated, but Michael knew it was a question.

"Yes, she is. She's the one, Lace, I know it, and I can feel it in every cell of my bones. I can't lose her when I've just found her!" Michael's hands shook. He'd spoken the truth. He hadn't realized it until that very second. It'd taken his entire life to find the woman who fit him perfectly.

Jamie was his woman. And she'd been snatched away by a killer.

Would he get her back? He closed his eyes. *Was she still alive?*

Two patrol cars stopped behind Chris's truck. One Luna County and one OSP.

Finally.

Michael ended his conversation with Lacey. Chris stood next to Michael with Brian peeking out at the cops from behind his father.

Michael mentally shook his head.

A boy should be racing down the walkway to check out the cool police cars, not hiding.

CHAPTER TWENTY

Jamie was in a trunk. An unbearable, cooking-the-bones, hot trunk. At least it was late in the evening. Thank God she wasn't being driven about with the sun beating directly on the metal above. This heat had to be radiating up from the hot blacktop and out of the underside of the car.

Her mouth was taped shut. Her hands were tied behind her, and her feet were bound together. She pounded on the side of the vehicle with both feet and kicked where she thought the tail-light should be. The damned vehicle had a glowing handle above her head, labeled for emergency trunk openings. A safety feature for kids who locked themselves in their parents' trunks.

It taunted her.

She continued kicking at the taillight area. A faint memory of reading a story about someone locked in a trunk, kicking the light out and signaling other drivers kept running through her brain. Fiction? Nonfiction? Didn't matter. It was her best damned solution at the moment. The car sounded fast. There hadn't been any turns or slowdowns since she'd come to consciousness a few minutes ago, so she suspected they were on a highway. Of course, ninety percent of Eastern Oregon's roads were probably long stretches of empty highways.

She kept kicking. Her legs had saved her before. Kicking at the tattooed man had saved her ass, and maybe they'd save her again. Sweat ran into her eyes and stung like a bitch.

Fuck.

What was Michael thinking? Her eyes watered. When he'd returned to their hotel room, what did he do? Did he panic? Was he angry? He had to know she hadn't left willingly.

And she wouldn't ever willingly leave Michael Brody. He made her laugh and see the world in a different way. He'd shown her she didn't always have to follow the rules. She'd simply done it for so long that she didn't know how to do anything else. Michael had opened her eyes. And opened her heart. She'd seriously fallen head over heels for the man.

Was she going to get the chance to be with him?

Or was she going to be found in a dirt pit in five years?

I'm sorry I'm putting you through this, Michael.

He must be frantic. He knew exactly why she wasn't waiting in their room. And that her odds of surviving were very slim.

Mr. Tattoo didn't leave witnesses.

She rubbed her face into the rough carpet and spit her hair out of her mouth. Her hair was sticking to her neck and face like she'd been swimming. If only she could take a deep breath.

Huffing though her nose without panicking took concentration. When she'd first woke, she'd felt like she was suffocating, unable to get the air her body needed. She'd seen stars in her vision in the dark trunk as she fought the panic and slowed her lungs. Thank God she wasn't claustrophobic. She had enough issues at the moment.

She paused her kicking and concentrated on her breathing again. She was getting a raw spot on her hip from the leg movements and the rough carpet. Her hip hurt, her hands were numb, and she was lying in a pool of sweat. The temperature in the trunk was a hairline from unbearable. Kicking was simply making it worse.

But she was still above ground.

The tattooed man's other victims were not. That poor old baker. And what about Chris? And Brian? Were they okay?

If he grabbed me, I suspect it's because he can't find Chris.

She prayed to God that was true.

When the phone in her room at the bed-and-breakfast had rung, she'd expected it to be Chuck. Instead, a man had whispered.

"Jamie? Are you okay?"

Jamie had sat up on the bed, phone pressed to her ear, because the voice was so faint. *Chris?*

"Chris? Is that you?"

"Shhh. I can't talk here." His whisper came from far away.

"Are you okay? Is Brian okay? You need to get to the police, Chris. Someone is trying to find you—"

"Shhh, I know. Look, I need you to take the boy for a few days. Can I leave him with you?"

Jamie's heart leaped. *Brian!* "Yes, of course. But you really should—"

"I'll meet you behind the bed-and-breakfast in two minutes. Back by the fence gate. He'll be safe with you." He disconnected.

Jamie slid her feet into her flip-flops and dashed out the door.

She hadn't thought about the obvious question of how Chris had known she was at the little hotel.

In the trunk, Jamie shook her head in the dark. How had she been so foolish? But she'd wanted to see the boy so bad. She'd pulled the B-movie heroine bit. The too-stupid-to-live move. She might as well have gone alone, down into the dark basement, to see if the killer was in there.

Instead, she'd left the room without telling Michael. Or anyone.

At the gate, it'd been quiet. Chuck had a small seating area outside with tables and umbrellas that Jamie had eyed wistfully earlier that day. It was simply too hot to sit outside. The backyard of the house was surrounded by a tall hedge, providing a sense of privacy to the large yard. At the far end, someone had removed a section of hedge and installed a wood gate. As far as Jamie could see from her room's window, the gate led to an alley that ran behind the row of houses. A one-truck-width alley where people kept their garbage cans.

She had darted out the rear door of the house and jogged the length of the yard to the gate. She'd pushed it open, stepped into the alley, and looked both ways. To her left was a sedan, facing her and blocking the alley, its engine running. She couldn't see anyone in the driver's seat. She took two steps in its direction.

That was all she remembered. Looking back, someone must have been to the right of the gate outside the hedge. When she pushed open the gate, she'd hidden him from her view. With the way her head was currently pounding and the painful spot behind her right ear, she had a good idea why she didn't remember what had happened.

And she knew it wasn't Chris who'd hit her over the head.

She was in Mr. Tattoo's trunk. She had no doubt.

The big question was *why had he grabbed her?*

She didn't know where Chris was. How would grabbing her help him find Chris?

The sheriff's description of the tortured baker entered her mind.

Jamie moaned, hiding her wet face in the carpet. *No. He can't do that to me.*

Detective Callahan had described some of the Polaroids. Those children…

Chris's nightmares…What had been done to him?

Was she next? As he fished for information she didn't have? Chris had always said it was best that she knew nothing.

Now she wasn't so sure.

She tried to take a slow, deep breath through her nose, and failed. The air felt heavier than it had two minutes ago. She exhaled abruptly, trying to clear her nostrils. Moisture was clogging her nose. Her heart pounded over the sounds of the car. *Calm down.* She inhaled slowly again, struggling to get air. It wasn't enough. Lights twinkled around the edge of her vision.

Oh shit.

Not enough oxygen. Sweat dripped from her back and chest as the sounds of the road started to fade in her ears.

★ ★ ★

Gerald didn't know where he was going. He'd tried calling his boss with no luck. And that had been over an hour ago. He'd tried four times.

270 • KENDRA ELLIOT

His boss had never missed his calls before, and that was making Gerald's acid reflux act up. His chest and the center of his back were on fire.

What was going on?

He twisted his hands around the steering wheel. An overwhelming sense of being up shit creek without a paddle was sinking into his brain.

Had his boss let him go?

He picked up his phone and called again. Nothing. He flung the phone on the passenger seat.

Maybe the mess in Eastern Oregon was making his boss uncomfortable. Had he already found out about the baker and teen boy? Had he decided Gerald was expendable?

Was he being left to sink or swim?

Gerald had always known this day was a possibility. And he was not goddamned expendable. If his boss was trying to distance himself from Gerald, he was in for a big surprise. Gerald had recordings. Video recordings and voice recordings of almost every phone call he'd ever had with the man that discussed Chris Jacobs or Daniel Brody. Recordings that would crush him. And destroy everything the man treasured. If his boss was letting him sink, he wasn't sinking alone.

He dialed the boss's cell again. Voice mail.

His gut burned.

The passenger in his trunk pounded with her feet. Thank goodness it was dark and there was virtually no traffic on the highway. He'd pull over and check her soon. As long as she kept kicking, it meant she wasn't dead.

It'd been a fast decision. After seeing Jamie Jacobs on TV and not knowing where to find Chris Jacobs, he figured he'd go back to the woman. At the very least, he had a gorgeous woman at his disposal. At the best, he had a lead to her brother.

When he'd seen Michael Brody stroll out of the bed-and-breakfast and down the street to the diner, he decided he had a few minutes. He circled the block once, spotted the gate in the alley, and searched for the phone number for the bed-and-breakfast. He'd planned to simply pose as her brother and tell her he needed some money. Even if she'd refused to give him money, he guessed she'd at least want to see him in person. It'd been obvious they didn't see each other. But when she asked about Brian, he'd known he had the perfect bait.

He'd hit her hard with the ax handle.

At first, he'd worried that he'd hit too hard. She'd collapsed instantly at his feet, a limp puddle of woman. But Jamie's pulse had stayed strong, so he tied her hands and dumped her in the trunk.

He'd done that once. Hit a victim so hard that he hadn't woken up. That'd been a waste of time and effort. He'd added the body to the hole in the woods along with his other victims. It'd been such a great hiding site.

A few miles out of Demming, he'd stopped and tied Jamie's feet and taped her mouth. She'd still been unconscious but breathing fine.

Some muffled screams came from the trunk, and he turned up the radio.

He could still feel the vibrations from her kicking in the trunk. It'd been nearly thirty minutes since he'd bound her feet. He shifted in his seat. It had to be hot in the trunk. A corpse in his trunk wasn't going to do him any good. Maybe he should check the temperature in there. He'd been blasting the air conditioner, but that wasn't going to stop Jamie from overheating.

The center console...

Ha! Gerald cheered up. He could access the trunk through the center of the backseat. If he lowered the console in back, that would put some cold air circulation into the trunk. A road sign indicated five miles until a rest stop. He'd find a quiet corner and check on his passenger.

Jamie chose that second to go silent.

The car's speed crept up to seventy-five. He'd be at the rest stop in a few minutes, and he could—

Red and blue lights flashed in his rearview mirror.

What the fuck?

Gerald's brain circuitry hit overtime. *They'd found him. They'd seen him grab her. They knew he'd killed the children. They knew he'd killed the Mexican and the teenager.*

His brain wouldn't stop firing off the panic messages. He looked down the deserted highway, and a brief thought of outrunning the cop car dashed through his head. Impossible. Those vehicles have amazing engines.

He studied his mirror. Only one police car. And he had been speeding a minute ago. He slowed and turned on his blinker.

Pull over. Be polite.

He wished he was armed. He'd left the Jacobs gun at the teen boy's death scene. Usually he carried two handguns, but tonight he had none. If he had to, he could take this officer down once he got out of the car.

Gravel crackled under his tires as he left the pavement and pulled to a stop. For a brief second, he thought the officer was going to pass him. Instead, the navy-blue car stopped close behind him. The ultimate in dorky hats was visible through the windshield. *State police.* No one else wore those wide-brimmed hats.

His trunk was silent.

What if she'd kicked out a light? Was there a foot hanging out the back of his car? Sweat poured off his temples. Gerald lowered his window and reached over to the glove box for his car-rental agreement. He looked in the rearview mirror. The trooper was still in his seat. Probably running his plates and calling in his location. That was okay. It would come back as a rental. And it didn't matter if he ran this driver's license. This identity was clean. He didn't even have a speeding ticket.

Until now. *Hopefully, that was all he was getting.*

The trooper was suddenly at his window. "Evening sir. License and registration please."

Gerald handed over the items. "I was going a little fast back there, wasn't I? It's a rental car. Here're the papers." He listened hard for any sounds coming from the trunk. It was silent.

Was Jamie passed out? Or dead? He needed to check the trunk. He swallowed hard, his heart pounding in his ears.

The trooper looked over his license. "No, Mr. Bennett. I pulled you over for cell phone use. You passed me a few miles back while talking on your cell phone."

Relief, amusement, anger, and disbelief shot through Gerald. "Seriously? The call didn't even go through."

The trooper's lips twitched. "Well sir, the law doesn't care if you didn't get connected or if someone hung up on you. I saw your phone at your ear. I'll be right back." He paused, taking a sharper look at Gerald. "You alright, sir?"

Gerald touched his cheekbone where the Mexican had whacked him with the rebar. "Pretty nasty, isn't it? Dropped my bar and weights on my face while bench-pressing today. That's the last time I don't use a spotter."

Disbelief crossed the trooper's face. "No spotter? Seriously? What were you thinking?"

Gerald tried to look ashamed. "I know. It was stupid. I figured since the weight wasn't too bad, I wouldn't ask anyone, but then my hand slipped."

The trooper shook his head and went back to his vehicle with Gerald's ID.

Gerald rested his head against his steering wheel. That could have gone far worse.

And a cell phone violation? He was being pulled over for using his cell phone? He gave a strangled laugh, suddenly lightheaded. *Holy fuck.*

If only the trooper knew what he'd left behind in Demming. And what he had in his trunk.

The trooper reappeared at his window and handed back his ID and paperwork. "I'm going to have to issue you a citation for the cell phone use. We're in the middle of a statewide crackdown because people aren't taking the law seriously. Get yourself a hands-free unit. Those are currently legal."

Gerald silently took the paperwork. *Don't say a word.* What he wanted to do was cram the ticket in the trooper's face. But he was getting a free pass. Take the ticket and get to the other side of the state. "I'll look into it."

The trooper touched the brim of his hat. "Drive safely, sir."

Gerald watched the trooper walk back to his car. He put on his blinker and pulled out onto the open highway. *How had the trooper seen his phone? The sun had been down for an hour.*

Don't look a gift horse in the mouth.

He kept an eye on the rearview mirror. The trooper's patrol car hadn't budged. It got smaller and smaller as Gerald increased his speed. Just before he couldn't see it anymore, it did an abrupt turn and headed in the opposite direction.

He looked at his ticket. One hundred forty-two dollars for talking on a cell phone?

Pissed and steaming about the fine, two miles later, Gerald took the rest stop exit.

Deserted.

He parked as far away as possible from the little bathroom buildings. He sat in the driver's seat, scanning the rest stop for a few minutes. Even though he'd watched the trooper head in the opposite direction, he half expected him to reappear. And not be alone. After the rest stop stayed quiet, he stepped out of the car and stretched. Every joint hurt. It'd been a hell of a long day.

First, the empty Jacobs house, then the old Mexican, the kid from the gas station, Jamie Jacobs, and then a fucking traffic ticket.

He stood behind his car, eyeing the trunk. He examined the taillights. Both looked intact. If she'd been kicking at them, it didn't show. He snorted, remembering his fear of a foot hanging out, visible to the trooper. He bent over the trunk, feeling the heat radiate from the metal against his face, listening.

All silent.

Ax in hand, he pushed the trunk release button on his key fob.

Jamie lay motionless. Her hair and shirt were soaked with sweat. He shoved at her legs with the ax handle, and her eyes opened. *Thank God, the bitch is still breathing.* She stared at him, her gaze studying his face and taking mental notes. She didn't move.

"You hot?" he asked.

Her eyebrows narrowed.

Probably a stupid question.

"I'll make you a deal."

The eyebrows rose a bit.

"Knock off the goddamned kicking, and I'll open the center console area. That'll let some of the air-conditioning into the trunk. Deal?"

Jamie blinked and gave one short nod.

"Yeah, I didn't think you were too stupid. You're no good to me barbecued or roasted."

She was silent.

He considered giving her some water, but that'd mean taking the tape off her mouth, and he didn't feel like acting like a nursemaid. She'd be okay without water for a few more hours. The air-conditioning should make a difference.

He poked at the inside of the trunk where the lights connected. All solid and covered up. She wasn't going to be able to damage them, no matter how hard she kicked.

Gerald slammed the trunk, opened the rear driver-side door, and yanked at the console that was tucked into the backseat. It moved forward. He could feel hot air from the trunk move into the cooler air of the car. He pointed the two wimpy rear vents at the center of the backseat.

He got back in the driver's seat and headed back to the highway. He hadn't seen a single vehicle in fifteen minutes. He took a long swallow from his bottle of water, sighed, and wiped at his mouth. He was gonna be driving most of the night.

It was a long drive back to the other side of the Cascade Mountains. Gerald was aiming a little farther south this time. He wasn't going back to Portland. He was headed toward home. Salem, the state's capital. Salem was his comfort zone.

The bunker had been closer to Salem, and his job was primarily in that city.

He took the highway turnoff toward a mountain range pass. Hopefully, he'd hear from his boss soon. He wasn't going to try calling while driving this time.

★ ★ ★

To Michael's relief, Spencer stepped out of the Luna County car. Nothing against the deputies of Luna County, but Spencer was the one with the brains. The rest seemed to be a bunch of local recruits who stood around a lot. One deputy tailed his boss. Hove opened his cruiser door but sat in the driver's seat, talking on his cell.

"Whatcha got?" Spencer asked as he strode up the walk. He nodded at Chris. "Jacobs. 'Bout time you turned up. I've got a couple of questions for you about Juan's place."

"Right now we've got to find Jamie. I know the Ghostman grabbed her," Chris said.

"Who?" Spencer scowled.

"I called him the Ghostman. Same guy who held me captive as a kid. Freaking ghostly, white-skin-colored asshole."

"Covered in ink now," Michael added.

"Mr. Tattoo is the Ghostman. Got it." Spencer's expression said he thought both of them were slightly nuts. "Who the fuck is he really?"

Michael shook his head. "Dunno."

Hove stepped forward. "According to your Detective Callahan, he's a former sexual predator known as Gary Hinkes. But the guy has vanished from the face of the earth. There's no driver's license, no tax records, nothing. He was arrested in the late eighties for some sex crimes, but no one can find any records. He was also arrested in conjunction with a murder of a Portland woman but went to prison on a lesser charge. There hasn't been a peep from him since he got out."

"Where are the records from the trial?" Spencer asked.

"Gone."

"And from his time in prison?"

"He was there for two months. Any scrap of paper relating to it has vanished."

Chris looked at Michael. "How does that happen?"

Michael's stomach thrummed. "Someone knows someone with the right connections."

"Well, the people who interacted with him shouldn't have disappeared…I hope. What about the warden from when he was in prison? He remember him?" Spencer crossed his arms on his chest.

Hove shook his head. "Retired. And he was only there two months. No one can tell us shit."

"How about the judge at his trial? Or his lawyer or prosecutor? Someone has to remember something besides Fielding. It was a fucking murder trial."

"The detectives in Portland are looking into that and some other possibilities. They'll find someone who knows what he's doing these days. Now, what do you got inside?" asked Hove.

"Absolutely nothing," Michael answered, but he waved the cops into the bed-and-breakfast. Michael was ready to crawl out of his skin. Standing around and waiting for the police wasn't how he operated. He liked action. He craved action. *He needed to DO something.*

But right now he had no fucking information to move on.

Chuck greeted the group of men and then watched them pound up the stairs. Spencer's deputy stayed back to question Chuck. Hove and Spencer made a quick survey of the bedroom and bathroom, identical to Michael's sweep. Hove scanned the backyard.

"Where's the gate go?" he asked Michael.

"Alley behind the property."

"Look in the alley?"

"No." Michael's mouth dried up. *Shit.* He started to dash out of the room.

"Hold up. We'll all go."

The three men marched through the bed-and-breakfast as Michael fought the urge to sprint ahead. *Why hadn't he checked the alley?*

Spencer pointed at the back door to the yard. "That been unlocked all day?" He directed the question to Chuck, who nodded.

If it hadn't been in the high nineties still, the backyard would have been inviting. The sun had nearly set, but the sky was still very light. Michael focused on the wood gate. It was open slightly into the alley. The hedge on either side had to be close to ten feet tall.

"Sucker is tall," muttered Hove, eyeing the hedge.

Spencer pushed the gate open, and the three men stepped into the empty alley.

Michael's heart plummeted. *What had he been expecting?*

The cops split up, one heading left and one to the right. Michael tailed Spencer. The alley was surprisingly clean. The other properties bordered the alley with wooden fences, hedges, or nothing. A few garbage cans stood in the alley but nothing else. Spencer peeked through a few gates and then turned around to head back to the bed-and-breakfast. Hove was doing the same from the opposite end.

"Pretty clean for an alley," said Spencer. "Won't find this in a big city."

Chris stepped through the gate into the alley. He nodded at Michael and scanned the alley both ways.

"Where's Brian?" Michael asked as the men regrouped at the gate.

"Got distracted by the bird feeders." Chris gestured behind him.

"There's some trash down that way." Hove gestured behind him. "But nothing else caught my eye."

"Trash?" Michael frowned. "Our end of the alley was clean enough to eat from." His legs started moving toward Hove's end. Up ahead, he could see some plastic cellophane litter next to the hedge. He drew closer and couldn't help but smile.

Some kid somewhere is gonna be upset.

The packages hadn't even been opened. At least a dozen Twinkies littered the concrete. He snorted. As a kid, that would have killed him to see all those go to waste. Too bad—

Michael whirled around when Chris violently retched into the hedge.

★ ★ ★

Mason barreled into the office. The traffic had finally let up. He'd passed a nasty-looking accident between a semi and one of those tiny Smart cars. The site had been crawling with cops and emergency personnel, so he hadn't stopped, but he'd done as much rubber-necking as all the other vehicles, adding to the slow-down. It was one thing to rubberneck at a simple fender-bender on the side of the freeway, but this was a sight he hadn't seen before.

The damned fairy-sized car was under the semi.

It appeared the truck had jackknifed, and the car had zoomed directly into the side of the trailer. And stuck underneath. It was about half of its original height now.

Mason didn't want to think about the driver.

He took off his hat, hooked it on its knob, and nodded at Ray, who was flipping through a stack of paperwork on his desk. Ray wore one of his two hundred polo shirts—his summer uniform. This one was a girly colored lavender. Mason didn't bother teasing him. Ray didn't give a shit about the color, and he easily pulled off the look. Mason didn't know crap about fashion, but somehow, Ray always looked like he'd stepped out of a men's health magazine.

Mason always felt like he'd stepped out of *AARP* magazine.

"Took you long enough," Ray greeted.

"Would you believe it was an accident like we'd never seen before?"

"Bullshit. Between you and me, we've seen everything"

"I shoulda took a picture. This was something else. A Smart car and a semi."

"Really?" Ray's brows shot up. "That's new."

"Told ya. What's going on?"

"I just finished up with the ME's office. Dr. Campbell got another positive ID on a pit body from her dental records. One of the women."

"Hooker?"

"No. This one walked the straight and narrow as far as I can tell."

Something odd in Ray's voice put Mason on high alert. "What?"

Ray reviewed his notes and cleared his throat. "Katy Darby. Reported missing fifteen years ago at age twenty-seven. Grew up and lived in Salem."

Mason's gut tightened. Ray's voice was off.

"She was into politics. Belonged to a half dozen political groups and was a paid employee for several of Senator Brody's reelection campaigns."

"She worked with the senator? For how long?"

"I'm trying to find out. People come and go during election time. I have a call in to his chief of staff to see what kinds of records they have. But employment records list Senator Brody as one of her employers for three different years in the 1990s. She also worked for two other members of congress from the state."

"Democrat or Republican?"

Ray looked up in disgust.

"I'm joking! Christ. Lighten up."

Ray rubbed at his nose. "Fucking long day. I've got calls to the other congressmen to see what they know about her. Only one of them is still in office. The other owns a Ford dealership in Medford now."

"Let me guess. That one was Republican."

Ray's gaze rolled toward the ceiling. "Anyway, she simply vanished off the face of the earth. Like the other ones. But she had more publicity and people looking for her. Her boyfriend was questioned pretty hard, but he had proof he was out of the state at the time of her disappearance. Her mother said she never believed the boyfriend was involved. Katy left work one evening as normal and didn't return the next day. Her car was still in the lot. No one started to ask questions until the afternoon of the next day, when someone clued in that her car was still there. They'd figured she was sick and didn't call."

"Was she working for Senator Brody at that time?"

"Yep. It was deep in reelection time. Not that Brody ever had anyone seriously oppose him. That guy's always been pretty popular. I have to imagine his campaigns weren't too difficult."

Elected office held no appeal for Mason. There was no way he wanted to beg for his job in public. It took a special type of person to be a politician. Senator Brody did it well; he was likeable and appeared honest. Mason had no personal problem with the senator or his politics; he just didn't trust any politician. They couldn't do their job without compromising something.

Mason didn't compromise. His job was black and white.

He thought he did it pretty well.

"You have the senator's personal cell, right?" Mason asked.

Ray rocked back in his chair, his face blank. "Yeah. So do you."

"You call him?"

"Hell no. It's eleven p.m."

"Probably the best time to reach him." Mason bit the inside of his cheek to keep from chuckling. Ray looked mildly ill at the thought of disturbing the senator at home this late. Ray had a hardcore set of social rules. Late-night phone calls were high on the list.

Mason enjoyed pushing Ray to break as many of his uptight rules as possible. Last month, he'd convinced the man to leave his garbage can at the curb two extra days after pickup. It cost Mason ten dollars for the bet, but he'd enjoyed watching Ray squirm over what the neighbors might think.

"This *is* a murder investigation."

"Well, I want to read his previous statements on Katy Darby before I question him."

"Good plan. Get reading."

"That's what I was doing when you walked in and started distracting me."

"What did he say back then?"

"Great employee, deeply saddened, didn't know her outside of a working relationship, yada, yada, yada."

"Cooperative?"

"Very."

Mason leaned back in his squeaky desk chair. "We need to talk to him again. Soon. Where's Darby's boyfriend these days?"

"New Hampshire. Married with two kids."

That didn't help much.

"As a cold case, it's been reviewed four different times. Looks like they call the boyfriend and some co-workers, ask the usual questions, then re-file it. There's been nothing new added."

"And now we've got the body...well, the remains," Mason corrected. "Anything unusual from the ME? Cause of death?"

"Dr. Campbell told me this is one of the bodies that had a broken hyoid, so they strongly suspect strangulation."

"What'd they get back on the gun found at the kid's murder?"

"Chris Jacobs says it was probably his. Says it was left at his home. Which was burgled, of course."

"I want to talk to Jacobs."

"Get in line."

"I want him here. Tomorrow. And I want one of us talking with the senator within the next twenty-four hours, too. I've got a good feeling about Katy Darby."

★ ★ ★

Chris explained the significance of the Twinkies, and Michael felt acid burn in the back of his throat. There was no doubt who had Jamie now.

In the hands of a fucking-psycho-freak.

Where were they?

How were they going to find them? Hove and Spencer didn't have any leads pointing them to the tattooed man. *Ghostman.* That was a better name. The guy had been invisible for twenty years, silently tormenting the families of his victims.

Michael's phone vibrated. Detective Callahan. Crap. He'd forgotten to call Callahan back after his surprise meeting with Chris. Maybe the detective had good news?

"Callahan. You got some information, I hope?"

"Did you find Chris Jacobs?"

Michael studied his brother. He was sitting on the porch with Brian's head in his lap, the boy half asleep. "Yes, and I found a hell of a lot more than that."

Michael shared Chris's story.

Callahan was stunned into a full five seconds of silence. "Where's the real Jacobs kid?" he finally asked.

"Dead. Daniel buried him. But Daniel goes by Chris now. It's his name."

It was getting easier for Michael to say. He was starting to think of his brother as Chris.

"Well, we've got an ID on one of the pit bodies who was a former employee of your father's. Katy Darby worked on a few of your father's reelection campaigns before she vanished. She doesn't fit the profile of the other victims. She seems to be squeaky clean."

Katy Darby?

"I remember the name," Michael said slowly, brain spinning. "I remember when she disappeared. My parents were pretty upset. They'd both liked her. I can remember my mother saying she was a very enthusiastic worker. I don't think anyone ever thought about her disappearance in conjunction with my brother."

"She's connected now. Looks like the same perpetrator who killed her killed those kids. That makes a double connection to your father."

"Chris said the Ghostman always threatened our family. He says he didn't harass the other kids in that way. Only him."

"Ghostman? You mean Mr. Tattoo?" Mason asked.

"Yep. That's what the kids called him."

"Formerly Gary Hinkes. We've got to figure out what name he's using now and what his connection is to your family."

"Christ. You don't think this is about The Senator's politics, do you? Don't tell me all these people have died because of the way he voted on a bill." Anger ricocheted through Michael's chest.

"I don't know why he has a hard-on for your family. I need to talk to your father again."

"That makes two of us."

"I was going to call him in the morning. You want to try reaching him tonight? We need to pull him in on this ASAP," said Mason.

"I'll call immediately. We need to figure out who the Ghostman is."

Michael ended the call, and Chris met his gaze. "It's linked to the senator?"

"I fucking hope not. But one of the bodies in the pit is a former campaign worker."

Both men turned as Hove jogged up the walk. "Got a sighting. He was headed west on Highway 22 about an hour ago. One of my troopers says he had the tattooed wrists we mentioned in the APB." Hove's eyes were bright. "We pulled him over for talking on his cell. He gave a fake ID. Well, he gave a legitimate ID, but now we know that it wasn't him. And the car is a rental. We've got the plates, and we're keeping an eye out for it."

Michael scanned a mental map of the state. Highway 22 crossed the Cascade Mountain Range and ended up in Salem. If he was going to Portland, the killer would have most likely taken a different highway pass. "Was he alone in the car? Was there a woman with him? He's not going back to Portland. I wonder why he's going to Salem? Did you pass this on to Callahan?" A million questions swirled in his head.

"Yes, he was alone, and I'm about to call Callahan."

"Fuck. *Where's Jamie?*"

"We'll find her."

Michael looked at Chris. "I'm heading to Salem. You coming?"

"You couldn't stop me. She's my sister."

CHAPTER TWENTY-ONE

With Brian asleep in the backseat and Chris riding shotgun, Michael tried to call his father as they raced across Central Oregon in the dark. The Senator's phone dumped into voice mail.

"Damn it!" He tried calling his parents' landline at their home, and his mother sleepily answered.

"Michael?"

"Sorry, Mom. I'm trying to reach Dad. It's important."

"Is it about Daniel?" Her voice was instantly alert.

"Uh…" His mind went blank. He wasn't ready to tell her about Chris. And Chris had asked to do it himself. "Not really. They've identified one of the female bodies from that pit as Katy Darby, remember her?"

Cecilia sucked in her breath. "Oh, that poor girl. We always wondered what happened to her. I had a gut feeling it wasn't good. She had such a zest for life, and she loved working with your father. She was really going places. I knew she didn't just run off."

"The police want to ask Dad some more questions about her. He's not answering his cell. Can I talk to him?"

"He's not here, Michael. He and Phillip are leaving first thing in the morning for Japan. He's staying at Phillip's tonight."

"At the governor's mansion? That's farther away from the airport."

"They're flying privately out of Salem to LA, meeting up with some other officials, and then flying out of LAX, I believe."

"How early are they going?"

"I don't know. He thought it was easier to stay down there than leave from here, so I had the impression it was a crack-of-dawn type flight."

"I guess I'll see if I can catch them before they go. I'm actually headed to Salem, but I'm several hours away."

Michael glanced at Chris as he ended the call. "Feel like seeing The Senator today?"

Chris stared back at him.

"Better get your story ready."

* * *

See the senator, thought Chris. In a few hours?

His life had completely turned upside down and inside out in a matter of hours. He'd put the senator and Cecilia out of his head years ago. It was the only way to keep his sanity.

He leaned back against the headrest and closed his eyes, a dizziness settling in his brain. For a few years as a kid, he'd fantasized about his reunion with his real parents, but he'd always felt a shadow watching over him, waiting for him to make one wrong move that would signal the Ghostman to kill them and Michael. So he'd stopped thinking about them, forcing himself to look at the Jacobses as his real parents, and he embraced Jamie as his sister.

But now it was time to own up to the truth.

His stomach churned, and he swallowed hard. He didn't want a repeat performance of the scene in the alley.

"They're gonna stop him, right? He's not going to hurt anyone else." He didn't clarify whom to Michael.

"If the police don't stop him, I will. They'll spot that car on the highway, and I'm not going to stop until I know what he's done with Jamie."

Chris opened his eyes and studied his brother in the dim light. Even though it'd been twenty years, he knew the determined set of that stubborn jaw. When Michael had his mind set on something, he didn't rest until he achieved it. Right now that obsession was Jamie.

He noted his brother didn't say "when I get Jamie back."

There was a very good chance his sister was dead.

Chris took a series of deep breaths. Everything was coming to a head. He was caught in the nightmare he'd been trying to prevent for twenty years. A killer had his sister.

He turned in his seat to check on Brian. The boy looked at ease with his head tipped back in the corner of a seat, his mouth slightly opened, deep in the sleep of childhood.

Brian was safe.

He might be able to put an end to his nightmares tonight. If he knew the Ghostman was behind bars, he'd be able to sleep.

Why him?

He'd asked that question for twenty years. Why had the Ghostman threatened his family and no one else's? Obviously, he'd kept Daniel and the real Chris alive the longest because he'd had a taste for young boys. How much longer would they have survived? The real Chris wouldn't have lasted another month. Maybe even a week.

"I still don't know why he took us," Chris told Michael. "We all asked him several times why he had to take all the kids from the bus. He never said why."

"How did it happen?" asked Michael. "I never understood how someone could make a whole group of people *and* a vehicle vanish the way he did."

"We were all back on the bus after touring the capitol building. The younger kids were getting whiny. It was a long day for them. I loved going there, you knew that. I loved visiting Dad's office, and Uncle Phillip's new representative office wasn't too far away. Other kids weren't excited about politics the way I was."

Michael snorted. "Politics suck."

"I wanted to be president one day."

"I remember," Michael laughed. "I was so fucking jealous of you. The Senator gave you so much more attention because you wanted to follow in his footsteps."

"No, I was jealous of you. You could do sports and didn't care what other people thought of you. Your mindset was always independent and cool. I wanted to be like that."

The two men locked gazes for a split second. Chris saw shock in Michael's eyes.

"Bullshit." Michael broke the moment. "You had nothing to be jealous of. Mom and The Senator thought you were perfect."

"Doesn't mean I thought I was. I wanted to be more like you."

"Jesus Christ. Once I realized you probably weren't coming back, I tried to turn myself into you. Tried to show more interest in The Senator's job, tried to make my schoolteachers happy. That lasted about a month.

"I had so much guilt. Did you know I lied about being sick to get out of that field trip? For years, I blamed myself for you getting taken. If I'd been there, maybe it wouldn't have happened. Or maybe I could have talked him into releasing you and taking me instead. *Fuck.* I figured Mom and The Senator hated me because you were gone and they were stuck with me. The lazy kid, the school skipper and skateboarder who nearly flunked out of math. How many times do you think they said, 'If only Michael had vanished instead of Daniel'?"

"They never said that!"

"They did in my brain. I believed they were too polite to say it out loud."

Chris stared at his brother. He'd often wondered how Michael had handled being left behind. As a kid, he'd figured his brother probably missed him on one level but cheered that he was an only child on another.

The Ghostman had wreaked havoc on everyone.

"I had no idea," Chris said quietly. "You know those are probably normal thoughts for a kid who experienced what you went through, but Mom and The Senator always loved you. They didn't wish you were gone."

Michael shrugged. "You have to love your own kid."

"No sane person wishes for their kid to be harmed."

"I couldn't keep the thoughts from occurring."

"Did you ever talk to someone?"

"A therapist? Yeah, I did that a few times. They wanted me to talk about my feelings too damned much. I just wanted them to help certain thoughts go away. I shoulda seen a hypnotist instead."

An overwhelming affection for his brother touched Chris. Michael had been in pain, too. They shouldn't have hurt alone.

He should have told the truth twenty years ago.

"You didn't finish your story," Michael prodded. "What happened to Sylvia Vasquez, the driver?"

"Oh." Chris struggled to focus. He was still thinking about Michael, young teenage Michael wishing he was dead instead of his brother.

"Sylvia coordinated the whole tour. She was a lot more than just a driver."

"I remember. She seemed to do a little bit of everything at the school."

"Well, we'd all gotten back on the bus and were starting to leave the parking lot when the Ghostman flagged us down. He was waving a jacket at us, like one of us had left something behind during the tour. And he was shouting her name like he was familiar with her."

"So maybe he knew her?"

"I saw her face. I don't think she knew him. But he got her attention, and she stopped the bus. When she opened the door for him, he said that one of us had left behind a coat, and he stepped on the bus."

"What were the kids doing?"

"Everyone sorta looked at each other, waiting to see who admitted leaving a coat. Sylvia turned in her seat to look at us, and that's when he crouched down and revealed the gun wrapped in the coat. He pointed it at Sylvia and told her to drive."

"Holy crap. And she just did what he said?"

"He eventually pointed the gun at Kendall, who was in the front seat. That made Sylvia drive."

"No one saw the bus leave," said Michael. "They asked for tips all over the city, and no one came forward to say they'd seen the bus. How in the hell did it just vanish?"

Chris shook his head. "We drove right through plenty of traffic. A million times, I wanted to flag someone and say we needed help, but he watched us like a hawk. Kendall was crying. He had the gun on her the whole way. Most of the kids were crying at one point or another. He kept saying he just needed a ride, and if we'd take him where he needed to go, he'd let us go safely.

"The first thing he did when we got to the woods was shoot Sylvia Vasquez. Then threaten to do the same to everyone else if we didn't obey him."

Michael was silent as he drove.

Chris looked out the window. How many times had he relived that bus ride? If he'd flagged another motorist. If he'd tackled the Ghostman as his attention waned for a second. His life and everyone else's could have been different.

"You were only a kid," Michael said. "Nothing you could have done would have made a difference."

Mind reader.

Chris wiped at his cheek. One day he might actually believe that.

CHAPTER TWENTY-TWO

It felt like she'd been in the trunk forever.

Jamie dozed in and out, the scenery never changing. Dark. Confined. The small access Mr. Tattoo had opened from the car to the trunk had probably saved her life. The cool air was heavenly. She was still thirsty, but at least she didn't need to pee. Thank God for small miracles, because she had a hunch he didn't want to be a bathroom escort.

Hopefully, she wasn't getting too dehydrated. No muscle cramps yet.

The car slowed and went through a series of turns. She continually lost her balance and rolled awkwardly several times in the trunk. Were they actually nearing a destination?

Please don't take me to the bunker.

She'd seen the faces of the cops who'd been in the bunker. And she'd read the descriptions in the newspaper. That'd been enough.

Surely he was taking her somewhere else. Only an idiot would go back to the scene of the crime. But would a new location be an improvement?

She was still alive and above ground. That was giving her hope. He had something in mind for her; otherwise, he would have killed her already.

That meant she had a chance. She was a fighter, and she'd fight with whatever she could get her hands on.

You're no good to me roasted or barbecued. That statement indicated he had something planned. But what? A ransom? Michael was probably loaded. He practically came from blue blood. Did her kidnapper know of her relationship with the reporter?

The tattooed man hadn't asked anyone for money when he had taken Chris and all those other kids. Ransom didn't sound like his style. It appeared he'd kept those kids for his own twisted purposes.

When he'd attacked her in her home, he'd wanted to know where Chris was. Did he think Chris would look for her? Did he think kidnapping her would bring Chris out in the open?

Why did he want Chris?

Chris didn't remember anything. Chris couldn't have identified Mr. Tattoo as his kidnapper. Why had he come out of the woodwork now? What could Chris do to him?

Another turn slammed Jamie's head against metal.

Shit.

She blinked away the wetness from her eyes. The car slowed and took a long turn. Then stopped. They idled for fifteen seconds and then slowly moved forward. Jamie listened hard, searching for any audible clue of where she could be. The roadway was smooth and paved, so at least they weren't near the bunker.

She exhaled slowly through her nose. *Like anywhere with him is okay.*

The car moved slowly for a short time and stopped. The engine turned off.

Jamie held her breath. She heard the car door open. He got out, slammed the door, and his footsteps grew fainter. He was leaving her alone. In the dark.

She strained her eyes to see in the dark. He'd left the space open to the trunk, but all she could see was a narrow view of cement walls, like the inside of a parking structure. An indirect light source gave the walls a soft glow.

Where was she?

Silence.

She relaxed and closed her eyes, thinking of Michael. If anyone could figure out where she was, he could.

★ ★ ★

Ray stretched in his chair, joints audibly popping. "Brody says the senator is spending the night at the governor's mansion and then leaving with the governor for Japan in the morning on some political trip. He tried to reach him, but his cell is probably off. He's heading to Salem to try to catch his father before they head to the airport."

"Looks like our killer is headed that way anyway." Mason rubbed at his eyes. It was four in the morning, and he wasn't going home anytime soon. There were too many irons in the fire that he wanted to keep an eye on.

"We've got his vehicle description and plates out to every trooper on the road. We'll find him," Ray said confidently.

"I want to know who this son-of-a-bitch really is. And I can't believe that trooper took a fake ID." Mason paced in the police building. He and Ray were the only ones on their floor working. Normal folks had gone home long ago.

"Wasn't fake. Was legit. Just wasn't him."

"I want to catch this asshole. Then I want to pull the lever on the electric chair."

"I suspect there'll be a brawl to be the lucky guy who gets that job."

"There's got to be something in that old murder case that points us in the right direction."

"You already talked to Lee Fielding. You think you could get any more out of him?"

Mason shook his head. "I've listened to that interview twice. Fielding doesn't know crap."

"What about the Darby file?"

"Until one of us talks to Senator Brody, I don't think we'll get much further there. I want to know what exactly his relationship was with the young woman."

Ray wrinkled his nose.

"For fuck's sake. You know as well as I do. Senators and their employees get it on all the time. Anytime a man has power like that, he's suddenly attractive to a lot of women. Especially the young ones," Mason stated.

"I don't like to think of anyone taking advantage of Cecilia Brody."

"Of course not. She's a very ill woman. But she's smart, and I've seen her and the senator interact. He cares. If he hurt her at some point in the past, she's forgiven him. But that doesn't mean she's forgotten about it."

"Are we gonna draw straws to see who gets to talk to him?"

"I'll do it. I wish he wasn't leaving the country. I'd rather talk to him in person again. I just can't get the same feel for a person on a cell phone. People are much more comfortable lying on a cell phone. I need to see his face so I know what he's not telling me."

Ray nodded. "Maybe we need to try to talk to him before he gets on a plane."

"Shit, I drove to Salem yesterday. I don't want to go again. And I haven't fucking slept." Mason rubbed a hand over his face, pulling at his cheeks. It felt like the blood had left his skin; there was an odd numbness to his face. Lack of sleep.

About three times a year, there'd be a case that would keep him and Ray up all night. A case where they were so close to something big that neither man could sleep because the answer might be right around the corner. This damned tattoo man was just out of their reach. If they didn't close their eyes, maybe they could sneak up on him.

"Let's both go. Let's just get in the car and head south. We'll hit Starbucks and be waiting at the Salem airport when the senator gets there. He'll have to take a few minutes to talk to us. Hell, he can catch a plane to Japan the following day if he needs to. Leave a message on his cell to call us back, saying we want to talk to him this morning. He'll get the message when he wakes up."

Ray was right. Standing around the office, staring at their phones wasn't helping. They might as well put themselves in the senator's path. At least it'd feel like they were doing something.

"You're right. But damn, I wish I could take a shower first." Mason discreetly sniffed at his armpits. "Christ! I reek."

"I've got some extra shirts. Go wash up, and I'll loan you one," Ray offered.

Mason eyed the width of Ray's weight-lifter chest. "Your stuff won't fit me. I'll look like an idiot."

"You want to stink for the senator? Or just look like you don't know your size? Your choice."

"I'll take the shirt."

★ ★ ★

Thirty minutes later, Mason and Ray were headed south out of Portland. Two coffees in Mason's sedan's cup holders and a file from Lee Fielding's murder trial on Ray's lap.

Mason was wearing an orange polo shirt. It had the damned little horse on it and everything. He felt like he glowed. Ray had offered him three different polo shirts. Pastel stripes, solid yellow, or solid orange. He went with the lesser of three evils. The shirt wasn't as baggy as he expected, probably because Ray had a tendency to wear them a little on the snug side.

Ray had referred to his shirt color as "tangerine." Mason had stared at him.

"It's orange."

"No, I have an orange one at home. This one's a little different."

Holy shit.

"You buy this stuff or does your wife shop for you?"

Ray looked hurt. "I buy my own stuff. Jillian likes how I dress. She'd tell me if I looked like an idiot. What the hell's your problem? There's other clothing in the world besides button-down collared dress shirts. Other colors besides blue, gray, and white."

"Drink your coffee." Translation: I'm ending this stupid line of conversation.

Ray took a sip of his Venti black coffee and dug through the papers in his lap. He cleared his throat. "Since all the stuff from Gary Hinkes's trial has vanished, I'm getting what references I can from Fielding's case."

"Right."

"We've already been through the transcript. Now I'm just looking at all the letters sent between the DA's office and Fielding's attorney and the judge. I can't believe how formal and long-winded all this crap is. It takes ten pages of letters to get everyone to agree on one little thing. It's like that over and over. No wonder attorneys rake in the big bucks. They charge three hundred dollars an hour to write a letter. I could send a text in ten seconds that accomplishes the same thing."

Mason grinned. "If only texts were nicely kept legal documents."

"Anyway, they spend a lot of time arguing back and forth. Most of this shit doesn't make any sense to me. I'm just looking for the Hinkes name. He's in here quite a bit. The prosecutor reprimands Fielding's attorney every time he mentions him. Says his case is separate and to keep his focus on Fielding only."

"Fielding's attorney was appointed, right?"

"Yeah, he couldn't afford one. Same with Hinkes. Glad to know we paid for their trials."

"Same guy from the DA's office prosecuted both?"

"No..." Ray shuffled through papers. "I'd thought so at first, but there's a reference somewhere for Fielding's attorney to take some issue up with a different prosecutor…I'm looking for it."

Ray sucked in a breath. "Well, I'll be damned."

★ ★ ★

Gerald jogged up the stairs from the parking area below the house. He'd let himself into the secured parking area and tapped the security code to disarm the house. He knew all the security; that was his job. He also knew that at five in the morning on a Saturday, his boss would still be asleep and the house empty of employees.

How was he going to be received? The boss wasn't going to be happy that he hadn't taken out Chris Jacobs. But he'd found some good bait to bring the man out into the open. Once Jacobs heard about his missing sister, he'd have a good idea who took her. And if the word about the pile of Twinkies got back to him, Jacobs would have no doubt.

Jamie had said she contacted her brother by leaving a phone message. He could get the number out of her and do the same if things didn't move fast enough.

He liked the idea of Jamie being locked in his trunk. And tied up. He'd experimented a bit with the bondage-type play but had never gotten turned on by it. But the long-haired woman in his car was sticking in his brain and distracting him in a big way.

Even if she never led him to Chris Jacobs, he still came out ahead.

He needed to find a different place to take the woman. He'd considered and rejected his own home or a hotel, and there was no way he could go back to the bunker. His boss had a few private vacation homes in the state that he could drive to in a couple of hours. He just needed a thumbs-up from his boss—and a key.

The big house was quiet and dark. Feeling a bit like a burglar, Gerald quietly sped through the halls and up another flight of stairs to the boss's bedroom. He raised his hand to quietly knock and then froze.

What if he wasn't alone?

He'd never walked in on his boss with anyone, but that didn't mean this couldn't be the first time. Gerald was often in the home at night, the boss knew that, but they'd never established a protocol for him needing to talk to the boss during sleeping hours. He still wasn't answering his cell phone.

The intercom.

There was an intercom system through the phone extensions on the house landline. He'd call from one of the other rooms first. His boss hated mornings. The man was a night owl and always struggled to wake up even on normal mornings.

He tiptoed away from the door. The intercom was a bit obnoxious sounding, but that should be better than Gerald appearing at the door if the boss wasn't alone. He headed back to the kitchen.

Nearing the kitchen, he stopped and sniffed the air. Coffee? Clinking of dishes told him someone was up. He pushed through the swinging door. His boss stood at the counter in front of the coffeemaker, his back to Gerald.

"Oh, I thought you'd still be asleep," said Gerald.

The man whirled around, his mouth in an O.

Not his boss.

"Sorry, Senator. I didn't know you were in town," Gerald apologized. His boss's brother was a common visitor in the governor's mansion. He tugged his jacket's sleeves down an inch and wished he'd worn his usual driving gloves.

"You scared the shit out of me, Prentice. You shouldn't sneak up on people like that."

"I didn't know anyone else was in the house."

"We're leaving for the airport in a couple of hours. I should wake Phillip up."

That would take care of Gerald's dilemma. "Good, I need to talk to him real quick. I was about to call him on the intercom. I'd rather you did the honors."

The senator chuckled with a smile, and Gerald understood why the man had never lost an election. He knew how to appear completely charming and relatable. "Phillip's never been a morning person. I'll let him know you're waiting to talk to him. Must be urgent if you're here this early on a Saturday morning."

Gerald shifted on his feet and pulled his sleeves again. "A personal matter, actually."

The senator nodded. "Got it. I'll let him know." He poured two mugs of coffee, adding plenty of cream to both, and backed through the swinging kitchen door. "A little peace offering. We were up till one last night packing and talking. Coffee should wake him up easier."

Gerald sincerely doubted coffee was going to help after his boss found out he hadn't completed his mission.

★ ★ ★

"What? What the hell is it?" Mason asked Ray again. The other detective was frantically rooting through his papers. Mason was about to pull the car over and grab the papers to see for himself.

"Hang on. I want to make sure I'm not totally wrong first."

"Christ, Ray, you're slower than my mother's dial-up."

Ray scanned a page. "Here it is. Here's the name again. Yep. Phillip Brody was the prosecutor for Hinkes's trial."

"*What the hell? Our Governor Brody?*"

"Yeah, our governor started out in the Multnomah County district attorney's office before moving into politics. Ran for state representative, succeeded, and moved up from there. But before that, he was a lowly assistant district attorney."

"Wait a minute." Mason's brain was making leaps and bounds. And somersaults. "So, Phillip Brody knew Hinkes at some point. Also had to learn what a scumbag he was."

"There's no way he'd keep up an association with that kind of person."

"Christ, I'd hope not. I like to think our elected officials have better taste."

"Governor Brody also has the type of power and access to make someone's past disappear."

"Shit." Mason didn't know if his brain could accept that step.

"Think the governor knows where to find Hinkes these days?"

"That'd be a big help. But wait a minute. Katy Darby."

"What about her?"

"She worked on Senator Brody's campaigns...maybe she also worked with Governor Brody? She seemed to be the type of person who would work with both men. Their politics are similar. I have to imagine that working on a campaign isn't a year-round job once the election is over. I wouldn't be surprised if she worked with both men. If one was happy with her work ethic, surely he'd recommend her to his brother. It'd make sense that she'd spend time during one man's off-season helping out the other one," said Mason.

"And she met up with Hinkes that way? That's implying Hinkes was still in association with the governor back then...or whatever position he held at that time."

"Why would the governor maintain a relationship with a scumbag he prosecuted? Especially a potentially murdering scumbag?" Mason was afraid to let his brain follow the possibilities presented by that train of thought.

Ray's brain zipped right up the path. "Because he needed someone to do some sort of dirty work."

"And he exchanged it for getting him off the murder charge," Mason finished. *Fuck.* "This isn't a TV show. Shit like that doesn't happen in real life."

"It shouldn't," agreed Ray. "But we have to look at this."

Mason glanced at his speedometer and saw he was over the speed limit by twenty-five miles per hour. He let up on the gas, his leg aching to push harder. "I don't like this theory."

"It's making my stomach cringe. This is our fucking governor. The people in this state are crazy about him. He seems to be a great guy."

"Well, people thought the same about Ted Bundy."

"Governor Brody isn't a serial killer."

"No, but I think he might have hung out with one."

CHAPTER TWENTY-THREE

The sky was barely lightening as Michael and Chris drove up the long, winding driveway to the governor's mansion. It looked like a manicured park. There were tall fir trees and flawless grassy slopes with large, artfully arranged boulders that looked like they'd always been part of the landscape. The huge Tudor house came into sight, and Chris craned his neck to see the entire home.

"I can't believe one of them made it this far."

Michael smiled. "They've both done real well. They're naturals for politics."

"I remember."

"How much have you followed them?"

Chris shrugged. "Here and there. I'd go through spurts and follow them online quite a bit for a few months. Then tell myself to not pay attention. That'd work for a while until one of them did or said something that got the press's attention."

"Yeah, they're pretty good at that." Michael studied his brother. "How long did you hold on to the politics dream?"

Chris snorted. "That vanished immediately. I never even considered it when I came back. The thought of all that spotlight made me want to puke. I did everything I could to stay off camera when they found me and continued that for years. I didn't want someone saying, 'Hey, you don't really look like Chris.' That was my biggest fear. That I would be found out, break my parents' hearts, and then *he* would find out. He'd destroy everyone if he knew I still lived. I'd lose my parents and your parents and you permanently."

"Christ."

"That's a heavy load for a kid to carry," Chris said. "I'm lucky I'm not too crazy. Just a little reserved."

Michael raised a brow at his brother. *Reserved?* Chris gave him a sarcastic half grin that speared him in the heart. It was eerily familiar yet unknown at the same time.

They'd lost so much time.

"You're a fucking hermit."

"Jesus, watch your mouth." Chris checked the backseat. Brian was still deep in the sleep of the very young.

Kids could sleep through anything.

"I was kidding. I know full well what I've done to my life," said Chris.

"You need to change it. You've got a kid who deserves to know his family. And we need to know him."

"I'm making the change. Once the ghost is gone, I'll bring Brian to meet everyone."

"What if we don't find the ghost? What if he slips away? Are you going back to living under a rock? That's no life for a kid. Shit, that's no life for anyone."

"I'm done hiding," Chris stated simply. He held Michael's gaze.

Michael stopped at a pole with a keypad and rolled down his window. "Better be. I'm not letting you go again," he muttered. He punched a six-digit code into the pad. A rolling gate with bars slid across the driveway.

The home was a tall two-story sprawling mansion. The driveway circled in front of the elegant entrance, but Michael veered sharply to the left and down a slope that angled to the back of the house. There was a basement level below the home, built into the slope.

"That's the garage? Below the house?"

Michael nodded. "There's room for a good ten vehicles under the house."

"You have the code?"

"I've been barging in here for the last four years. Uncle Phil hosted a hell of a birthday party for me at the mansion last year. Security is very tight. He has a full-time bodyguard-slash-personal assistant, but family has all the codes." *Except you.*

Chris didn't say anything. Michael suspected he was experiencing the same odd disconnected feeling that he was. Chris was his brother...but he wasn't. He was part of his family...but he wasn't.

The man had missed out on a lot.

Did he want to be fully embraced back into their high-profile family?

"It's gonna be a big deal in the press." Michael didn't expand.

"I know," Chris said quietly.

"You're gonna be everywhere. Everyone is going to want a piece of you and Brian."

His brother shifted in his seat. "I know."

"Is that what you want?"

Chris was silent.

Michael pulled the Range Rover under the house, found an empty spot next to a sedan, and parked. Four other vehicles silently filled other parking slots. One looked like his father's Mercedes, but Michael wasn't certain. They all looked alike to him. He turned to his brother.

"Is that what you want? Do you want the hoopla? Can you handle the exposure and press?"

Chris turned to him, his eyes hard and determined. "No, I don't want all that shit," he said hoarsely. "What I want is my family back. I want to go for beers with you and talk till they close the bar down. I want to go camping and scare the crap out of you in the middle of the night with cheesy sounds and shadows like I used to. I want Brian to sit on the floor in front of the Christmas tree while Jamie and Cecilia take pictures and spoil him with every holiday cookie they can bake. *That's* what I want. I don't want all the other crap."

The wave of emotion poured out of Chris and slapped Michael in the face. He blinked. Hard. The brothers stared at each other.

"Mom is sick," Michael said. "Did you know that?"

Chris paled. "How sick?"

"It's bad. She needs a new kidney. She doesn't get out much these days. She resigned at the hospital. She's still on all the big boards, of course, but she doesn't make it to the meetings." Michael studied his brother. *Does Chris think of her as his mother still?*

Chris was silent. Michael could see thoughts spinning through his head.

How did it feel to know the mother you haven't seen in two decades was extremely ill?

"I want to see her. Today. Once we talk to the senator, I want to go see her today," he repeated.

To Michael, the words sounded difficult for Chris. How hard was it for him to step out of his cocoon of protection? Seeing their mother and explaining his story was a huge step.

Michael finally spoke. "We'll make that Christmas scene happen. I have no doubt."

"I'm gonna have to choose," Chris said. "I don't know if I can survive the publicity."

Determination to protect his little brother welled up in Michael. Here was something he could do for his brother. Finally. "Leave that part to me."

Uncertainty filled Chris's gaze. "We'll see. I'll know what I need to do when it starts happening."

Michael put his hand on the door. "Are you coming upstairs?"

Chris glanced in the backseat. "I'm gonna stay here. Let him sleep."

Michael nodded. His brother wasn't ready to face his father yet. But he would do it. On his own time. At least he was ready to see their mother.

"Okay. Come on up if he wakes or you feel like it. I don't know how long this will take."

★ ★ ★

Chris watched Michael jog across the parking garage toward the stairs, and he felt like a big pussy. He was going to have to face the senator. Soon. But waking him up first thing in the morning didn't seem the right way to accomplish it. And they needed to see Cecilia. Chris had already lost one set of parents after not seeing them for years. He wasn't going to let that happen again. If Cecilia was as ill as Michael said, Chris needed to see her now. She deserved to know her son was still alive.

Had he done the right thing? Should he have contacted them years ago?

He blew out a lungful of air and relaxed into the seat. The soft breathing in the backseat calmed him.

He'd done what he had to do. Sure enough, the Ghostman had proved that he'd still been out there and had been keeping an eye out for him. If he'd suddenly decided to tell the world who he really was, he could have risked the lives of all the Brodys.

But now he was going to put an end to the Ghost. He and Michael weren't going to give up until Jamie was back and the Ghost was gone. Then Brian would be safe.

Chris frowned. Would there ever be a time he could let Brian out of his sight and be relaxed? He couldn't keep an eye on the boy forever. What if Michael wanted to take him out for ice cream? Would he let Brian go?

Chris's stomach churned.

But this was Michael. Michael would protect the boy with his life. Chris had no doubt. *But would he be diligent in watching him?*

It just took one second. One second where your gaze was distracted and things happened to a child. He rubbed his wet palms on his shorts. *Christ.* He needed therapy.

If he was going to jump back into the mainstream, he would need to let Brian have some space. He'd taught him well. The boy knew how to be careful and not to trust strangers.

But he's a child.

Chris closed his eyes and tipped his head against the seat. What he really wanted to do was bang it against the wall. He knew what was right. He knew what to do. But the thought of doing it was making him ill. *Time to grow a pair.*

A faint thumping sound made his eyes open. He turned to look at Brian. All quiet.

The sound thumped again. Twice.

He scanned the parking garage, every nerve in his body on alert. *Who else was in the garage?* The garage was well lit, brighter than the hazy morning outside the walls. No one moved.

Thumping.

A movement out of the corner of his eye jolted his gaze to the adjacent sedan. *Did that car just move?* No one was in the seats. Chris stretched a bit to see down into the foot area of the backseat, but couldn't. He glanced at Brian and opened his door.

The car rocked slightly in time to two thumps.

He slowly slid out of the SUV, leaving his door open, took three steps to the sedan, and peered through the windows into the darkness of the backseat. The car was empty. No one in the backseat.

Someone's in the trunk.

Instant sweat moistened Chris's armpits and upper lip. "Fuck," he whispered. He stared hard at the trunk. The car was a newer American sedan.

He waited for more thumps.

All quiet.

He moved behind the sedan and bent over the trunk, listening hard.

Nothing.

Had he imagined the noise? No. He'd definitely heard something and had seen the car vibrate with the sound. He held out a hand four inches above the trunk, as if he could hear better through his palm. Still quiet.

He straightened. *Now what?*

He looked at Michael's SUV and couldn't see through the privacy glass to Brian in the backseat. His passenger side door hung open, waiting for anyone to hop in the vehicle. He strode back to the SUV and cupped his hands around his eyes against the glass to see his son.

Brian was sleeping. Head sideways, mouth ajar.

Chris commanded his heart rate to slow.

Thumping shook the car behind him. Chris whirled around and saw the movement. He walked to the back of the car and pounded on the trunk. "Hey! Someone in there?"

Frenzied thumping answered him.

And faint screams?

"*Jesus Christ!*" Chris ran his hands along the back edge of the trunk, his fingers frantically feeling for the release mechanism. He pushed and tugged at each little piece of metal until he felt the trunk give a popping sensation. The lid smoothly eased open, and Chris stared into his sister's wild eyes.

★ ★ ★

The bright lights blinded Jamie. She dug her face into the carpet at the pain in her eyes. It hadn't been too dark in the trunk since he'd opened the access hole, but now little knives stabbed at her eyes. A shadow hovered over her.

"Jamie?" It spoke and strong hands covered her, tugging at her bindings, feeling the tape on her mouth. *"Oh my God!"*

Chris? She squinted up at the form as it morphed into her brother. He got his fingernails under the tape over her mouth and tugged. Every minor hair ripped out from around her mouth, along with the outer skin cells of her lips. She cried as the tape came off.

"God damn it," Chris said. "How in the hell...?" He felt her bindings at her wrists and ankles. "I need something to cut these. Hang on." He darted away.

Jamie panted in the clean air and blinked away her tears. She breathed deep and rested her head. "Chris," she croaked.

"Hang on." He didn't sound too far away.

He reappeared with a Leatherman-type tool. He fumbled with it, searching for a blade. "How in the hell did you get in there? Is this the Ghost's car? You're okay, right?" He hammered her with questions, not waiting for an answer. He found a blade that satisfied him and went to work on the binding around her wrists.

Jamie licked at her lips and winced at the pain. Her wrists suddenly released, and shocks of agony shot up her arms and back down to her hands. Burning took over the numbness in her fingers. She moaned.

"You okay?" Chris paused his sawing at her ankle bindings, his gaze frantic on her face.

She nodded and tried to clear her throat.

"I'm okay," she croaked.

"How'd you get in here? Who—"

"Tattoo," she croaked again.

Chris halted. "Did he drive you here?"

Jamie nodded. Rage and fear fought for dominance on Chris's face. He attacked her bindings again.

"Where—" She broke off into a coughing fit.

"We're in the parking garage of the governor's mansion. *Fuck!* That means the tattooed Ghost is upstairs. With Michael!"

"*What?*" Jamie's mind froze. *Michael? Here?*

"Do you know who he is?" Chris asked fiercely, sawing at her bindings.

"The tattooed guy? He took the kids."

Chris nodded, concentrating on his work. "And he just killed my best friend back in Demming. He wants me."

"I know. I know about the baker. I'm sorry, Chris. You think Michael—" Her mind leaped ahead. "Where's Brian?"

"Right here," answered a young voice.

Both Jamie and Chris started at the new voice. The boy peeked into the trunk from the side.

"Brian, get back in the truck."

"But Dad, why—"

"*Get back in the truck.*"

The face vanished, and Jamie's heart dropped. Her nephew.

"We've got to get out of here. I've got to get him out of here."

Jamie felt her ankles release. "Brian? But where's Michael?"

Chris bent to help her out of the trunk. He hooked his arms around her shoulders and knees and hoisted her easily. He set her on her feet, and her legs shook. She hung on to him.

"Where's Michael?" she asked again.

"Upstairs."

"But you think the tattoo—what the hell is his name?"

"Gary Hinkes. But I call him the Ghostman."

"You think he's upstairs? With Michael? Does Michael know?"

"Fuck no, we came to talk to the senator. He's staying here with his brother. Michael went up, and I was waiting in the car when I heard your thumps from the trunk."

Jamie clung to Chris. "We've got to warn him. What will happen—"

"We're getting the hell out of here. I won't let him near Brian."

"We've got to get Michael—"

"I won't leave my brother. I'm going up there first."

Jamie couldn't speak for two seconds. She stared at Chris, her fingers digging into his arms. "What did you just say?"

Chris met her gaze. "Michael is my brother."

Her world tipped and shattered. Jamie lost the feeling in her legs and started to collapse. Chris held on and kept her upright.

"I had to do it," he said. Hazel eyes the same shape as Michael's green ones stared at her, pleading with her to understand.

Images bombarded her. Images of Chris, images of Michael.

She understood. She didn't know why, but she understood, and all that mattered was that he was safe and here now. The why could come later. She nodded, and relief passed over his eyes.

"I'll explain everything later. Can you drive?"

Jamie tried to take a step, but numbness prevailed in her feet. "No."

"Okay. Get in the backseat." He shook her shoulders to get her to look at him. "I'm leaving you to watch Brian. I've never left him with anyone. Do you understand?" His eyes were deadly serious. Jamie could only nod; the magnitude of what Chris was entrusting her with was overwhelming.

"I want you guys to get down on the floor of Michael's SUV and stay there until we come back. Okay?"

Jamie started to shake. "You can't go up there. You can't let him see you."

"Daddy?" Brian's shrill voice reflected Jamie's fears.

"It's okay, Brian. Jamie is going to stay with you. I'll be right back with Michael."

Brian peeked out of the SUV. Jamie's heart melted.

"Brian, this is your aunt Jamie who I told you about."

The solemn face nodded at her, his eyes scared.

"Hey, Brian." Jamie soaked up the sight of the little boy. There was so much of both Chris and Michael in his face. She let the tears flow.

Concern crossed Brian's face. "Is she hurt?"

"She's a little banged up. And tired and scared." Chris helped Jamie into the back of the Range Rover. "Take good care of your auntie. I'll be back in a minute."

"Chris!" Jamie stopped the car door as he started to slam it shut. He stared at her.

"You've got to be careful. He's dangerous." She whispered the last word, mindful of little ears.

"I'm good." He reached into a deep pocket in his cargo shorts and showed her the butt of a gun.

Jamie gasped. "What are you—where did you get that?"

"This one is Michael's. I found it in his console when I got the tool to cut your bindings. I have my own, too." He patted a bulge at the side of his waist. "We were both boy scouts at one time, you know. We believe in always being prepared."

"I didn't know," she whispered. And she hadn't known that fact. There was a hell of a lot about Michael Brody that she didn't know. And Chris.

"He's not armed. He's up there with that man, and he isn't armed." Terror climbed up her spine.

Chris nodded, determination on his face. He dug into his other pocket and handed her his cell. "Call the police. I need to go." He looked at Brian, and Jamie's heart cracked at the love for the boy on his face. "Love you, buddy. I'll be right back." He slammed the truck door. Jamie listened to his running footsteps fade away.

Jamie crouched on the floor, dialed 911, and forced a smile at her nephew. "Why don't you get down on the other side, and I'll tell you about your dad when he was a boy as soon as I'm done on the phone." Her neck, ankles, and wrists were in some serious pain. And her brother just ran off to meet a killer. Not just any killer, but the killer from his nightmares.

Please be careful, Chris.

Brian cautiously moved off the seat to the floor, his serious eyes studying her. She tried to get comfortable, stretching out her legs and rubbing at her wrists.

And bring back Michael in one piece.

★ ★ ★

Michael jogged up the stairs from the parking garage. There was an elevator, but the governor only used it for hauling awkward items into the home. He strode through a few halls, heading toward the kitchen, feeling a bit like an intruder but not too bad. He'd had the run of the house since Uncle Phil had been elected to office years ago. He'd spent a full two months living here during the summer of his uncle's first term while he did some investigative pieces on a bill in the Senate.

He needed to wake up his uncle and father. He inhaled deeply, smelling coffee. Someone was already up.

Coffee before anything.

He suddenly felt his exhaustion and rubbed at his eyes. The effects of driving all night and his stress over Jamie were about to catch up with him in a bad way. Coffee held a promise of making everything better. He pushed open the swinging door to the kitchen. Empty. Except for a steaming coffeemaker. Michael grabbed the pot, noticing it was half full. Someone had been caffeinating already. He'd fill a cup and head upstairs. He poured the steaming liquid into a cup. Now if only the police would call and say they'd spotted the car the tattooed man was driving. If they could just get their hands on him. Maybe—

The kitchen door swung open, and his uncle's head of security stepped in, froze, and blinked at Michael. His mouth actually dropped open. Michael tried not to laugh at the man's surprise. Wasn't easy to shock the unflappable man. But wow, what had caused the bruise on his cheek?

"Hey, Gerald. I'm trying to catch my father before he takes off. Sorry so early, but Mom said they were leaving at the crack of dawn. You know what time? You're driving them, I assume?"

Gerald blinked a few more times, glanced at the clock on the coffeemaker, and tugged at his sleeves. He always reminded Michael of an owl. He was wide-eyed and blinked frequently, his lanky body constantly hidden in oversized brown or black jackets that gave the impression of wings. "I think they're leaving in thirty minutes."

"Great. I'm glad I didn't miss them. Wow. Do I need to worry for the other guy? Who did a number on your cheek?"

"Accident." The owly man stared at Michael for a few more seconds.

Okay. None of my business.

"Want some coffee?" Michael asked to fill the silence. Stupid. Gerald had probably made it, and Michael was politely offering him his own coffee?

Gerald started to back toward the swinging door, his gaze never leaving Michael's. He buried a hand in his coat pocket. Unease crawled up Michael's spine, and he frowned.

Someone's not happy I let myself in. Which made no sense; Michael always let himself in. He probably popped in every other month. What was up with this morning? Should he apologize?

Gerald's back touched the door, and he reached back with his other hand to push it open the rest of the way. His baggy sleeve slid up his arm an inch.

Michael stared at the narrow burst of color on his skin.

Time stopped.

How had he not noticed the tattoos? *Because he always wears the stupid coats. And driving gloves.*

Michael lunged, flinging his cup of hot coffee at the man's face. Gerald crashed backward through the door, howling at the hot liquid in his eyes. His pocket hand pulled out a gun, but Michael tackled him. They crashed to the floor, and the gun went off. Michael felt a burn rip his ribs under his arm, and his ears instantly rang.

With Gerald underneath him, he slammed the man's right arm against the ground, and the gun spun across the floor. The entire right side of Michael's chest was on fire. They'd landed in a large formal dining room, its wood floor polished to a high sheen and slick as ice.

Michael threw his body after the gun, scrambling across the slippery floor on his hands and knees, feeling warm wetness seep through his shirt. He grabbed the firearm and spun around, his fingers settling into the comfortable familiarity of the Glock. With shaking arms, he pointed the gun at Gerald.

Michael swallowed hard at the sight of Gerald in a mirrored position.

Both on their knees, both with a gun, both aiming at the other.

★ ★ ★

Gerald breathed hard, his hands tight on his backup weapon as he locked in on the bleeding man in front of him. One of the first things he'd done after arriving at the mansion was arm himself; he'd felt naked in front of the trooper who'd given him the cell phone ticket. In the past, Phil had made fun of him for preferring to carry two guns. He wouldn't be laughing now.

Coffee dripped down Gerald's face. The heat had stung at first, but shock had replaced the pain. Michael Brody had surprised the shit out of him in the kitchen. *How the fuck did he get from Eastern Oregon so fast?* Gerald had assumed he was still moping around the town looking for his girlfriend. Now he was oozing blood on the governor's floor, looking ready to pass out.

He'd seen the recognition on Brody's face as he spotted his tattoos. In the past, Brody hadn't spared him a second glance. An occasional greeting, that was about it. Gerald had always been careful to keep his arms covered as much as possible. The governor had felt his tattoos were unprofessional, even for someone who worked security, and he urged him to wear driving gloves and long sleeves, especially around other politicians.

The woman must have reported that he had ink. She could have gotten a glimpse.

"Where's Jamie?" Michael panted.

Gerald laughed.

"*Where is she? What did you do to her?*"

He smiled back at Brody.

"If you've hurt her, I will kill you."

"Then I better keep my mouth shut for now."

"You're a fucking sick asshole." Brody spit the words. "You killed all those kids."

Gerald raised one eyebrow and sighted his weapon again. Center of mass. Brody's right arm drooped an inch.

"I heard about the pictures."

"What pictures?"

"The police have Polaroids of you…and the kids…"

Those pictures. "Big fucking deal."

"What did you do with Jamie?" Brody's gun quivered.

One side of Gerald's mouth turned up. He saw no need to answer questions.

"*Is she dead? Did you kill her, you fucker?*" Brody's arms shook violently with his question. "*Where is she?*"

Gerald wanted to just shoot the asshole again and be done with it. But part of his brain knew the governor would be livid. Livid at the political scandal. Right now everything that had just happened could be written off as an accident.

He needed to get Brody out of the house. Blood pooled near his knee. He could wait and Brody would be unconscious in minutes.

"What I want to know is why that bus of kids?" A different voice spoke from Gerald's right. From the corner of his eye, he saw a man step into the dining room with a gun pointed at him. *What the fuck?* Gerald didn't take his eyes off Brody.

"I'll kill him! I'll shoot him right now!" Gerald yelled at the newcomer. "Shoot me and I'll have a bullet in Brody's heart a split second later." He had a solid wall four feet behind him. The other man couldn't move behind him for an advantage.

"Chris. Don't shoot." Brody breathed hard. "He needs to tell me where Jamie is."

"Jamie's downstairs. She's fine."

Chris Jacobs? Gerald grinned. "You boys got together? You must have a lot in common." Gerald saw Brody's gun waver the slightest bit, relief touching his eyes.

"More than you know," snarled Brody. "Put your gun down."

"No, fucker! Why don't you?" Gerald kept his gaze on Brody.

"Go back downstairs," Brody ordered Chris. "I need to be the one to do this."

"No, I'm going to put a bullet in his brain," Chris insisted. "I will make him pay for what he did to me and my friends. *Do you know how often I wished I was dead?* While I was in that bunker and after? I've been looking over my shoulder *all my life* for this guy! And now he's right in front of me."

A new voice spoke. "Let's not get ahead of ourselves." Gerald smiled at the sound of his boss.

★ ★ ★

Thank God. Michael exhaled. Uncle Phillip had spoken from his left.

Now Gerald would back down.

Michael's rigid stance made his muscles shake, and his right side burned like a red-hot bitch. But he wouldn't remove his focus from Gerald. He couldn't.

"No!" Jamie's voice rang from Uncle Phillip's direction.

"Here's something for you, Gerald! Look what I found in the garage," Phillip said. Brian shot into the dining room, tripping over his feet and sprawling in front of Gerald. "This is the shit that happens when you don't *follow orders!*"

Chris leaped forward but was too late. Gerald had already snatched the boy, scrambled to his feet, and held his gun at Brian's temple. Michael glanced at Chris, who had his gaze locked on his son and his gun locked on Gerald's head. Chris looked stricken. His son was in the hands of his nightmare.

"*Brian.*" Chris choked out the name.

Michael realized Phillip had shoved the boy into the room and now had a long blade at Jamie's neck. Her furious green gaze met Michael's.

He stared from Jamie to his uncle. "She's okay, Uncle Phil, she's with me."

Phillip had Jamie as a shield. Her eyes were bloodshot, her usually sleek hair raggedy, and she rocked on her feet like she could barely stand. Phillip met his gaze and shook his head.

Michael couldn't breathe; his lungs had no function. *No, Uncle Phil...why?* He swung his gun toward his uncle and faltered. "Uncle Phil..." His uncle didn't let go.

Michael swayed. "Let her go. It's Gerald, Uncle Phil. Gerald is the one—"

His uncle looked at Gerald. "*I can't believe you fired a gun in my home!*"

Gerald blinked. "Accident."

"There are no fucking accidents. Look where you've put us!" Phillip's face darkened.

Michael's vision narrowed, and events snapped neatly into place as his stomach heaved. "You knew," he accused his uncle,

326 • KENDRA ELLIOT

his gun shaking. "You knew what Gerald did!" Michael looked at Jamie. "I'm gonna get you out of here, princess."

Her gaze held his, and she silently moved her lips. *Don't call me princess.*

God damn. He blinked rapidly, realizing he would do anything for her. Give up any possession, any job, any friends to simply spend the rest of his life in her presence and have her smile at him with those eyes.

"Now, Michael," Phillip said with a patient voice. "I don't know what's going on here, but barging into my home with a gun is uncalled for." His uncle wore his politician's smile, but his usually lively eyes were dead. The up and down of his emotions was unnatural.

"*Uncalled for?*" Michael's head buzzed, and his limbs quivered. "This isn't a political debate! A killer is your head of security. A killer who murdered children, stole children. *My brother and Jamie's! Your nephew!* Why didn't you do something?"

"Don't make me hurt your beautiful woman, Michael. We can work this out."

Michael swung his gun back to Gerald. Skin bulged where the muzzle of the gun dug into Brian's temple. Red fury hazed Michael's vision, and he heard Chris suck in a hoarse breath.

Brian was silent. His gaze darting between his father and Michael.

"Shoot me and he'll slice the woman," Gerald threatened.

Both Michael and Chris shifted their aim to the governor, who pressed the blade against Jamie's neck. A drop of blood ran down to her collarbone. His uncle stared back at him, his eyes cold. *Why does he still protect Gerald? Over his own nephew?* Chris's gun swung back to Gerald.

Michael's mind raced. If he shot at his uncle, he could miss and hit Jamie. Either way, Gerald would shoot Brian.

If he or Chris shot at Gerald, the tattooed man's gun could go off and shoot Brian. Phillip would slice Jamie's neck.

There was no winning situation.

He met Chris's eyes. A deathly fury shone in his brother's gaze, but no answer of what to do.

For the first time in his life, Michael couldn't take a chance. His gut wasn't telling him what to do. There was too much at stake. It wasn't just his life; it was Jamie's, Brian's, and Chris's lives. Sweat ran down his spine, and he winced trying to clear his eyes. Fog started at the edges of his sight. He had to make a decision.

"Oh my God." Phillip's voice was ragged. Michael moved his gun in his direction and saw his uncle staring at Chris, his mouth slightly open. "Daniel."

"What?" Gerald frowned and studied Chris. His eyes widened. "Jesus Christ. Where is Chris Jacobs?"

Jamie let out a breathy sob. Tears streamed down her cheeks, and Michael's heart split in pain for her.

"Chris didn't make it," she whispered.

"God damn it! You told me Daniel was dead!" Phillip shouted at Gerald.

The room went deathly silent. Chris met Michael's gaze, and he knew they had the same thought. *Why did Phillip care if Daniel was dead?*

Both men swung their weapons toward their uncle.

"It was you," Michael stated quietly, locking eyes with his uncle. "You ordered Daniel killed. And all those other children got caught in the middle. You had Gerald do it. He was acting under your orders."

Phillip said nothing, and the blade bit deeper in Jamie's flesh. She gasped. Anger flushed his face.

"Why? *Why? What did I do?*" Chris screamed at his uncle.

Phillip said nothing, and Chris's finger trembled on the trigger. Brian sniffled in the silence. Chris swerved his weapon at Gerald again.

"You're a ghost," Chris spat at Gerald. "You're the Ghostman who killed my friends and ruined my life. My life and my family's lives...both of my families."

The Ghostman gave Chris a slow smile and moved his gun under Brian's neck, pointing it up into the child's soft skin. "I was just following orders."

"*Gerald!*" the governor roared.

"*You ordered it!*" the Ghostman shouted back, veins popping on his neck. "You wanted the boy dead. You said he saw you strangle that woman."

Jamie sucked in a loud breath, and Michael stared at his uncle.

★ ★ ★

Jamie felt another drop of blood run down her neck. The bite of the blade stung, and the man behind her frequently trembled. She smelled his sour sweat under the fresh scent of soap. He'd showered recently, but it wasn't enough. The tension sucked the oxygen from the room, and she quietly gulped for air.

The governor had found her and Brian in Michael's vehicle. She'd been telling Brian stories, talking quietly, trying to distract the boy and massage some feeling back into her feet at the same time. Brian's gaze had shot over her shoulder an instant before she lost her balance and fell backward out of the vehicle as the governor yanked the door open. Her hands had grabbed frantically at the SUV, but her head hit the concrete floor, and she'd stared up at an angry man.

Now she watched Michael sprawl on his knees in the huge dining room. His arms were taut as his weapon weaved between his two targets. Chris did the same gun choreography as the men shouted and threatened each other. Michael looked ready to collapse. The pool of blood by his knees slowly expanding. His entire right side was drenched in red. *How badly was he hurt?* Every few seconds, his arms quivered.

Jamie wanted to vomit. There was no scenario in her head where this ended well.

"What woman?" Michael shouted at his uncle.

"No woman."

Jamie felt the governor's arm tighten across her chest. She wanted to do something. Kick him or elbow his gut. *Do something!* She was a strong woman, but he was a large, fit man, and she'd spent the last several hours locked in a trunk with her limbs bound. She was lucky to be upright.

"You said he saw everything!" the Ghostman shouted. His pale face flushed with an odd luminescence, like his blood was lighter in color than anyone's. Brian was holding steady. He watched everyone with his wide, dark eyes, not missing a thing. He sniffled occasionally, but Jamie was proud of her nephew. He was keeping his head.

Chris looked near the end of his rope. His feet were spread, his weight evenly balanced, and his gaze often locked with his son's. When he looked at the Ghostman, Jamie saw death rise in his eyes.

How can he handle seeing Brian with that man?

"I'm going to get you out of here, son," Chris said softly to Brian, ignoring the shouts of the other men. Brian tried to nod at his father and winced as the gun jammed farther under his jaw.

330 • KENDRA ELLIOT

"Chris." Jamie spoke. She wanted to warn him to hold still, not be a hero. But how do you say that to a man whose son is being held hostage by a killer? Instead, she just looked at him. Chris met her eyes and gave an imperceptible nod, his gaze going back to his son and the Ghostman.

He understood what she'd wanted to say.

"*Shut up!*" the governor yelled at the Ghostman. His body felt hot and damp through the back of Jamie's shirt.

"You fucked up, not me. You started this whole mess."

"You'd be sitting in prison for murder for the last twenty years if it wasn't for me!" The governor's voice shot up an octave on the last word. "*You owe me!*"

"I paid my dues. I got rid of that kid!"

"No, you fucking didn't! He's right there!"

What had Chris seen?

Her brother listened intently. "You're talking about the trip, aren't you? The trip where we went to the capitol building. I showed up at your office, and there was a woman on the floor. You said you were trying to help her! You thought I'd seen you strangle her? Is that what you thought?"

The governor sputtered.

"I saw nothing! I saw a woman who needed help, and I thought you were doing that!" Chris's gun wavered. "You had all those kids killed because you thought I saw you kill someone? *And I didn't!*" Tears poured down Chris's cheeks. "I saw *nothing! Do you hear me? You ordered your own nephew killed, and I saw nothing!*" Chris wiped at his face with one hand, the other keeping the gun on the Ghost. "Ah, fuck me. All this...*all this for nothing!*"

★ ★ ★

Michael couldn't breathe. Tiny spots sprouted at the edge of his vision.

Uncle Phil did this. He did it to all of us.

"Let Jamie go, Uncle Phil." His uncle's name burned on his tongue, but he said it on purpose, reminding the man who was in the room. His family. "Things can't get better if something happens to Jamie or Brian. There's no way to spin this to get the public's support. This is over."

His uncle clenched his jaw, and Jamie winced. Michael focused on her face, blinking, trying to clear his head of the mess he'd just learned. All that mattered now was getting her out safely. Before loss of blood had him dropping his gun.

"Put down the knife, Uncle Phil."

"No. This isn't my fault."

He sounded like a defiant child.

"I've done valuable things for this state. Just think what might not have been achieved if I wasn't governor. Or during my years as a representative. I am *important*."

He's nuts. A new spike of fear rose in Michael's chest.

"That woman was nobody. The type of person who wanted to use me to better herself. Two fucking dates, and she tells me she's pregnant? And it's mine? I couldn't risk it." His uncle tightened his grip on Jamie, his pupils huge.

Something moved in Michael's peripheral vision.

Phillip's body slammed forward, and his head whipped back as he was tackled from behind. The momentum knocked him and Jamie to the floor, and she cried out as Michael's father landed on top of them. The knife vanished between the wrestling brothers. Michael crawled across the floor to the group, his right arm collapsing under his weight. A gunshot thundered from behind him in the room, but his focus stayed on Jamie. He pulled up, lunged, and grabbed Phillip's ankle. The man kicked, his heel catching Michael in the mouth. He tasted blood and spit.

The Senator straddled his brother's back and slugged him in the right ear. Phillip thrashed, nearly throwing Maxwell Brody off to the side. Jamie twisted and shoved and pushed at the two men, trying to escape from underneath.

The knife appeared in Phillip's hand, and he frantically stabbed backward at his brother's thigh. Michael's father shouted and grabbed at the knife, the blade slicing his hand. Blood quickly covered the floor and group.

Michael grabbed Jamie's hand and tried to haul her out from under the men. His right arm screamed at the effort. His left hand held the gun, useless in his untrained hand, but he was unwilling to set it down. She rolled onto her back and kicked at both men, who fought each other on top of her covered legs.

Michael's gaze locked on his father's thigh. The blood wasn't seeping; it was spurting in time to a heartbeat. Phillip had sliced the artery, and Maxwell's heart would force the blood out of his body until it was gone.

He only had minutes to stop the blood flow.

★ ★ ★

Chris spotted the senator behind Phillip Brody a split second before the man rushed and tackled the governor. The action distracted the Ghost for a split second as the governor hit the floor. Chris bent over and charged. The Ghost jerked his gun away from Brian and pointed it at Chris. Chris saw the gun swing his way as if in slow motion. The muzzle coming into focus, aiming at his brain. He lunged forward and came up under the Ghostman's gun arm, shoving it skyward as it went off.

The explosion made his ears ring.

Chris grabbed Brian's shirtfront, ripping him from the Ghost's slack arm, and flung him to the side. Chris pressed forward, chest-to-chest with his nightmare, tripping the Ghost backward into the wall, struggling with the man's gun arm still trapped and pointing at the ceiling.

The Ghost's hot breath covered his face as Chris pressed the tip of his gun into the man's neck and dug. The Ghost fought, thrusting his knee and slamming his head forward. Chris ducked the head strike and shifted his weight to miss the knee. Distantly, he heard Brian scream for the man to let go of his dad.

"Brian, run!"

★ ★ ★

Jamie's breath shot out of her as she crashed to the floor. The weight of two large male bodies crushed her, and she went into panic mode. She fought. Memories of her last attack ricocheting through her head. She clawed, she screamed, she kicked. She didn't know where the knife was, and she didn't care. A gunshot boomed, and she looked for Michael.

He was on the floor, crawling toward her. He had the gun in his left hand, slamming it against the floor as he moved. Michael's right arm collapsed twice under his weight, his mouth bleeding.

Had he been shot in the mouth?

He grabbed her hand with his right and pulled, but the two fighting older men pinned her. She kicked harder, not caring who she hit. Dimly, she noticed the second man was Michael's father, the senator. Grunting, the two brothers wrestled, the knife flashing between them. Warm, wet blood coated her legs and slicked the floor.

Was she cut? Had she not felt it?

Glancing at Michael, she saw his mouth was open, shock in his eyes. But he wasn't looking at her. She followed his gaze and saw the blood spurting out of his father's leg. She froze.

Tourniquet. Now.

"Shoot him!" she screamed at Michael. "Shoot him, now!"

He shook his head; it was too dangerous. She yanked her hand out of his, and alarm flashed across his face. With both hands, she shoved at the closest male body and the men rolled off her, thrashing and stabbing. She kicked at the governor, and he slashed at her legs. Michael's father panted hard, his face crimson, and she saw an awareness of his injury in his eyes as he wrestled with his brother. The senator's movements slowed, and Phillip gave a wallop to his chest that sent him flying onto his back. The senator lay still, gasping for breath as he stared at the ceiling.

He's lost too much blood.

The governor froze, staring at his brother's leg. He dropped the knife and reached for his belt buckle. Michael shot up from the floor and took his uncle down, slamming his head into the floor.

"Bind his leg," Phillip yelled from beneath Michael. "He's bleeding out."

Michael scrambled off his uncle, who yanked his belt out of his loops. Phillip thrust the leather into Michael's hands, who tore at his father's pants, trying to see the wound. Blood spurted in arcs. Michael whipped the belt around his father's leg at the groin and wrenched it tight, the blood slowing. Phillip moved to his knees, his gaze locked on his brother. The governor's shoulders sagged, and he buried his face in his hands.

Jamie grabbed Michael's gun.

★ ★ ★

Blood pounding in his ears, Chris swallowed hard, pressed into the Ghostman, and rested his finger on the gun's trigger, grinding the weapon into the man's jaw. The noise in the room faded away. Just Chris and his personal devil existed. The Ghostman stopped fighting and held perfectly still, trapped by Chris's body against the wall. No safety on the Glock. Chris simply had to pull firmly. Once.

Nightmare over.

"Chris. Don't do it." Jamie's voice came from behind him.

Chris's finger twitched

"You're better than this. Don't start new nightmares."

Chris stared into the eyes of his personal hell-creator. He could see the edge of the man's contacts. He could see where he needed to touch up the hair dye. He could see the man's fear. He could smell the Ghost, menthol and dusty, his scent eerily familiar and revolting.

"I've got him covered," Jamie said. "You can back away."

"Brian?" Chris croaked.

"Safe. I saw him run out of the room."

"Michael?"

"He's taking care of his father." Jamie paused. "He and the governor are trying to stop the senator's bleeding."

Chris continued to lock stares with the Ghost, adrenaline pumping into his stomach, making him nauseous. He swallowed hard, fighting back visions of this man touching him as a child. He could feel the man's heartbeat against his own. "Drop your gun."

The Ghostman's gun arm was still above his head, held motionless by Chris's strength. Strength that he felt waning.

"Let go," the Ghost sneered back, his lips exposing yellowed teeth.

"Gun first."

"Fuck you."

"You've got two guns pointed at your head. Drop yours." Jamie sounded like she was disciplining one of her students. Her voice had moved closer. The sound of Michael talking frantically to his father entered Chris's awareness.

The Ghost broke eye contact and looked over Chris's shoulder. Presumably at Jamie. Resignation crossed his features. The Ghost's arm muscles moved under Chris's hand, and the Ghost's gun fell to the ground.

Chris released his arm, took a half step back, and struck the Ghost across the face with his gun. His nose exploded in a shower of blood, and the Ghost dropped to his knees with a wail, his hands on his face.

"Chris!" Jamie cried.

Chris stood with his feet planted apart, his gun at his side, staring at the destroyer of his life, gasping deeply. He'd never seen the man grovel at his feet before.

Shoot him.

Do it.

He shook his head.

You have cause. Protect your son.

The Ghost cowered on his knees, blood seeping through his fingers, his shoulders shaking.

Chris swallowed hard and turned away. Jamie stood behind him, her gun still trained on the wretch of a human being. Her hair was tangled and smears of blood covered her body, but she stood strong. She met his gaze, and tears shone at the corners of her eyes.

"You did the right thing."

Chris wondered.

She started to smile, but her gaze bolted behind him. Her mouth opened.

Chris whirled, raised his gun, and shot.

A mist of blood covered the wall as the Ghostman slumped onto his side, his fingertips on his gun.

CHAPTER TWENTY-FOUR

Mason had placed one foot on the stairs to the governor's front door when he heard the gunshot. He didn't even look at Ray; he simply ran up the steps, pulling out his weapon. "Call for back-up!" He hit the front door running.

Locked.

He pounded on the door in frustration. "Police!"

Shit.

He jogged back down the steps and looked up at the big mansion, scanning the windows, wondering where another entrance could be. Ray was on his cell phone, rattling off instructions.

Damn it! They had to check around the side of the home. Mason wished the backup would instantly appear. He jerked his head at Ray and had started to move to the right side of the building when a movement near the front door caught his eye. He stopped. Two wide eyes peered out from a decorative window beside the huge double doors. Mason had already reversed direction back to the doors when he realized it was a child. He lowered his weapon and pulled out his badge to show the child.

The boy vanished.

Mason sprinted up the stairs and pressed his face against the same section of glass and saw a small figure step farther out of his sight. "I'm with the police! I heard the gunshot. Are you hurt?" he hollered at the boy. "Can you open the door?"

The boy stepped back into his line of vision, caution etched in his face. Mason didn't see any wounds and gave a mental sigh of relief.

"Is everyone okay?"

The boy simply stared at him, and Mason wondered if he could hear. He pressed his badge and ID against the glass. "I've called for more police. Can you get the door open?"

The boy still didn't move. Mason was about to give up and head around the side of the house again when the boy started at something and glanced over his shoulder. A second later, he ran at the door, terror on his face, and Mason could hear him fumbling with the locks.

"He's letting us in!" he yelled at Ray.

The door opened, and an alarm screeched a warning.

"Jesus Christ." The sound was worse than a teenager's car stereo.

The boy shrank back, clearly shaken by the continuous siren. "Good boy. You did the right thing."

The kid didn't look like he believed him, and he put his hands over his ears, his eyes gigantic. Mason wanted to do the same. The squawking split his eardrums.

"Where's the gunshot? Do you know?" Mason yelled. The boy nodded, spun around, and started to dash away.

"Wait!" Mason grabbed at the boy's shoulder and tried to lead him out of the house. His first priority was the kid's safety. The boy fought back.

"My dad's in there! I can't leave!"

Mason held tight to the boy's shirt. "Who's your dad?"

Ray jogged up the steps, wrapped an arm around the boy's ribcage, and lifted him up. The boy screamed and kicked as they moved away from the house.

"We're the police, kid. We're here to help, and I can't let you back in where there're gunshots." Over the alarm, Ray spoke calmly in the boy's ear and carried him back to the vehicle. The kid ignored him and proceeded to pound away. On one hand, Mason admired the kid's smarts for fighting back against strangers; on the other hand, he wanted the kid to shut up and hold still.

"Look in the car," Ray said to the boy as they neared the car door. "You see all that equipment? We're police."

The kid stilled. Ray set him on his feet but kept a firm grip on him.

"That's better," Mason said. He squatted down to get on eye level with the boy. Near the car, the alarm sounds were a bit more bearable. "Now, where are the people in the house?"

Dark brown eyes studied Mason. The child was way too serious. "They're in a dining room. Uncle Michael got shot. He's bleeding. And my dad was fighting with the ghost. The ghost pushed his gun in my neck." The boy touched his neck, and Mason saw the red circle. Anger burned in his gut.

"You're Brian Jacobs," Mason stated. *Ghost? The albino guy? Mr. Tattoo is here?*

The boy's eyes widened, and he nodded. New sirens sounded in the distance. The cavalry was coming. "I want you to stay outside with the other police officers. Ray and I are gonna go get your dad."

"And Aunt Jamie is hurt. She's bleeding, too."

Mason felt a wave of relief that the woman was still alive. But what hell were he and Ray about to walk into?

Two local police units pulled in, lights flashing, sirens adding to the din. Mason took Brian's hand and led him to the officer stepping out of the car.

"I want two of you with me and—"

"Someone's coming out!" an officer at the second car yelled.

All the men turned to the house, weapons ready, eyes sharp. Mason pushed Brian behind him and squinted at the figure at the door. It was female.

"We need an ambulance!" Jamie shouted. "At least three!"

CHAPTER TWENTY-FIVE

Two Months Later.

Jamie followed the two men single file through the woods. The air was warm, but she could smell fall creeping into the air. A few more weeks and a definite chill would permeate the forest. She concentrated on placing her feet as she walked. If this was a trail, it didn't get much use. Chris had been the only one to track it a few times. Maybe some deer.

Chris and Michael moved silently ahead of her, glancing back occasionally to see if she was keeping up. Or to make certain she didn't vanish. The three of them had a hard time being out of each other's sight for very long. There were daily phone calls or texts, simple check-ins for no reason, other than the mental well-being that their loved ones were still safe.

The Ghostman was dead.

The police had linked several cold cases to Gary Hinkes, aka Gerald Prentice, with the governor's help. The crimes ranged from murder to rape. Katy Darby and the others in the pit from the forest had been just a few of the bodies he'd left in his invisible wake. The local and national media had gone on about the Ghostman for weeks, hounding Chris and Jamie. They'd refused all comments and tried to live normal lives. Michael and the senator had made statements to the media requesting privacy for a family who'd been to hell and back.

The governor sat in the county jail. He'd confessed to the death of the woman in his office twenty years before, and his lawyers were arguing over what to do next. His confession had solved a cold case involving a woman's body who'd been dumped near the capitol building. The senator had spent a week in the hospital after surgery to repair his femoral artery. Luckily, the artery was only nicked, and the governor's fast action with his belt as a tourniquet on his brother's thigh had probably saved his life.

Michael's family struggled to comprehend that a beloved relative had their son murdered and then had callously let them wallow in depression and grief for two decades. Helping to save his brother hadn't redeemed Phillip in his family's eyes, especially since he'd nearly killed him first. Armchair psychiatrists claimed Phillip suffered from a God complex, believing he was privileged and his actions unquestionably correct. His family abandoned all contact with the governor.

Jamie glanced ahead at her brother, leading the way. If Chris was suffering emotionally, he never showed it. He'd stayed at her house for the first two weeks and then moved into a rental close by. She'd loved having Brian in her home. He'd brought a light into the house that had never existed before. He loved to talk to his aunt. They talked for hours at her kitchen table, and Jamie had learned he was smart as a whip. School started in a week, and he was both excited and nervous to attend public school for the first time. Chris hated the idea but hadn't fought her; deep down he knew school was the right place for his son. Brian would be at Jamie's school, and she'd sworn to check in on him several times a day.

The nights had been silent, not like the nights she recalled as a kid with her brother waking up the household with his screams. She'd immediately put Brian in counseling with the best child therapist she knew. Brian had blossomed and seemed to put his incident with the Ghostman behind him. He'd talked freely to Jamie about "the bad man" and accepted his father's need to have him in sight most of the time. Jamie knew he'd do well in school. Chris was the one who would struggle with his son out from under his wing. She urged Chris to see a therapist too.

"We'll see," he'd answered with a half smile. She'd brought it up two more times and then given up. She had a hunch he was seeing a therapist on his own, not wanting to discuss it with family. He never said a word about the Ghostman, but Jamie would catch him studying his surroundings and faces of strangers when they were out in public, searching for something. He maintained a high level of constant alertness that had to be exhausting.

At the hospital, Michael had told his parents who Chris really was. Both Cecilia and her husband had stared from Michael to Chris and back again. Cecilia burst into tears and nearly collapsed onto her husband's hospital bed. The senator had reached out a hand to Chris.

"Is it true?" he'd asked.

Jamie heard his voice shake and watched him scan Chris's face, gripping his hand, searching for a hint of the boy he'd known. He must have found it, because recognition suddenly shone in his eyes.

"Daniel," he whispered.

Cecilia rushed him, wrapping her arms around him and wiping tears on Chris's shirt.

"I…I think I need to go by Chris," Chris mumbled. He slowly wrapped his arms around his mother and closed his eyes.

His arms trembled slightly, and Jamie felt the pain of how hard that intimate contact was for her reclusive brother.

"I don't care what you want to be called," Cecilia stated. "You're back. I always knew you'd come back. I never gave up hope. Never!"

The frail woman got more than her son back; she got her life back. Chris had been a match for her kidney transplant. The only male in her family with two strong kidneys had immediately undergone surgery for his mother. Six weeks had passed, and Chris moved like he'd never been under the knife.

Brian had been delighted to find he had an extended family and took to his grandparents right away. He'd confided in Jamie that he'd always wanted grandparents, but his dad had said they'd died in a car wreck. "Just like my mom," he'd said with solemn eyes.

Jamie did her best to step into that mothering role that Brian had needed so desperately. Chris had tried hard to create a young man, but every young man also needs some coddling. Every boy needed a dog, too. Sheriff Spencer had found Juan's missing dog and turned him over to Brian. The pair was inseparable. Brian was a happy boy who laughed and loved to share his imagination.

He drew, like his father had, and dreamed up stories, which he shared with Jamie day after day. Most of the stories were of a young boy, his dog, and his exciting adventures, but occasionally the boy faced evil demons.

In his stories, the boy always conquered the demons.

Jamie loved him. She'd given Chris a piece of her mind about keeping the boy's existence from her and then promptly forgiven him. Chris had provided her with an incredible gift in her nephew. It was odd. Her real brother was long dead. But when she looked at Chris, she couldn't feel the loss. She'd searched for the emotions, combed through old pictures, trying to remember the real Chris, but this man had been her brother for the last eighteen years. The real Chris she'd known for eight short years.

Her left leg gave a small spasm, and she glanced down at the scars from the governor's knife. They'd fade in time. A few stitches had put her back together. Therapy sessions had done away with most of the nightmares of being kidnapped by a vicious killer and locked in a car trunk. The sudden claustrophobia at weird times was new but nothing she couldn't deal with. She simply avoided small, enclosed spaces.

Michael had installed a top-of-the-line alarm system in her home. They'd discussed moving in together, and agreed it was too soon, but he spent every night and day at her house. When Chris moved out, they'd approached the moving-in idea again. They agreed it was still too soon, and things were going great, so why mess up a good thing?

Then Michael put his house on the market.

Jamie's eyes had nearly popped out of her head as she'd pulled up to his home and seen the sign. "What? When did you do that? *Why* did you do that?"

He'd shrugged. "I'm never home."

"But...but..."

"Why am I paying someone to clean a house and a service to take care of the yard if I'm never there?"

"Well...but, I mean..."

"Don't worry, princess. I've got a nice apartment picked out not too far from you. I feel like renting for a bit." Then he'd given her a look. A look that plainly told her he had no intention of renting. Ever.

His house hadn't sold yet. But he'd moved half his belongings into her little home. For a man, he had an incredible amount of stuff. Maybe they should considered living in his...

"Doing okay?" Michael asked over his shoulder as he held a branch out of her way.

Jamie looked up, smiled, and nodded. And felt her heart beat a little faster. Michael made her feel good. For a man with a wild streak, he was all seriousness when it came to the two of them. He put her first, he made her try new things, he made her leave the dishes on the kitchen counter overnight, proving that life goes on even if everything isn't in its place.

For her, he was steadfast.

She'd fallen head over heels for the man. And had no idea when it'd happened. It'd crept up on her and snuck under her heart when she wasn't paying attention. When she'd been locked in that trunk, he'd been all she could think about and all she'd worried about. Obviously, her love for him had started before that. Maybe it'd been that steamy night at the bed-and-breakfast, or when he'd arrived to take charge after her attack. It didn't matter.

She was in love with Michael Brody.

It was the biggest leap she'd ever taken.

He waited for her to pass him on the deer trail and took her hand, walking side-by-side as their space had widened.

"Hey, gorgeous." His green gaze held hers.

"Hey," she whispered back. The forest was silent except for the crush of the dirt under their feet. Jamie embraced the peace of the woods and simply smiled at her man, moving in unison with him as they hiked. She'd never felt a connection like this one.

★ ★ ★

Damn, she had eyes that didn't let him look away. Freaking blue as oceans. Michael took a deep breath to recalibrate his brain, which was suddenly full of images of Jamie. Some clothed, some not. The last two months had been the most intense of his life. A red-hot roller coaster that he didn't want to end. Well, the good parts anyway. He could do without the vanishing girlfriend or gunshot parts.

His ribcage still ached if he took a deep breath or twisted a certain way. The bullet had run along a few ribs, removing a little bone and a lot of skin. No surgery needed, but it'd been an awkward place to heal, and the pain had stretched from his sternum to his spine. The stitches on his lips hadn't been pleasant either. Hard to kiss the woman you love when your mouth hurts like hell. It didn't help that the black stitches had looked like they'd been sewn by a five-year-old.

The stitches were gone, but he still had a weird numbness in some spots that the doctors assured him would return to normal. Then he wouldn't be distracted when he kissed his woman.

His woman.

He didn't dare say it out loud. She'd roll her eyes, but that didn't matter. He knew what she meant to him, and he made certain she knew it, too. He knew exactly what he wanted in his future. *Her.* All of her. But she had some weird idea about going slow. *Why?* He knew they were fated to be together. Why did they have to dance around and learn about each other? They could do all that later. He wanted one hundred percent of her *now.*

Putting his house on the market might have spooked her a bit, but hey, *he was living at her place.* She seemed to be in denial. She had some socially acceptable idea of the path a relationship should follow, and moving in together after knowing each other for two weeks didn't fit in her perfect world.

Screw her perfect world. He'd show her *perfect.*

Chris supported him completely. As did Brian and his parents. They all loved Jamie. She and Brian had brought an openness and affection out of his uptight parents that he'd never seen before. His father had resigned from the Senate and stood by his mother's bedside as she healed from her surgery. And they'd never looked happier.

Brian was spending the day with his grandparents while Michael, Jamie, and Chris tramped through the forest. Chris stopped, staring at a fallen tree off to the right. Michael felt a brief shudder shoot through Jamie, and he squeezed her hand.

In front of the fallen tree was a pile of river rocks, which surrounded a thin, concrete-like marker. It wasn't large, maybe eighteen inches high by a foot wide.

How had Chris hauled that into the woods?

Jamie let go of his hand and ran her knuckles under her eyes, moving closer to the marker. She squatted down and touched the pale concrete.

"I made the marker," said Chris. "I've been here maybe five times over the years. The first time I managed to find him, I buried him." He swallowed hard, his voice unnaturally hoarse. "I don't know what you want to do, Jamie. Do you want him moved?"

Her fingers traced the letters, her face hidden by her long hair. *Christopher Jacobs. Brother and Friend.* There were no dates. Michael's heart ached for her.

She picked up a small rock from the pile, wrapped her fingers around it, and stood, turning to face both the men. She looked lost. Michael watched her study Chris's face. She had to be searching for the brother she remembered. Could she see the difference? Or had the years combined the two men into one? Her gaze locked with Chris's, and she gave a small smile.

"Look around," she said, her focus moving to the towering firs. "It's beautiful here. It's quiet and peaceful and calm. I feel a happiness and restfulness in the air. I can't think of a better place to be. He needs to stay here."

Michael felt the calmness, too. The forest was still and tranquil, almost welcoming. He studied the small marker, hating and loving the simpleness of it simultaneously. Part of him ached for it to be a huge monument, but most of him knew it was utterly appropriate.

He felt a kinship with the young man buried under the earth; it could have easily been his own brother. In a way, it was. Daniel hadn't returned; Daniel had died, too. But the man next to him was definitely his brother. And Jamie's brother, too.

"She's right," Michael said. "This is perfect."

Chris looked from one of them to the other and back. His shoulders slumped a bit in relief, and he nodded. "I'd hoped I'd done the right thing. It seemed right."

Jamie hugged him hard. "Thank you for taking care of him."

Michael slapped his brother on his back. "You did good." Chris surprised him by fiercely pulling him into the hug. Michael hugged him back and laid his cheek against Jamie's hair, inhaling her scent.

"You've got a family here, princess."

She met his gaze and smiled. "Always."

ACKNOWLEDGMENTS

I have an amazing group of people who support my writing in different ways. My agent, Jennifer Schober, who handles the legal wrangling of my books. My acquiring editor, Lindsay Guzzardo, who guides me every step of the way through the production of my books. Charlotte Herscher, my developmental editor, who gently lets me know when I've created unlikeable characters. Jessica Poore, my author-relations guru, who promptly answers my million e-mails and sends me chocolate. Melinda Leigh, fellow Montlake author, who shares my roller coaster ride of tears and squees on the publishing journey. My husband, Dan, who suggested I quit my day job and hire someone to clean the house. He's a keeper.

ABOUT THE AUTHOR

Born and raised in the Pacific Northwest, Kendra Elliot has always been a voracious reader, cutting her teeth on classic female sleuths and heroines like Nancy Drew, Trixie Belden, and Laura Ingalls before proceeding to devour the works of Stephen King, Diana Gabaldon, and Nora Roberts. She graduated with a degree in journalism but went on to become a licensed dental hygienist. Her debut novel, *Hidden*, was an overall top 100 Kindle bestseller for 2012. Elliot shares her love of suspense in her third novel, *Buried*. She still lives in the Pacific Northwest with her husband and three daughters.